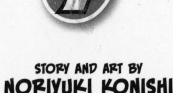

WITHDRAWN

# YO·KAI WATCH
## 7

STORY AND ART BY
# NORIYUKI KONISHI

ORIGINAL CONCEPT AND SUPERVISED BY LEVEL-5 INC.

# YO-KAI WATCH™
## Volume 7
### A HAIRY SITUATION
Perfect Square Edition

## Story and Art by Noriyuki Konishi
## Original Concept and Supervised by LEVEL-5 Inc.

Translation/Tetsuichiro Miyaki
English Adaptation/Aubrey Sitterson
Lettering/John Hunt
Design/Izumi Evers

YO-KAI WATCH Vol. 7
by Noriyuki KONISHI
© 2013 Noriyuki KONISHI
©LEVEL-5 Inc.
Original Concept and Supervised by LEVEL-5 Inc.
All rights reserved.
Original Japanese edition published by SHOGAKUKAN.
English translation rights in the United States of America,
Canada, the United Kingdom and Ireland arranged with
SHOGAKUKAN.

Printed in the U.S.A.

Published by VIZ Media, LLC
P.O. Box 77010
San Francisco, CA 94107

10 9 8 7 6 5 4 3 2 1
First printing, May 2017

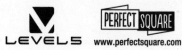

LEVEL5     PERFECT SQUARE     VIZ media
www.perfectsquare.com     www.viz.com

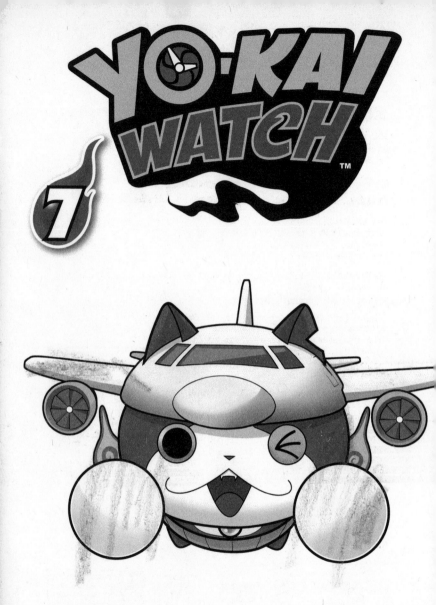

# YO-KAI WATCH

## 7

STORY AND ART BY
**NORIYUKI KONISHI**

ORIGINAL CONCEPT AND SUPERVISED BY LEVEL-5 INC.

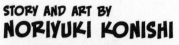

# CHARACTER INTRODUCTION

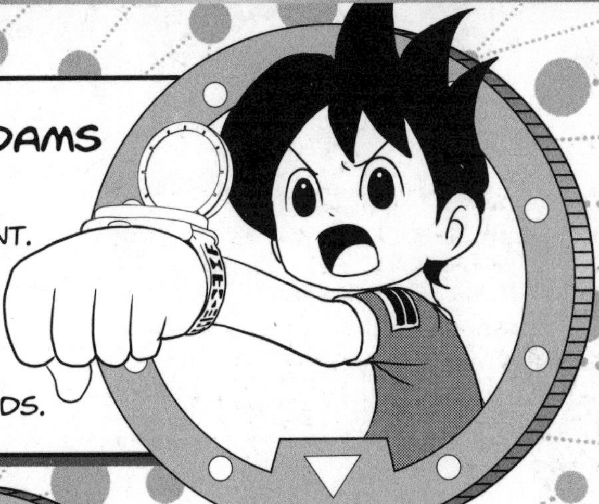

## NATHAN ADAMS

AN ORDINARY ELEMENTARY SCHOOL STUDENT. WHISPER GAVE HIM THE YO-KAI WATCH, AND THEY HAVE SINCE BECOME FRIENDS.

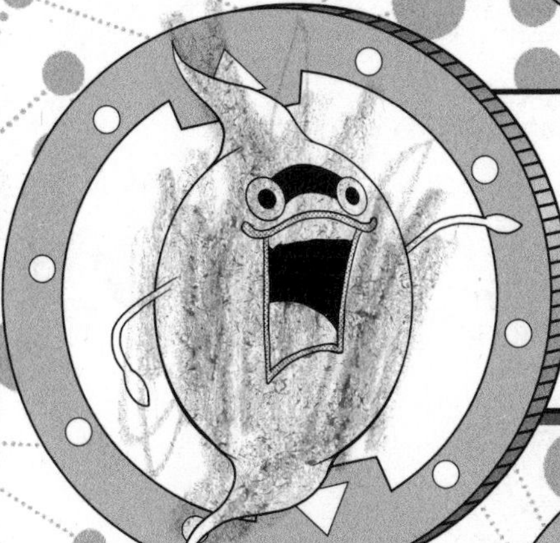

## WHISPER

A YO-KAI BUTLER FREED BY NATE, WHISPER HELPS HIM BY USING HIS EXTENSIVE KNOWLEDGE OF OTHER YO-KAI.

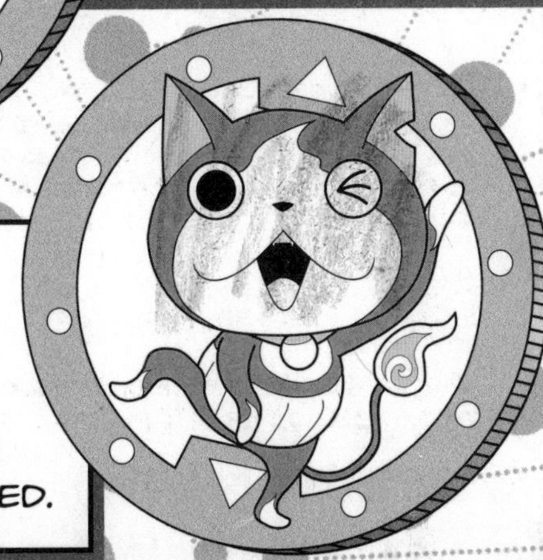

## JIBANYAN

A CAT WHO BECAME A YO-KAI WHEN HE PASSED AWAY. HE IS FRIENDLY, CAREFREE AND THE FIRST YO-KAI THAT NATE BEFRIENDED.

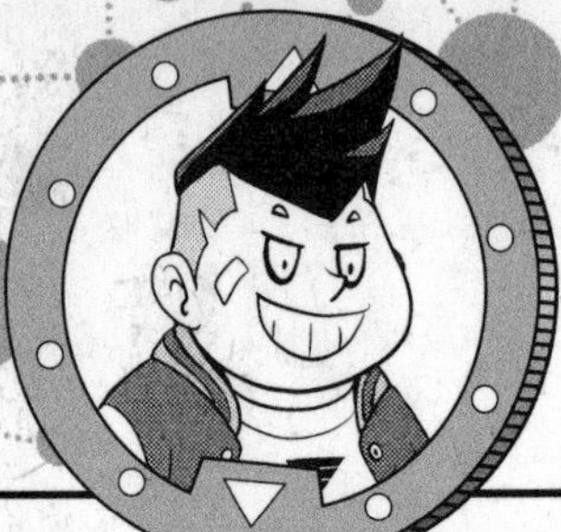

EDWARD ARCHER
NATE'S CLASSMATE.
NICKNAME: EDDIE. HE
ALWAYS WEARS HEAD-
PHONES.

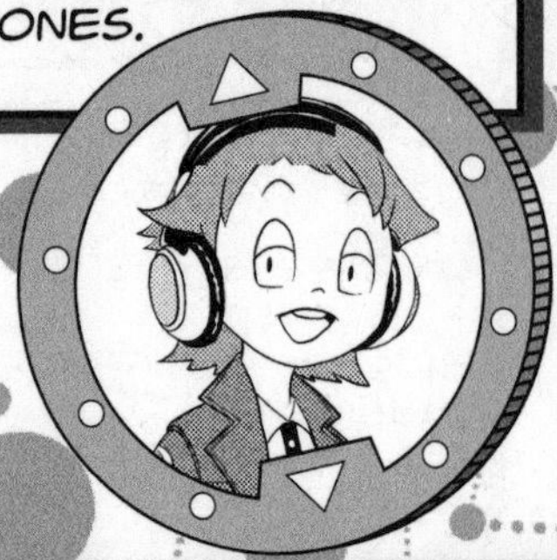

BARNABY BERNSTEIN
NATE'S CLASSMATE.
NICKNAME: BEAR.
CAN BE MISCHIEVOUS.

# TABLE OF CONTENTS

# CHAPTER 59
# THE WANDERING YO-KAI HAS APPEARED!
## FEATURING MYSTERIOUS WANDERING YO-KAI VENOCT

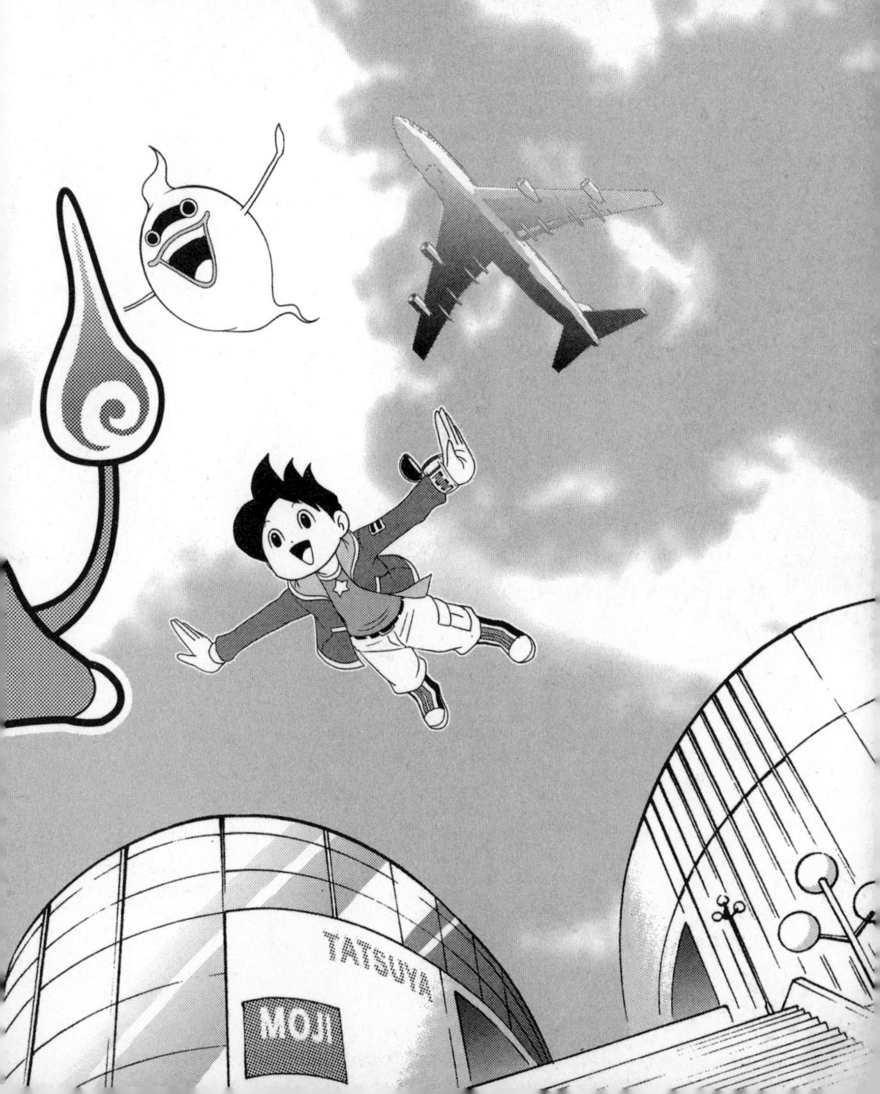
TATSUYA
MOJI

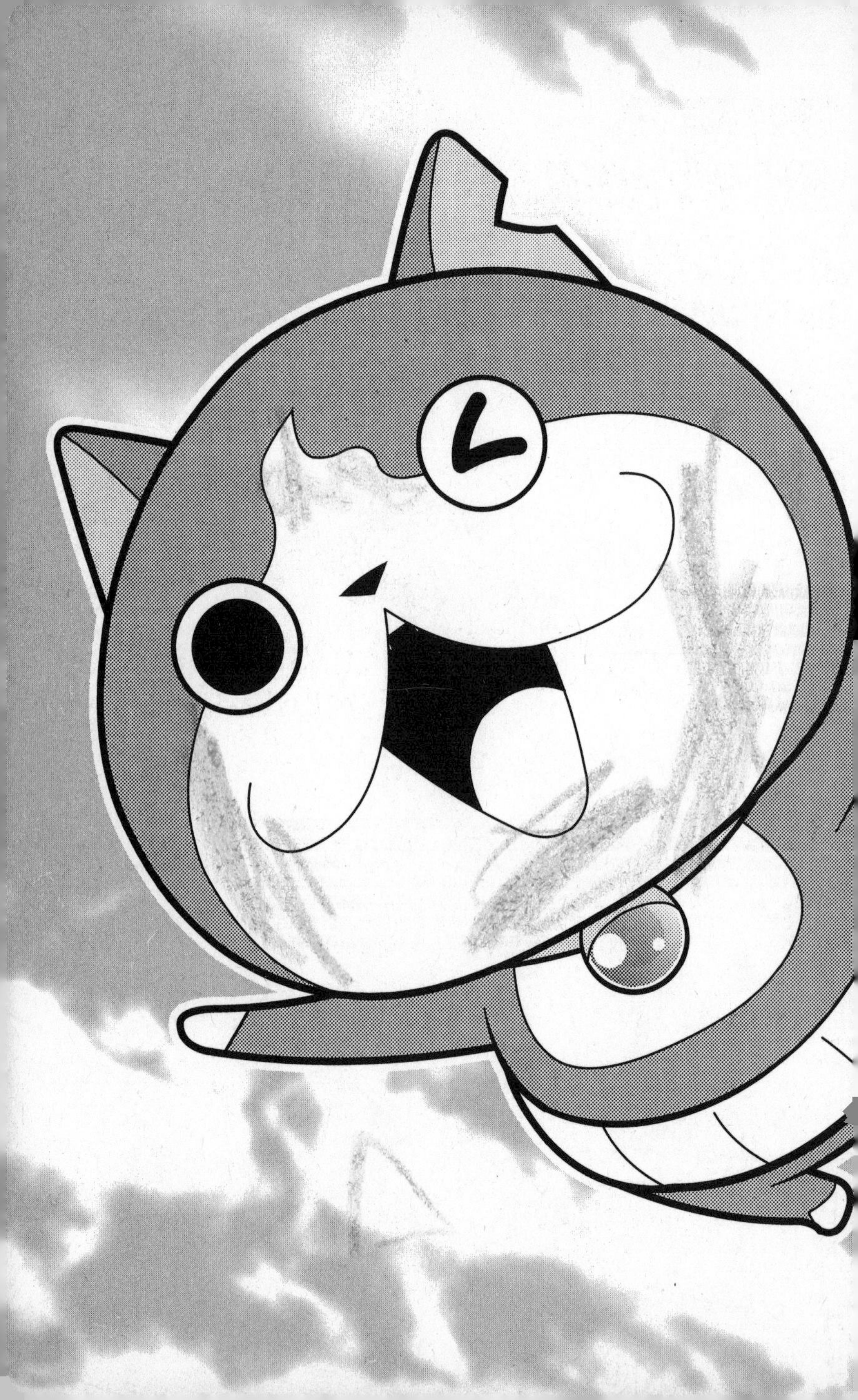

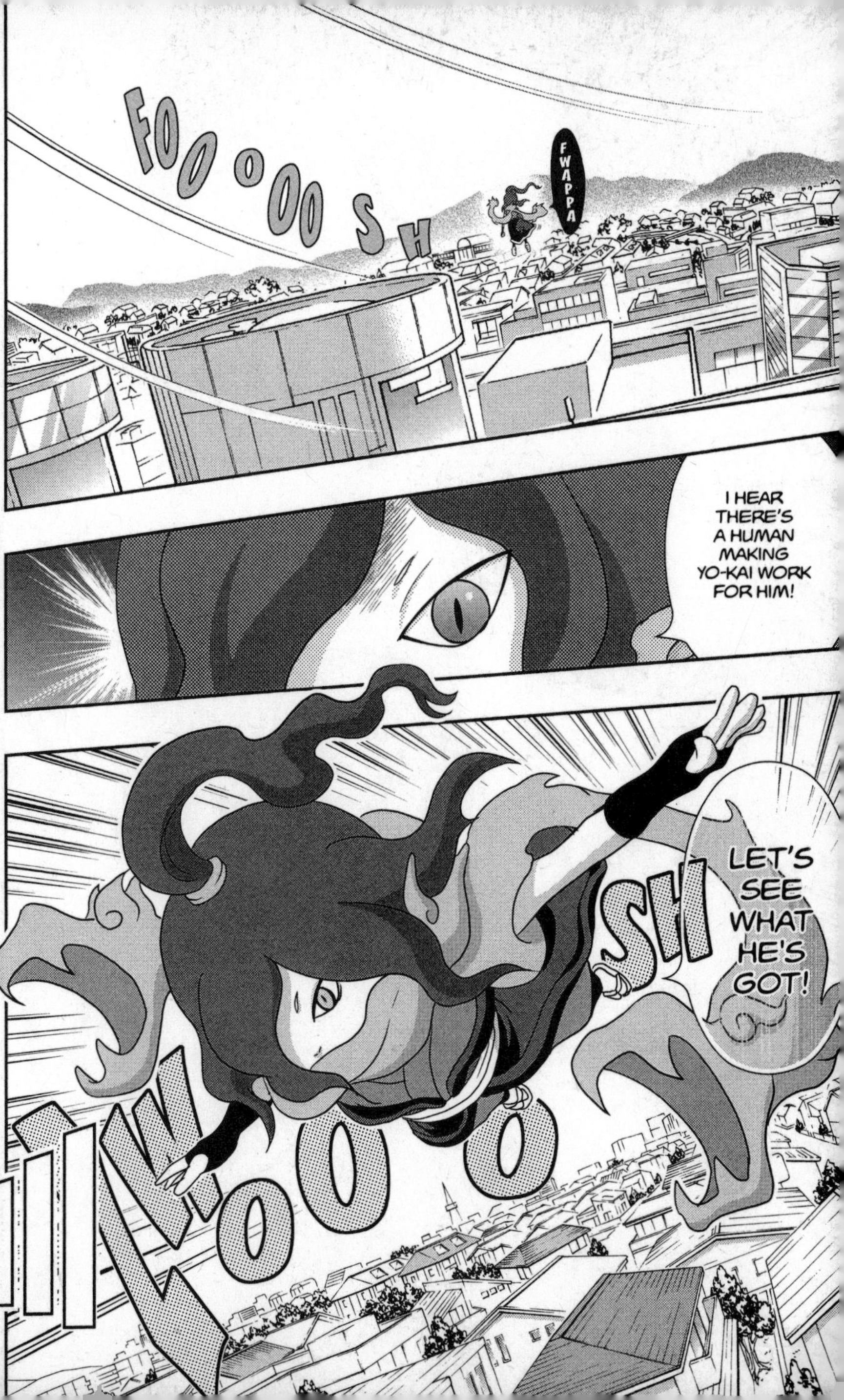
FOOOOOOSH
FWAPPA
I HEAR THERE'S A HUMAN MAKING YO-KAI WORK FOR HIM!
LET'S SEE WHAT HE'S GOT!
WHOOOOSH

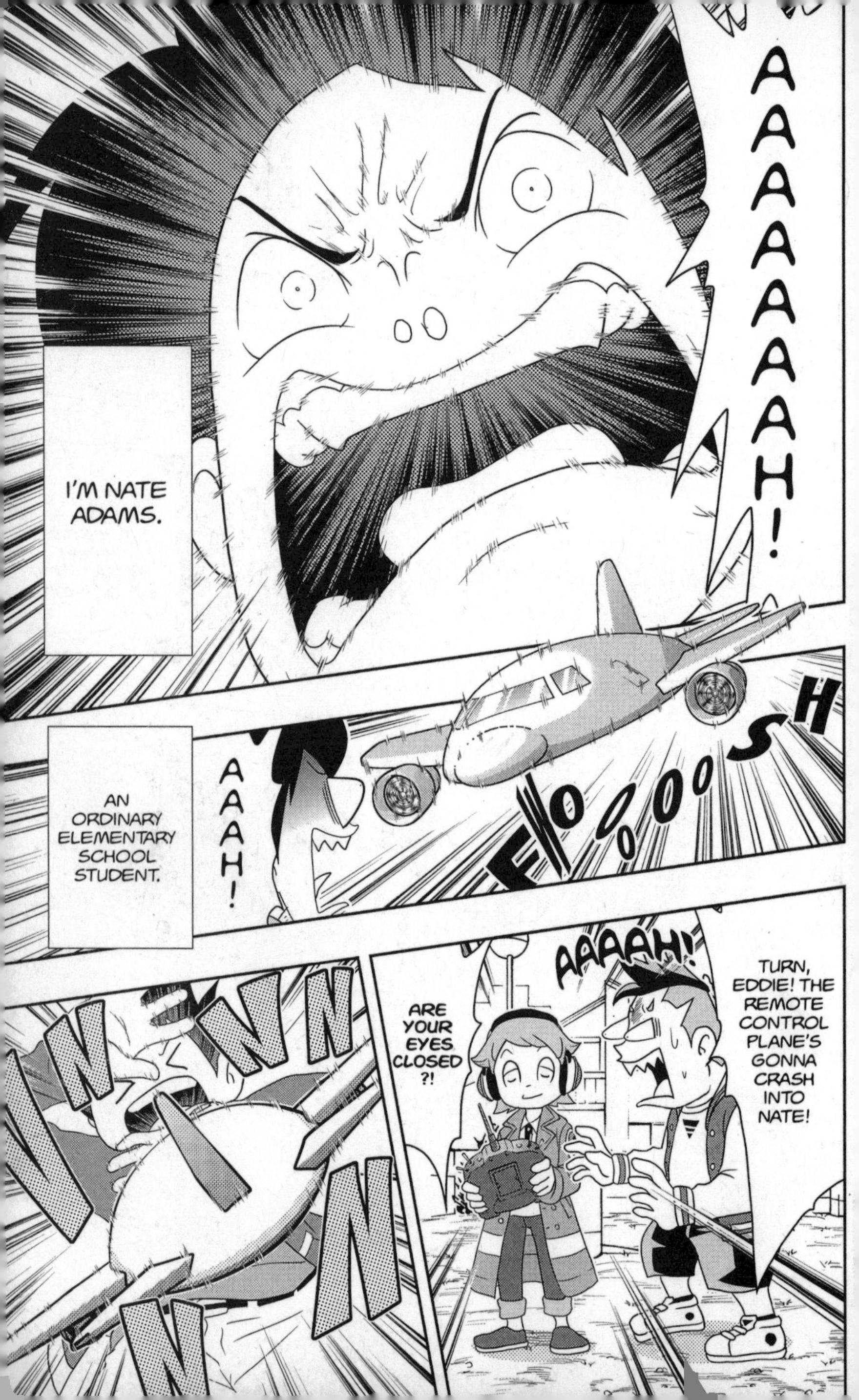
AAAAAAAH!
I'M NATE ADAMS.
FWOOOOSH
AAAH!
AN ORDINARY ELEMENTARY SCHOOL STUDENT.
AAAAH!
TURN, EDDIE! THE REMOTE CONTROL PLANE'S GONNA CRASH INTO NATE!
ARE YOUR EYES CLOSED?!
WNNN

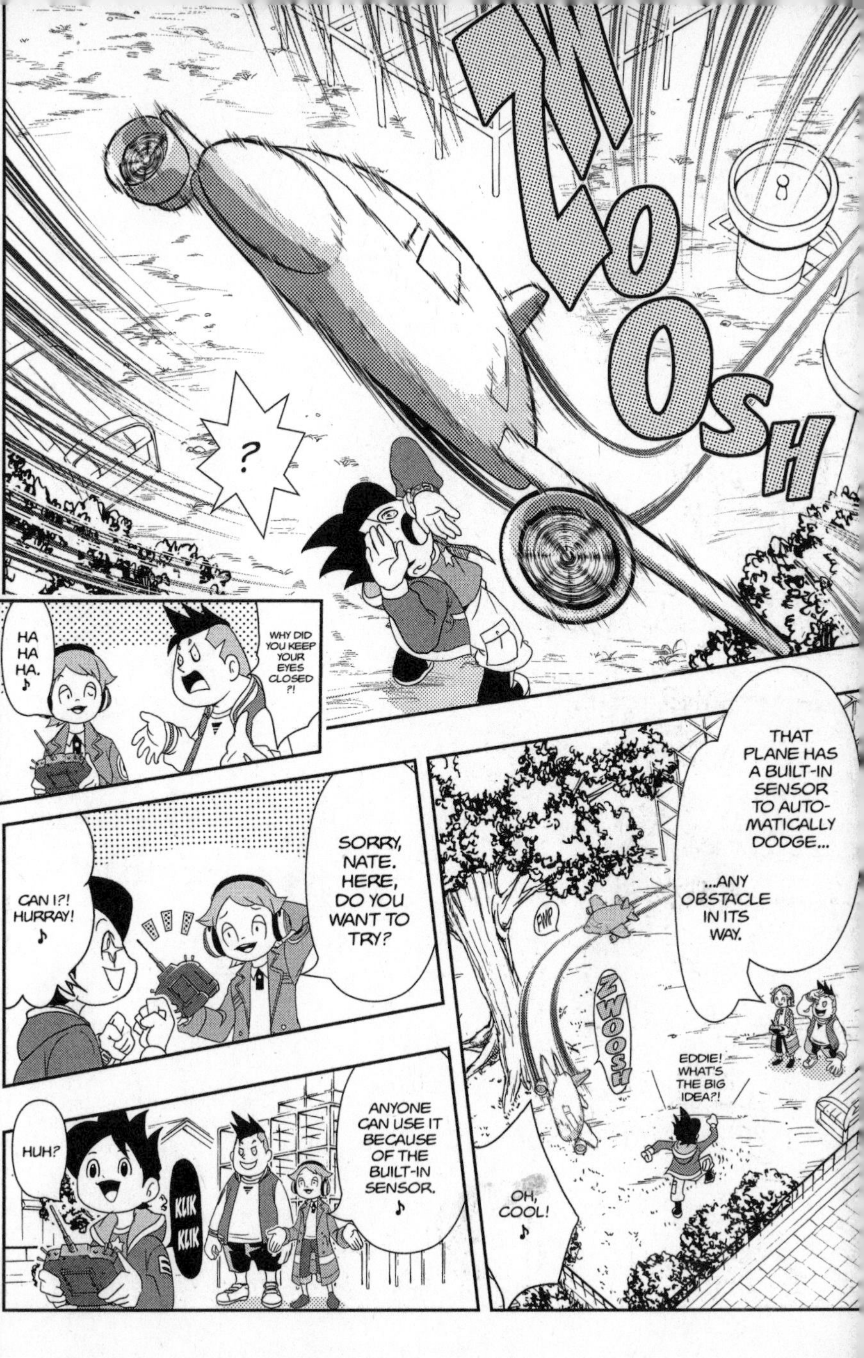
ZWOOSH
?
HA HA HA. ♪
WHY DID YOU KEEP YOUR EYES CLOSED?!
THAT PLANE HAS A BUILT-IN SENSOR TO AUTOMATICALLY DODGE...
...ANY OBSTACLE IN ITS WAY.
FWP
ZWOOSH
EDDIE! WHAT'S THE BIG IDEA?!
OH, COOL! ♪
SORRY, NATE. HERE, DO YOU WANT TO TRY?
CAN I?! HURRAY! ♪
ANYONE CAN USE IT BECAUSE OF THE BUILT-IN SENSOR. ♪
KLIK KLIK
HUH?

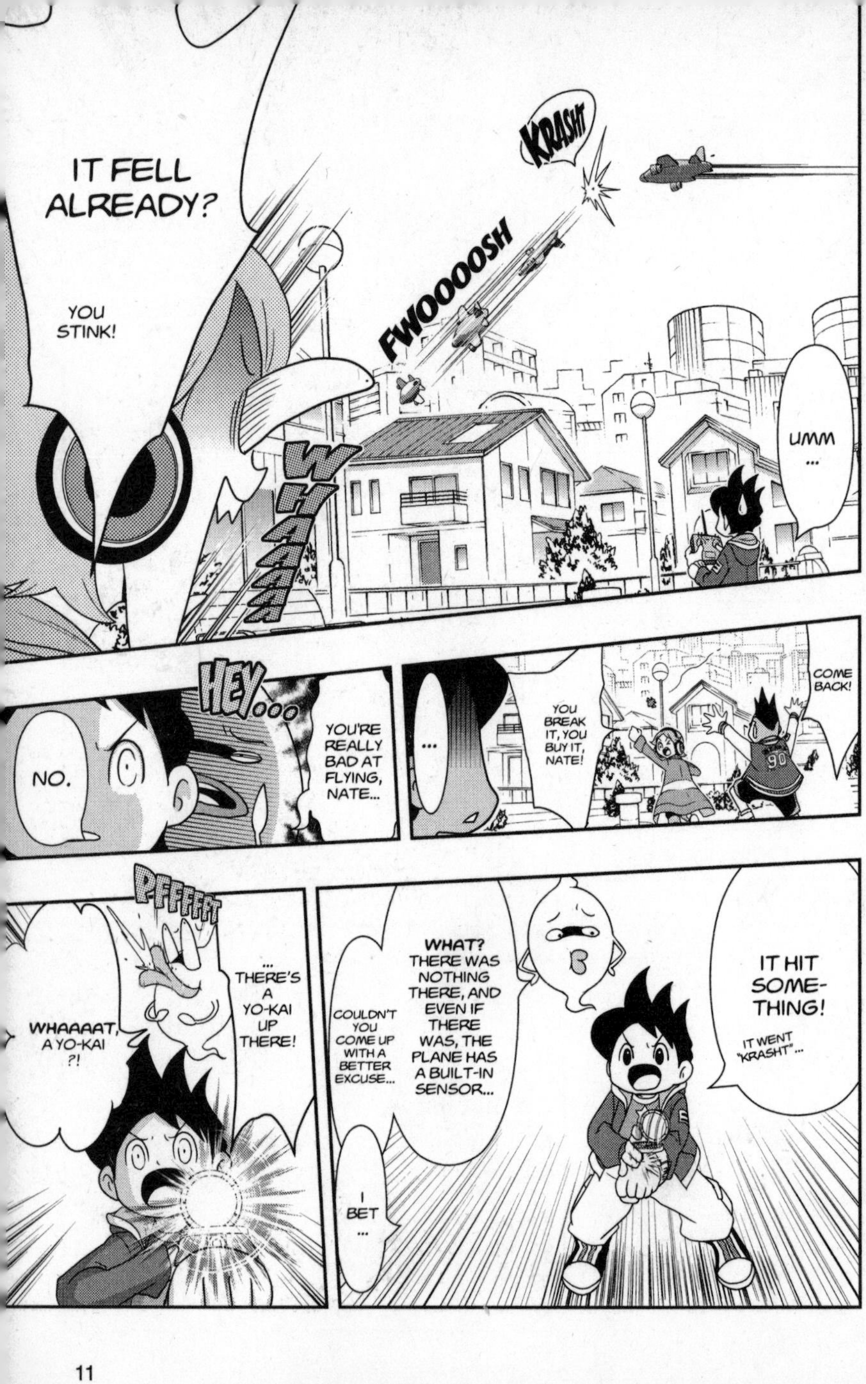
KRASHT
UMM ...
FWOOOOSH
WHAAAAA
IT FELL ALREADY?
YOU STINK!
COME BACK!
YOU BREAK IT, YOU BUY IT, NATE!
...
YOU'RE REALLY BAD AT FLYING, NATE...
HEY...
NO.
IT HIT SOME-THING!
IT WENT "KRASHT"...
WHAT? THERE WAS NOTHING THERE, AND EVEN IF THERE WAS, THE PLANE HAS A BUILT-IN SENSOR...
COULDN'T YOU COME UP WITH A BETTER EXCUSE...
I BET ...
PFFFFFT
... THERE'S A YO-KAI UP THERE!
WHAAAAT, A YO-KAI ?!

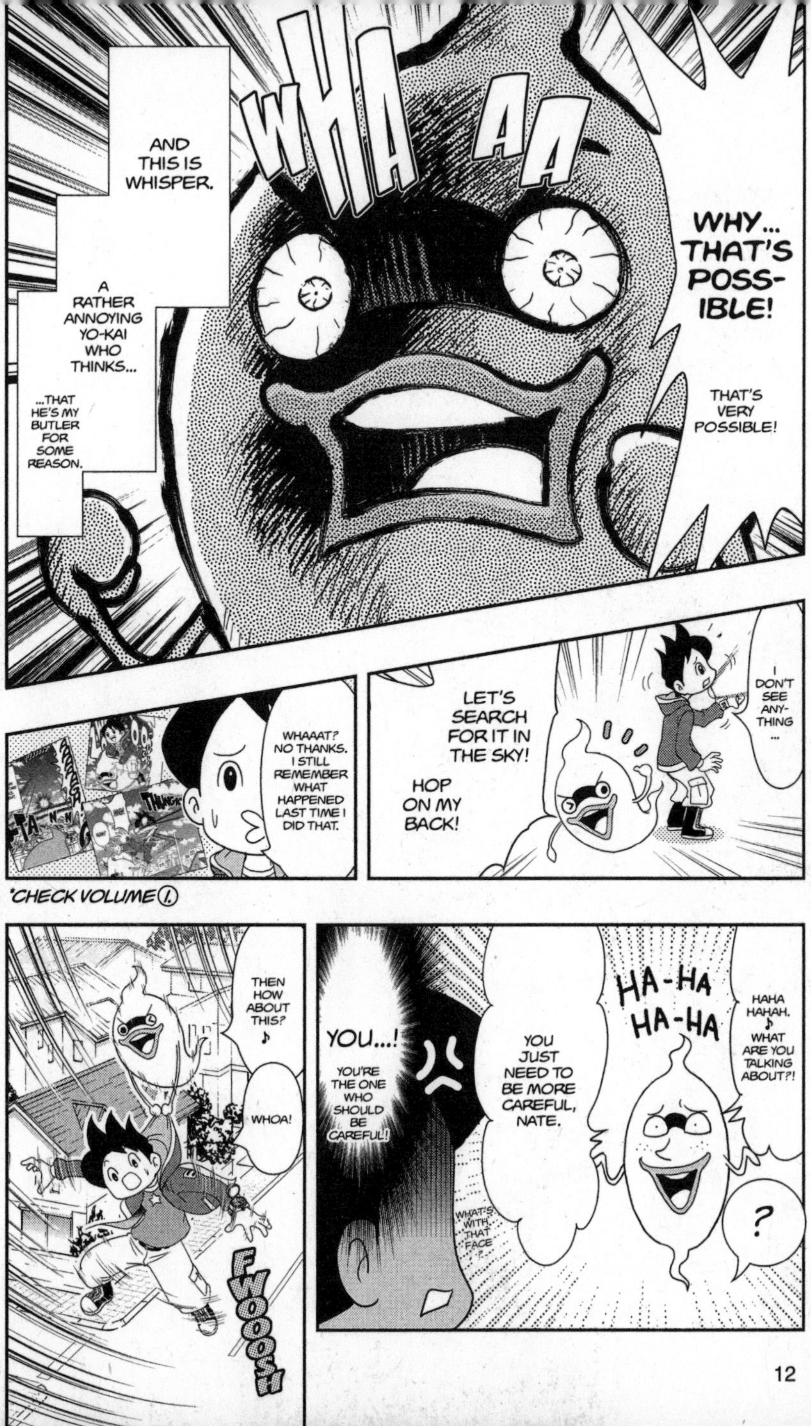
WHAAAA
WHY... THAT'S POSS-IBLE!
THAT'S VERY POSSIBLE!
AND THIS IS WHISPER.
A RATHER ANNOYING YO-KAI WHO THINKS...
...THAT HE'S MY BUTLER FOR SOME REASON.
I DON'T SEE ANY-THING...
LET'S SEARCH FOR IT IN THE SKY!
HOP ON MY BACK!
WHAAAT? NO THANKS. I STILL REMEMBER WHAT HAPPENED LAST TIME I DID THAT.
*CHECK VOLUME ①.
HAHA HAHAH. ♪ WHAT ARE YOU TALKING ABOUT?!
HA-HA HA-HA
?
YOU JUST NEED TO BE MORE CAREFUL, NATE.
YOU...!
YOU'RE THE ONE WHO SHOULD BE CAREFUL!
WHAT'S WITH THAT FACE?
THEN HOW ABOUT THIS? ♪
WHOA!
FWOOOSH

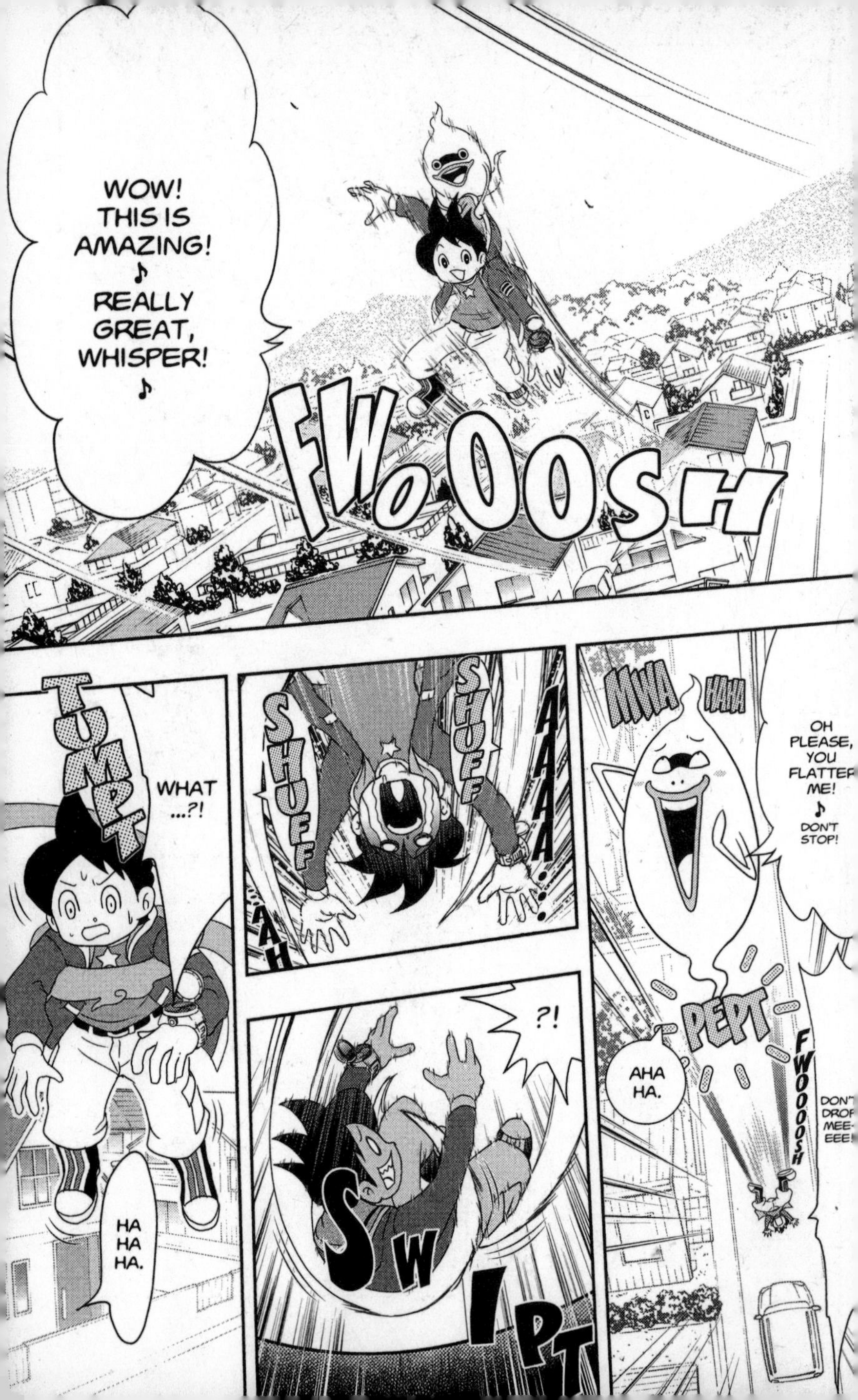
WOW! THIS IS AMAZING! ♪ REALLY GREAT, WHISPER! ♪
FWOOOSH
MWA HAHA
OH PLEASE, YOU FLATTER ME! ♪
DON'T STOP!
AHA HA.
PEPT
FWOOOOSH
DON'T DROP MEE-EEE!
AAAAA...!
AAH
SHUFF
SHUFF
?!
SWIPT
TUMPT
WHAT ...?!
HA HA HA.

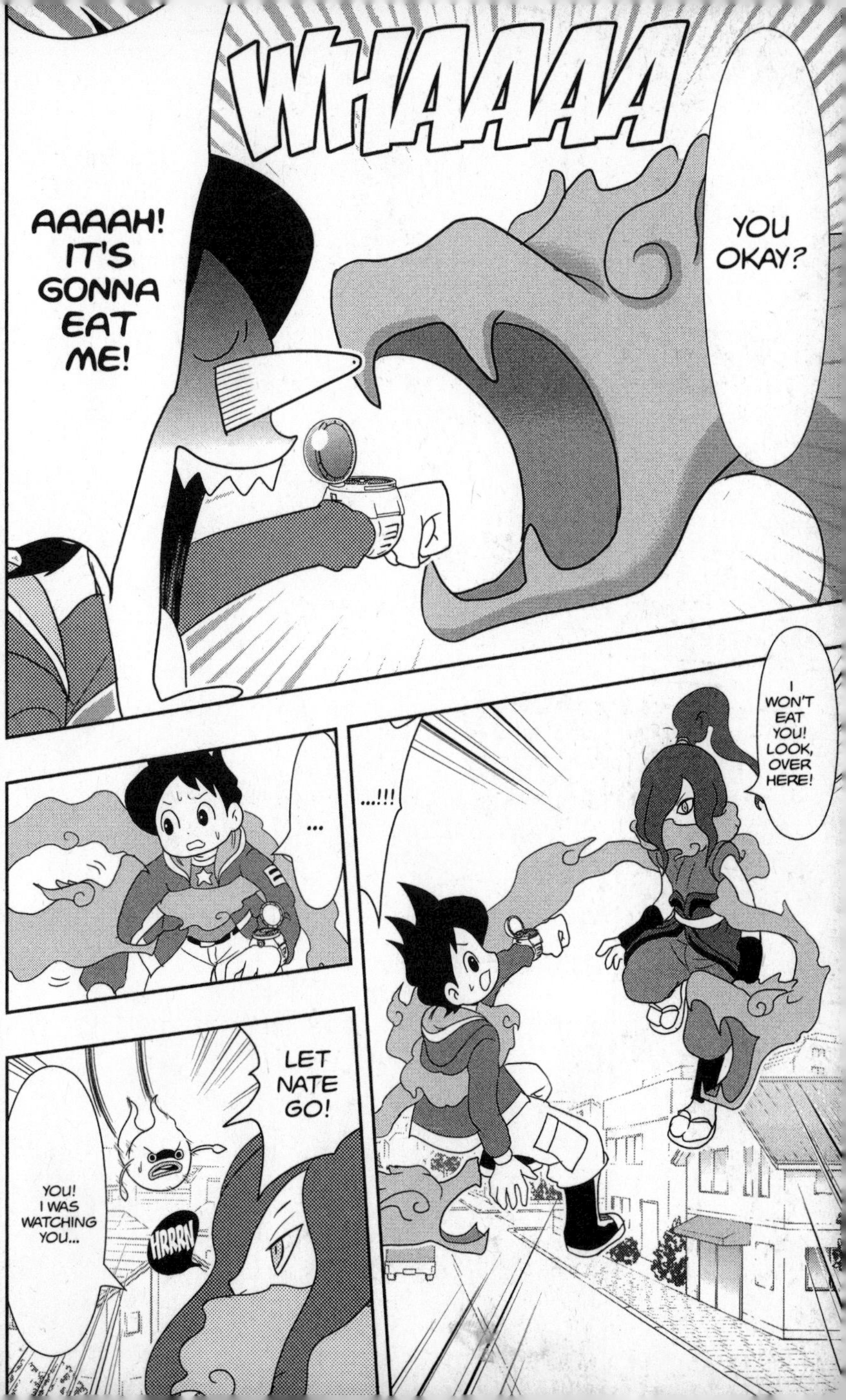
WHAAAAA
YOU OKAY?
AAAAH! IT'S GONNA EAT ME!
I WON'T EAT YOU! LOOK, OVER HERE!
...!!!
...
LET NATE GO!
YOU! I WAS WATCHING YOU...
HRRRN

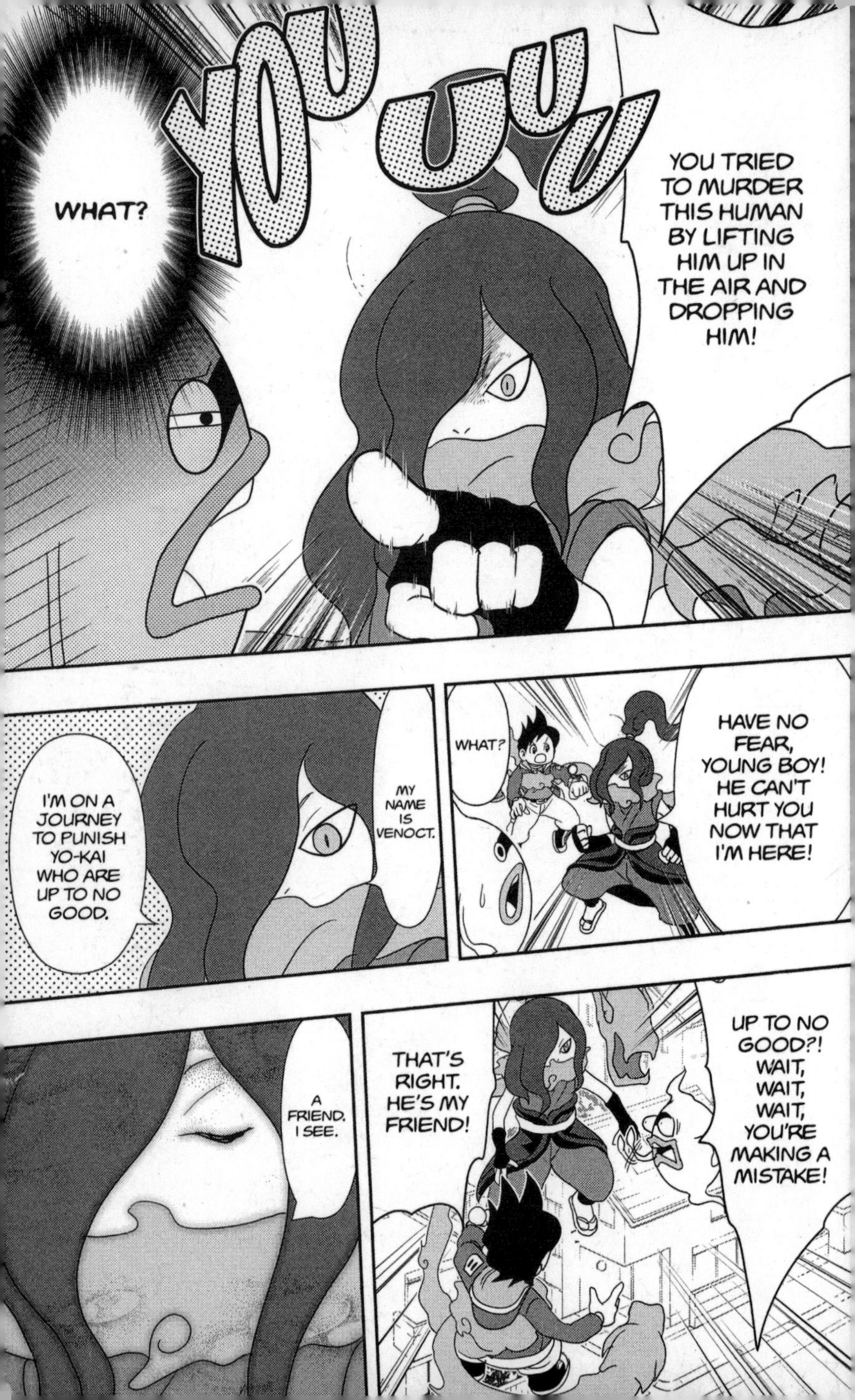
YOUUUU
YOU TRIED TO MURDER THIS HUMAN BY LIFTING HIM UP IN THE AIR AND DROPPING HIM!
WHAT?
HAVE NO FEAR, YOUNG BOY! HE CAN'T HURT YOU NOW THAT I'M HERE!
WHAT?
MY NAME IS VENOCT.
I'M ON A JOURNEY TO PUNISH YO-KAI WHO ARE UP TO NO GOOD.
UP TO NO GOOD?! WAIT, WAIT, WAIT, YOU'RE MAKING A MISTAKE!
THAT'S RIGHT. HE'S MY FRIEND!
A FRIEND. I SEE.

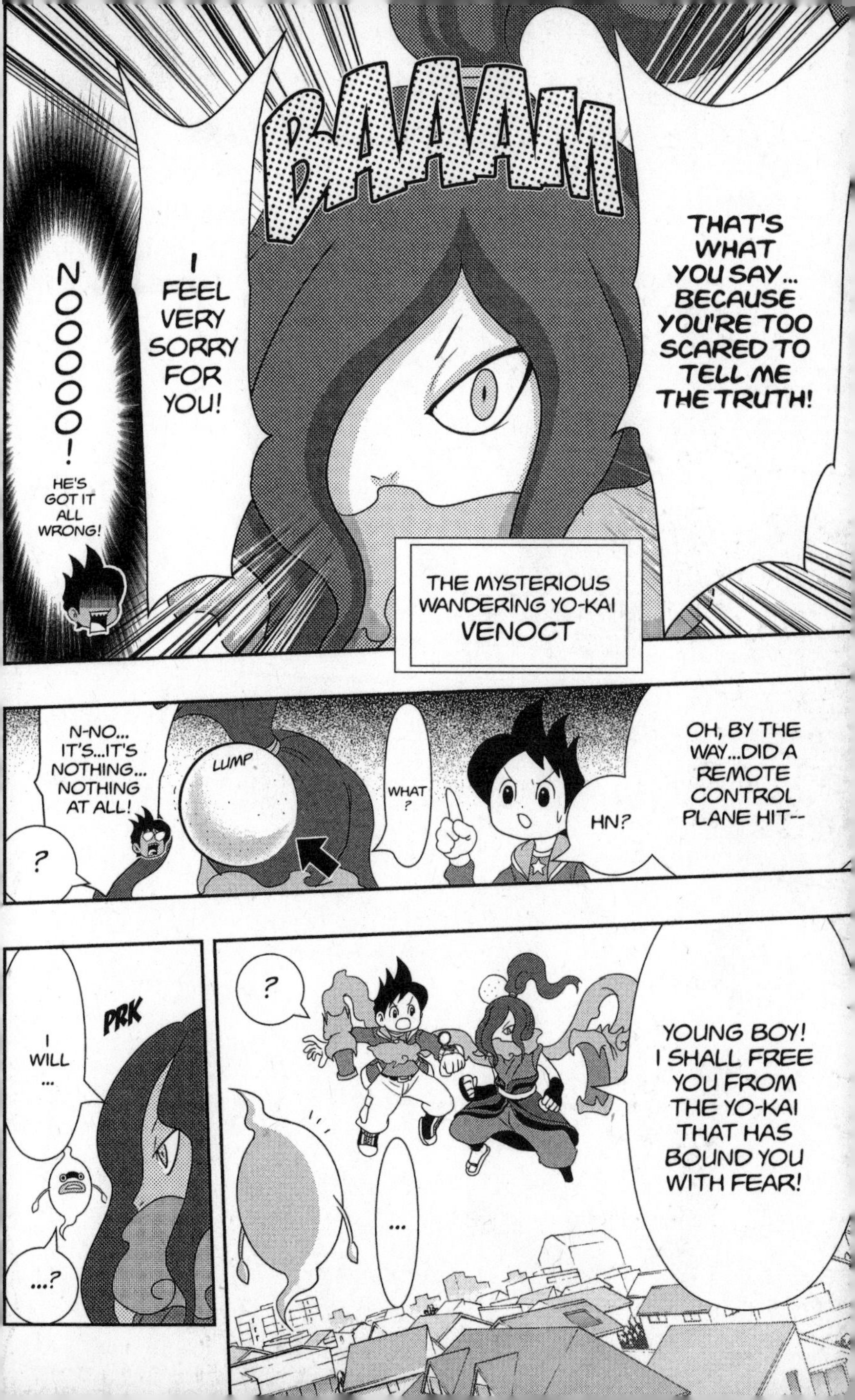
THAT'S WHAT YOU SAY... BECAUSE YOU'RE TOO SCARED TO TELL ME THE TRUTH!
BAAAM
THE MYSTERIOUS WANDERING YO-KAI VENOCT
I FEEL VERY SORRY FOR YOU!
NOOOOOO!
HE'S GOT IT ALL WRONG!
OH, BY THE WAY...DID A REMOTE CONTROL PLANE HIT--
HN?
WHAT ?
LUMP
N-NO... IT'S...IT'S NOTHING... NOTHING AT ALL!
?
YOUNG BOY! I SHALL FREE YOU FROM THE YO-KAI THAT HAS BOUND YOU WITH FEAR!
?
...
I WILL ...
PRK
...?

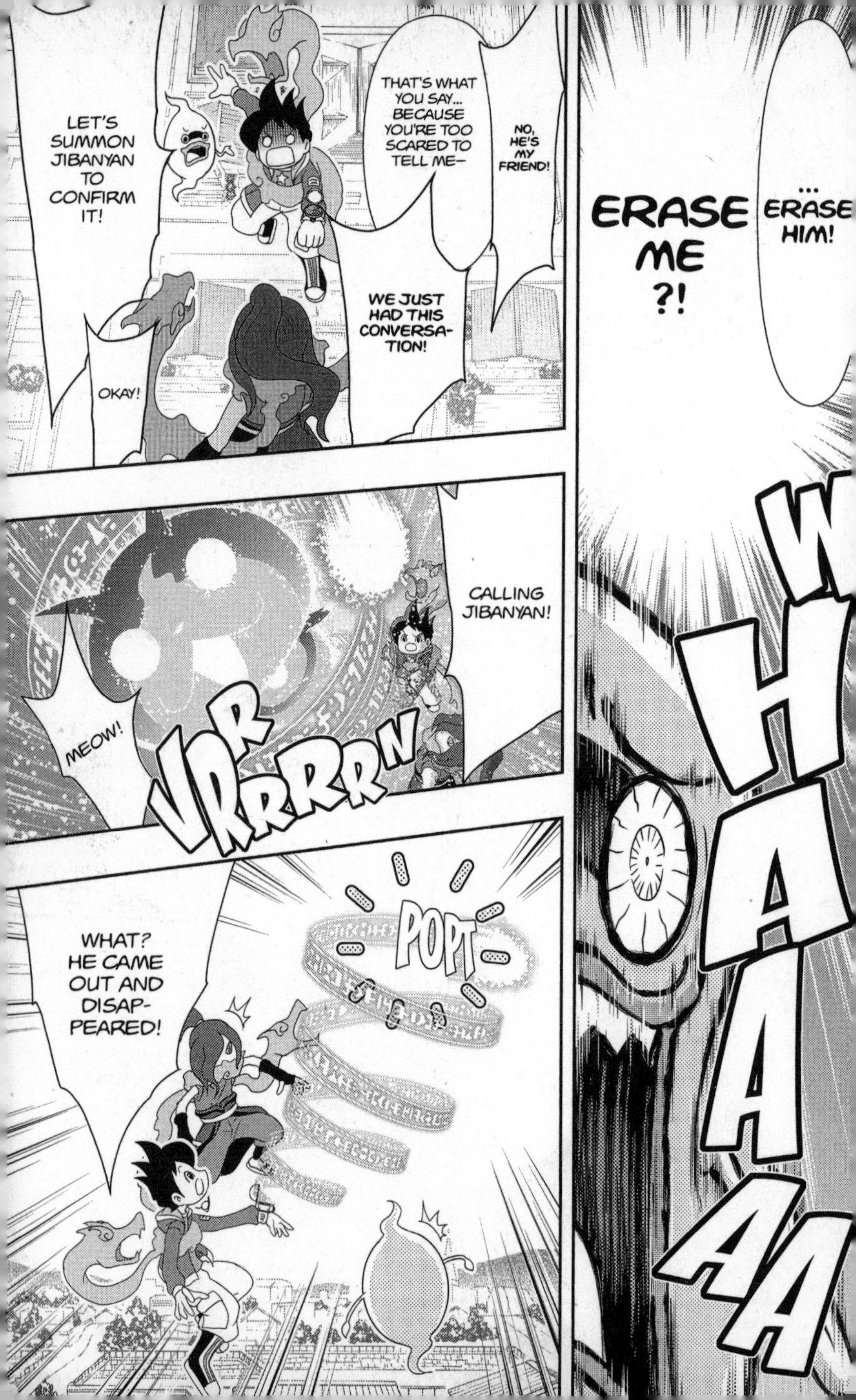
... ERASE HIM!
ERASE ME ?!
WHOAAAAA
THAT'S WHAT YOU SAY... BECAUSE YOU'RE TOO SCARED TO TELL ME–
NO, HE'S MY FRIEND!
WE JUST HAD THIS CONVERSATION!
LET'S SUMMON JIBANYAN TO CONFIRM IT!
OKAY!
CALLING JIBANYAN!
VRRRRRN
MEOW!
POPT
WHAT? HE CAME OUT AND DISAPPEARED!

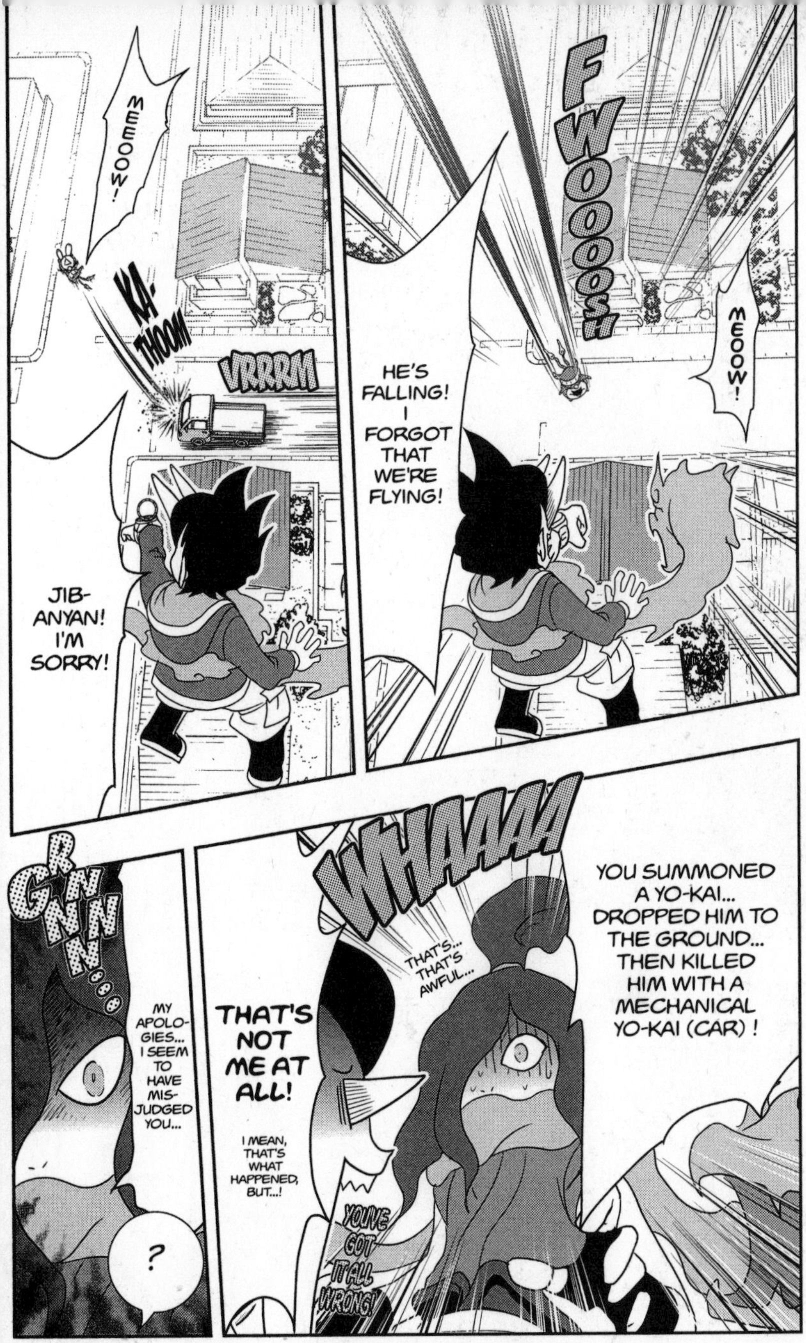
FWOOOOSH
MEOOW!
HE'S FALLING! I FORGOT THAT WE'RE FLYING!
MEEOOW!
KA-THOOM
VRRRM
JIB-ANYAN! I'M SORRY!
WHAAAAA
YOU SUMMONED A YO-KAI... DROPPED HIM TO THE GROUND... THEN KILLED HIM WITH A MECHANICAL YO-KAI (CAR)!
THAT'S... THAT'S AWFUL...
THAT'S NOT ME AT ALL!
I MEAN, THAT'S WHAT HAPPENED, BUT...!
YOU'VE GOT IT ALL WRONG!
GRNNN...
MY APOLO-GIES... I SEEM TO HAVE MIS-JUDGED YOU...
?

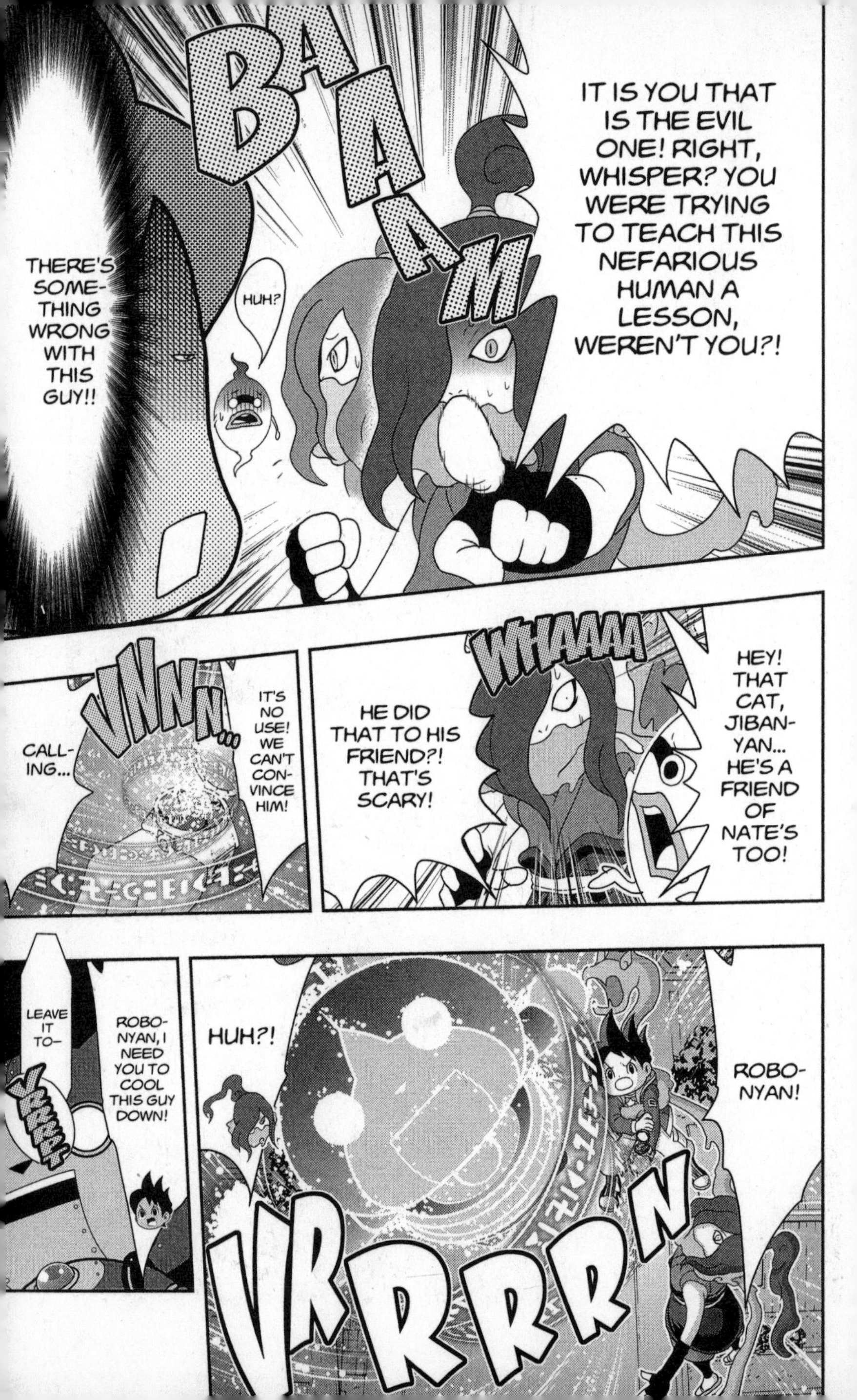

IT IS YOU THAT IS THE EVIL ONE! RIGHT, WHISPER? YOU WERE TRYING TO TEACH THIS NEFARIOUS HUMAN A LESSON, WEREN'T YOU?!
BAAAM
HUH?
THERE'S SOME-THING WRONG WITH THIS GUY!!
WHAAAA
HEY! THAT CAT, JIBAN-YAN... HE'S A FRIEND OF NATE'S TOO!
HE DID THAT TO HIS FRIEND?! THAT'S SCARY!
IT'S NO USE! WE CAN'T CON-VINCE HIM!
VNNNN...
CALL-ING...
ROBO-NYAN!
HUH?!
VRRRRN
ROBO-NYAN, I NEED YOU TO COOL THIS GUY DOWN!
LEAVE IT TO—

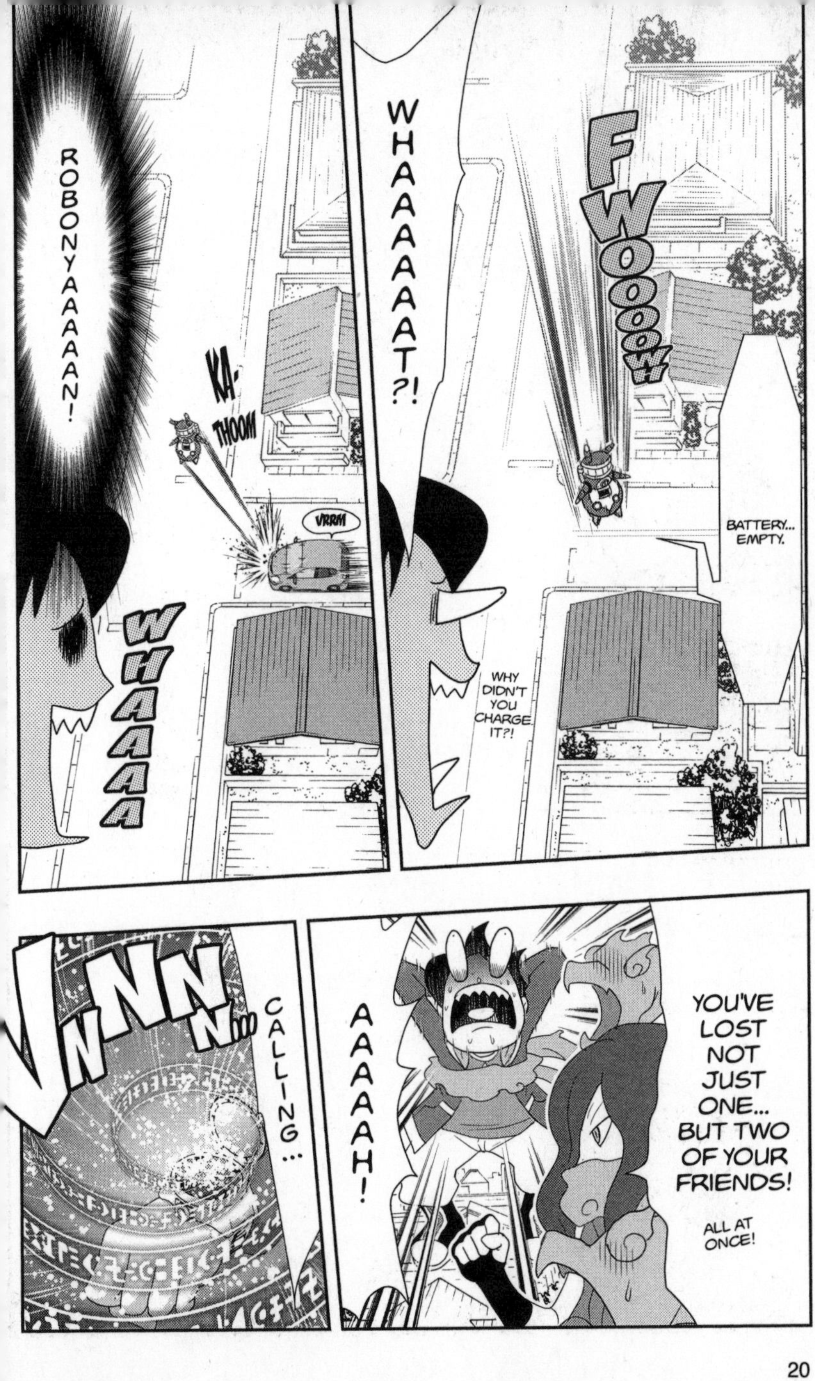
FWOOOOOW
BATTERY... EMPTY.
WHAAAAAAAAT?!
WHY DIDN'T YOU CHARGE IT?!
ROBONYAAAAAAAN!
KA-THOOM
VRRM
WHAAAAAA
YOU'VE LOST NOT JUST ONE... BUT TWO OF YOUR FRIENDS!
ALL AT ONCE!
AAAAAAAH!
JNNNN...
CALLING...

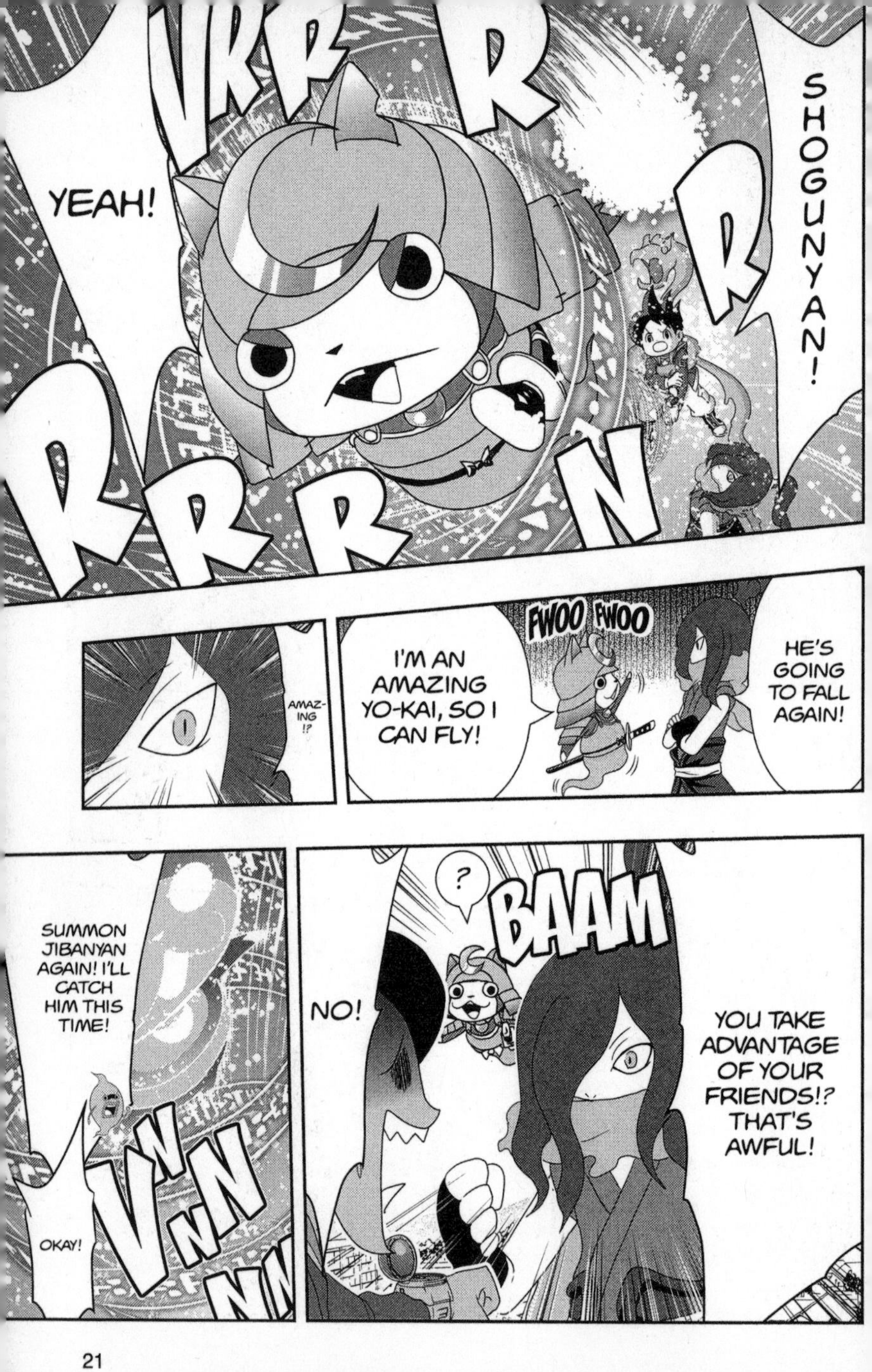
SHOGUNYAN!
VRRRR
YEAH!
RRRRN
HE'S GOING TO FALL AGAIN!
FWOO FWOO
I'M AN AMAZING YO-KAI, SO I CAN FLY!
AMAZ-ING !?
YOU TAKE ADVANTAGE OF YOUR FRIENDS!? THAT'S AWFUL!
BAAM
?
NO!
SUMMON JIBANYAN AGAIN! I'LL CATCH HIM THIS TIME!
VNNNN
OKAY!

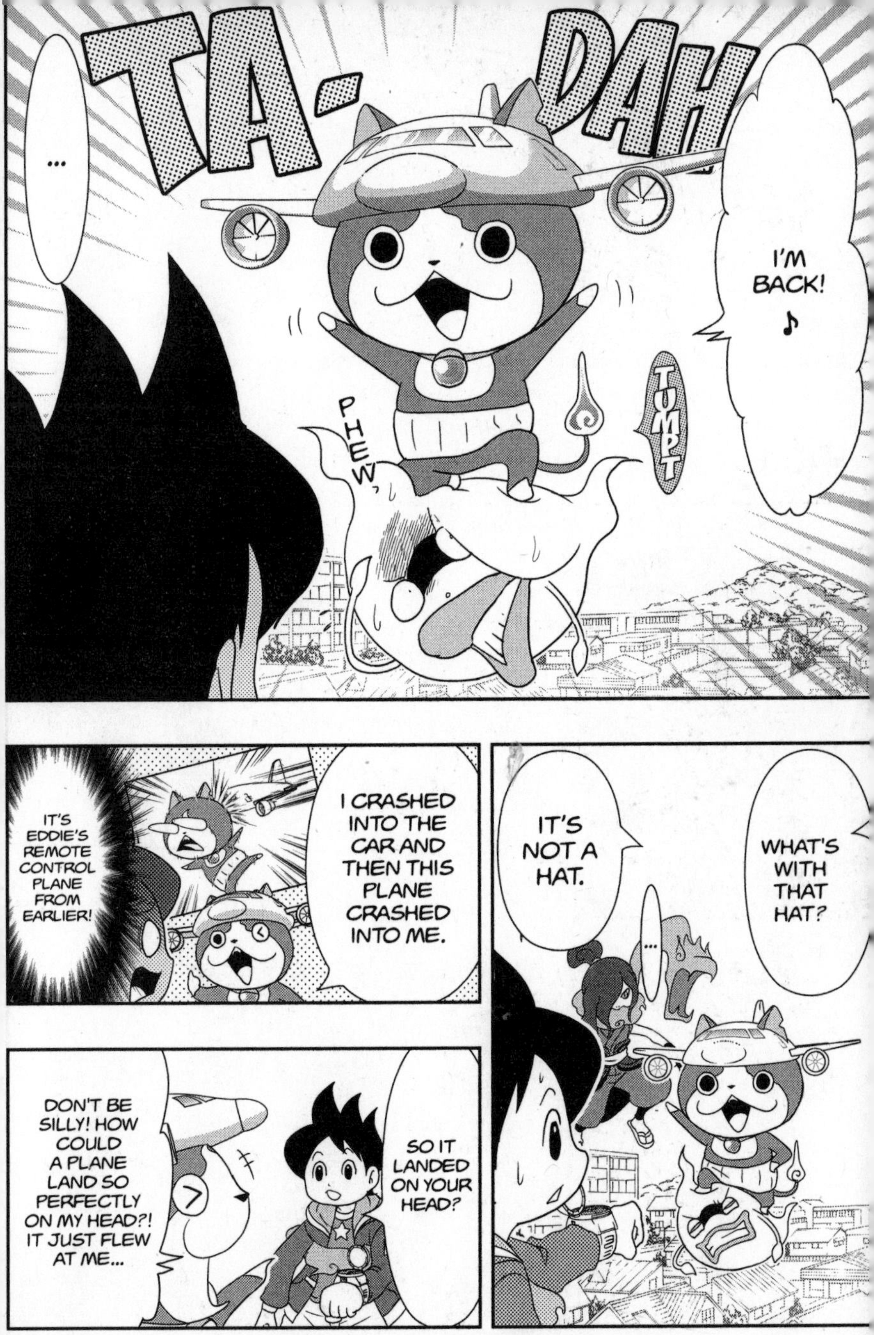
TA-DAH
I'M BACK! ♪
TUMPT
PHEW
...
WHAT'S WITH THAT HAT?
IT'S NOT A HAT.
...
I CRASHED INTO THE CAR AND THEN THIS PLANE CRASHED INTO ME.
IT'S EDDIE'S REMOTE CONTROL PLANE FROM EARLIER!
SO IT LANDED ON YOUR HEAD?
DON'T BE SILLY! HOW COULD A PLANE LAND SO PERFECTLY ON MY HEAD?! IT JUST FLEW AT ME...

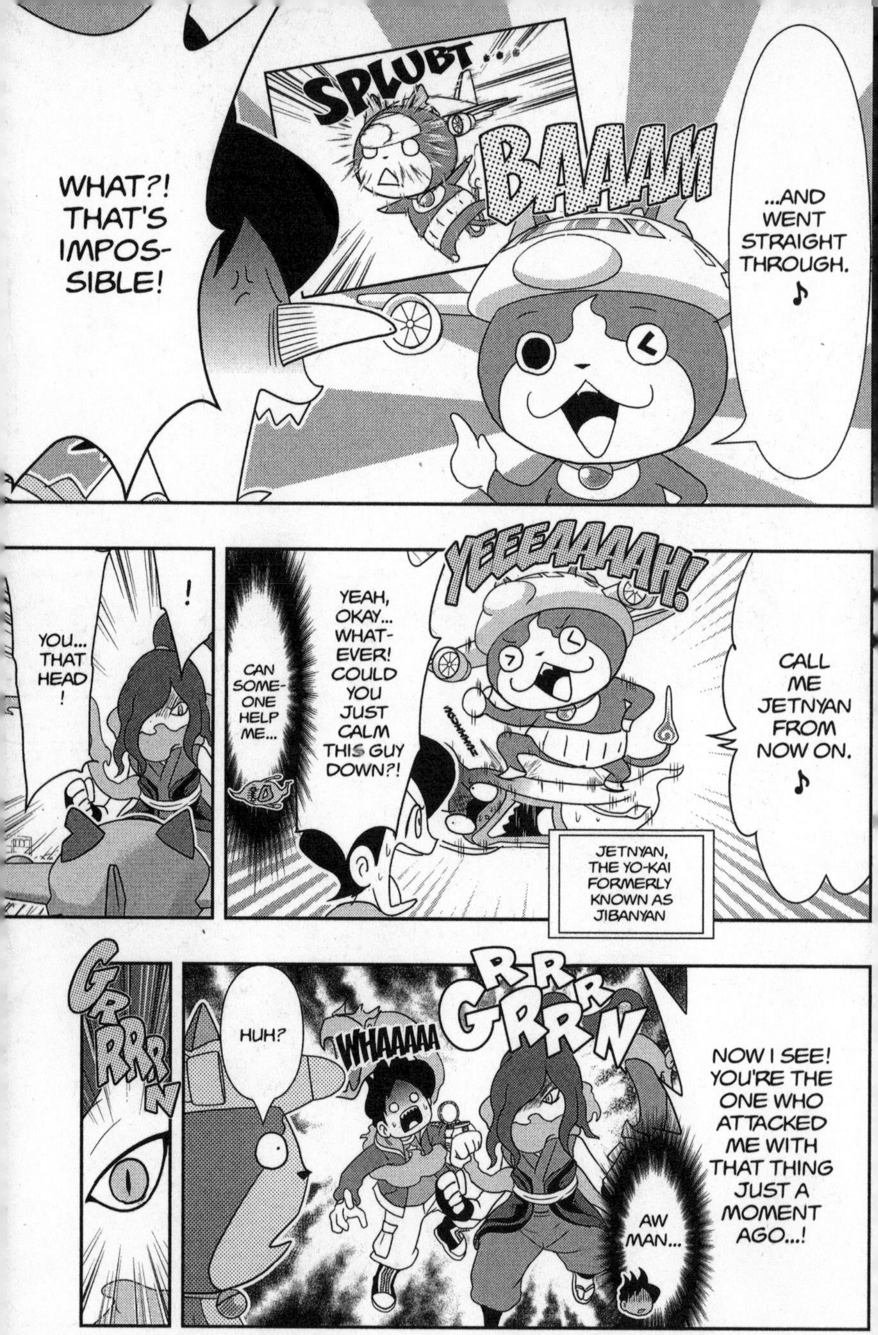
...AND WENT STRAIGHT THROUGH. ♪
SPLUBT
BAAAAM
WHAT?! THAT'S IMPOS-SIBLE!
CALL ME JETNYAN FROM NOW ON. ♪
YEEEAAAAAH!
YEAH, OKAY... WHAT-EVER! COULD YOU JUST CALM THIS GUY DOWN?!
CAN SOME-ONE HELP ME...
JETNYAN, THE YO-KAI FORMERLY KNOWN AS JIBANYAN
!
YOU... THAT HEAD!
NOW I SEE! YOU'RE THE ONE WHO ATTACKED ME WITH THAT THING JUST A MOMENT AGO...!
GRRRRRN
WHAAAAA
HUH?
AW MAN...
GRRRN

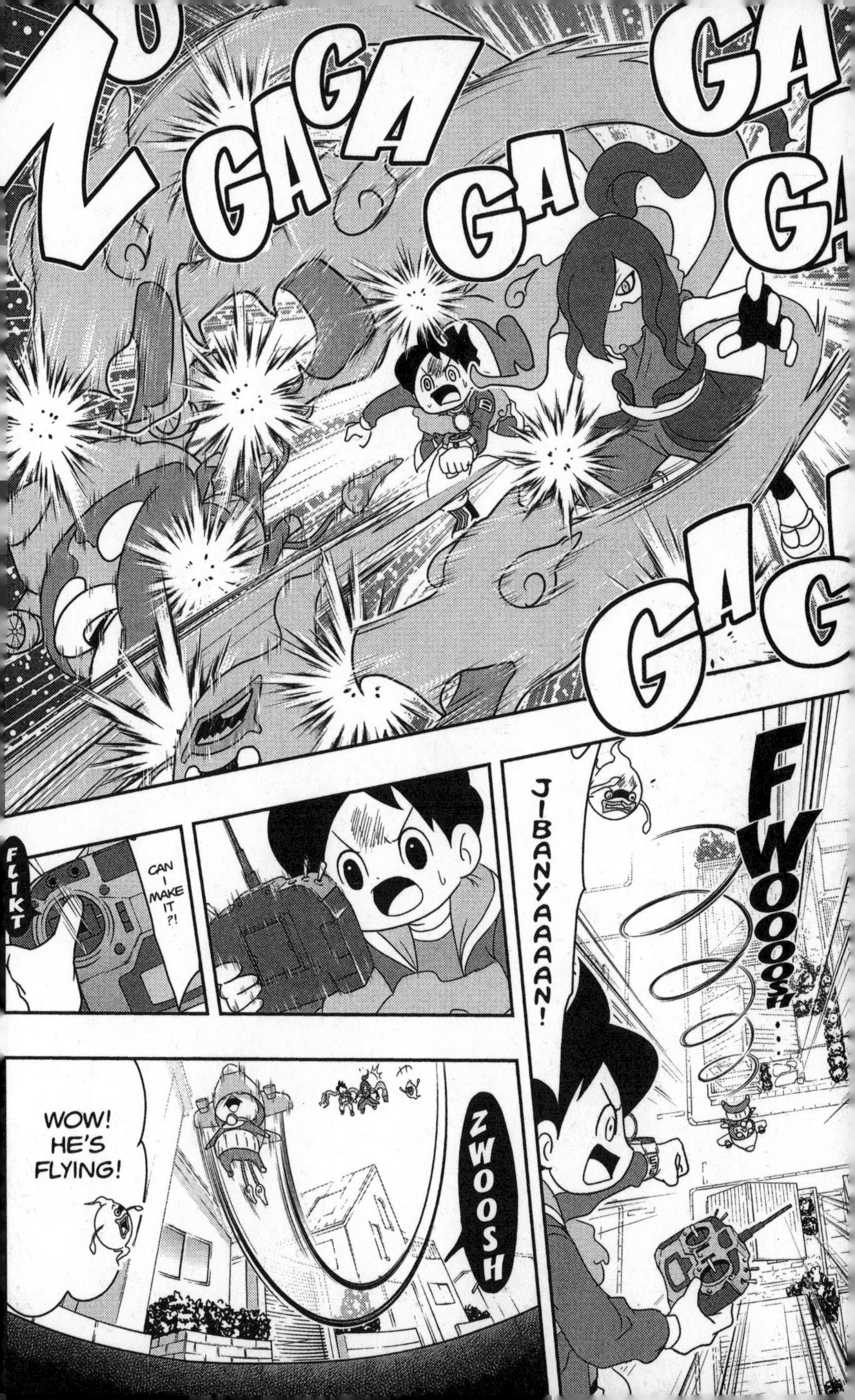

GA GA
GA GA
GAGAGA
GAGA
JIBANYAAAAAN!
FWOOOOSH...
CAN I MAKE IT?!
FLIKT
ZWOOSH
WOW! HE'S FLYING!

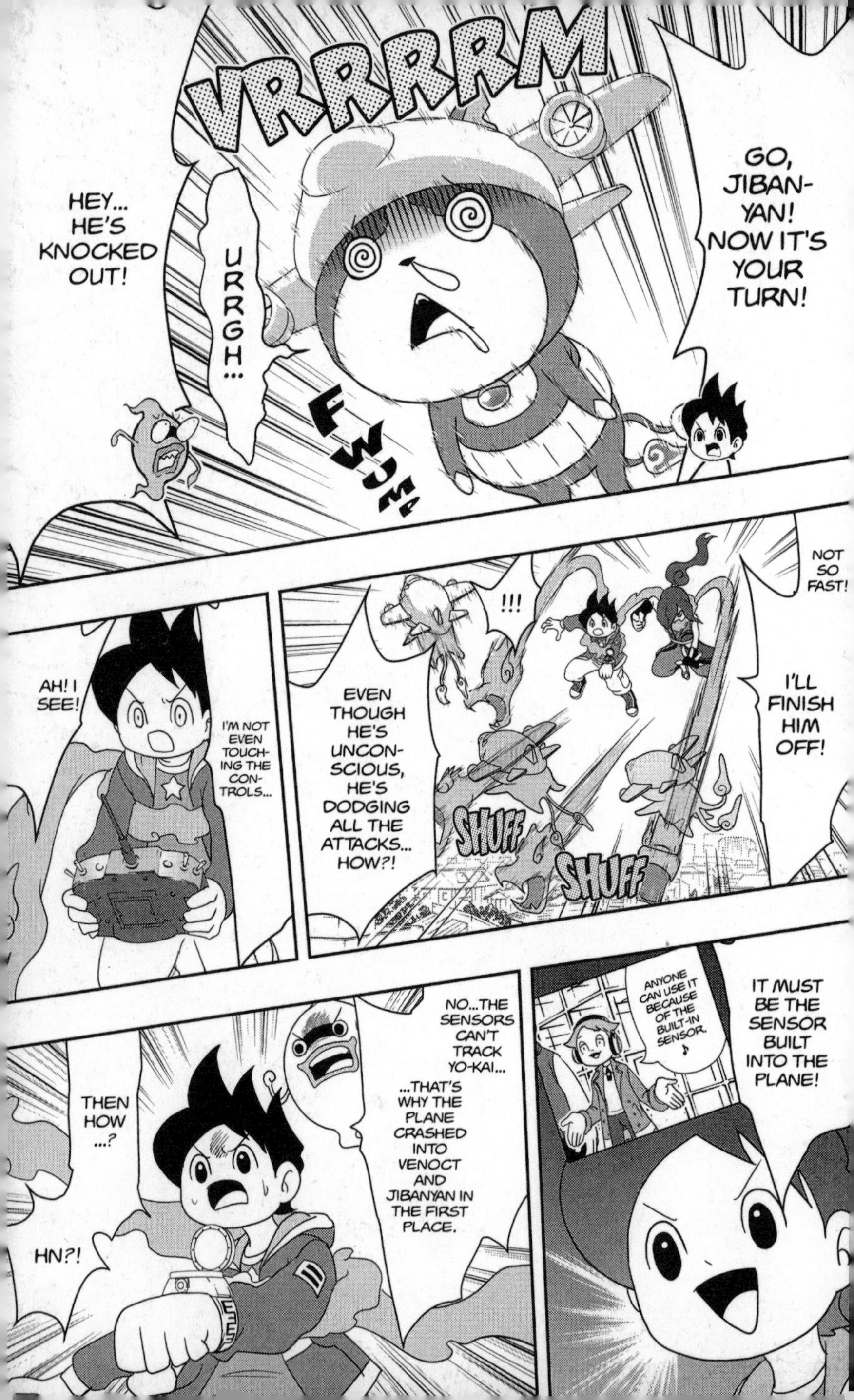
VRRRRM
GO, JIBAN-YAN! NOW IT'S YOUR TURN!
URRGH...
HEY... HE'S KNOCKED OUT!
FWUMP
NOT SO FAST!
I'LL FINISH HIM OFF!
!!!
EVEN THOUGH HE'S UNCONSCIOUS, HE'S DODGING ALL THE ATTACKS... HOW?!
SHUFF
SHUFF
I'M NOT EVEN TOUCHING THE CONTROLS...
AH! I SEE!
IT MUST BE THE SENSOR BUILT INTO THE PLANE!
ANYONE CAN USE IT BECAUSE OF THE BUILT-IN SENSOR. ♪
NO...THE SENSORS CAN'T TRACK YO-KAI...
...THAT'S WHY THE PLANE CRASHED INTO VENOCT AND JIBANYAN IN THE FIRST PLACE.
THEN HOW ...?
HN?!

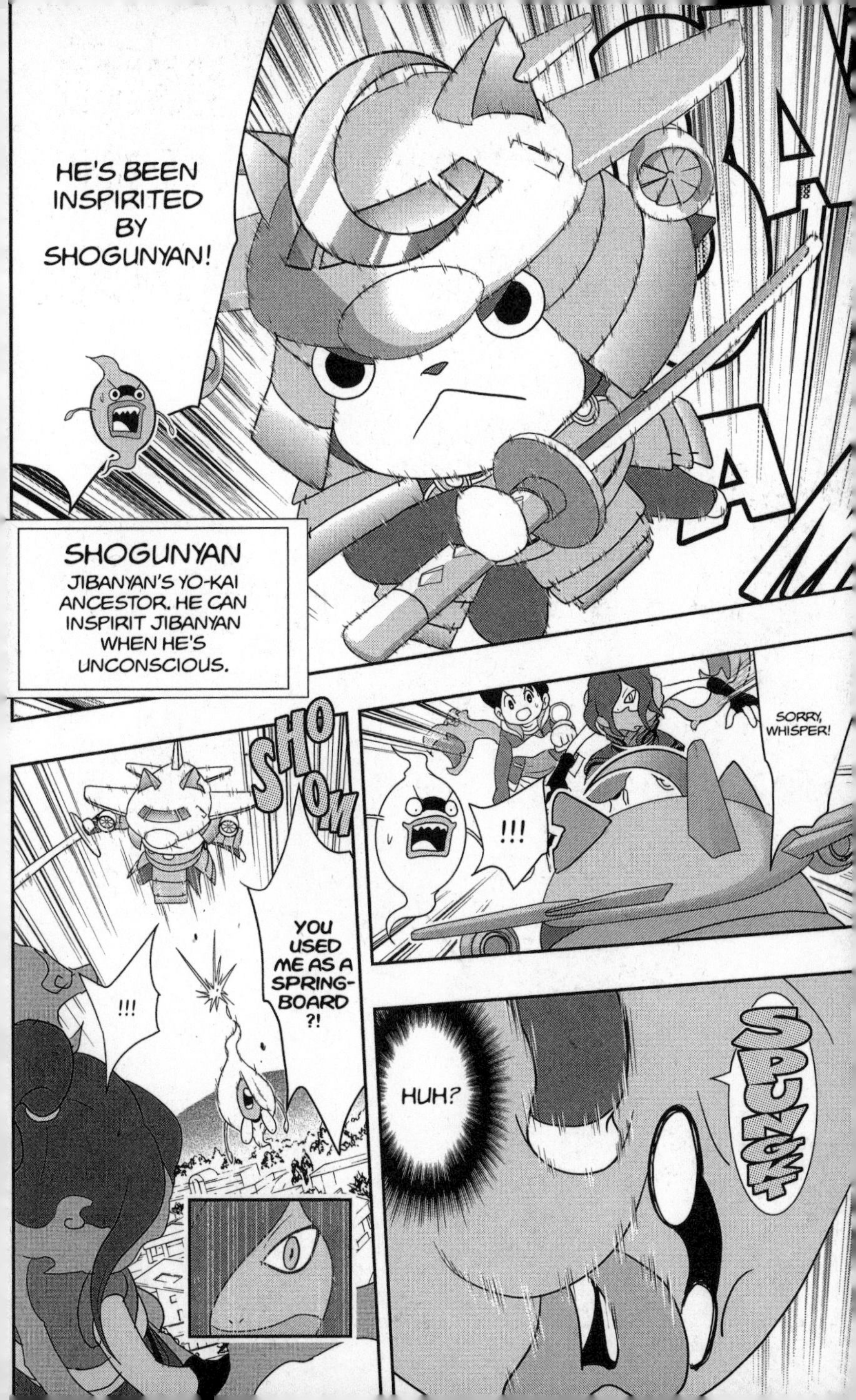
HE'S BEEN INSPIRITED BY SHOGUNYAN!
SHOGUNYAN
JIBANYAN'S YO-KAI ANCESTOR. HE CAN INSPIRIT JIBANYAN WHEN HE'S UNCONSCIOUS.
SORRY, WHISPER!
!!!
HUH?
SHOOM
YOU USED ME AS A SPRING-BOARD?!
!!!

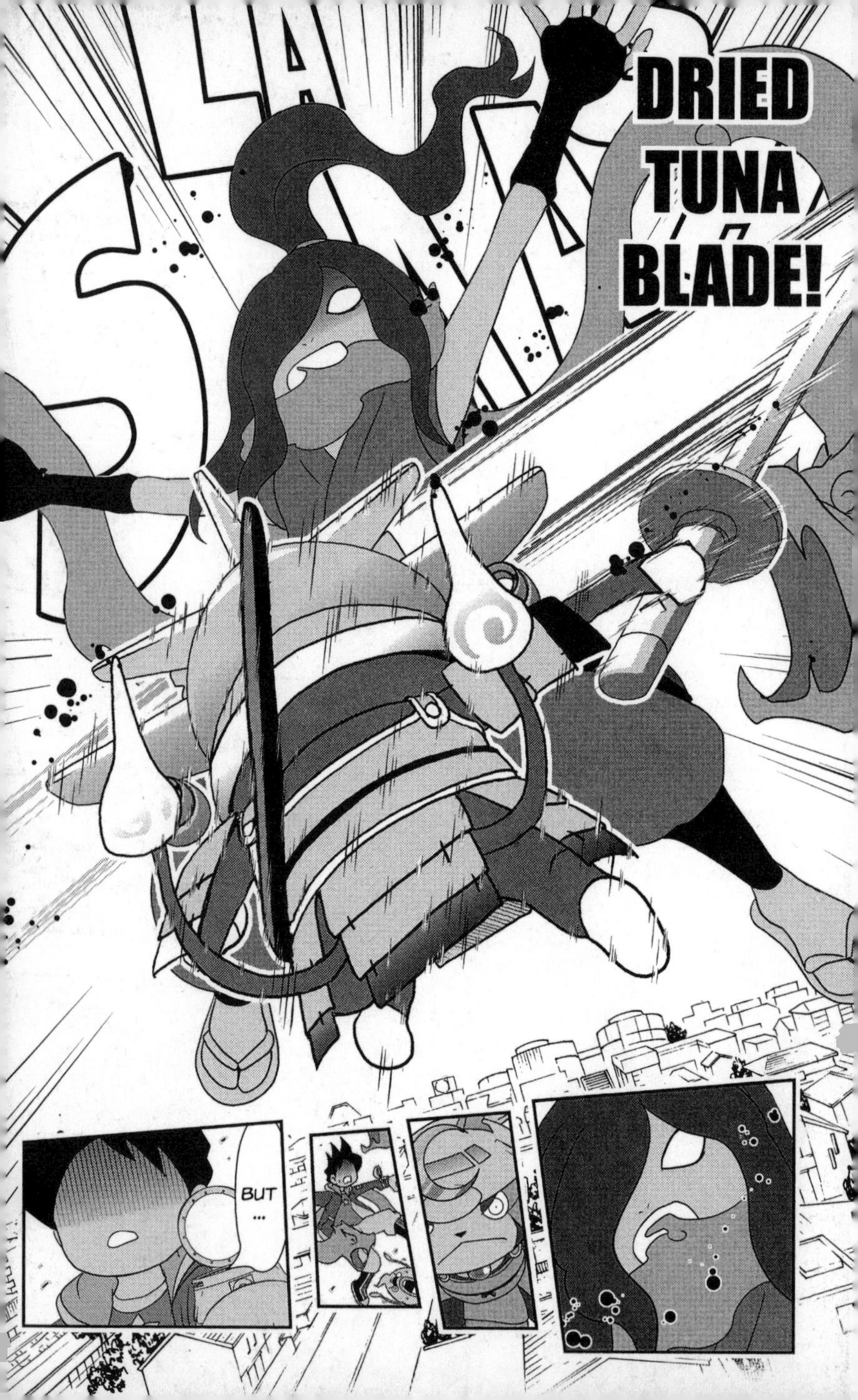
DRIED TUNA BLADE!
BUT ...

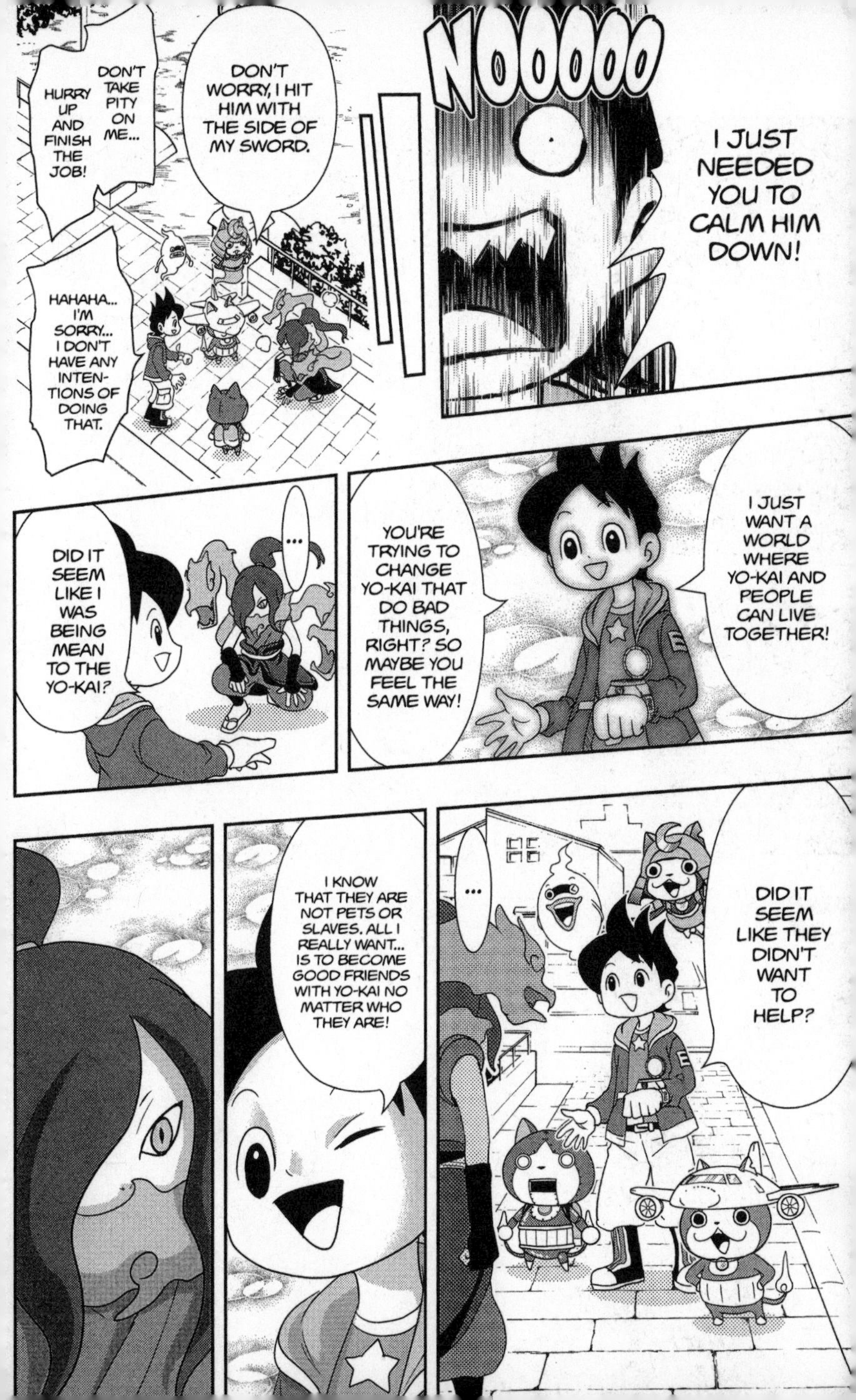
NOOOOO
I JUST NEEDED YOU TO CALM HIM DOWN!
DON'T WORRY, I HIT HIM WITH THE SIDE OF MY SWORD.
DON'T TAKE PITY ON ME...
HURRY UP AND FINISH THE JOB!
HAHAHA... I'M SORRY... I DON'T HAVE ANY INTEN-TIONS OF DOING THAT.
I JUST WANT A WORLD WHERE YO-KAI AND PEOPLE CAN LIVE TOGETHER!
YOU'RE TRYING TO CHANGE YO-KAI THAT DO BAD THINGS, RIGHT? SO MAYBE YOU FEEL THE SAME WAY!
...
DID IT SEEM LIKE I WAS BEING MEAN TO THE YO-KAI?
DID IT SEEM LIKE THEY DIDN'T WANT TO HELP?
...
I KNOW THAT THEY ARE NOT PETS OR SLAVES. ALL I REALLY WANT... IS TO BECOME GOOD FRIENDS WITH YO-KAI NO MATTER WHO THEY ARE!

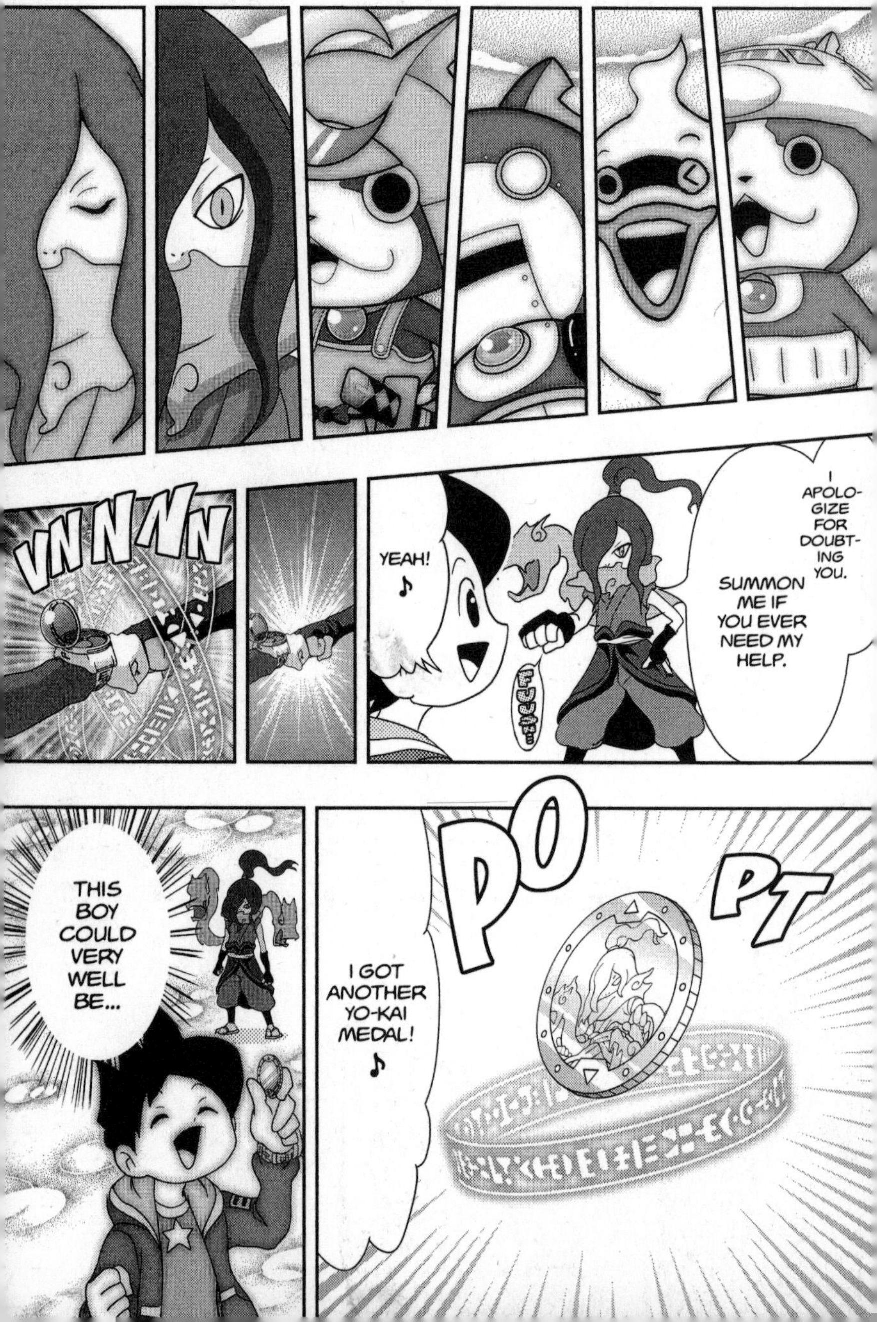
I APOLOGIZE FOR DOUBTING YOU.
SUMMON ME IF YOU EVER NEED MY HELP.
YEAH! ♪
VNNNNN
POPT
I GOT ANOTHER YO-KAI MEDAL! ♪
THIS BOY COULD VERY WELL BE...

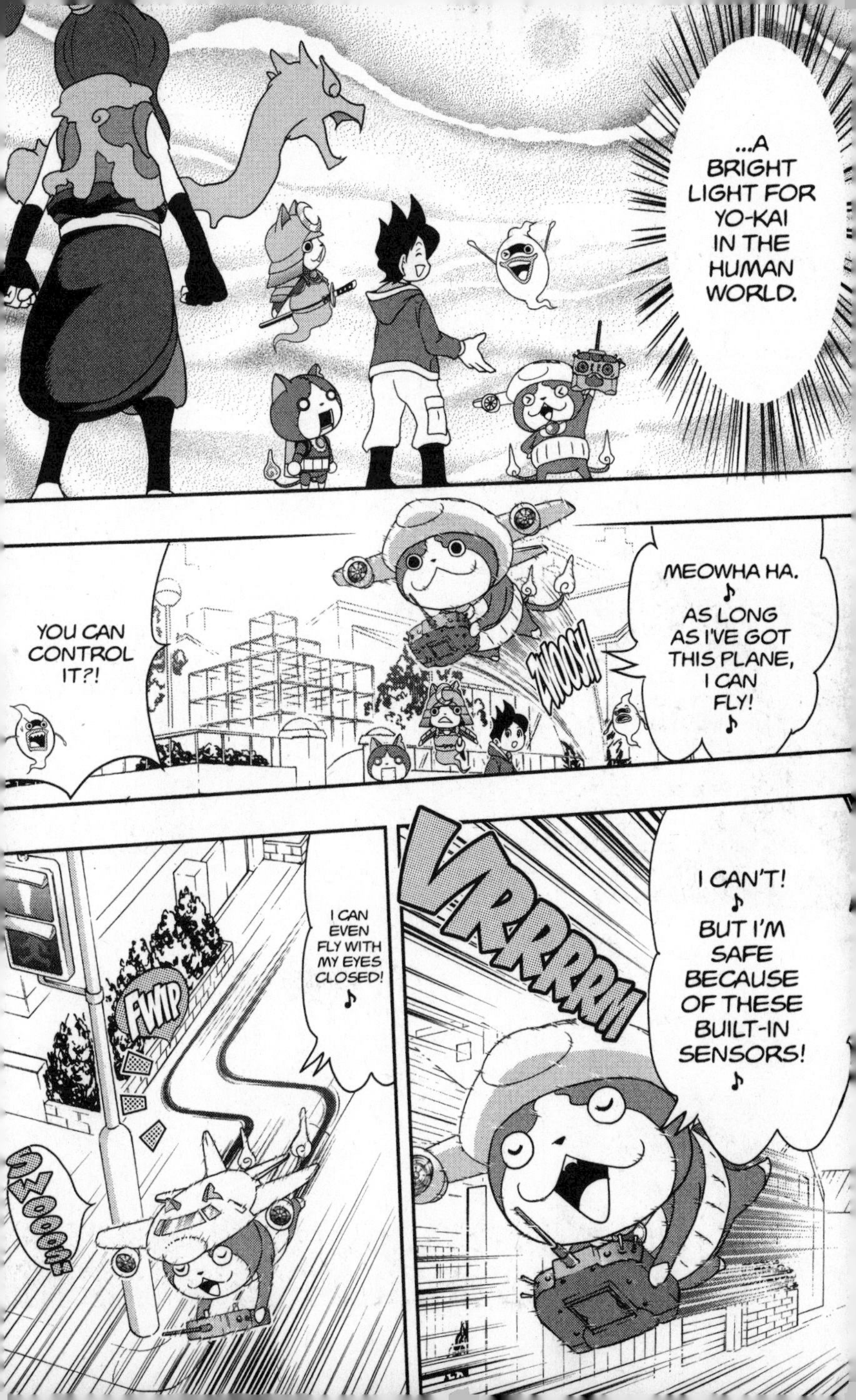
...A BRIGHT LIGHT FOR YO-KAI IN THE HUMAN WORLD.
MEOWHA HA. ♪ AS LONG AS I'VE GOT THIS PLANE, I CAN FLY! ♪
ZWOOSH
YOU CAN CONTROL IT?!
VRRRRRM
I CAN'T! ♪ BUT I'M SAFE BECAUSE OF THESE BUILT-IN SENSORS! ♪
I CAN EVEN FLY WITH MY EYES CLOSED! ♪
FWIP
SWOOOSH

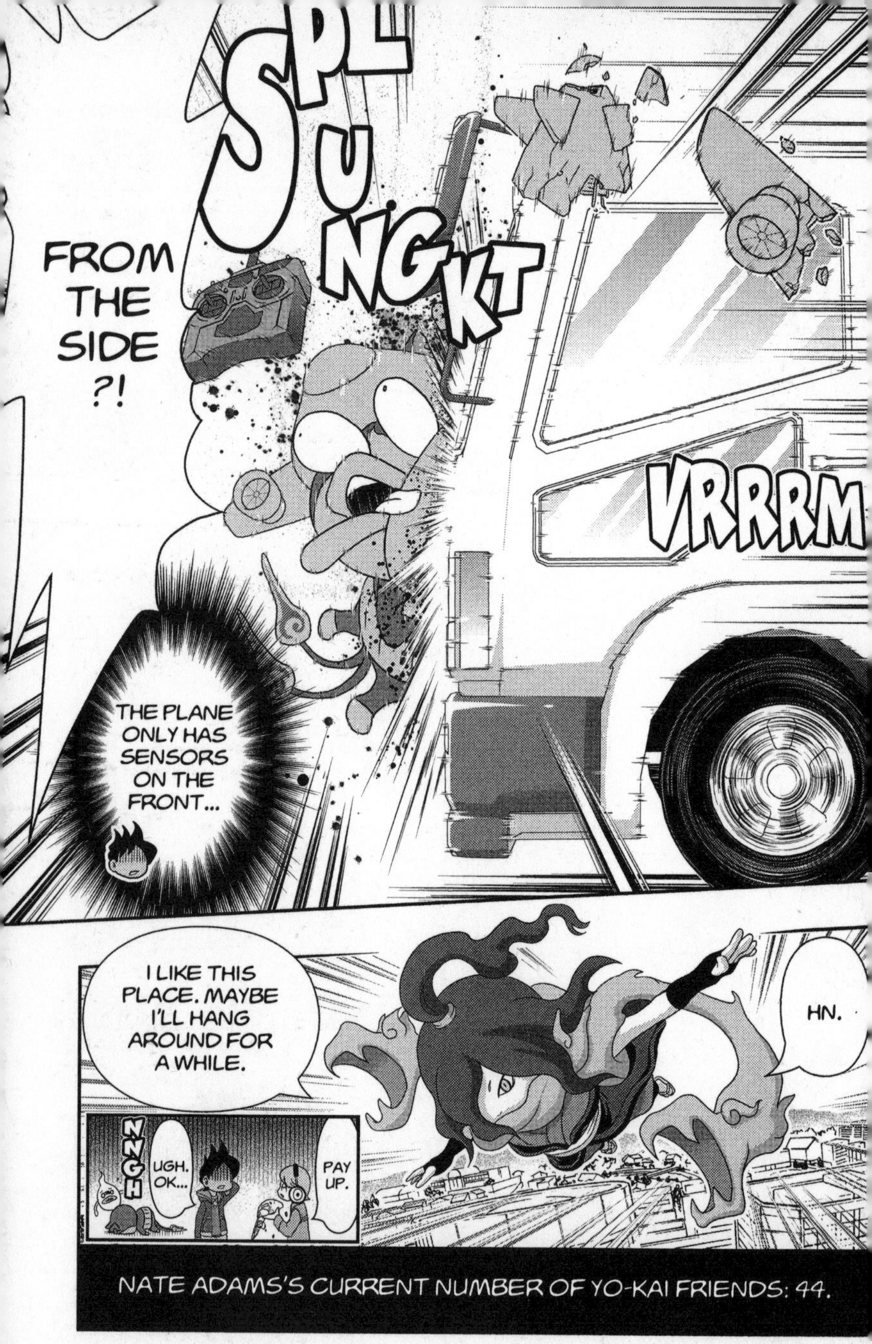
VRRRM
SPLUNGKT
FROM THE SIDE ?!
THE PLANE ONLY HAS SENSORS ON THE FRONT...
HN.
I LIKE THIS PLACE. MAYBE I'LL HANG AROUND FOR A WHILE.
PAY UP.
UGH. OK...
NNGH
NATE ADAMS'S CURRENT NUMBER OF YO-KAI FRIENDS: 44.

## VENOCT

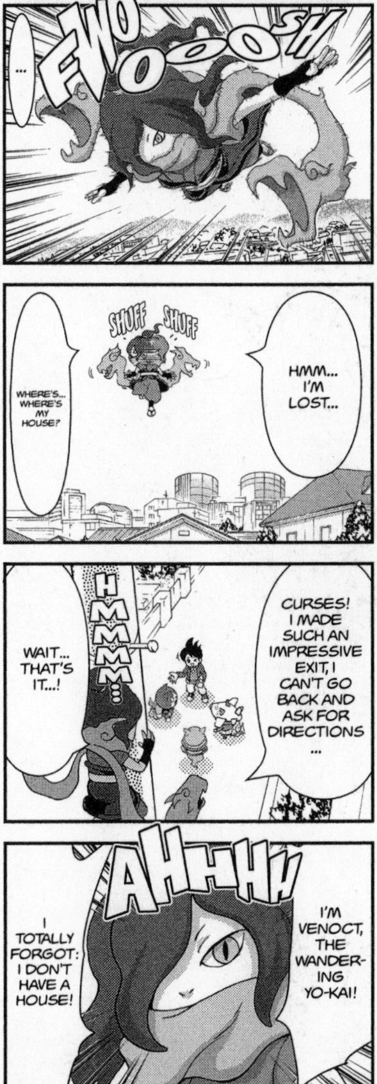
FWOOOOSH
...
SHUFF SHUFF
HMM... I'M LOST...
WHERE'S... WHERE'S MY HOUSE?
CURSES! I MADE SUCH AN IMPRESSIVE EXIT, I CAN'T GO BACK AND ASK FOR DIRECTIONS ...
HMMMM...
WAIT... THAT'S IT...!
AHHHHH
I'M VENOCT, THE WANDER-ING YO-KAI!
I TOTALLY FORGOT: I DON'T HAVE A HOUSE!

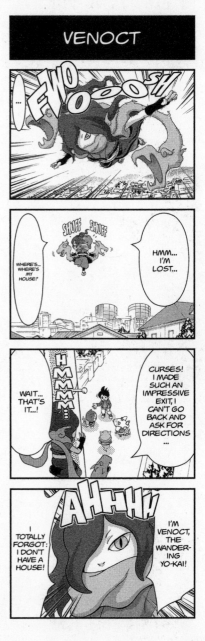

# CHAPTER 60
# STOP BRAGGING!
## FEATURING BOASTING YO-KAI PAPA WINDBAG

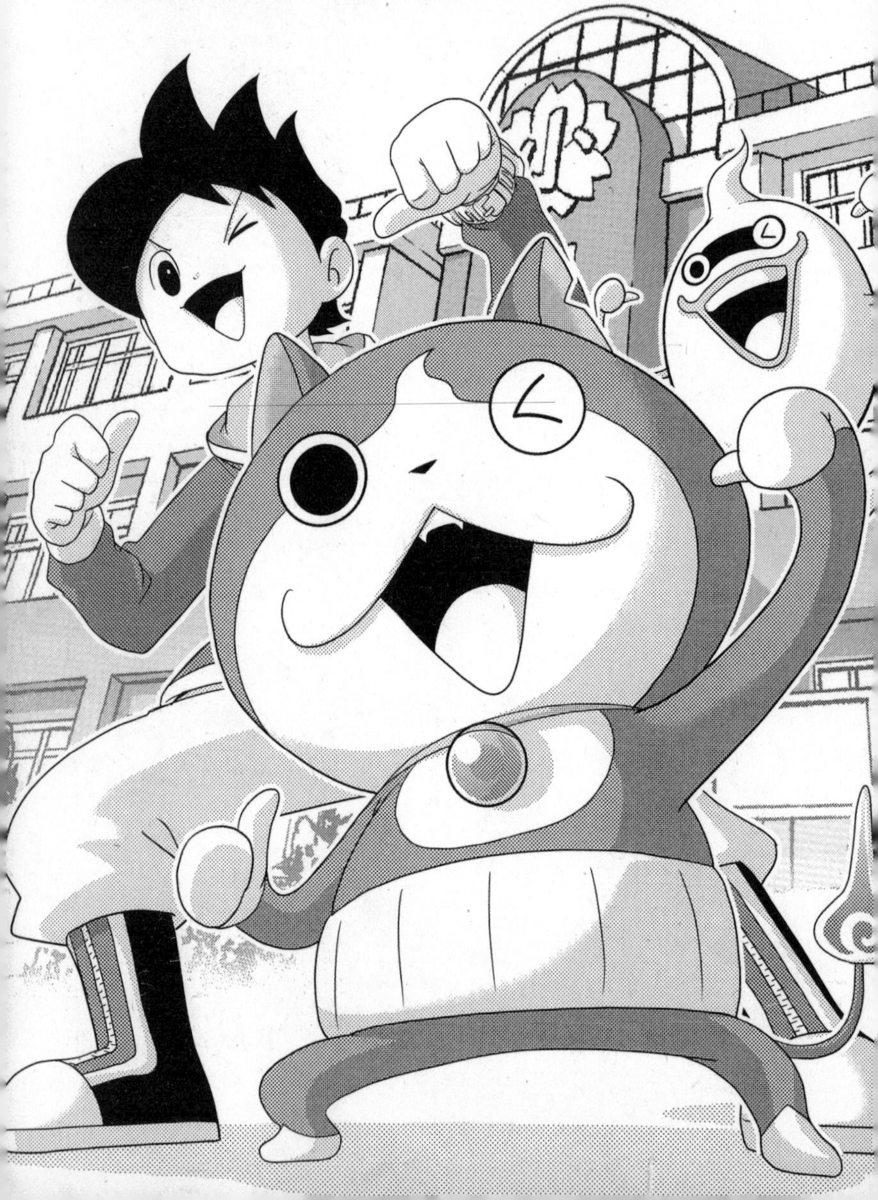

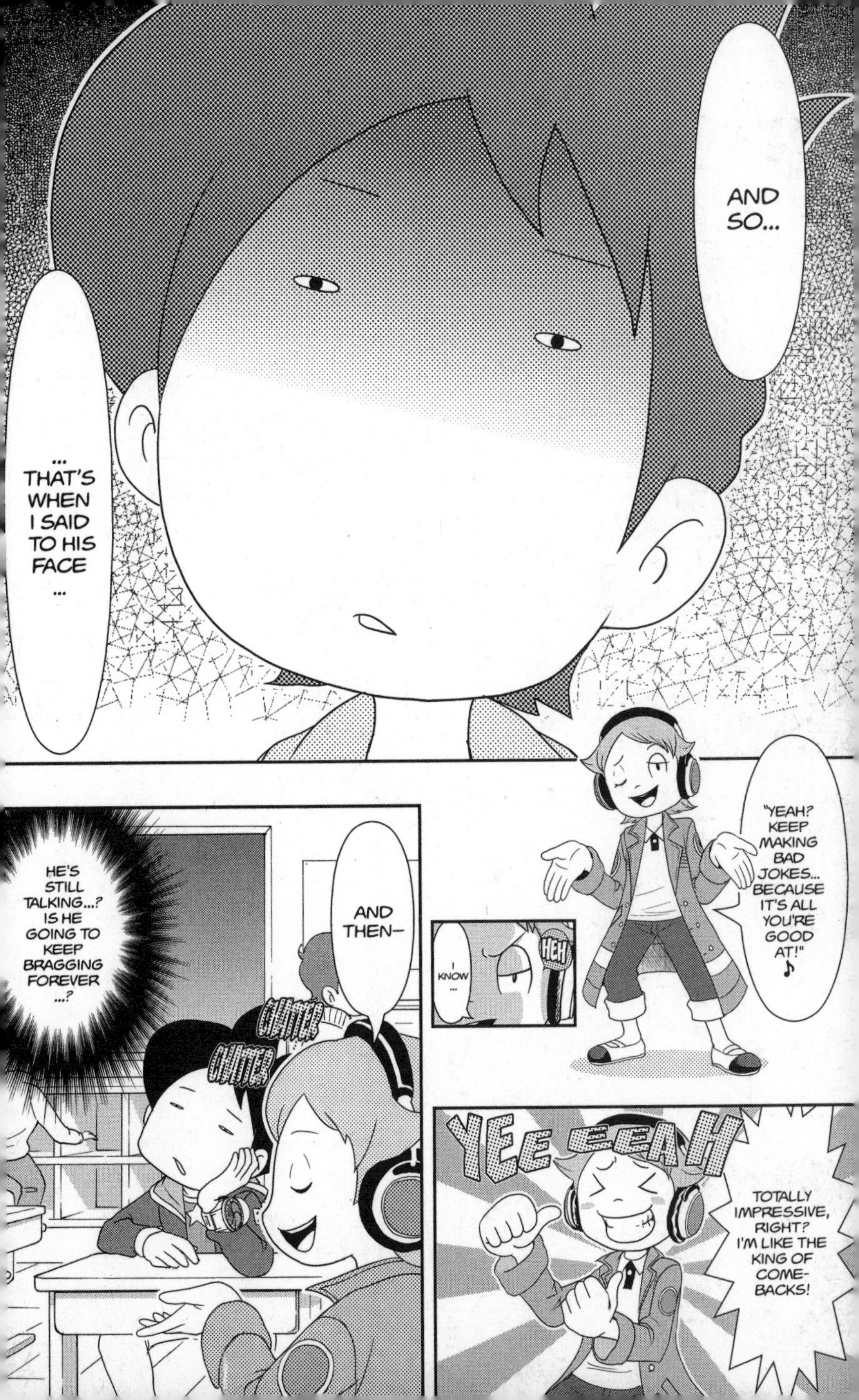
AND SO...
...THAT'S WHEN I SAID TO HIS FACE...
"YEAH? KEEP MAKING BAD JOKES... BECAUSE IT'S ALL YOU'RE GOOD AT!" ♪
HEH
I KNOW...
YEE-EEAH
TOTALLY IMPRESSIVE, RIGHT? I'M LIKE THE KING OF COME-BACKS!
AND THEN—
HE'S STILL TALKING...? IS HE GOING TO KEEP BRAGGING FOREVER...?
CHATTER
CHATTER

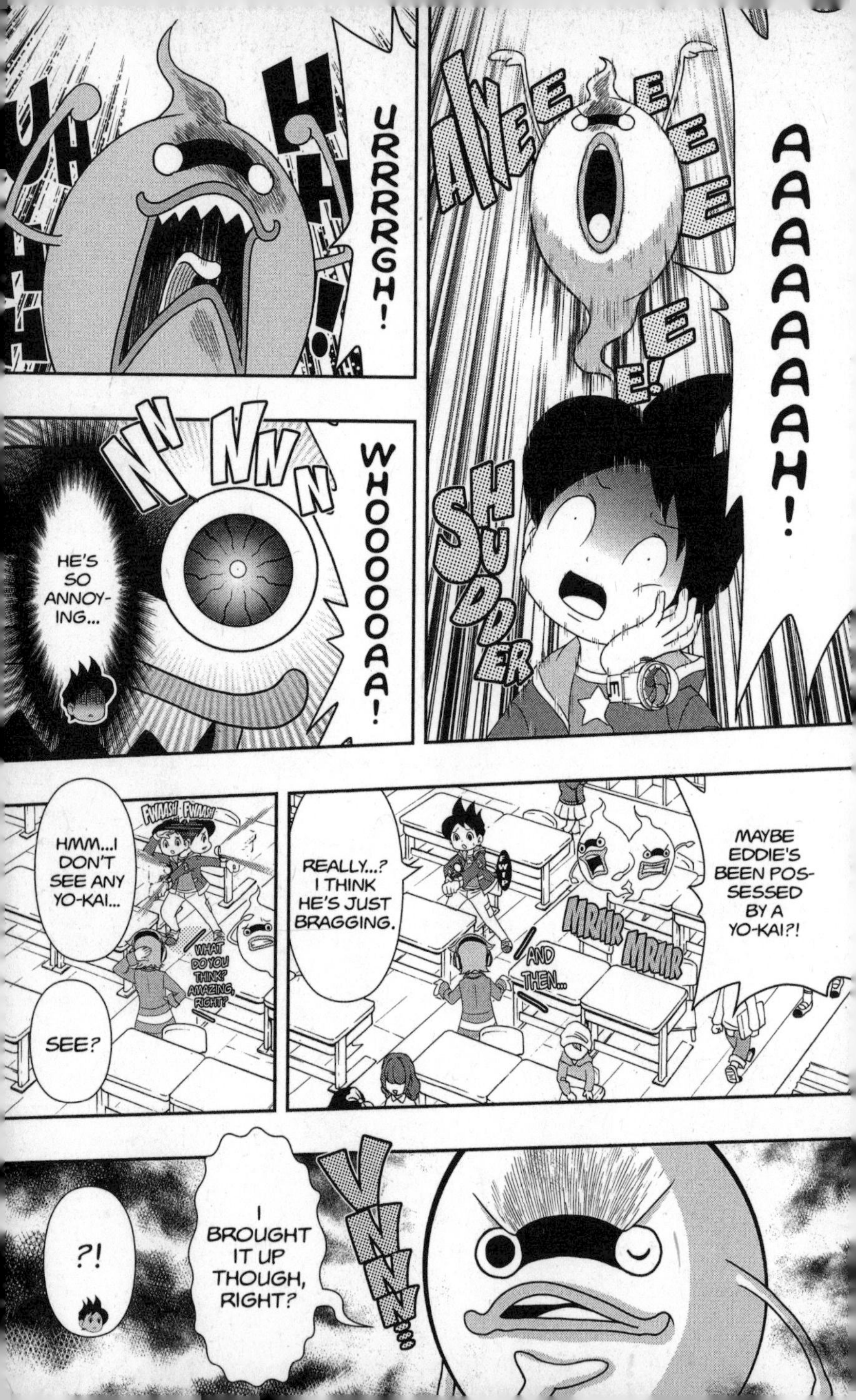
AAAAAAAAH!
AYEEEEEEE!
SHUDDER
URRRRGH!
WHOOOOOOAA!
NNNNNN
HE'S SO ANNOYING...
MAYBE EDDIE'S BEEN POSSESSED BY A YO-KAI?!
MRMR MRMR
REALLY...? I THINK HE'S JUST BRAGGING.
FWIP
AND THEN...
HMM...I DON'T SEE ANY YO-KAI...
FWAASH FWAASH
WHAT DO YOU THINK? AMAZING, RIGHT?
SEE?
VNNN...
I BROUGHT IT UP THOUGH, RIGHT?
?!

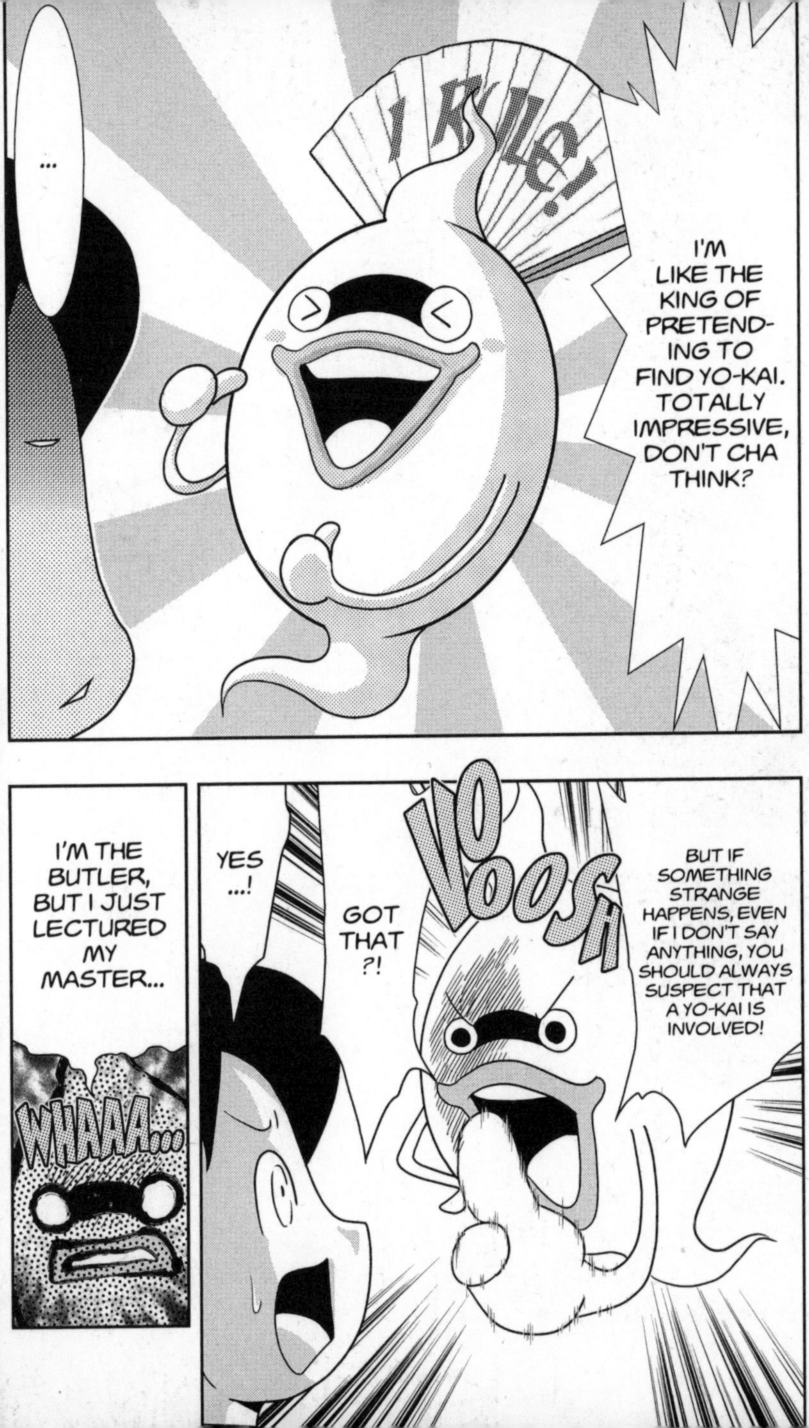
I RULE!
I'M LIKE THE KING OF PRETEND-ING TO FIND YO-KAI. TOTALLY IMPRESSIVE, DON'T CHA THINK?
...
BUT IF SOMETHING STRANGE HAPPENS, EVEN IF I DON'T SAY ANYTHING, YOU SHOULD ALWAYS SUSPECT THAT A YO-KAI IS INVOLVED!
VOOSH
GOT THAT?!
YES...!
I'M THE BUTLER, BUT I JUST LECTURED MY MASTER...
WHAAAA...

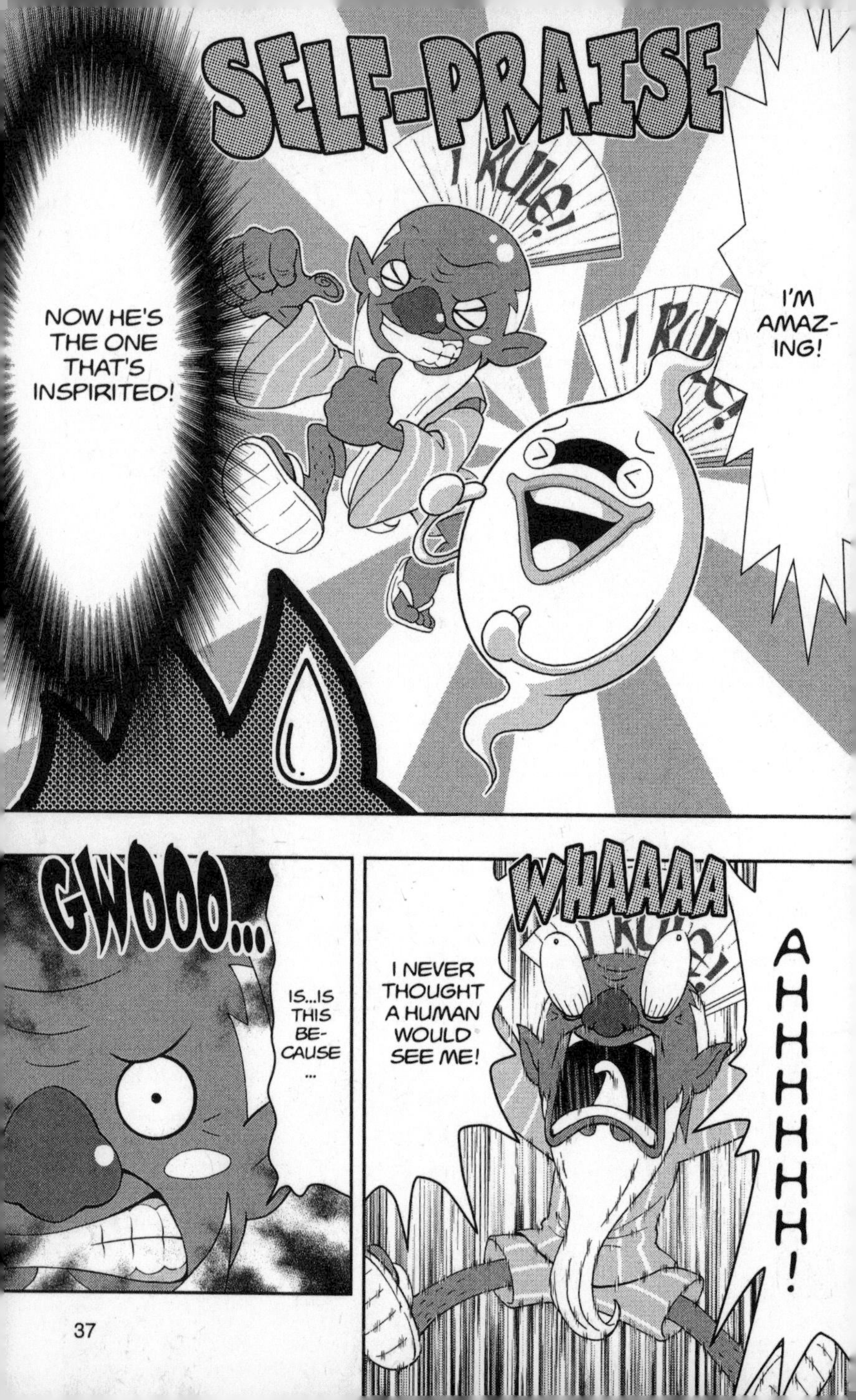
SELF-PRAISE
I RULE!
I'M AMAZ-ING!
NOW HE'S THE ONE THAT'S INSPIRITED!
WHAAAA
AHHHHHH!
I NEVER THOUGHT A HUMAN WOULD SEE ME!
GWOOO...
IS...IS THIS BE-CAUSE ...

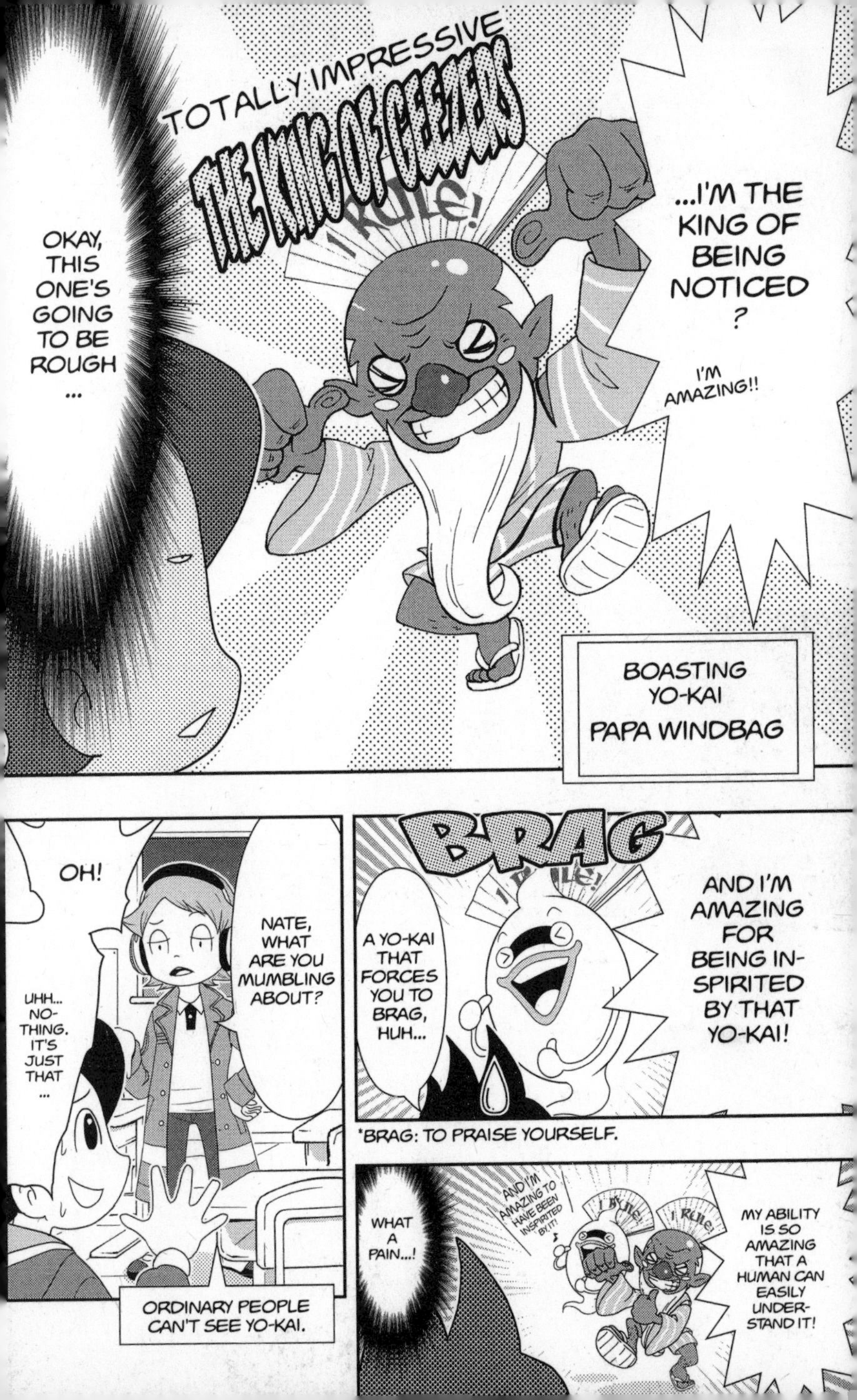

...I'M THE KING OF BEING NOTICED?
I'M AMAZING!!
TOTALLY IMPRESSIVE
THE KING OF GEEZERS
I RULE!
BOASTING YO-KAI PAPA WINDBAG
OKAY, THIS ONE'S GOING TO BE ROUGH...
BRAG
AND I'M AMAZING FOR BEING IN-SPIRITED BY THAT YO-KAI!
A YO-KAI THAT FORCES YOU TO BRAG, HUH...
*BRAG: TO PRAISE YOURSELF.
MY ABILITY IS SO AMAZING THAT A HUMAN CAN EASILY UNDER-STAND IT!
AND I'M AMAZING TO HAVE BEEN INSPIRITED BY IT!
WHAT A PAIN...!
NATE, WHAT ARE YOU MUMBLING ABOUT?
OH!
UHH... NO-THING. IT'S JUST THAT...
ORDINARY PEOPLE CAN'T SEE YO-KAI.

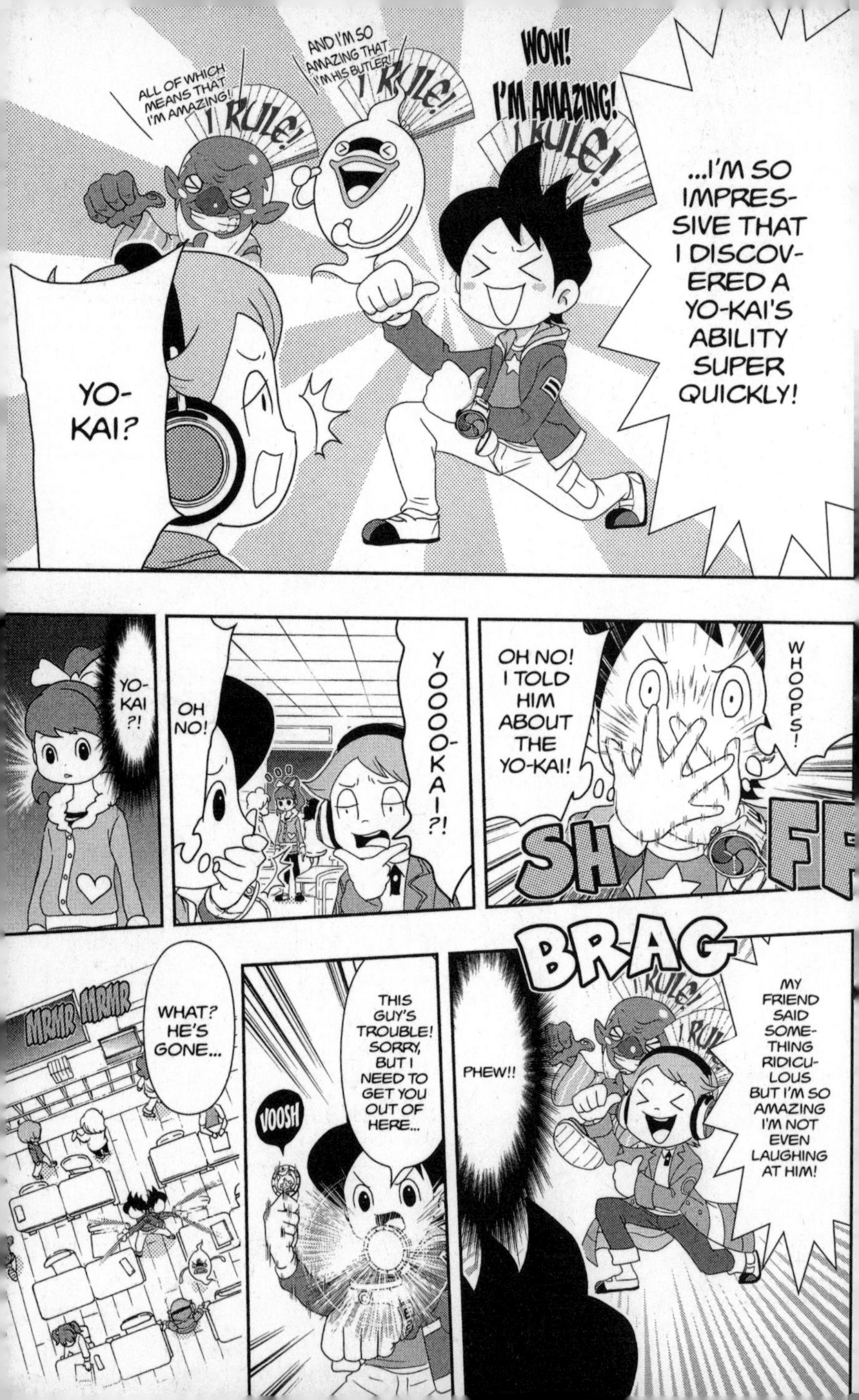
...I'M SO IMPRESSIVE THAT I DISCOVERED A YO-KAI'S ABILITY SUPER QUICKLY!
WOW! I'M AMAZING!
I RULE!
AND I'M SO AMAZING THAT I'M HIS BUTLER!
I RULE!
ALL OF WHICH MEANS THAT I'M AMAZING!
I RULE!
YO-KAI?
WHOOPS!
OH NO! I TOLD HIM ABOUT THE YO-KAI!
SH
FF
YOOOOO-KAI?!
OH NO!
YO-KAI?!
BRAG
MY FRIEND SAID SOMETHING RIDICULOUS BUT I'M SO AMAZING I'M NOT EVEN LAUGHING AT HIM!
I RULE!
I RULE!
PHEW!!
THIS GUY'S TROUBLE! SORRY, BUT I NEED TO GET YOU OUT OF HERE...
VOOSH
WHAT? HE'S GONE...
MRMR MRMR

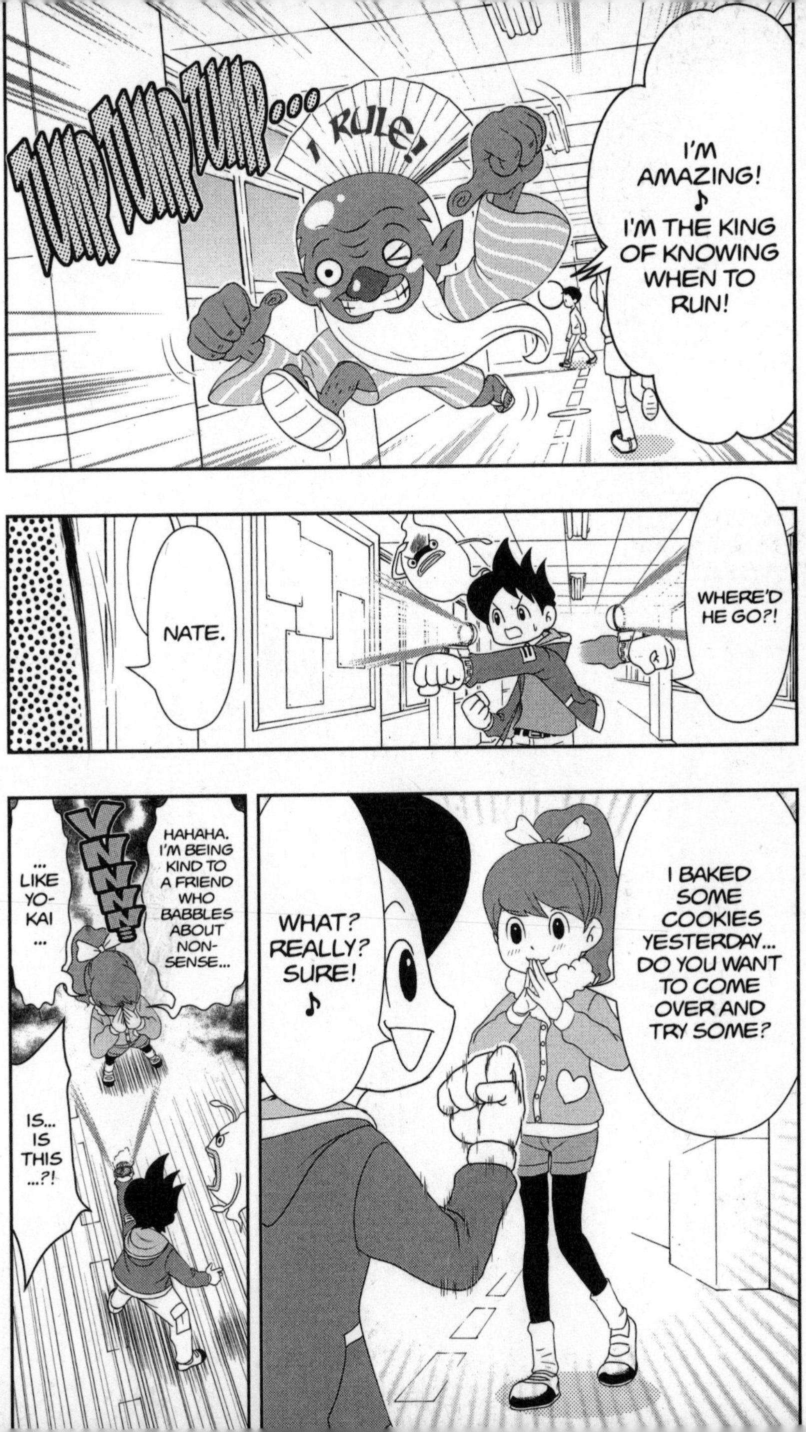
I'M AMAZING! ♪ I'M THE KING OF KNOWING WHEN TO RUN!
I RULE!
TUMP TUMP TUMP...
WHERE'D HE GO?!
NATE.
I BAKED SOME COOKIES YESTERDAY... DO YOU WANT TO COME OVER AND TRY SOME?
WHAT? REALLY? SURE! ♪
HAHAHA. I'M BEING KIND TO A FRIEND WHO BABBLES ABOUT NON-SENSE...
... LIKE YO-KAI ...
VNNNN
IS... IS THIS ...?!

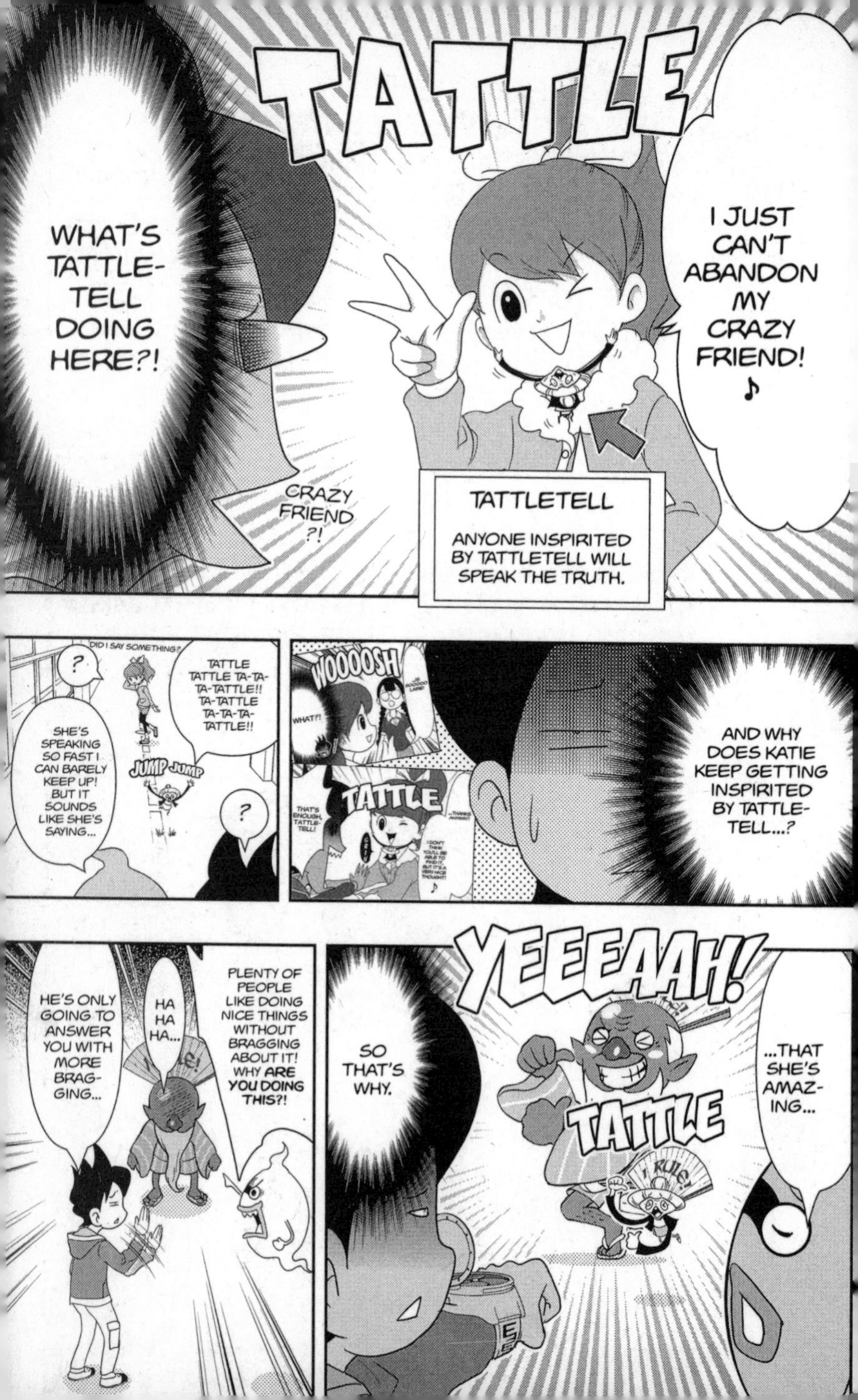
TATTLE
I JUST CAN'T ABANDON MY CRAZY FRIEND! ♪
WHAT'S TATTLE-TELL DOING HERE?!
TATTLETELL
ANYONE INSPIRITED BY TATTLETELL WILL SPEAK THE TRUTH.
CRAZY FRIEND ?!
AND WHY DOES KATIE KEEP GETTING INSPIRITED BY TATTLE-TELL...?
WOOOOSH
WHAT?!
TATTLE
THAT'S ENOUGH, TATTLE-TELL!
DID I SAY SOMETHING?
?
TATTLE TATTLE TA-TA-TA-TATTLE!! TA-TATTLE TA-TA-TA-TATTLE!!
SHE'S SPEAKING SO FAST I CAN BARELY KEEP UP! BUT IT SOUNDS LIKE SHE'S SAYING...
JUMP JUMP
?
YEEEAAH!
...THAT SHE'S AMAZ-ING...
TATTLE
I RULE!
SO THAT'S WHY.
PLENTY OF PEOPLE LIKE DOING NICE THINGS WITHOUT BRAGGING ABOUT IT! WHY ARE YOU DOING THIS?!
HA HA HA...
HE'S ONLY GOING TO ANSWER YOU WITH MORE BRAG-GING...

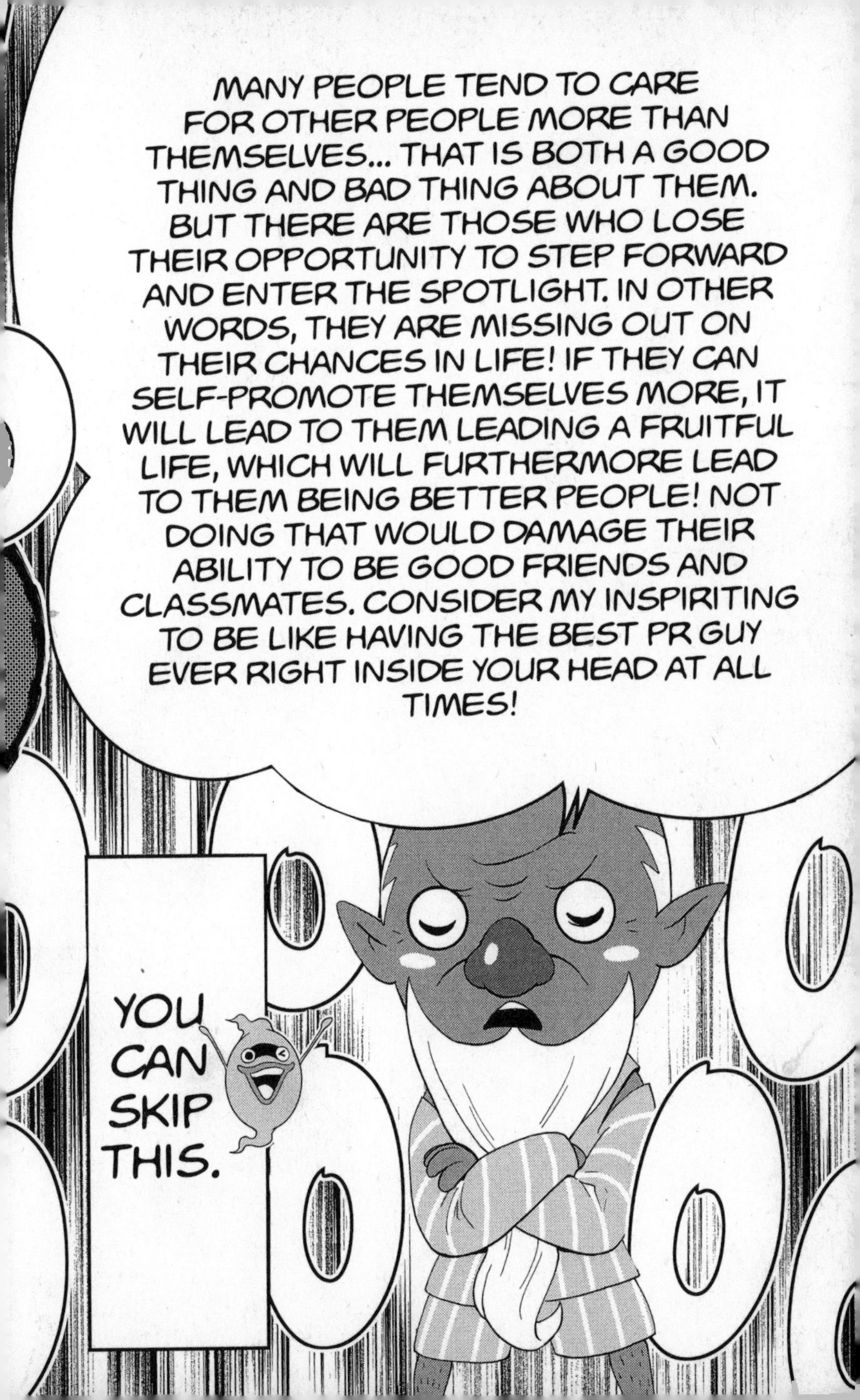
MANY PEOPLE TEND TO CARE FOR OTHER PEOPLE MORE THAN THEMSELVES... THAT IS BOTH A GOOD THING AND BAD THING ABOUT THEM. BUT THERE ARE THOSE WHO LOSE THEIR OPPORTUNITY TO STEP FORWARD AND ENTER THE SPOTLIGHT. IN OTHER WORDS, THEY ARE MISSING OUT ON THEIR CHANCES IN LIFE! IF THEY CAN SELF-PROMOTE THEMSELVES MORE, IT WILL LEAD TO THEM LEADING A FRUITFUL LIFE, WHICH WILL FURTHERMORE LEAD TO THEM BEING BETTER PEOPLE! NOT DOING THAT WOULD DAMAGE THEIR ABILITY TO BE GOOD FRIENDS AND CLASSMATES. CONSIDER MY INSPIRITING TO BE LIKE HAVING THE BEST PR GUY EVER RIGHT INSIDE YOUR HEAD AT ALL TIMES!
YOU CAN SKIP THIS.

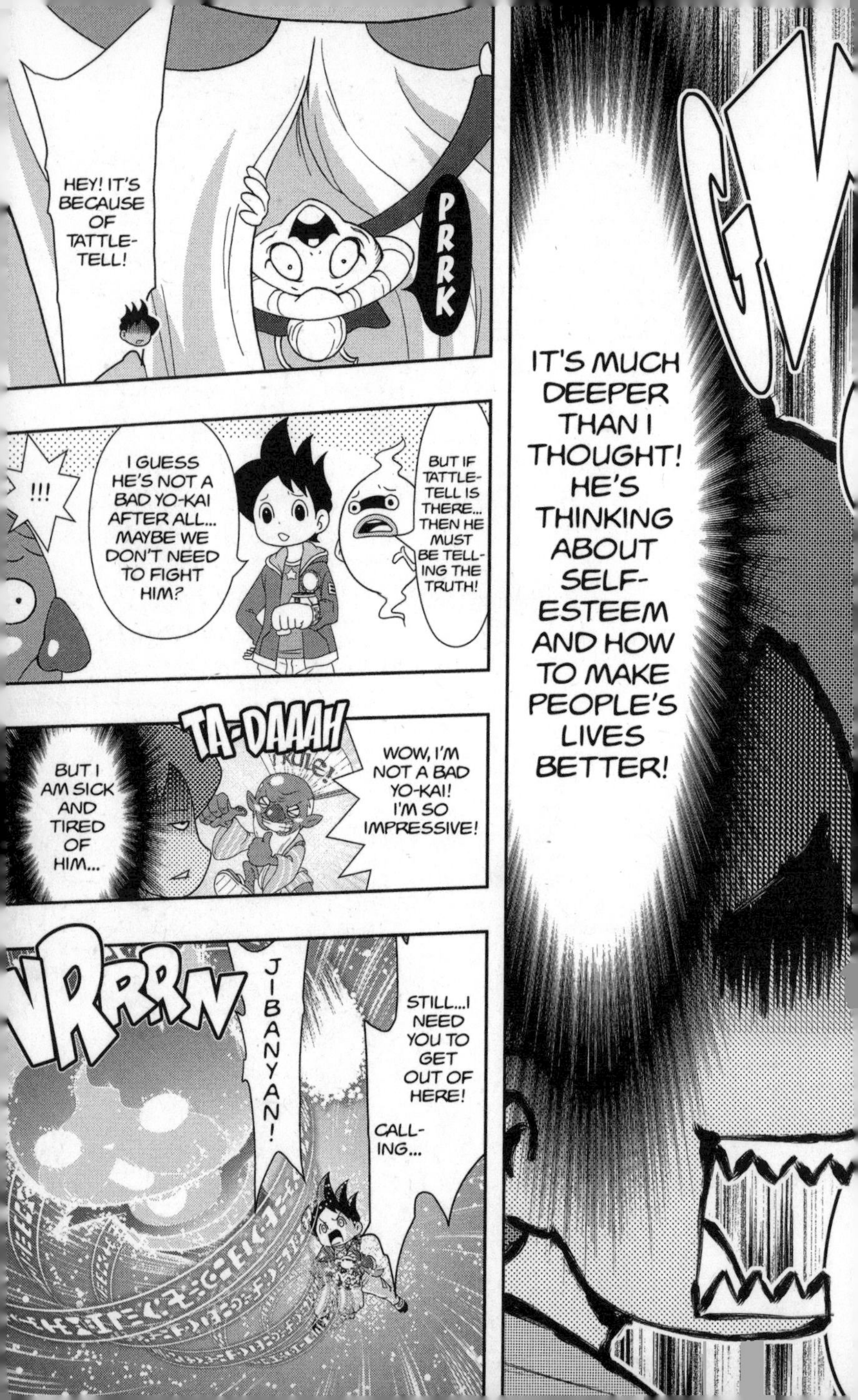
IT'S MUCH DEEPER THAN I THOUGHT! HE'S THINKING ABOUT SELF-ESTEEM AND HOW TO MAKE PEOPLE'S LIVES BETTER!
PRRK
HEY! IT'S BECAUSE OF TATTLE-TELL!
BUT IF TATTLE-TELL IS THERE... THEN HE MUST BE TELLING THE TRUTH!
I GUESS HE'S NOT A BAD YO-KAI AFTER ALL... MAYBE WE DON'T NEED TO FIGHT HIM?
!!!
WOW, I'M NOT A BAD YO-KAI! I'M SO IMPRESSIVE!
TA-DAAAH
BUT I AM SICK AND TIRED OF HIM...
STILL...I NEED YOU TO GET OUT OF HERE!
CALLING...
JIBANYAN!
VRRRN

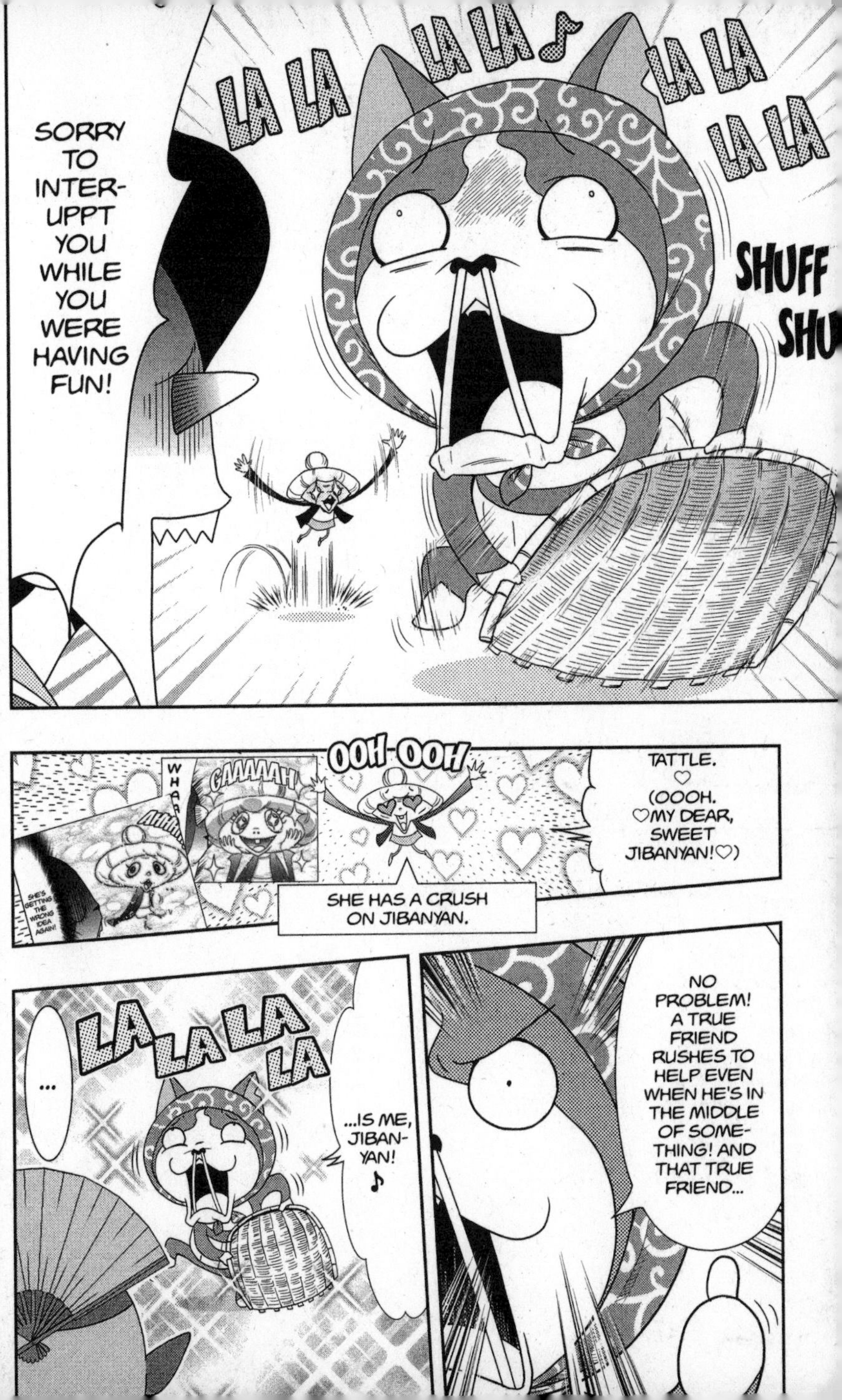
LA LA LA LA♪ LA LA LA LA
SHUFF SHU
SORRY TO INTER-UPPT YOU WHILE YOU WERE HAVING FUN!
LA LA
TATTLE. ♡ (OOOH. ♡MY DEAR, SWEET JIBANYAN!♡)
OOH-OOH
SHE HAS A CRUSH ON JIBANYAN.
GAAAAAH
WHA
AHHH
SHE'S GETTING THE WRONG IDEA AGAIN!
NO PROBLEM! A TRUE FRIEND RUSHES TO HELP EVEN WHEN HE'S IN THE MIDDLE OF SOME-THING! AND THAT TRUE FRIEND...
...IS ME, JIBAN-YAN! ♪
LA LA LA LA
...

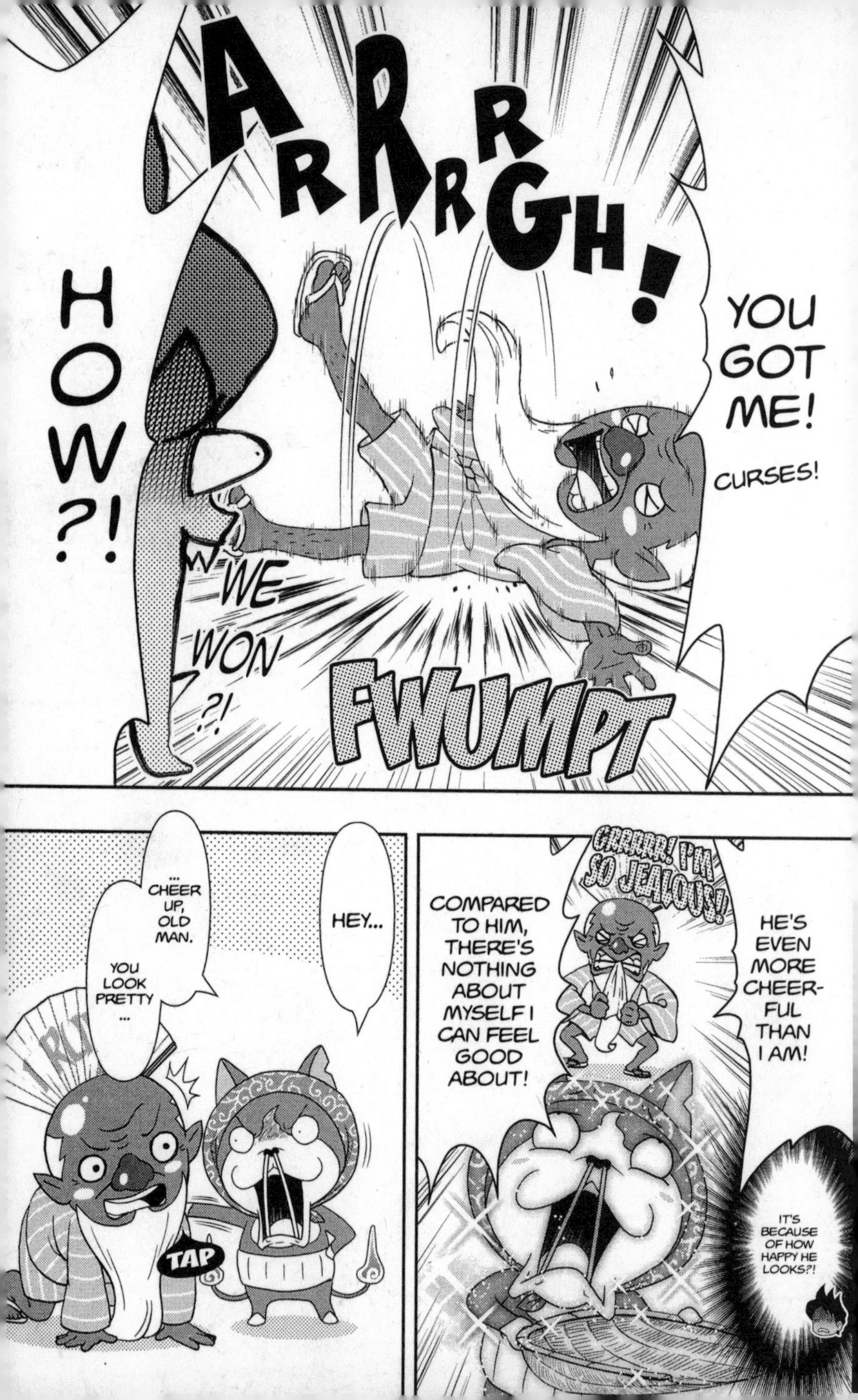
ARRRRGH!
YOU GOT ME!
CURSES!
HOW?!
WE WON?!
FWUMPT
GRRRRR! I'M SO JEALOUS!!
HE'S EVEN MORE CHEER-FUL THAN I AM!
COMPARED TO HIM, THERE'S NOTHING ABOUT MYSELF I CAN FEEL GOOD ABOUT!
IT'S BECAUSE OF HOW HAPPY HE LOOKS?!
HEY...
... CHEER UP, OLD MAN.
YOU LOOK PRETTY ...
TAP

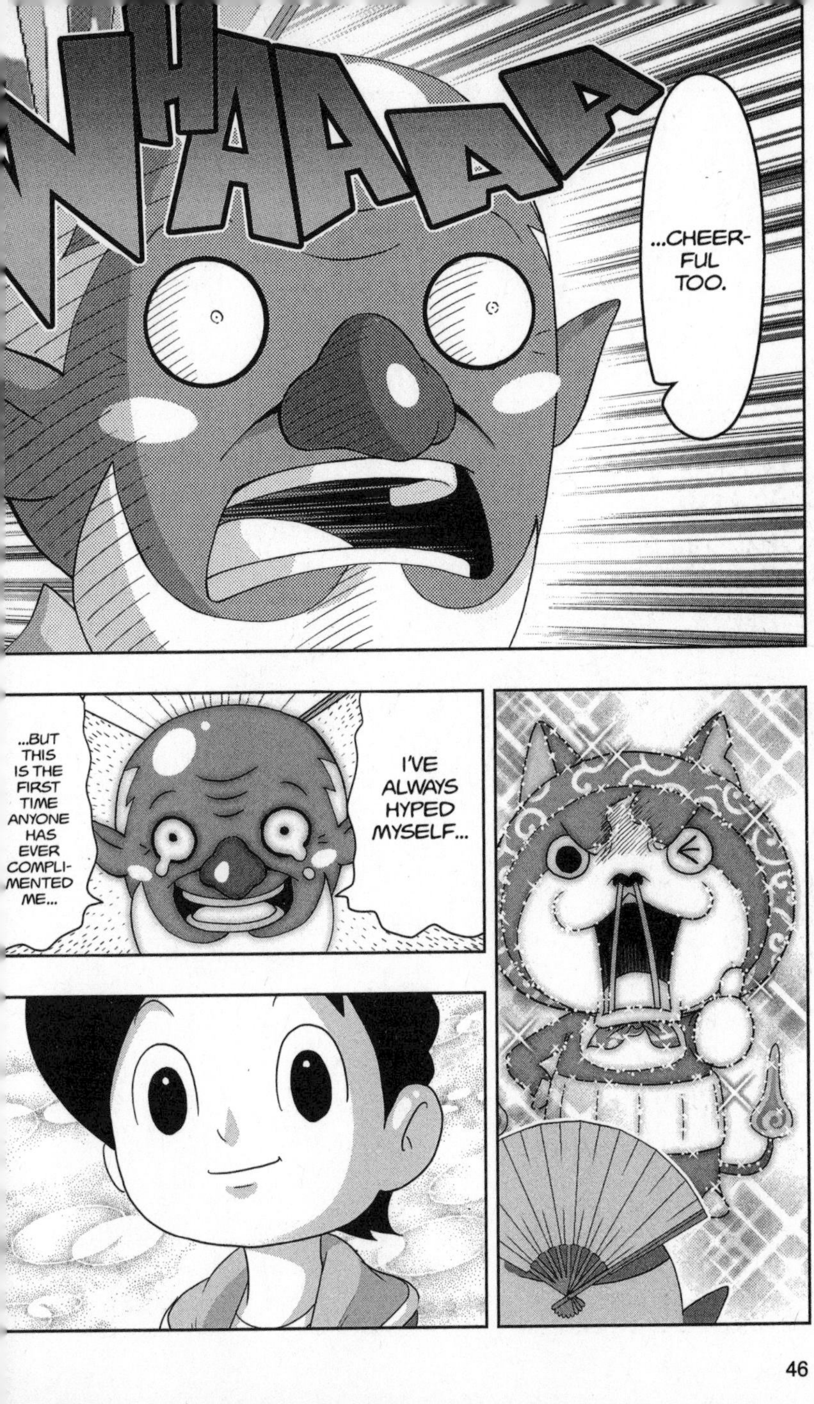
...CHEER-
FUL
TOO.
WHAAAA
I'VE ALWAYS HYPED MYSELF...
...BUT THIS IS THE FIRST TIME ANYONE HAS EVER COMPLI-MENTED ME...

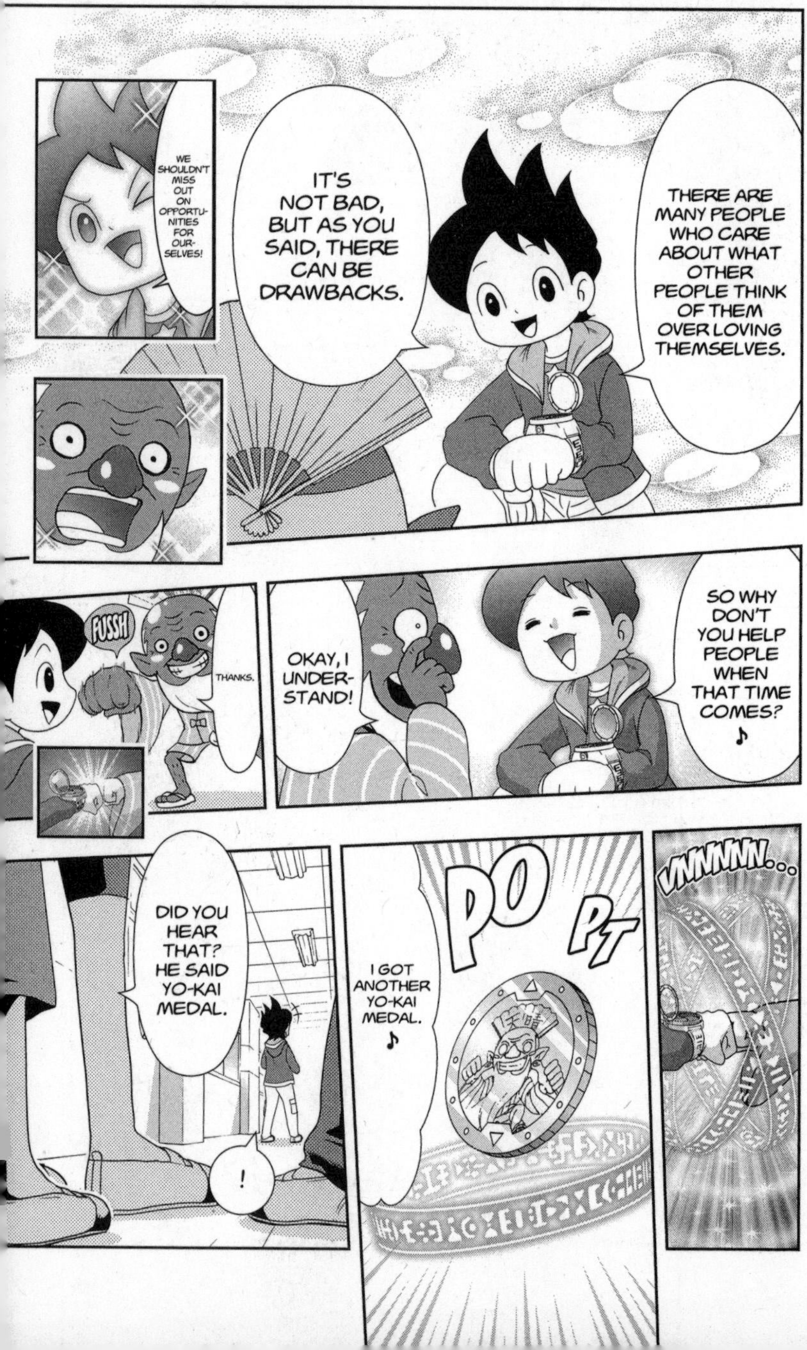
THERE ARE MANY PEOPLE WHO CARE ABOUT WHAT OTHER PEOPLE THINK OF THEM OVER LOVING THEMSELVES.
IT'S NOT BAD, BUT AS YOU SAID, THERE CAN BE DRAWBACKS.
WE SHOULDN'T MISS OUT ON OPPORTU-NITIES FOR OUR-SELVES!
SO WHY DON'T YOU HELP PEOPLE WHEN THAT TIME COMES? ♪
OKAY, I UNDER-STAND!
THANKS.
FUSSH
VNNNNN...
POPT
I GOT ANOTHER YO-KAI MEDAL. ♪
DID YOU HEAR THAT? HE SAID YO-KAI MEDAL.
!

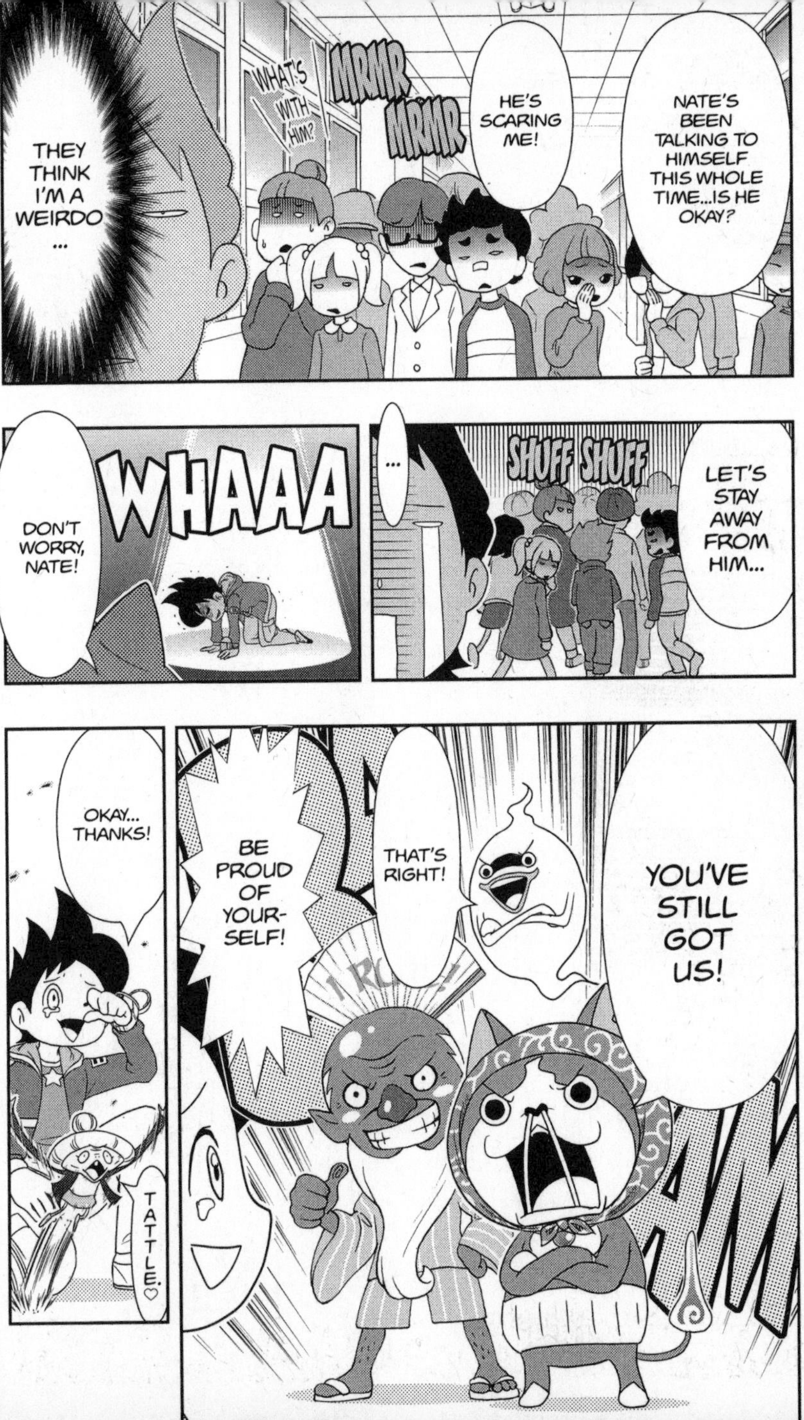
NATE'S BEEN TALKING TO HIMSELF THIS WHOLE TIME...IS HE OKAY?
HE'S SCARING ME!
MRMR MRMR
WHAT'S WITH HIM?
THEY THINK I'M A WEIRDO ...
LET'S STAY AWAY FROM HIM...
SHUFF SHUFF
...
WHAAAA
DON'T WORRY, NATE!
YOU'VE STILL GOT US!
THAT'S RIGHT!
BE PROUD OF YOUR-SELF!
OKAY... THANKS!
TATTLE.♡

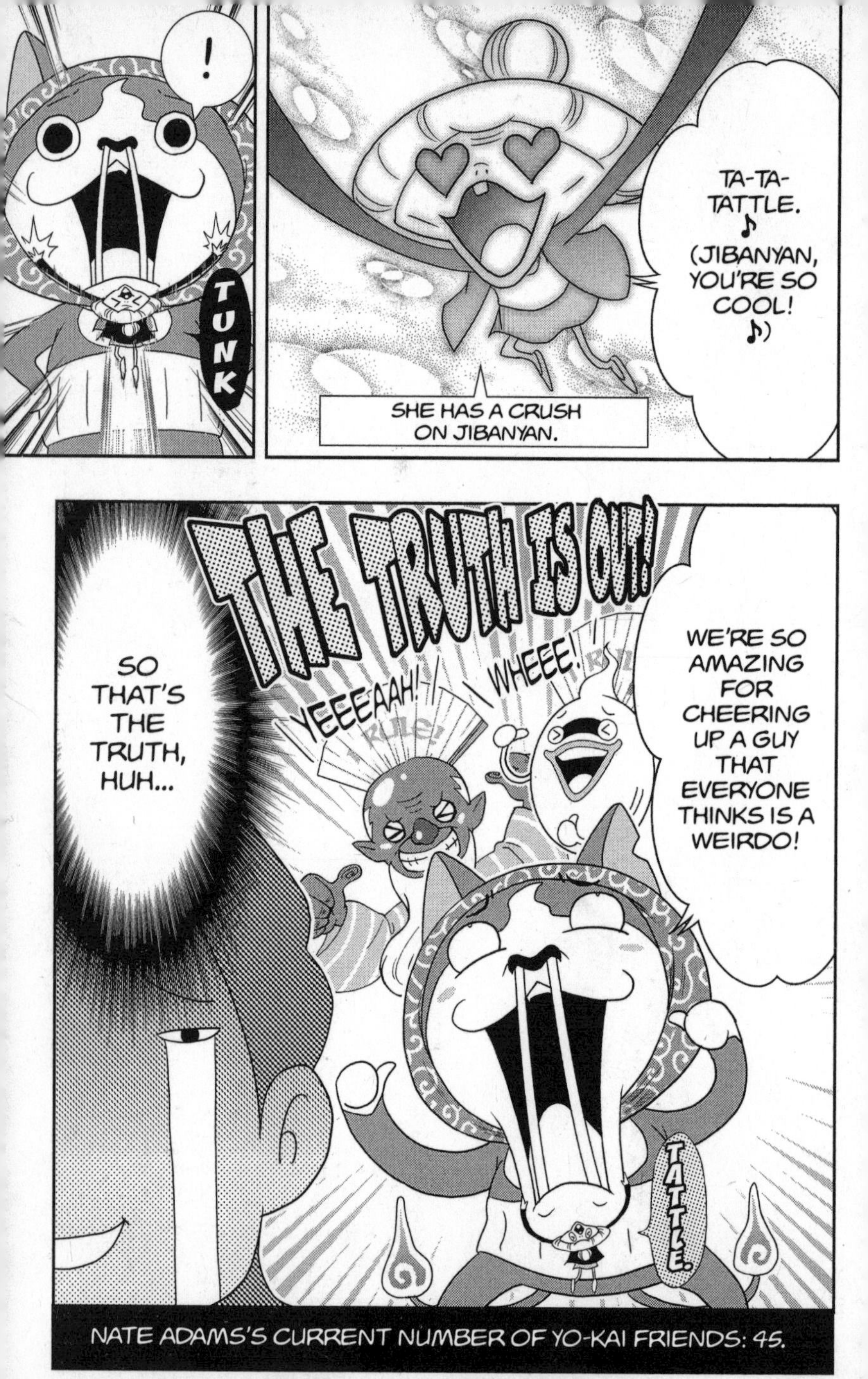
TA-TA-TATTLE. ♪ (JIBANYAN, YOU'RE SO COOL! ♪)
SHE HAS A CRUSH ON JIBANYAN.
!
TUNK
THE TRUTH IS OUT!
WE'RE SO AMAZING FOR CHEERING UP A GUY THAT EVERYONE THINKS IS A WEIRDO!
WHEEE!
YEEEAAH!
SO THAT'S THE TRUTH, HUH...
TATTLE.
NATE ADAMS'S CURRENT NUMBER OF YO-KAI FRIENDS: 45.

# CHAPTER 61
# STOP MY NOSEBLEED!

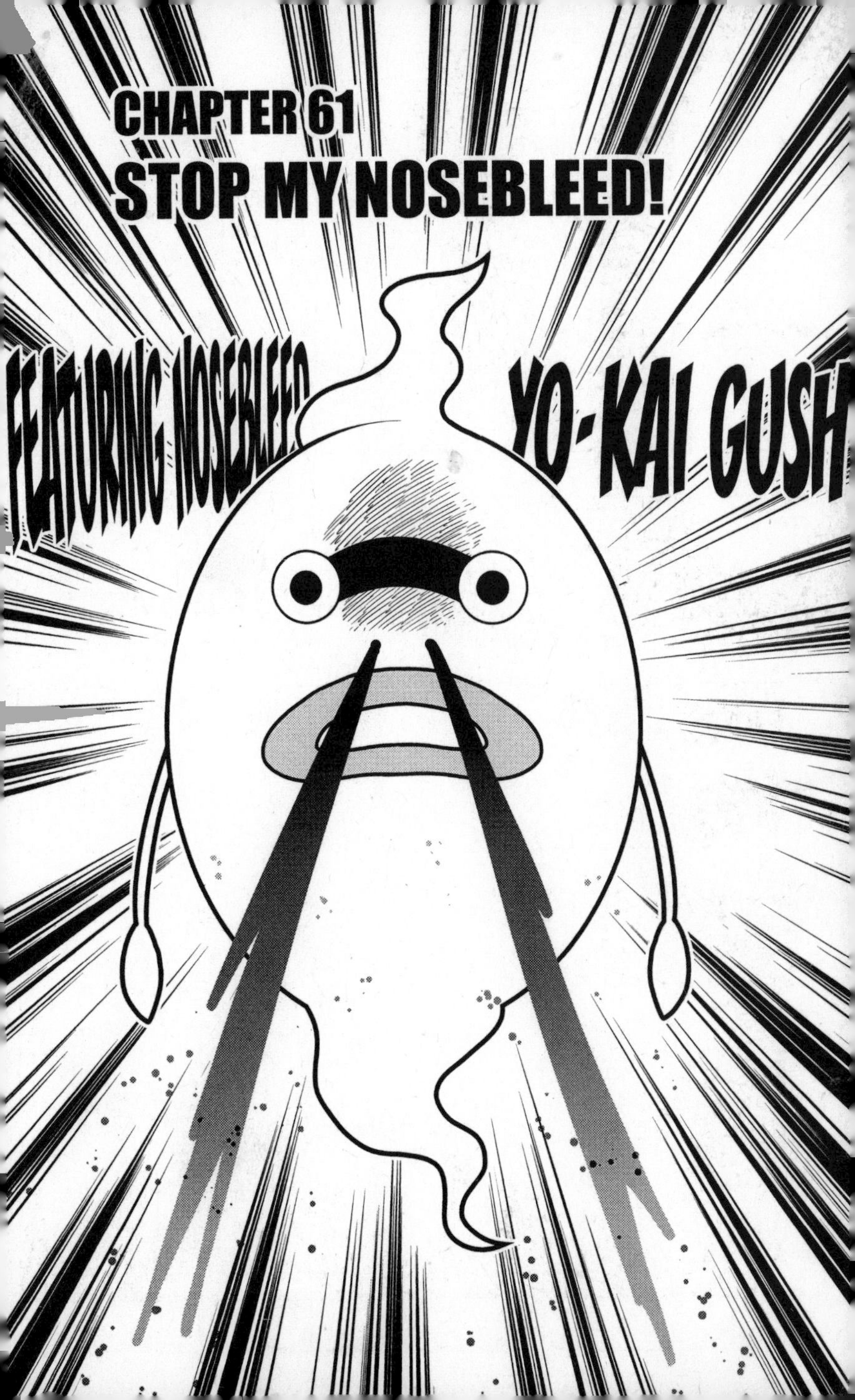

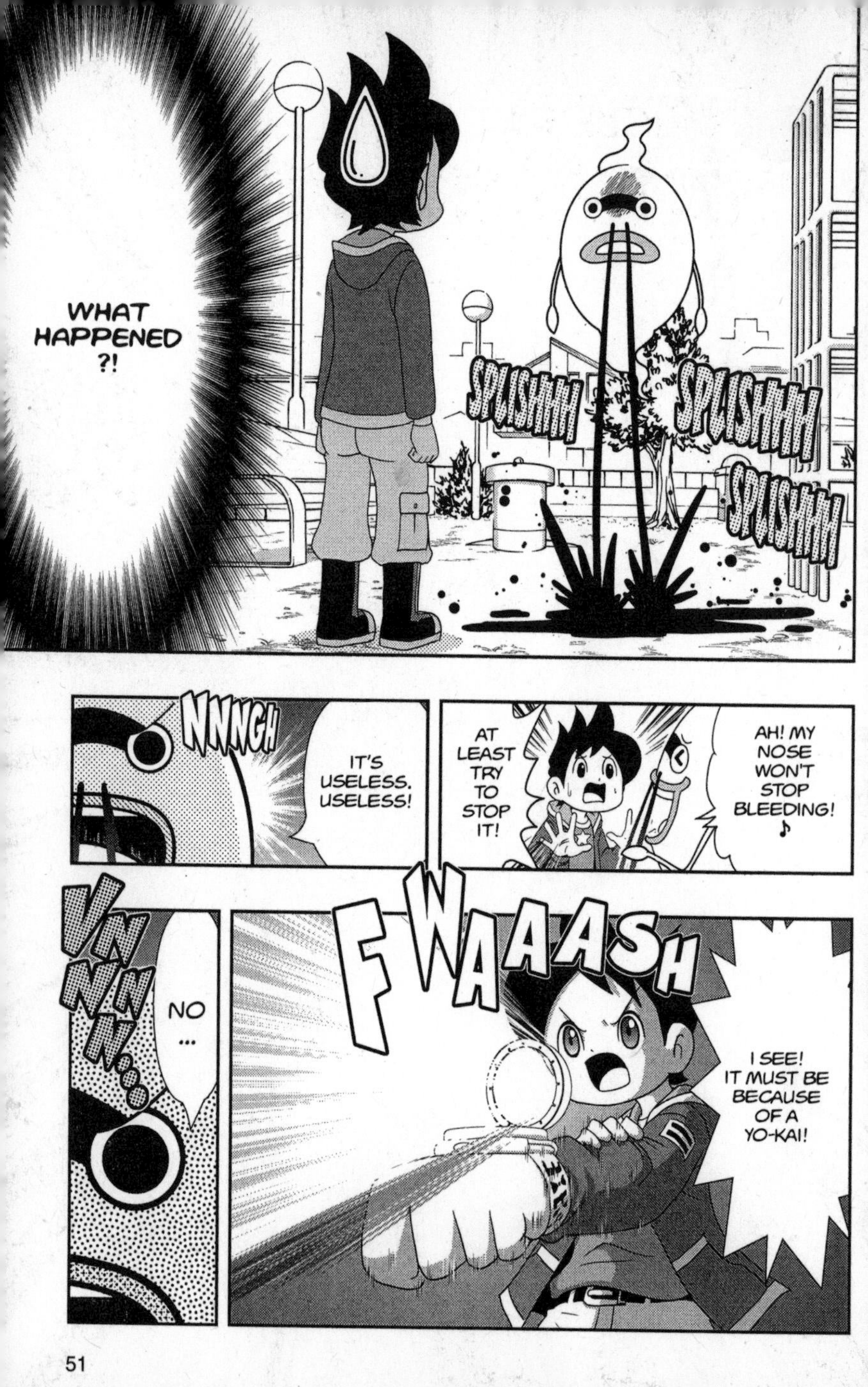
WHAT HAPPENED ?!
SPLISHHH
SPLISHHH
SPLISHHH
AH! MY NOSE WON'T STOP BLEEDING! ♪
AT LEAST TRY TO STOP IT!
NNNGH
IT'S USELESS. USELESS!
FWAAASH
I SEE! IT MUST BE BECAUSE OF A YO-KAI!
NO ...
VINNNNN...

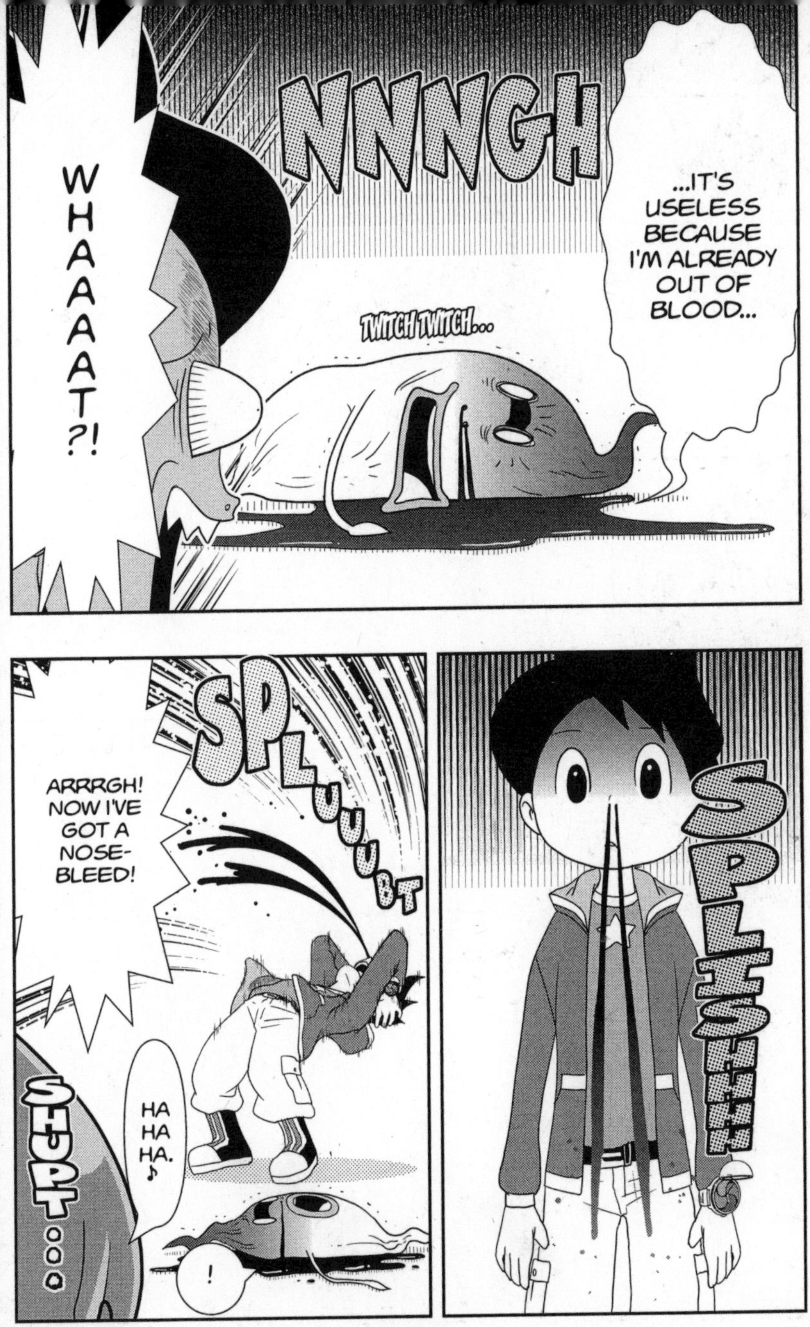
NNNGH
...IT'S USELESS BECAUSE I'M ALREADY OUT OF BLOOD...
TWITCH TWITCH...
WHAAAAAT?!
SPLISHHH
SPLUUUBT
ARRRGH! NOW I'VE GOT A NOSE-BLEED!
HA HA HA. ♪
SHUPT...
!

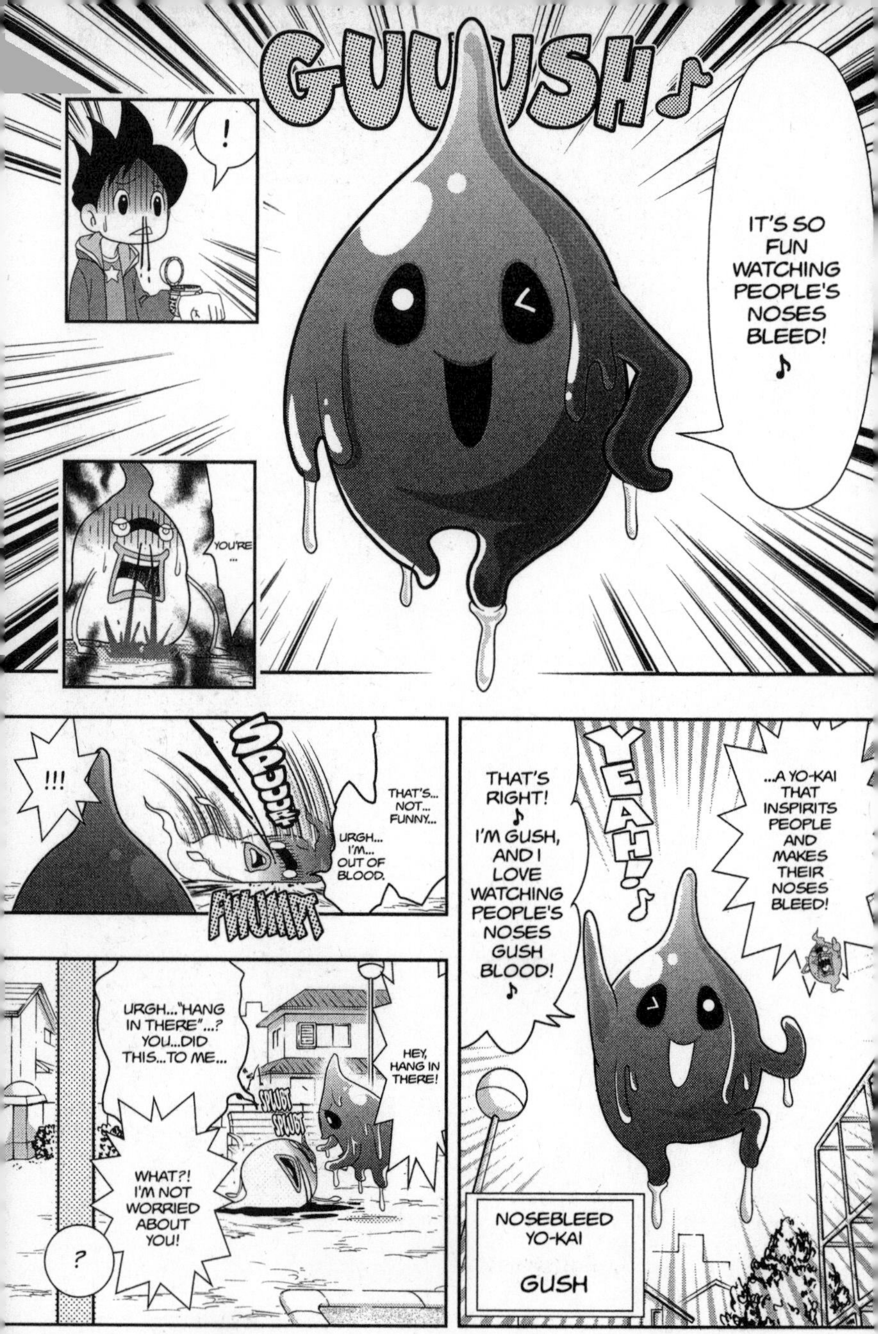
GUUUSH♪
IT'S SO FUN WATCHING PEOPLE'S NOSES BLEED! ♪
!
YOU'RE ...
...A YO-KAI THAT INSPIRITS PEOPLE AND MAKES THEIR NOSES BLEED!
YEAH!♪
THAT'S RIGHT! ♪ I'M GUSH, AND I LOVE WATCHING PEOPLE'S NOSES GUSH BLOOD! ♪
NOSEBLEED YO-KAI
GUSH
SPUUUT
THAT'S... NOT... FUNNY...
URGH... I'M... OUT OF BLOOD.
!!!
FWUMPT
HEY, HANG IN THERE!
SPLUBT
SPLUBT
URGH..."HANG IN THERE"...? YOU...DID THIS...TO ME...
WHAT?! I'M NOT WORRIED ABOUT YOU!
?

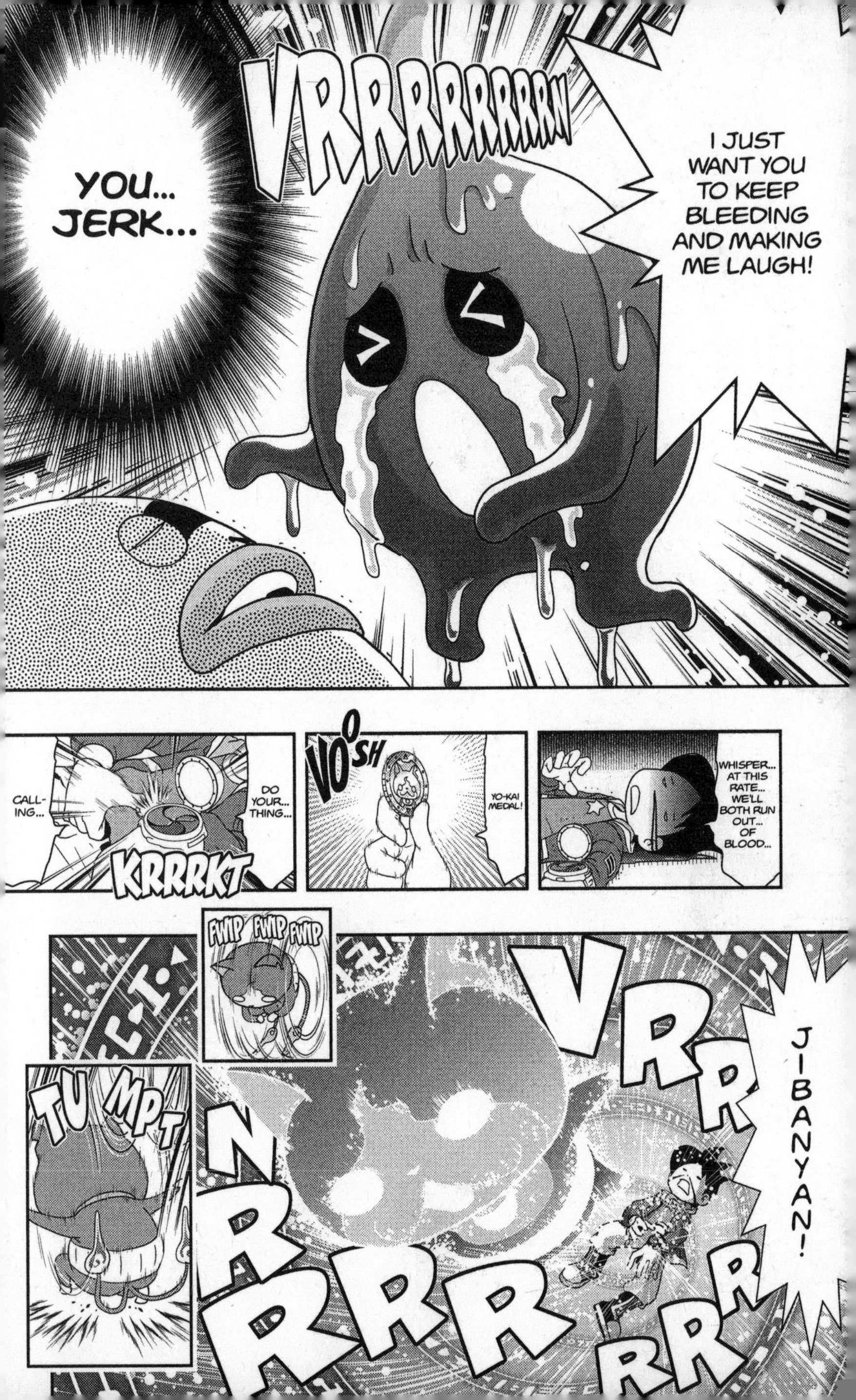
I JUST WANT YOU TO KEEP BLEEDING AND MAKING ME LAUGH!
VRRRRRRRRN
YOU... JERK...
WHISPER... AT THIS RATE... WE'LL BOTH RUN OUT... OF BLOOD...
YO-KAI MEDAL!
VOOOSH
DO YOUR... THING...
CALLING...
KRRRKT
JIBANYAN!
VRRNRRRRRRRR
FWIP FWIP FWIP
TUMPT

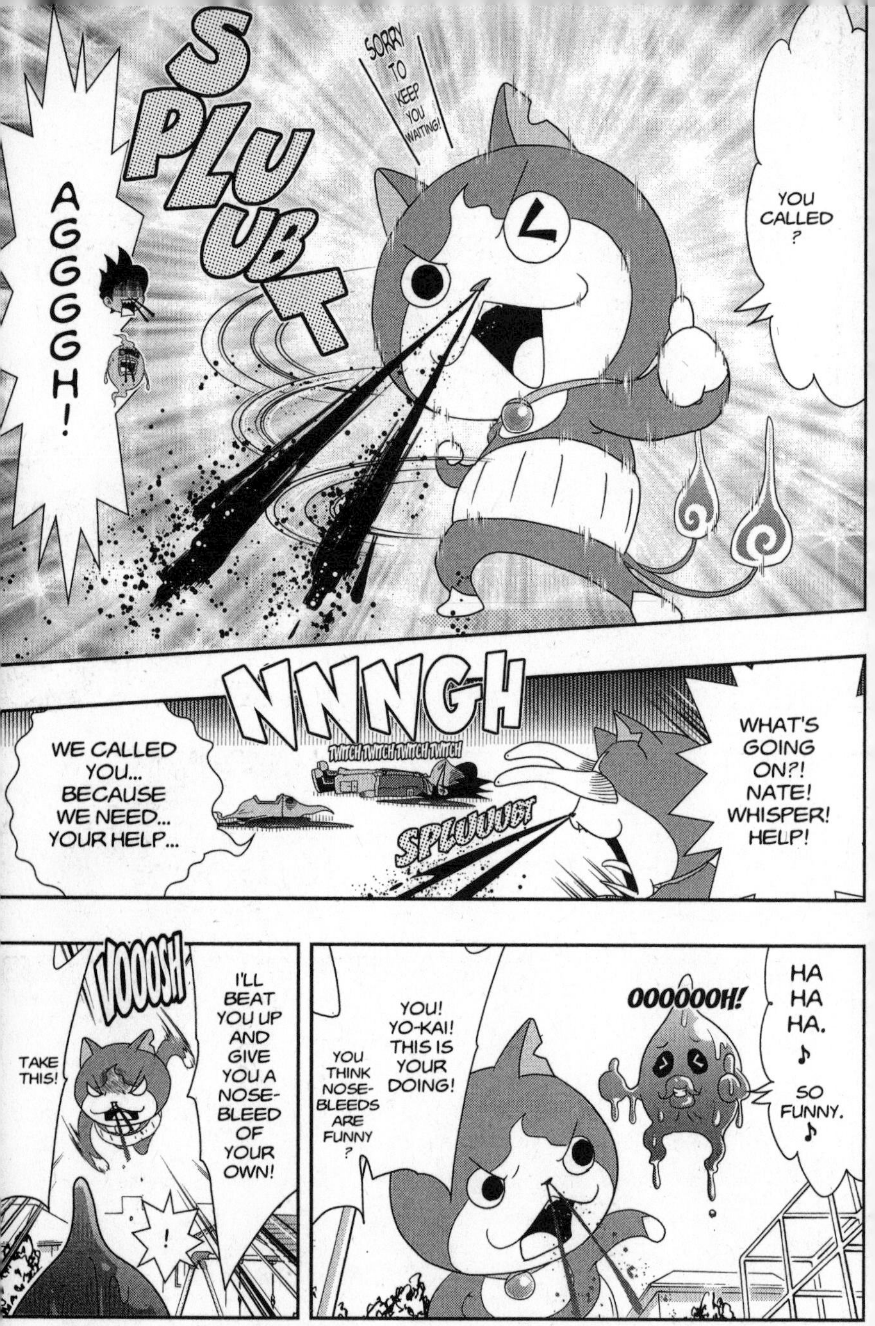
YOU CALLED?
SORRY TO KEEP YOU WAITING!
SPLUUBT
AGGGGH!
WHAT'S GOING ON?! NATE! WHISPER! HELP!
NNNGH
TWITCH TWITCH TWITCH TWITCH
SPLUUUBT
WE CALLED YOU... BECAUSE WE NEED... YOUR HELP...
HA HA HA. ♪ SO FUNNY. ♪
OOOOOOH!
YOU! YO-KAI! THIS IS YOUR DOING!
YOU THINK NOSE-BLEEDS ARE FUNNY?
VOOOSH
I'LL BEAT YOU UP AND GIVE YOU A NOSE-BLEED OF YOUR OWN!
TAKE THIS!
!

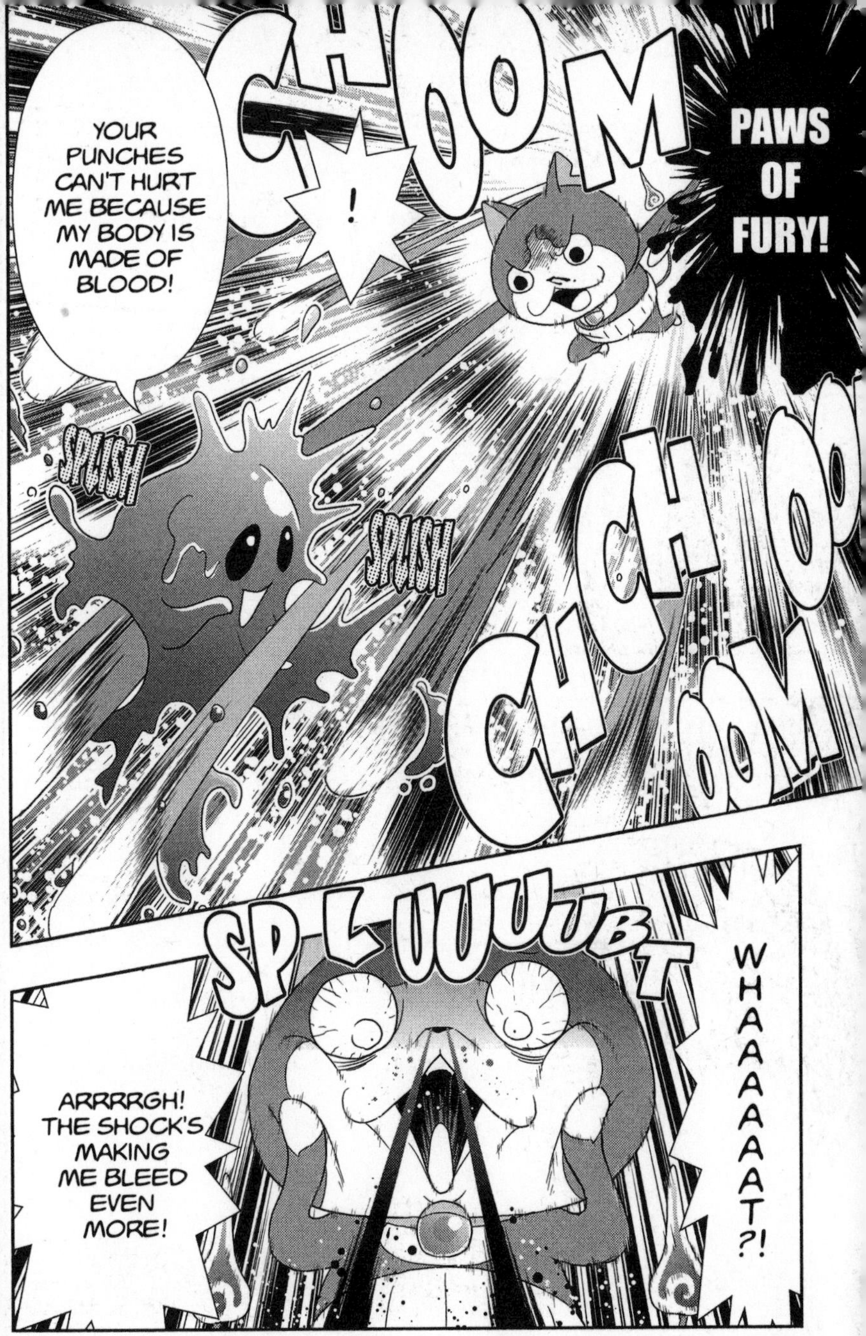

PAWS OF FURY!
CHOOOM
!
YOUR PUNCHES CAN'T HURT ME BECAUSE MY BODY IS MADE OF BLOOD!
CHOOOM
CHOOOM
SPLISH
SPLISH
SPLUUUUBT
WHAAAAAAT?!
ARRRRGH! THE SHOCK'S MAKING ME BLEED EVEN MORE!

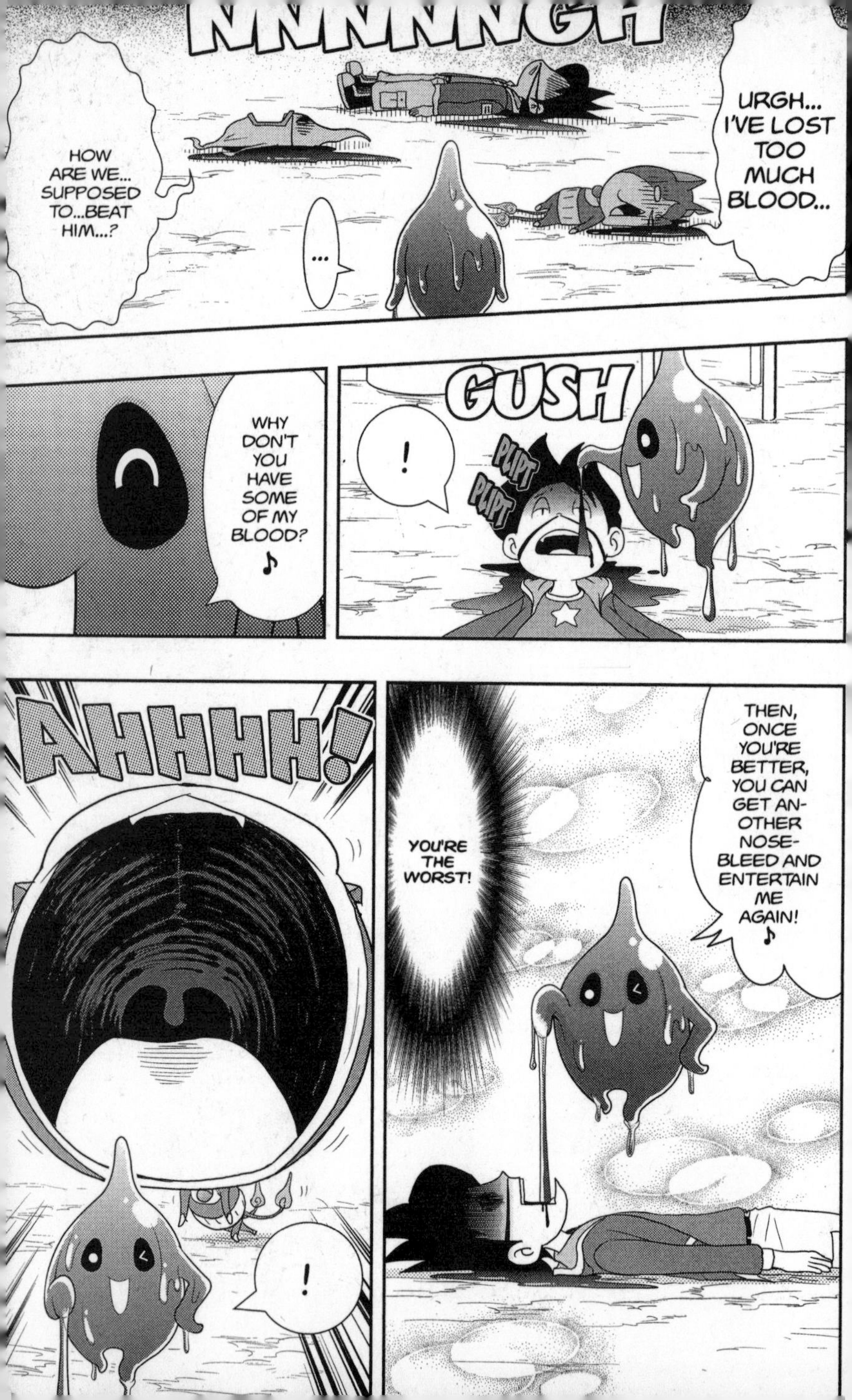
NNNNNGH
URGH... I'VE LOST TOO MUCH BLOOD...
...
HOW ARE WE... SUPPOSED TO...BEAT HIM...?
GUSH
PLIPT PLIPT
!
WHY DON'T YOU HAVE SOME OF MY BLOOD? ♪
THEN, ONCE YOU'RE BETTER, YOU CAN GET AN-OTHER NOSE-BLEED AND ENTERTAIN ME AGAIN! ♪
YOU'RE THE WORST!
AHHHHH!
!

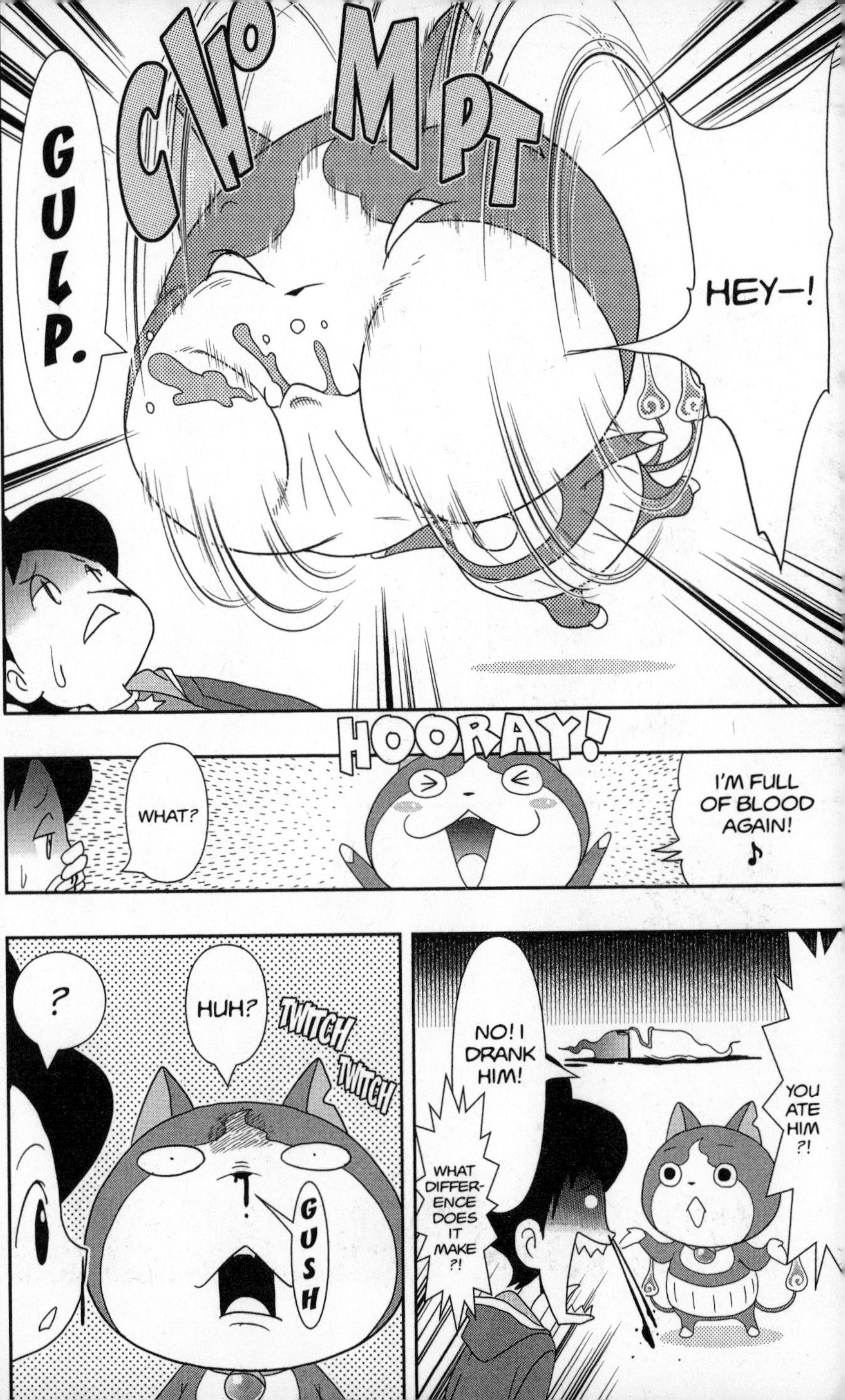
HEY—!
CHOMPT
GULP.
HOORAY!
I'M FULL OF BLOOD AGAIN! ♪
WHAT?
YOU ATE HIM?!
NO! I DRANK HIM!
WHAT DIFFERENCE DOES IT MAKE?!
TWITCH TWITCH
HUH?
?
GUSH

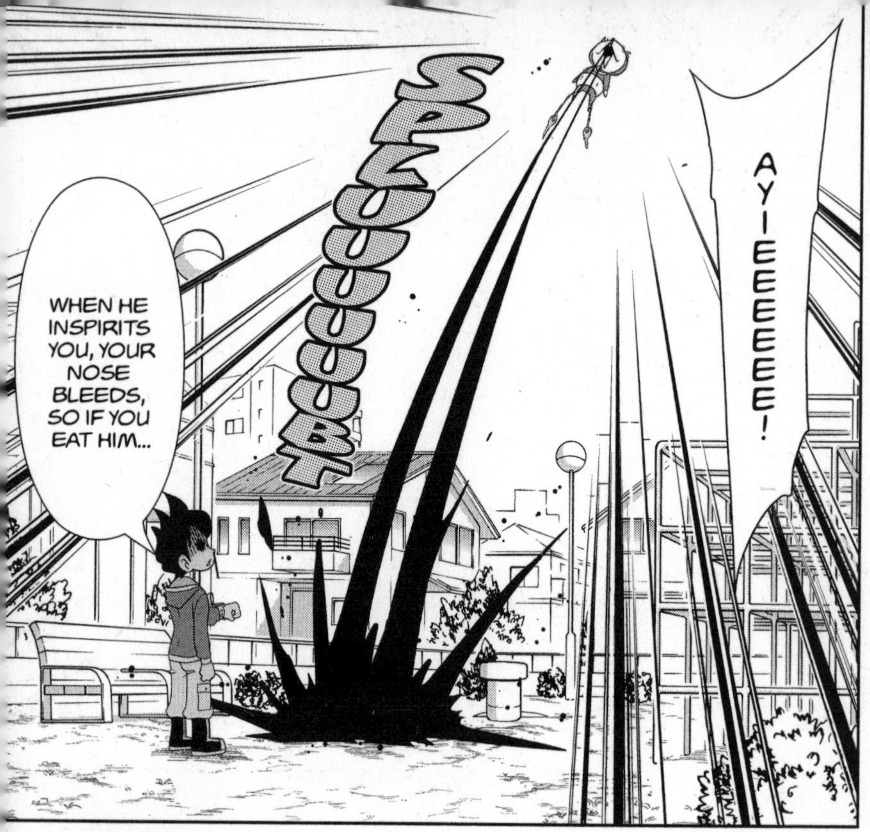
AYIEEEEEE!
SPLUUUUUUUBT
WHEN HE INSPIRITS YOU, YOUR NOSE BLEEDS, SO IF YOU EAT HIM...

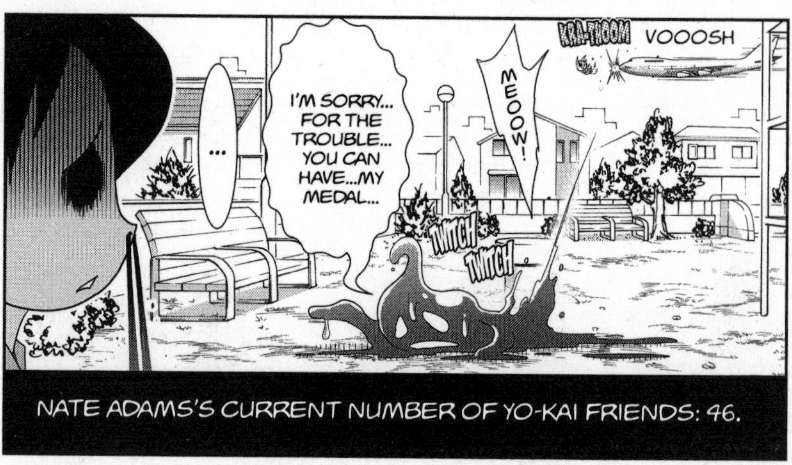
VOOOSH
KRA-THOOM
MEOOW!
I'M SORRY... FOR THE TROUBLE... YOU CAN HAVE...MY MEDAL...
...
TWITCH
TWITCH
NATE ADAMS'S CURRENT NUMBER OF YO-KAI FRIENDS: 46.

# GUSH!

FWEEEE
MEOW ...?!
SHUPT
WHAAA...
MY BATTERY'S DEAD! I CAN'T FLY!
KLIKT
KLIKT
WALK-ING'S SUCH A PAIN. I WANT TO FLY!
TUMPT TUMPT
HUH?
HEY, JIBANYAN! LONG TIME NO SEE! ♪
NOT LIKE THIII-IIIIIS!
SPLUUUUBT
WOOSH
HE FLEW.

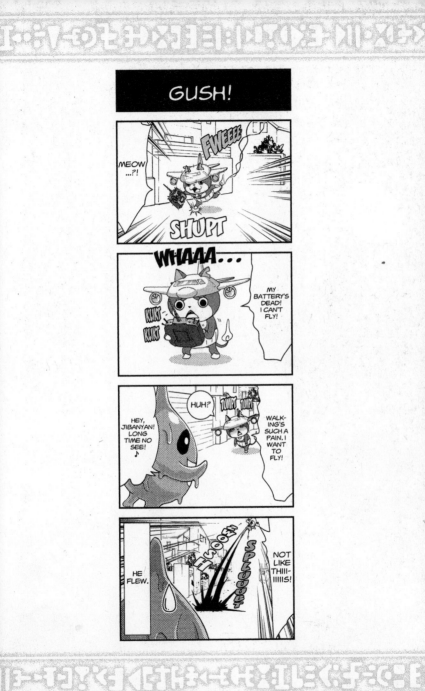

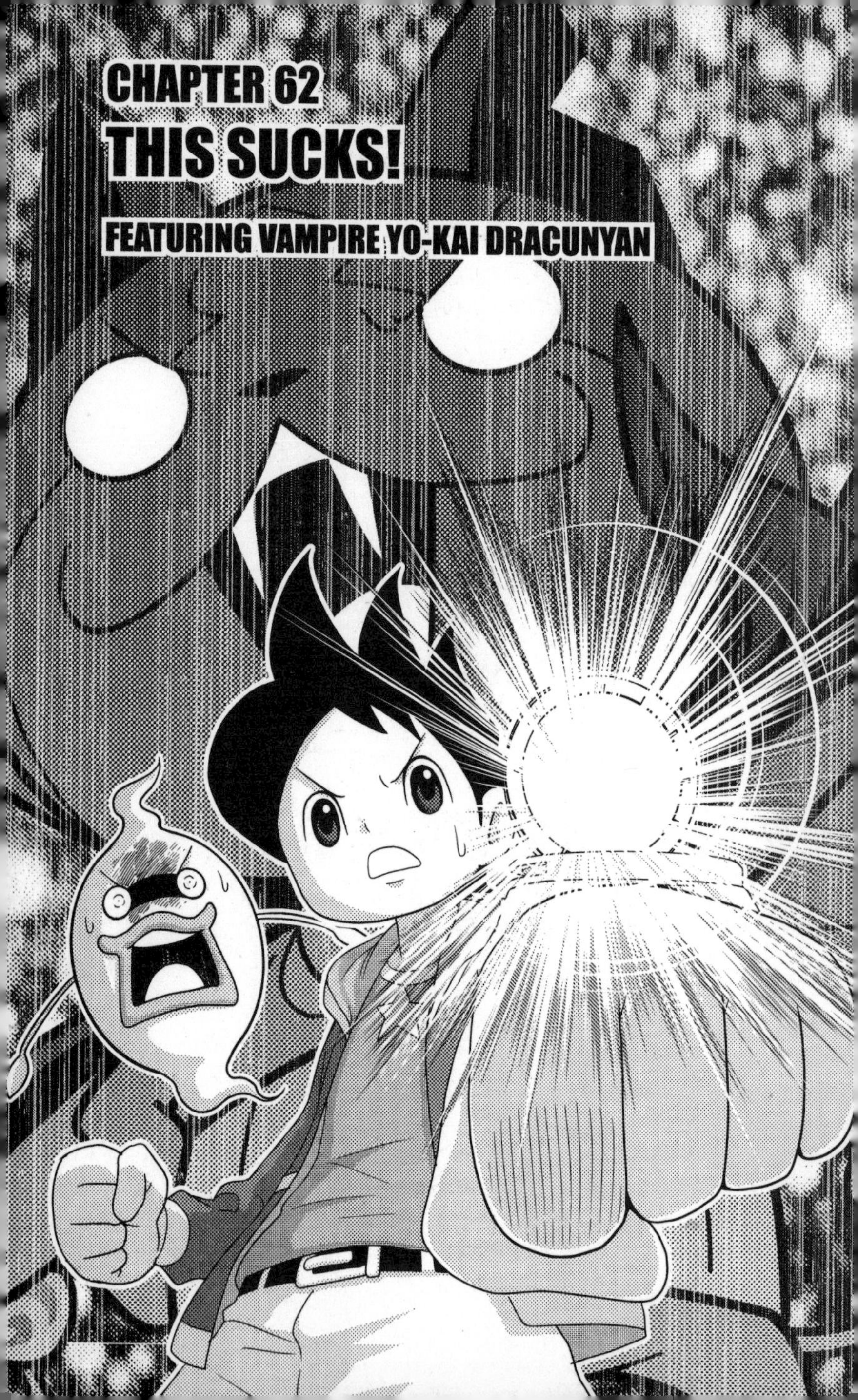
CHAPTER 62
THIS SUCKS!
FEATURING VAMPIRE YO-KAI DRACUNYAN

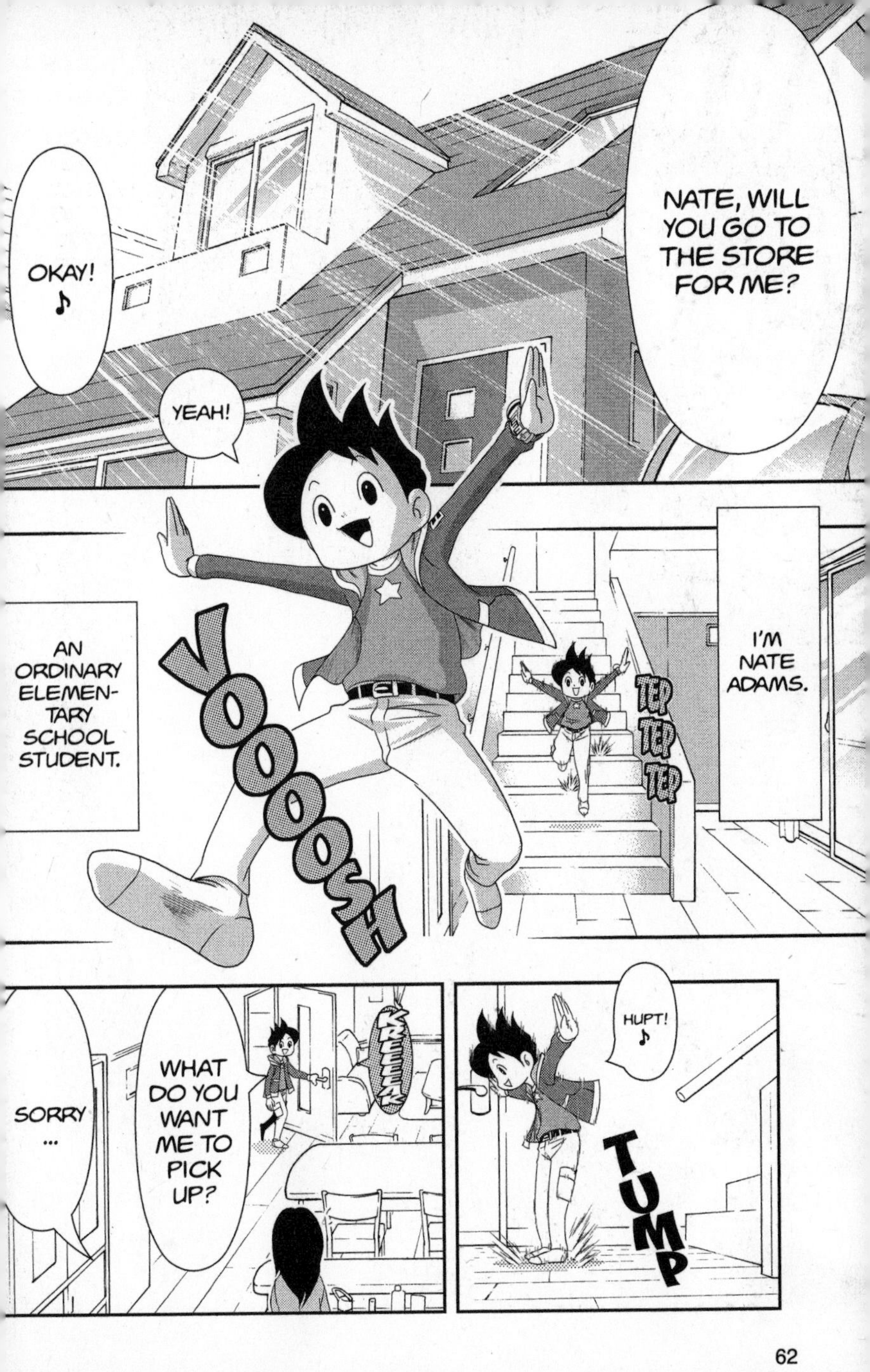
NATE, WILL YOU GO TO THE STORE FOR ME?
OKAY! ♪
YEAH!
I'M NATE ADAMS.
TEP TEP TEP
YOOOOSH
AN ORDINARY ELEMENTARY SCHOOL STUDENT.
HUPT! ♪
TUMP
KREEEAK
WHAT DO YOU WANT ME TO PICK UP?
SORRY ...

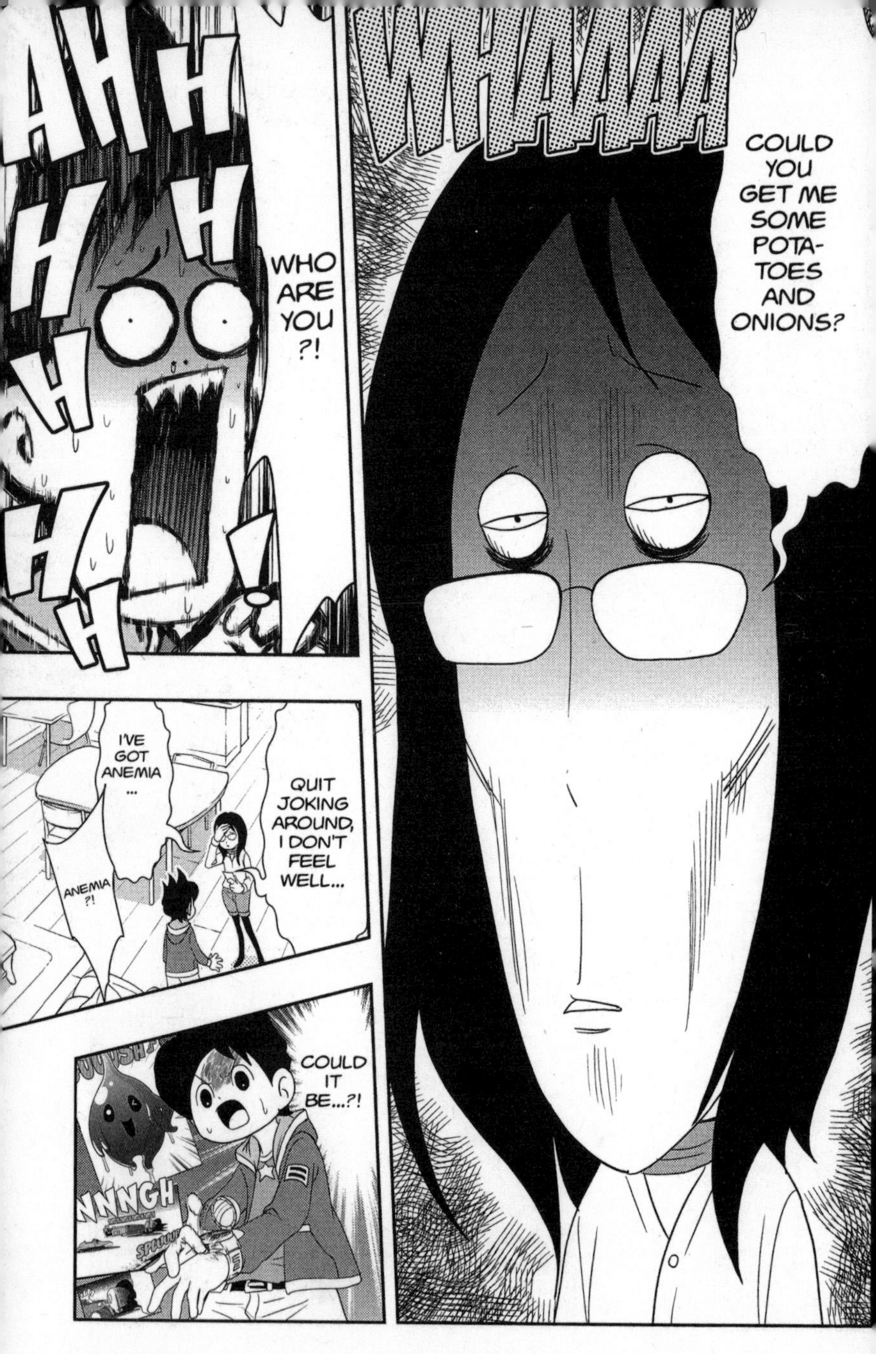
WHAAAA
COULD YOU GET ME SOME POTATOES AND ONIONS?
AHHHHHHHH
WHO ARE YOU ?!
QUIT JOKING AROUND, I DON'T FEEL WELL...
I'VE GOT ANEMIA ...
ANEMIA ?!
COULD IT BE...?!
NNNGH

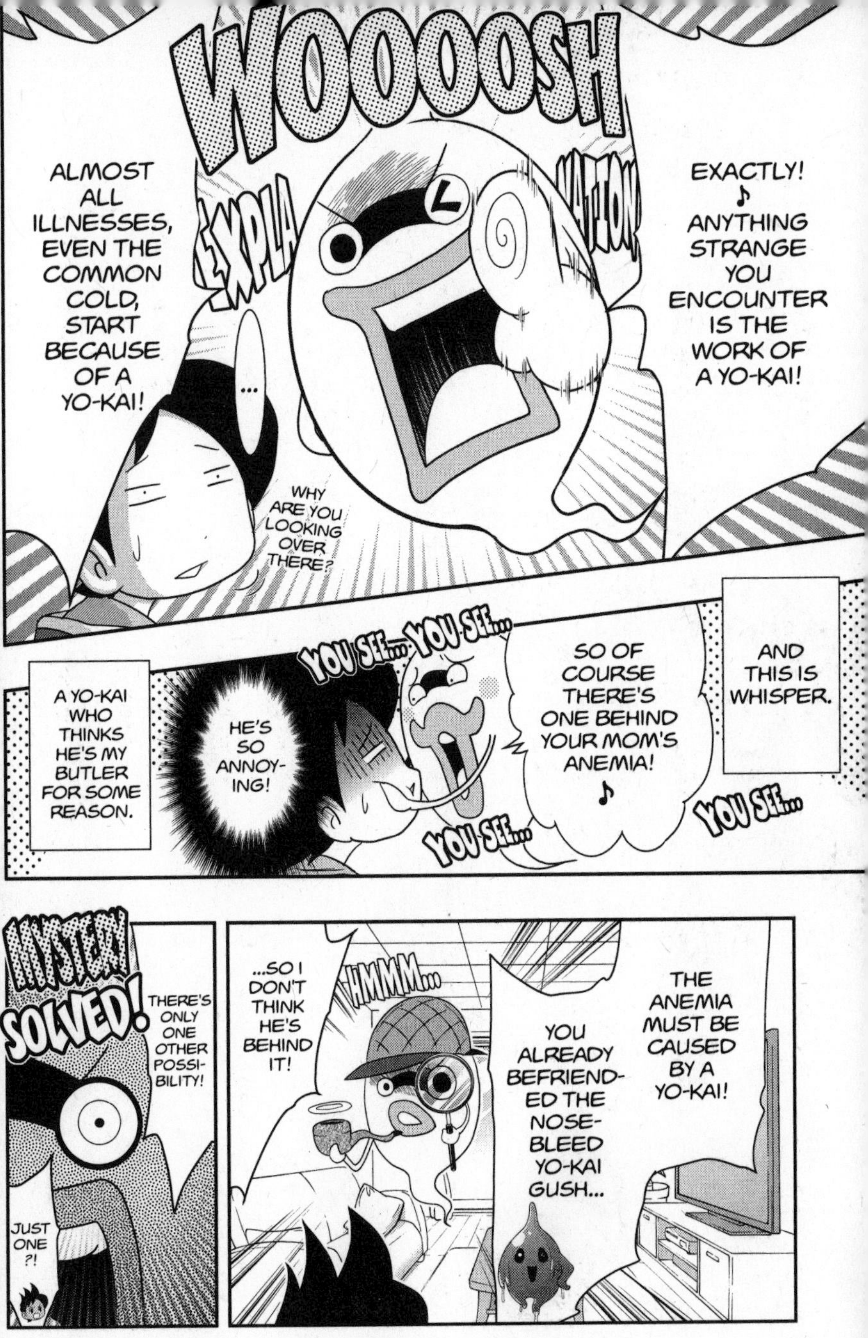
EXACTLY! ♪ ANYTHING STRANGE YOU ENCOUNTER IS THE WORK OF A YO-KAI!
WOOOOSH
EXPLANATION
...
ALMOST ALL ILLNESSES, EVEN THE COMMON COLD, START BECAUSE OF A YO-KAI!
WHY ARE YOU LOOKING OVER THERE?
AND THIS IS WHISPER.
YOU SEE...
SO OF COURSE THERE'S ONE BEHIND YOUR MOM'S ANEMIA! ♪
YOU SEE... YOU SEE...
YOU SEE...
HE'S SO ANNOY-ING!
A YO-KAI WHO THINKS HE'S MY BUTLER FOR SOME REASON.
THE ANEMIA MUST BE CAUSED BY A YO-KAI!
YOU ALREADY BEFRIEND-ED THE NOSE-BLEED YO-KAI GUSH...
HMMM...
...SO I DON'T THINK HE'S BEHIND IT!
MYSTERY SOLVED!
THERE'S ONLY ONE OTHER POSSI-BILITY!
JUST ONE ?!

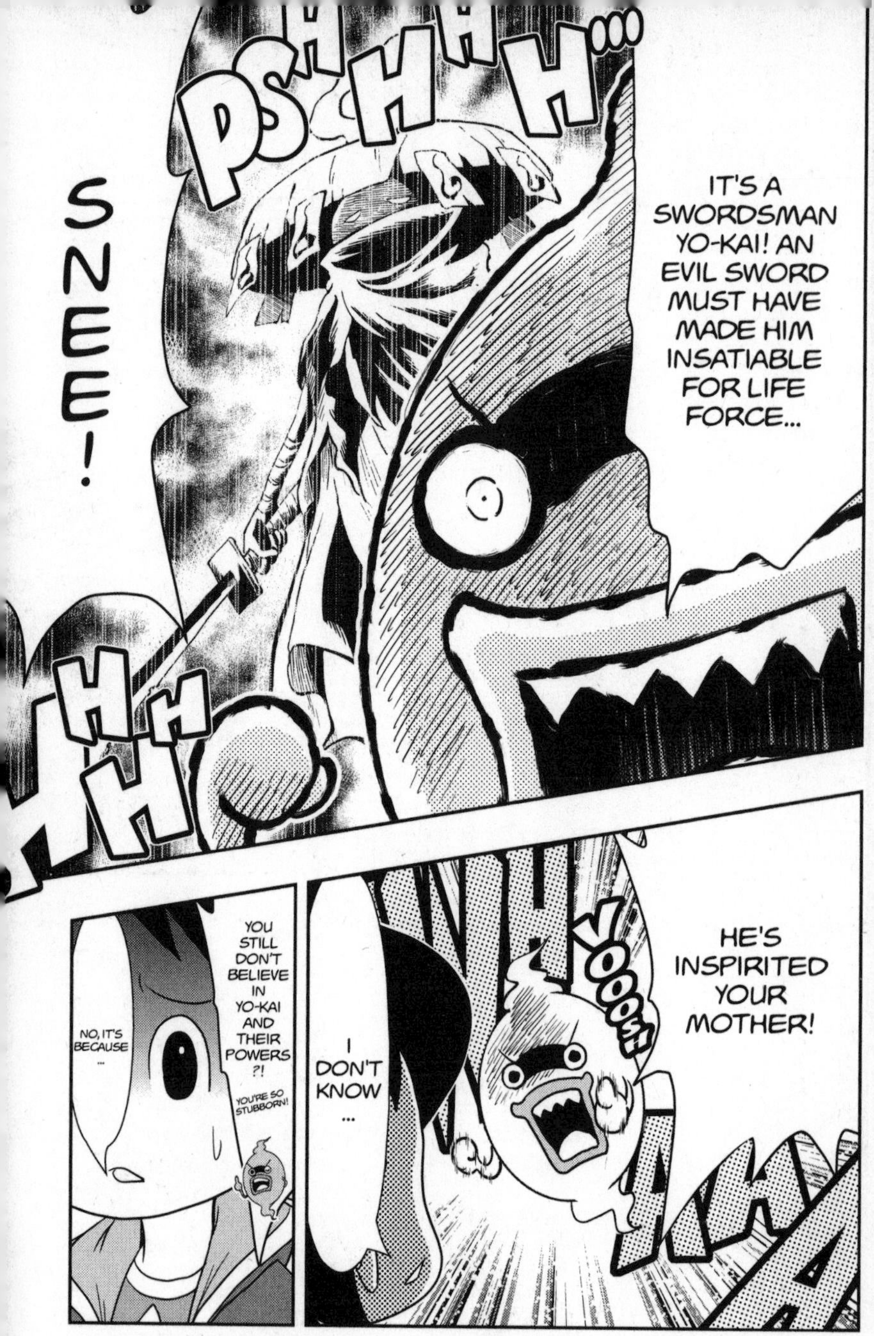
PSHHHH...
IT'S A SWORDSMAN YO-KAI! AN EVIL SWORD MUST HAVE MADE HIM INSATIABLE FOR LIFE FORCE...
SNEEE!
HHHH
HE'S INSPIRITED YOUR MOTHER!
VOOOM!
I DON'T KNOW ...
YOU STILL DON'T BELIEVE IN YO-KAI AND THEIR POWERS?!
YOU'RE SO STUBBORN!
NO, IT'S BECAUSE ...

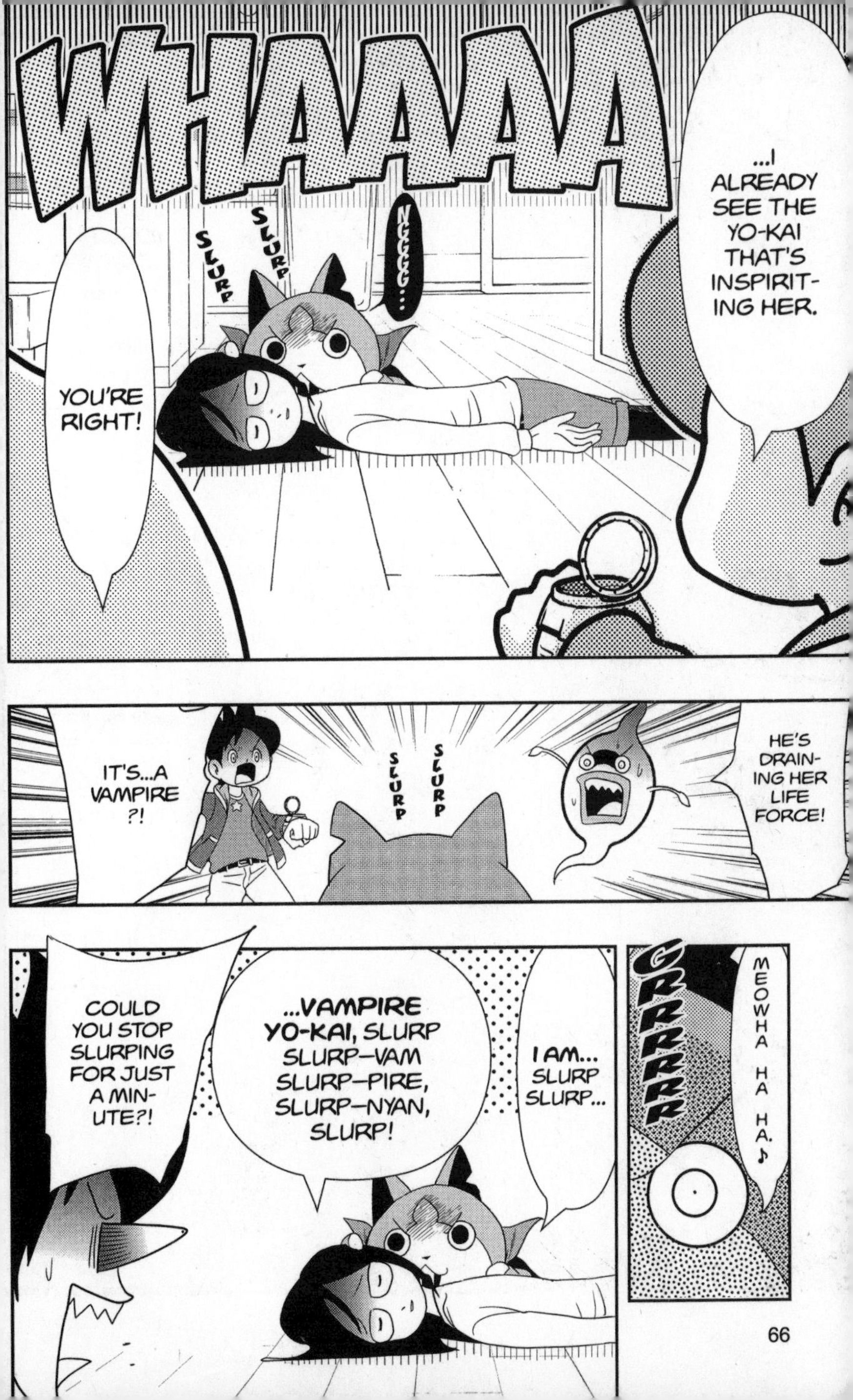
...I ALREADY SEE THE YO-KAI THAT'S INSPIRIT-ING HER.
WHAAAA
NGGGG...
SLURP
SLURP
YOU'RE RIGHT!
HE'S DRAIN-ING HER LIFE FORCE!
SLURP
SLURP
IT'S...A VAMPIRE?!
MEOWHA HA HA.♪
GRRRRR
I AM... SLURP SLURP...
...VAMPIRE YO-KAI, SLURP SLURP—VAM SLURP—PIRE, SLURP—NYAN, SLURP!
COULD YOU STOP SLURPING FOR JUST A MIN-UTE?!

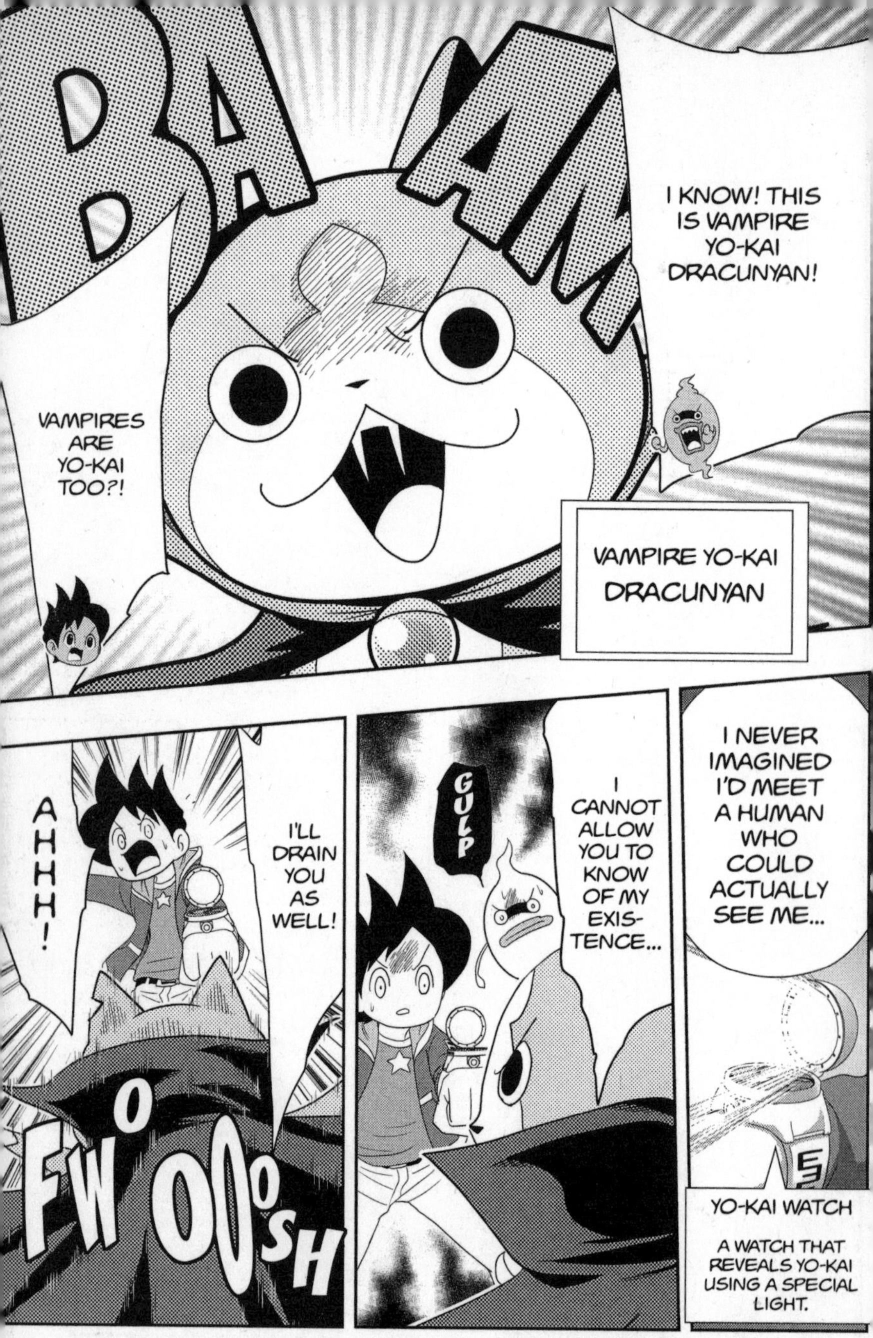
BAAM
I KNOW! THIS IS VAMPIRE YO-KAI DRACUNYAN!
VAMPIRE YO-KAI DRACUNYAN
VAMPIRES ARE YO-KAI TOO?!
I NEVER IMAGINED I'D MEET A HUMAN WHO COULD ACTUALLY SEE ME...
YO-KAI WATCH
A WATCH THAT REVEALS YO-KAI USING A SPECIAL LIGHT.
I CANNOT ALLOW YOU TO KNOW OF MY EXISTENCE...
GULP
I'LL DRAIN YOU AS WELL!
AHHHH!
FWOOOOSH

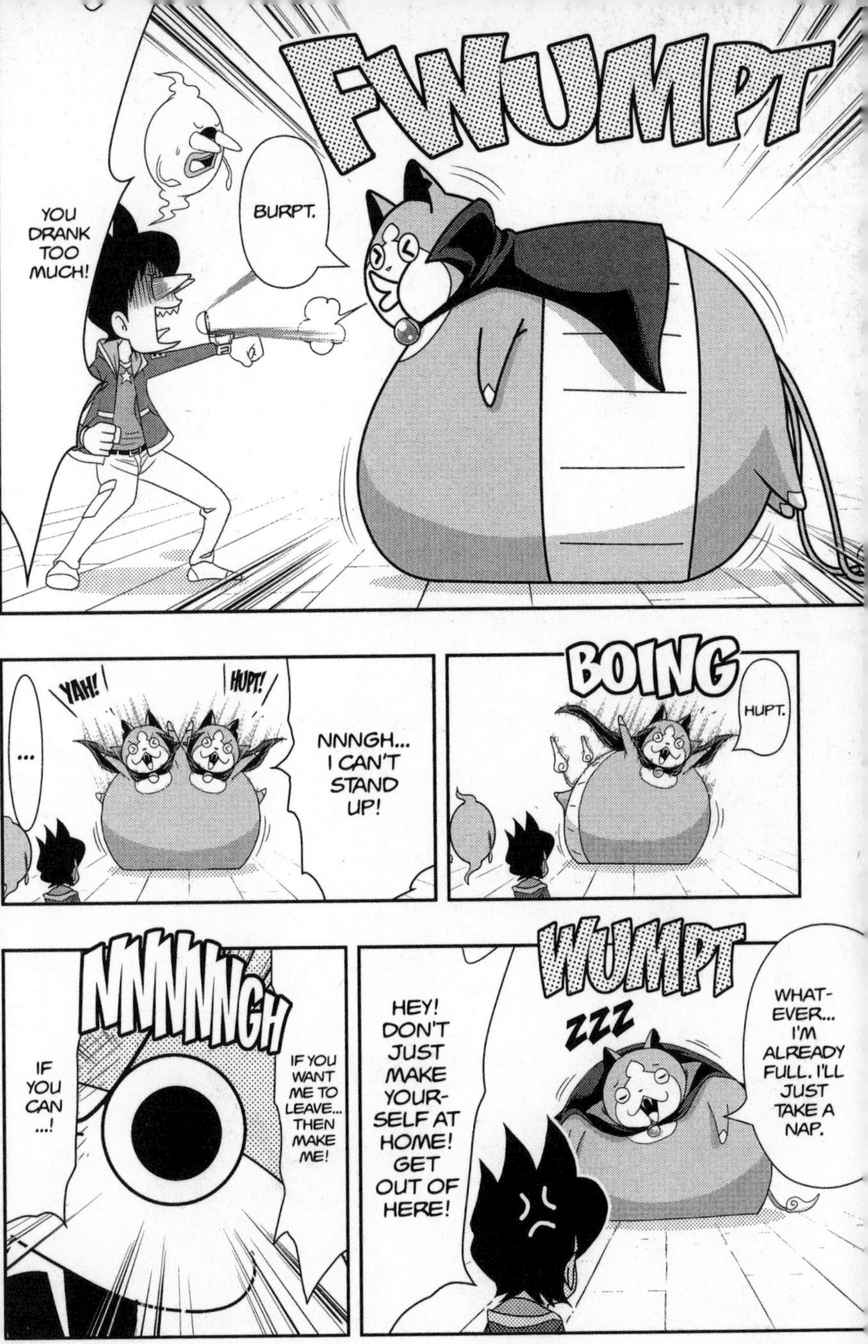
F-WUMPT
BURPT.
YOU DRANK TOO MUCH!
BOING
HUPT.
HUPT!
YAH!
NNNGH... I CAN'T STAND UP!
...
WUMPT
WHAT-EVER... I'M ALREADY FULL. I'LL JUST TAKE A NAP.
ZZZ
HEY! DON'T JUST MAKE YOUR-SELF AT HOME! GET OUT OF HERE!
NNNNNNGH
IF YOU WANT ME TO LEAVE... THEN MAKE ME!
IF YOU CAN ...!

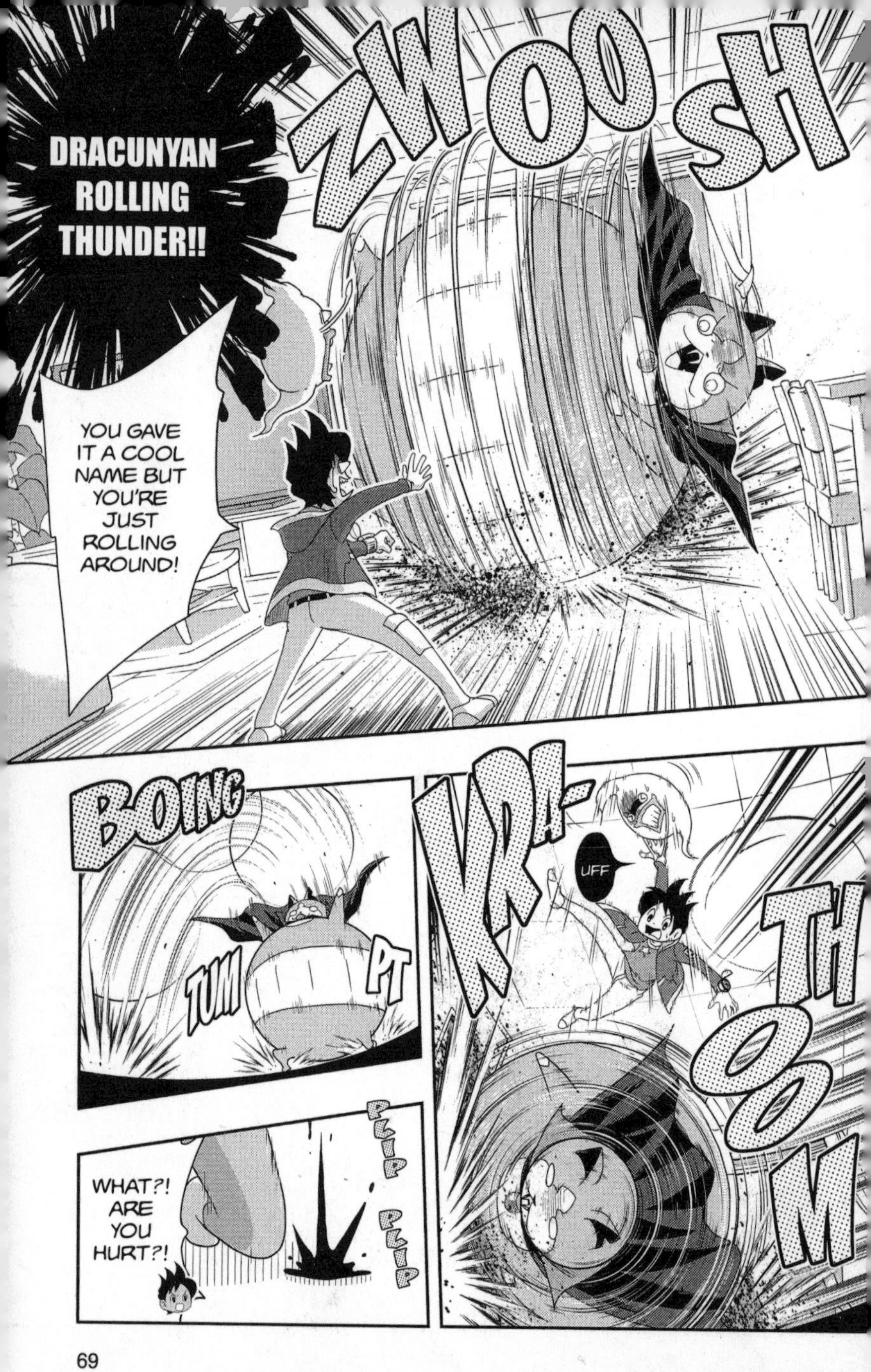
ZWOOSH
DRACUNYAN ROLLING THUNDER!!
YOU GAVE IT A COOL NAME BUT YOU'RE JUST ROLLING AROUND!
KRA-
UFF
THOOM
BOING
TUMPT
PLIP PLIP
WHAT?! ARE YOU HURT?!

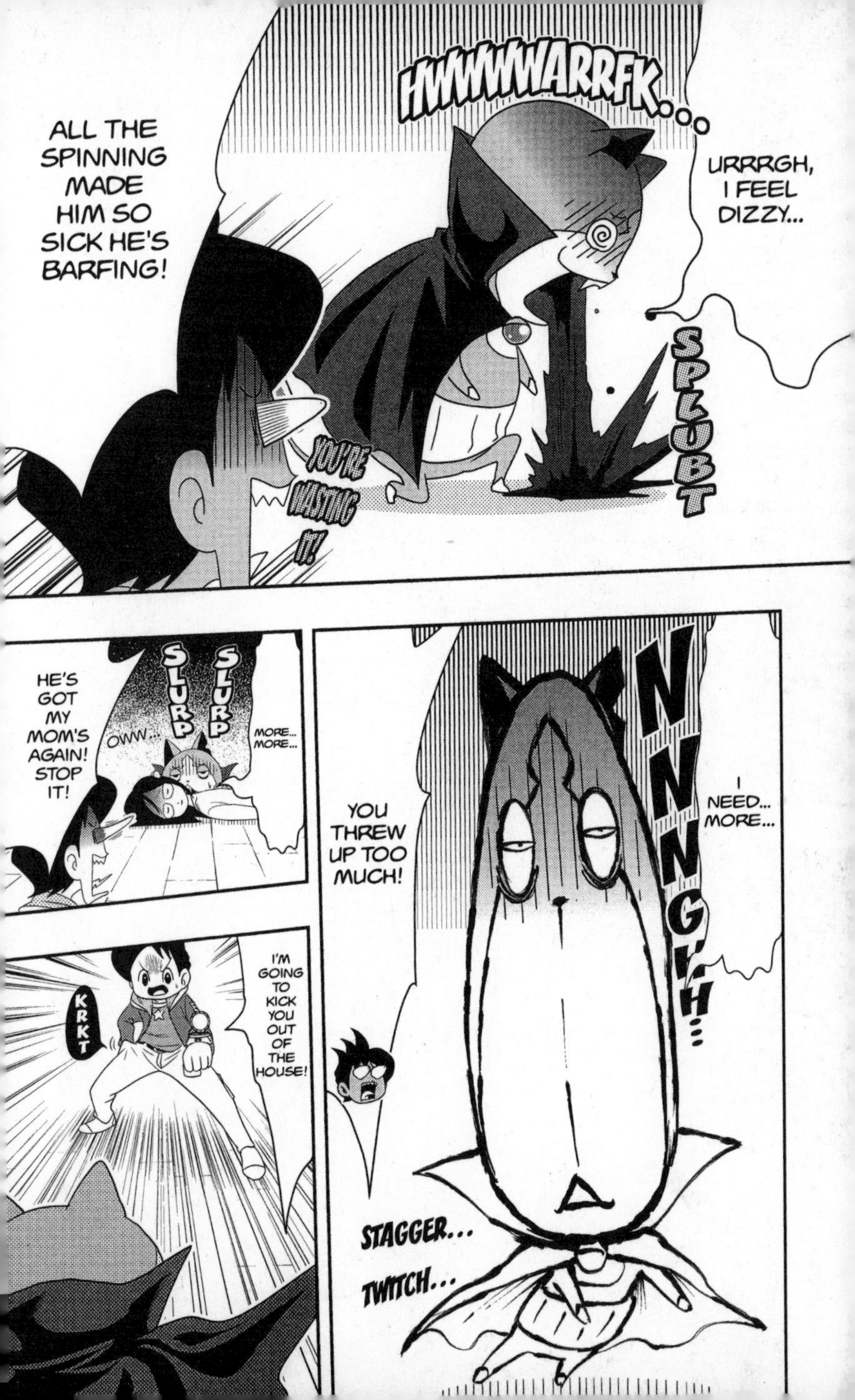
HWWWWARRFK...
URRRGH, I FEEL DIZZY...
ALL THE SPINNING MADE HIM SO SICK HE'S BARFING!
SPLUBT
YOU'RE WASTING IT!
NNNNGH...
I NEED... MORE...
YOU THREW UP TOO MUCH!
STAGGER...
TWITCH...
MORE... MORE...
SLURP
SLURP
OWW...
HE'S GOT MY MOM'S AGAIN! STOP IT!
I'M GOING TO KICK YOU OUT OF THE HOUSE!
KRKT

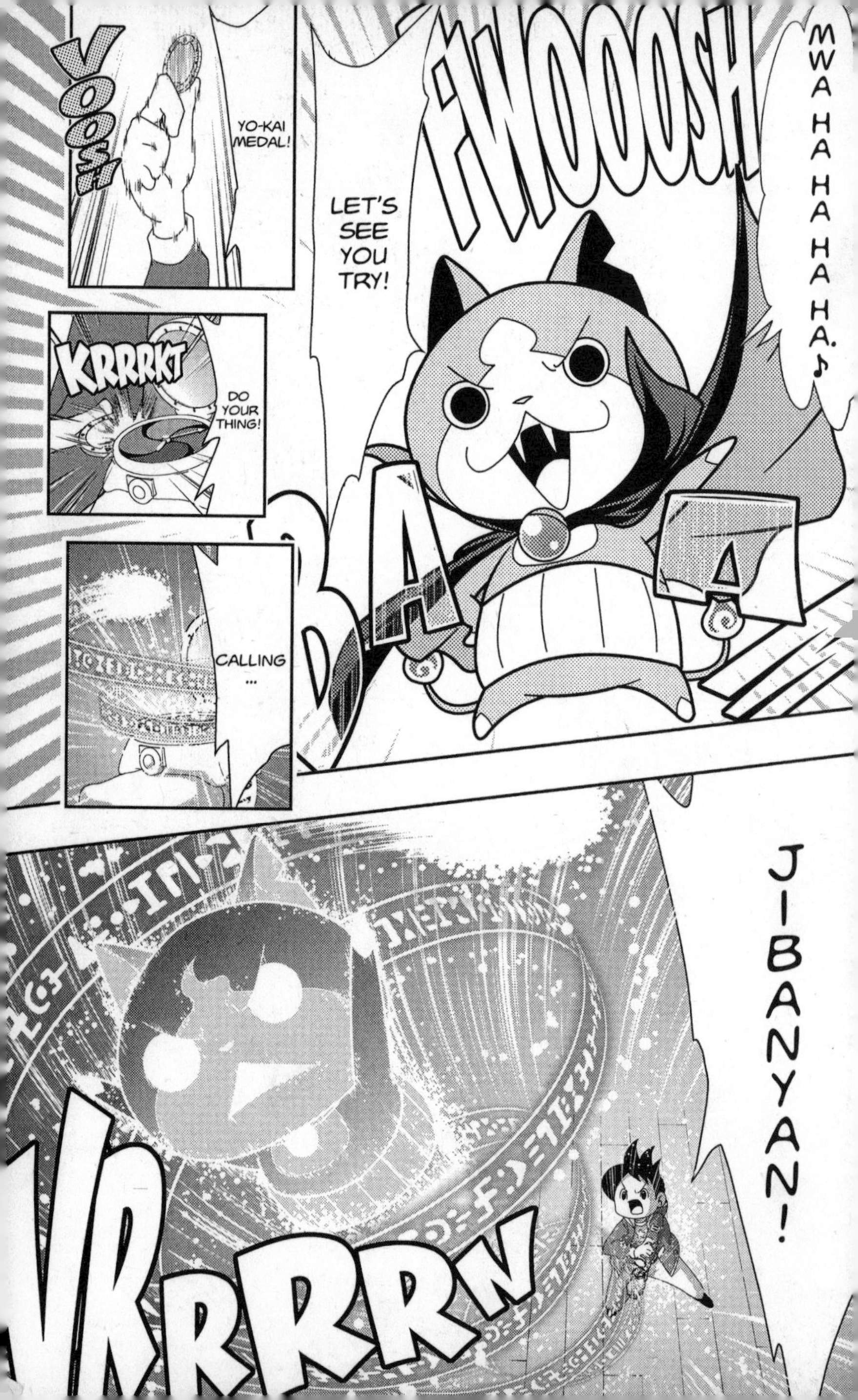
MWA HA HA HA HA HA HA♪
WOOOSH
LET'S SEE YOU TRY!
VOOSH
YO-KAI MEDAL!
KRRRKT
DO YOUR THING!
CALLING ...
JIBANYAN!
VRRRRN

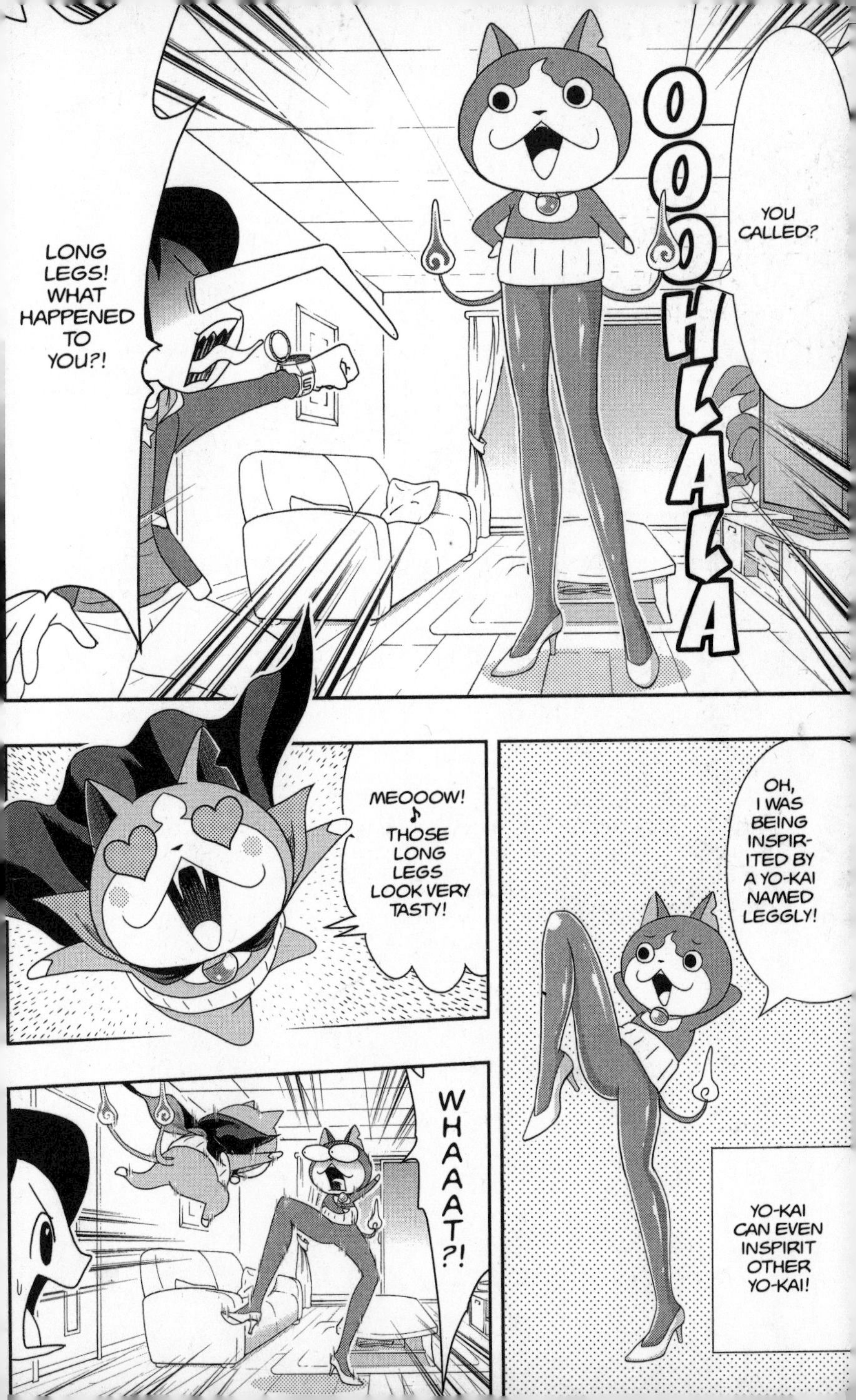
YOU CALLED?
OOOHLALA
LONG LEGS! WHAT HAPPENED TO YOU?!
OH, I WAS BEING INSPIR-ITED BY A YO-KAI NAMED LEGGLY!
YO-KAI CAN EVEN INSPIRIT OTHER YO-KAI!
MEOOOW! ♪ THOSE LONG LEGS LOOK VERY TASTY!
WHAAAT?!

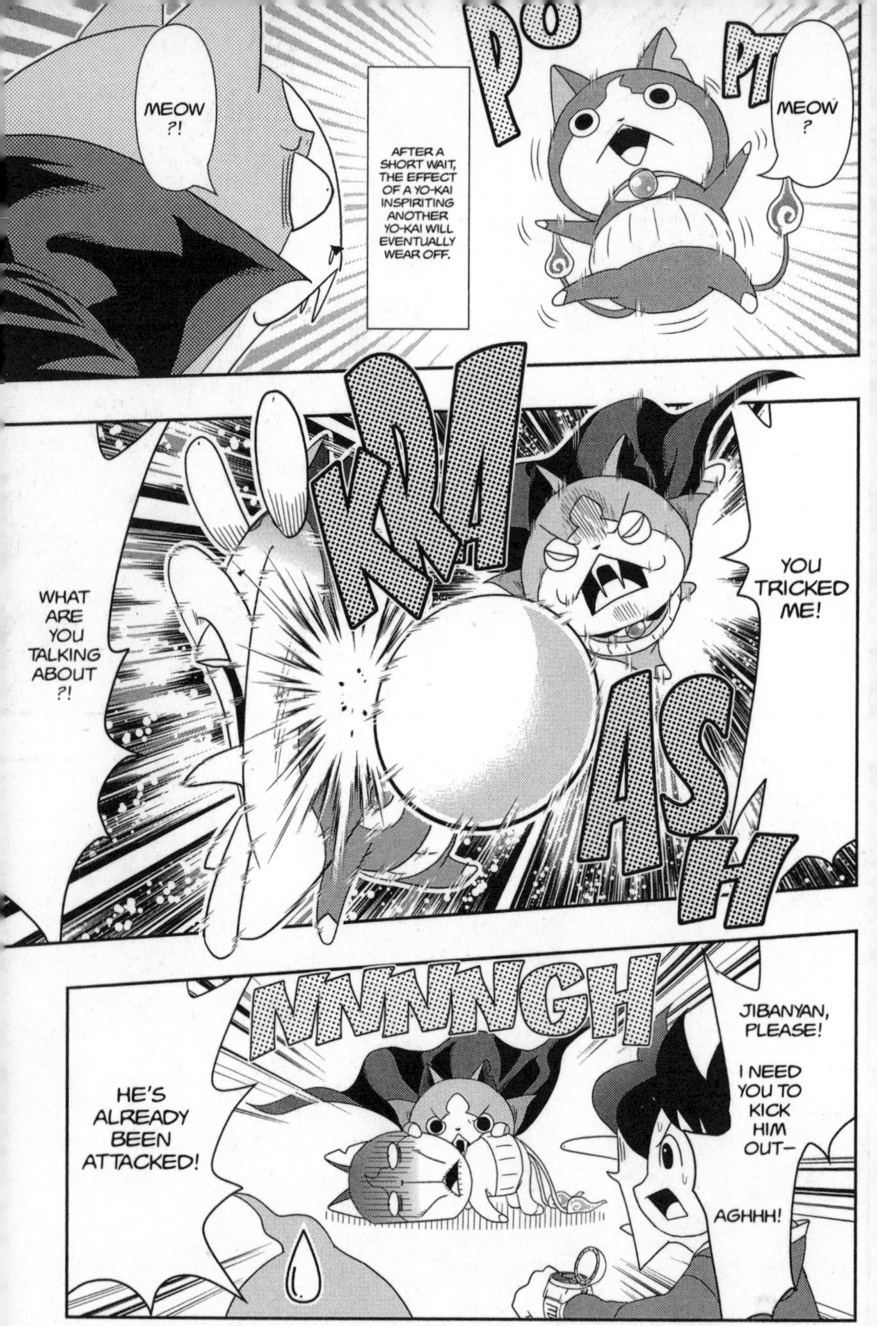
POPT
MEOW ?
AFTER A SHORT WAIT, THE EFFECT OF A YO-KAI INSPIRITING ANOTHER YO-KAI WILL EVENTUALLY WEAR OFF.
MEOW ?!
YOU TRICKED ME!
KRAASH
WHAT ARE YOU TALKING ABOUT ?!
JIBANYAN, PLEASE!
I NEED YOU TO KICK HIM OUT–
AGHHH!
NNNNNGH
HE'S ALREADY BEEN ATTACKED!

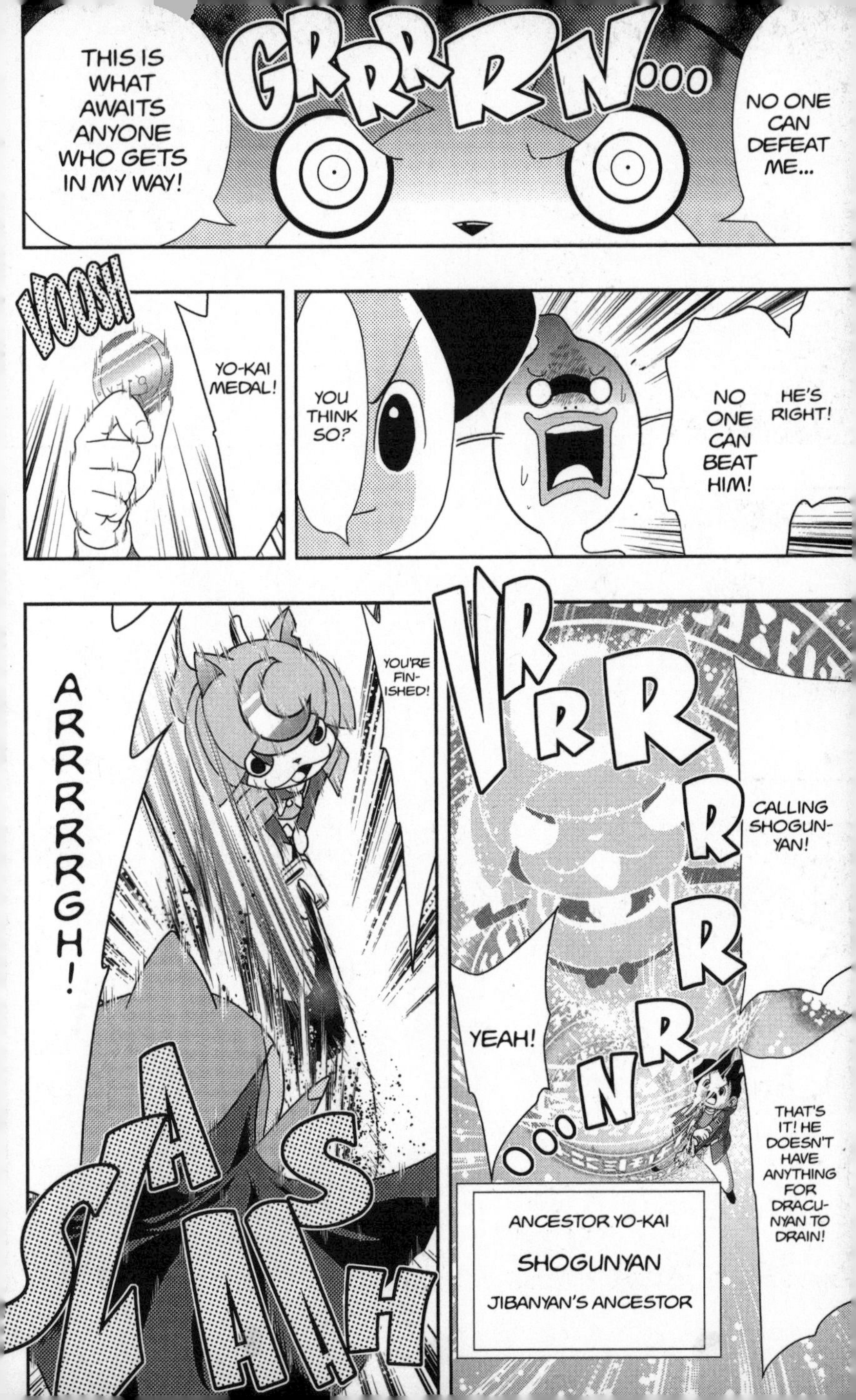
NO ONE CAN DEFEAT ME...
GRRRRN...
THIS IS WHAT AWAITS ANYONE WHO GETS IN MY WAY!
HE'S RIGHT!
NO ONE CAN BEAT HIM!
YOU THINK SO?
YO-KAI MEDAL!
VOOSH
THAT'S IT! HE DOESN'T HAVE ANYTHING FOR DRACU-NYAN TO DRAIN!
CALLING SHOGUN-YAN!
VRRRRRRRN...
YEAH!
ANCESTOR YO-KAI
SHOGUNYAN
JIBANYAN'S ANCESTOR
YOU'RE FIN-ISHED!
ARRRRRRGH!
SLAAASH

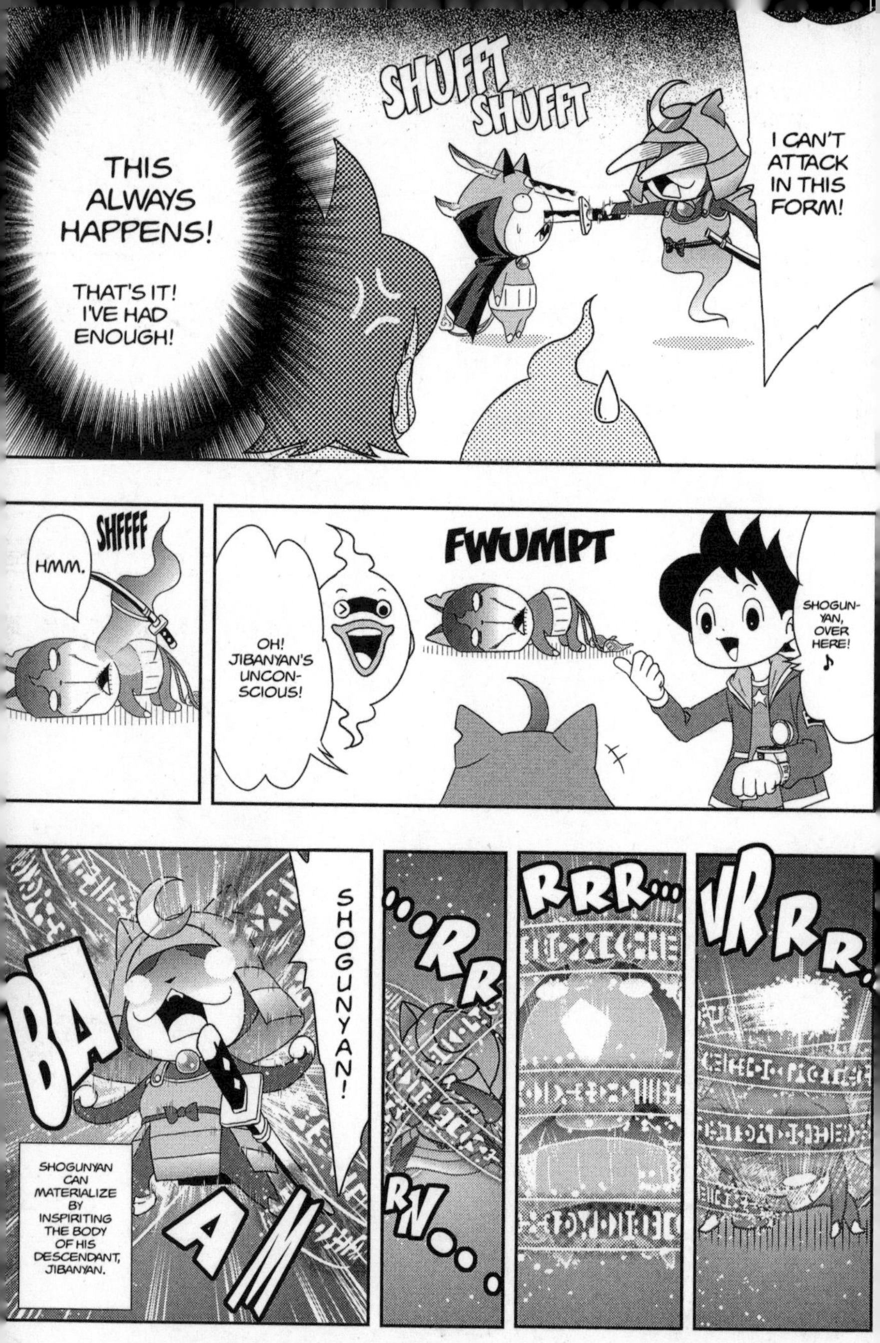
I CAN'T ATTACK IN THIS FORM!
SHUFFT SHUFFT
THIS ALWAYS HAPPENS!
THAT'S IT! I'VE HAD ENOUGH!
SHOGUN-YAN, OVER HERE! ♪
FWUMPT
OH! JIBANYAN'S UNCON-SCIOUS!
SHFFFF
HMM.
VRRRR..
RRR...
...RR
RN...
SHOGUNYAN!
BAAM
SHOGUNYAN CAN MATERIALIZE BY INSPIRITING THE BODY OF HIS DESCENDANT, JIBANYAN.

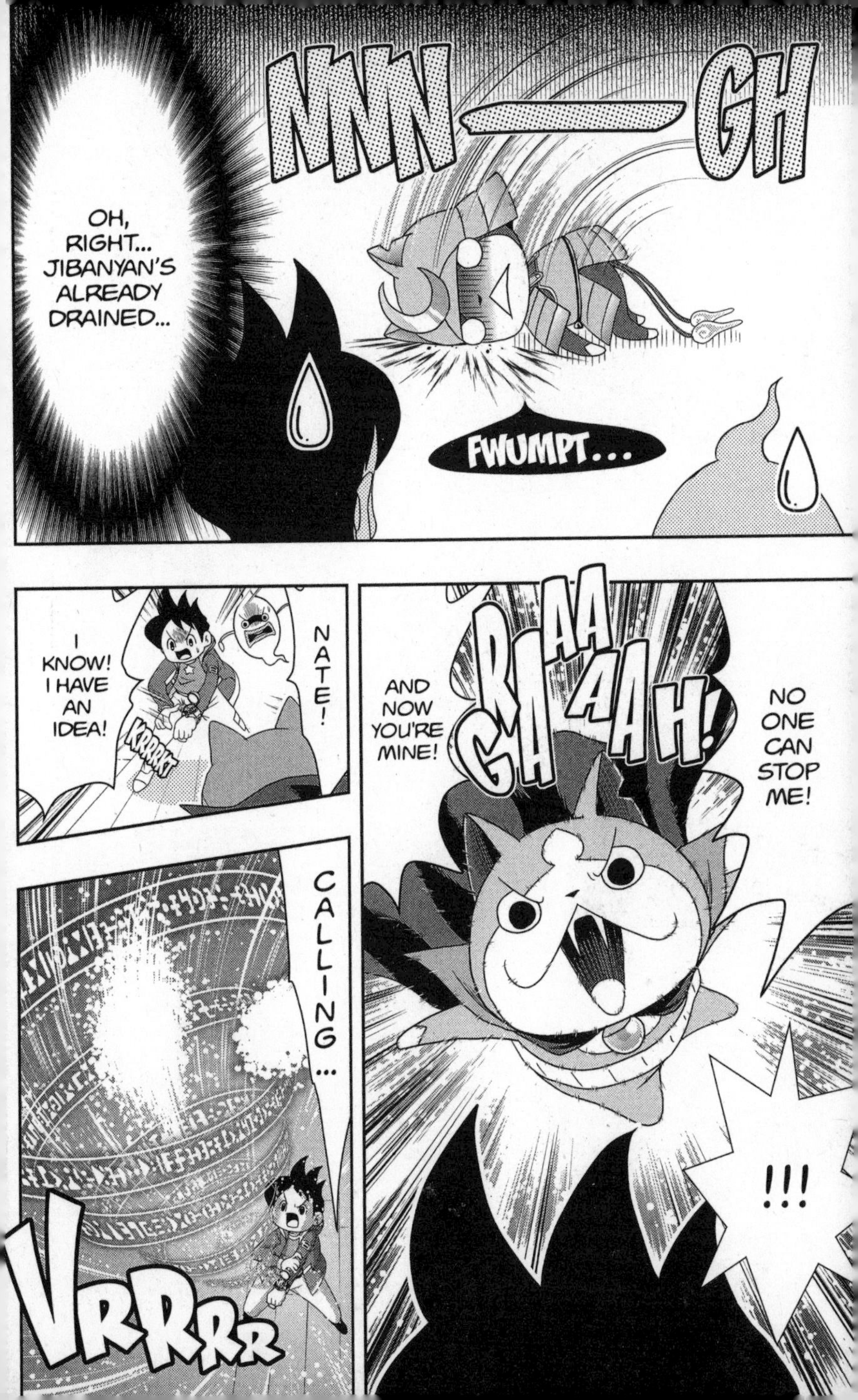
NNNN—GH
OH, RIGHT... JIBANYAN'S ALREADY DRAINED...
FWUMPT...
NO ONE CAN STOP ME!
GRAAAAH!
AND NOW YOU'RE MINE!
!!!
NATE!
I KNOW! I HAVE AN IDEA!
KRRRKT
CALLING...
VRRRR

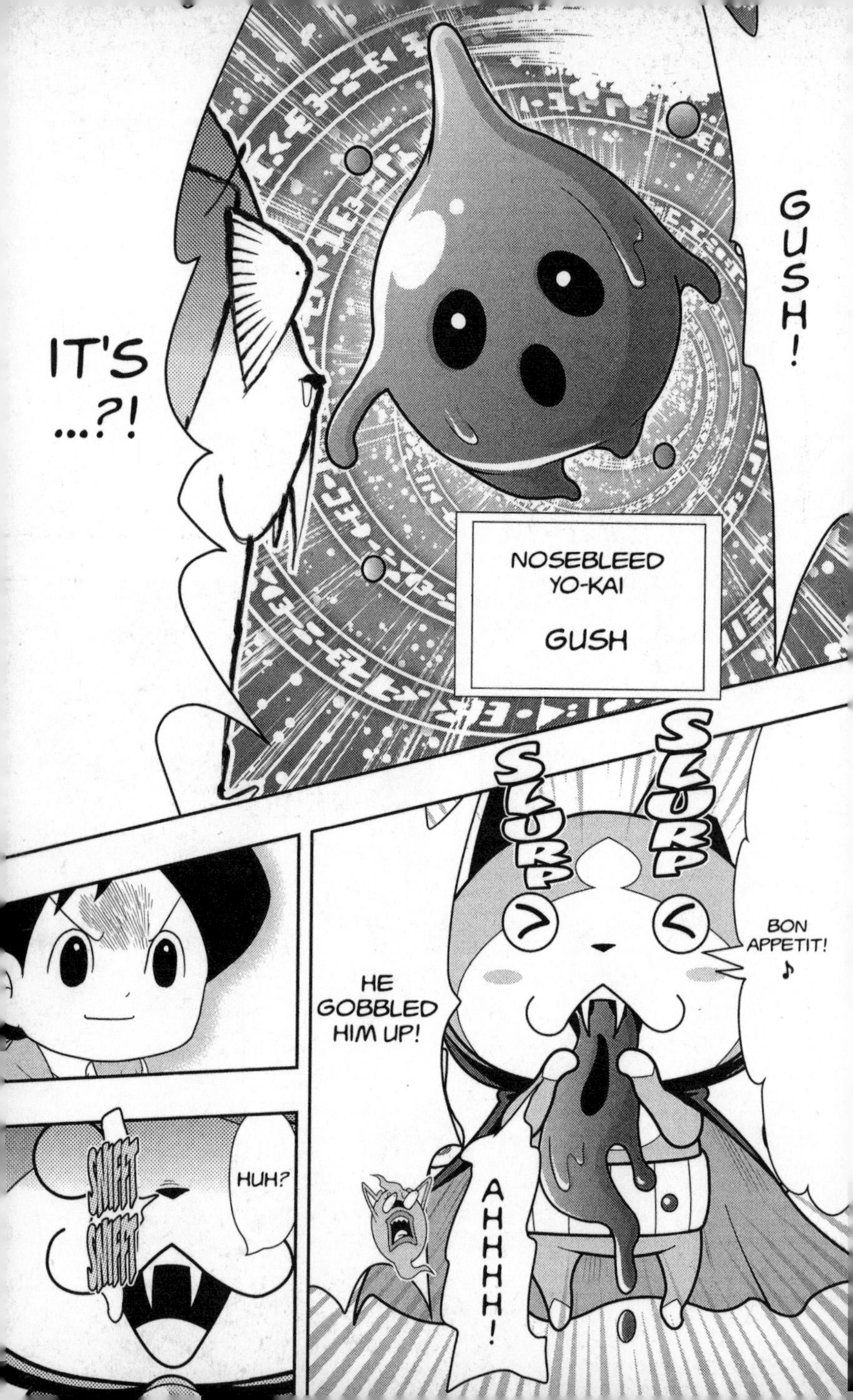
GUSH!
NOSEBLEED YO-KAI
GUSH
IT'S ...?!
SLURP
SLURP
BON APPETIT! ♪
HE GOBBLED HIM UP!
AHHHH!
HUH?
SNIFF
SNIFF

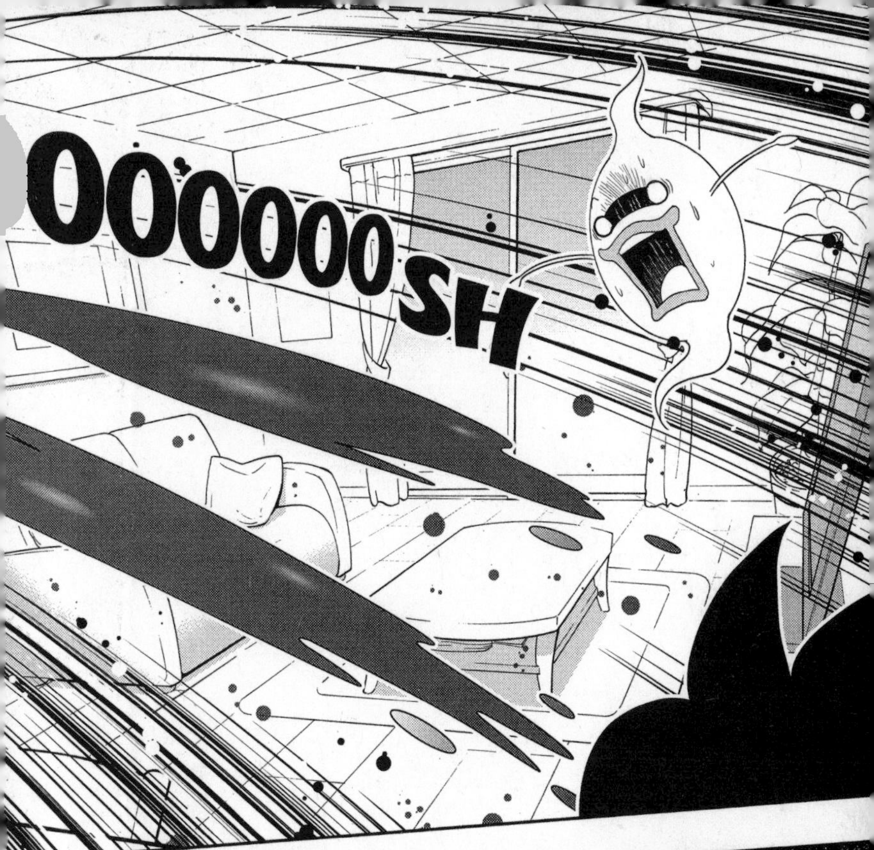
OOOOOOSH

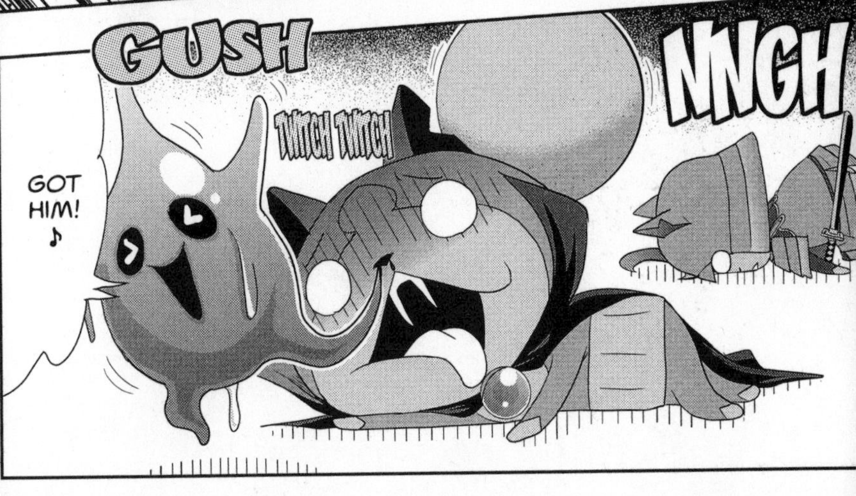
NNGH
TWITCH TWITCH
GUSH
GOT HIM! ♪

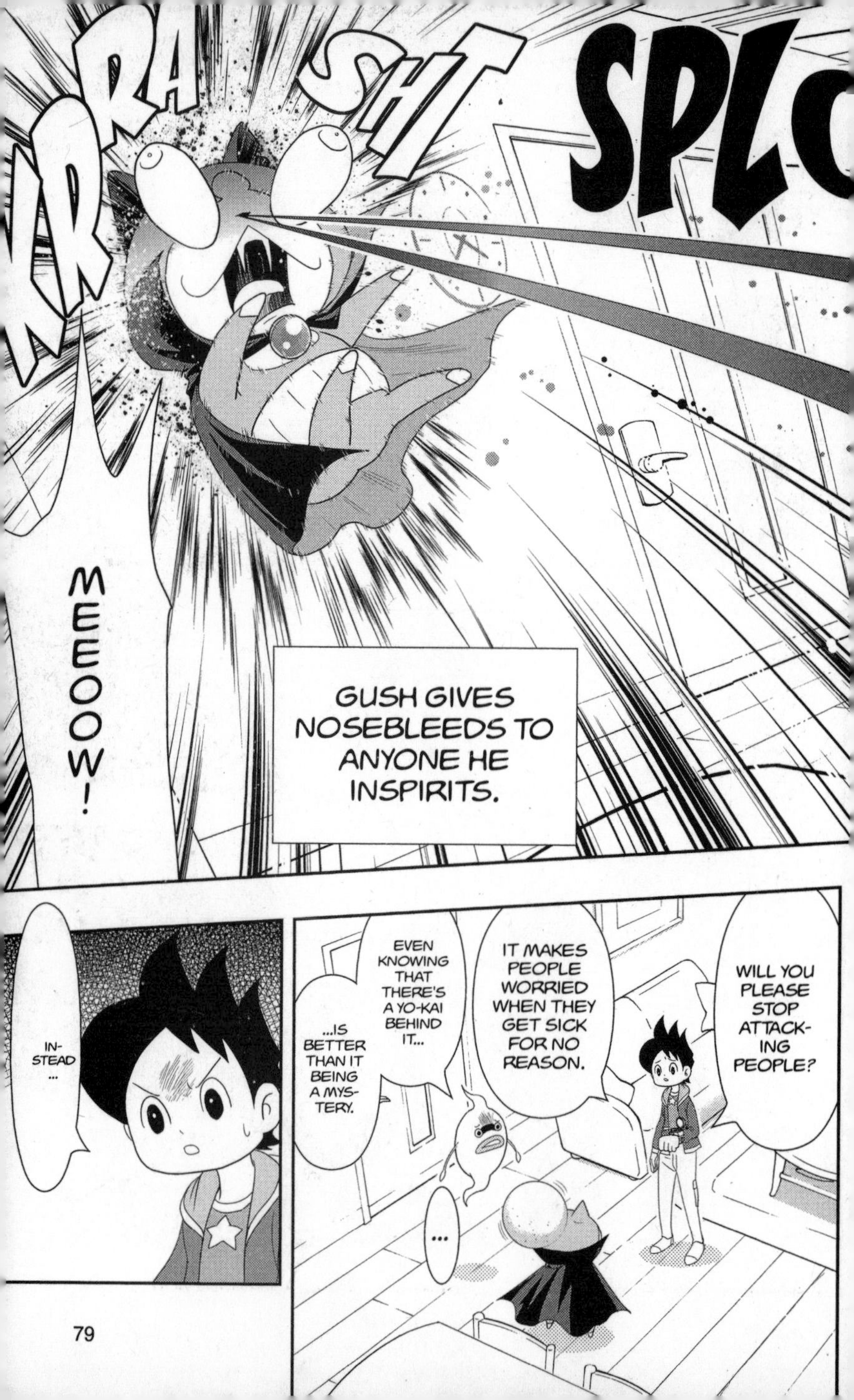
SPLO
WRASHT
MEEOOOW!
GUSH GIVES NOSEBLEEDS TO ANYONE HE INSPIRITS.
WILL YOU PLEASE STOP ATTACKING PEOPLE?
IT MAKES PEOPLE WORRIED WHEN THEY GET SICK FOR NO REASON.
EVEN KNOWING THAT THERE'S A YO-KAI BEHIND IT...
...IS BETTER THAN IT BEING A MYSTERY.
...
INSTEAD...

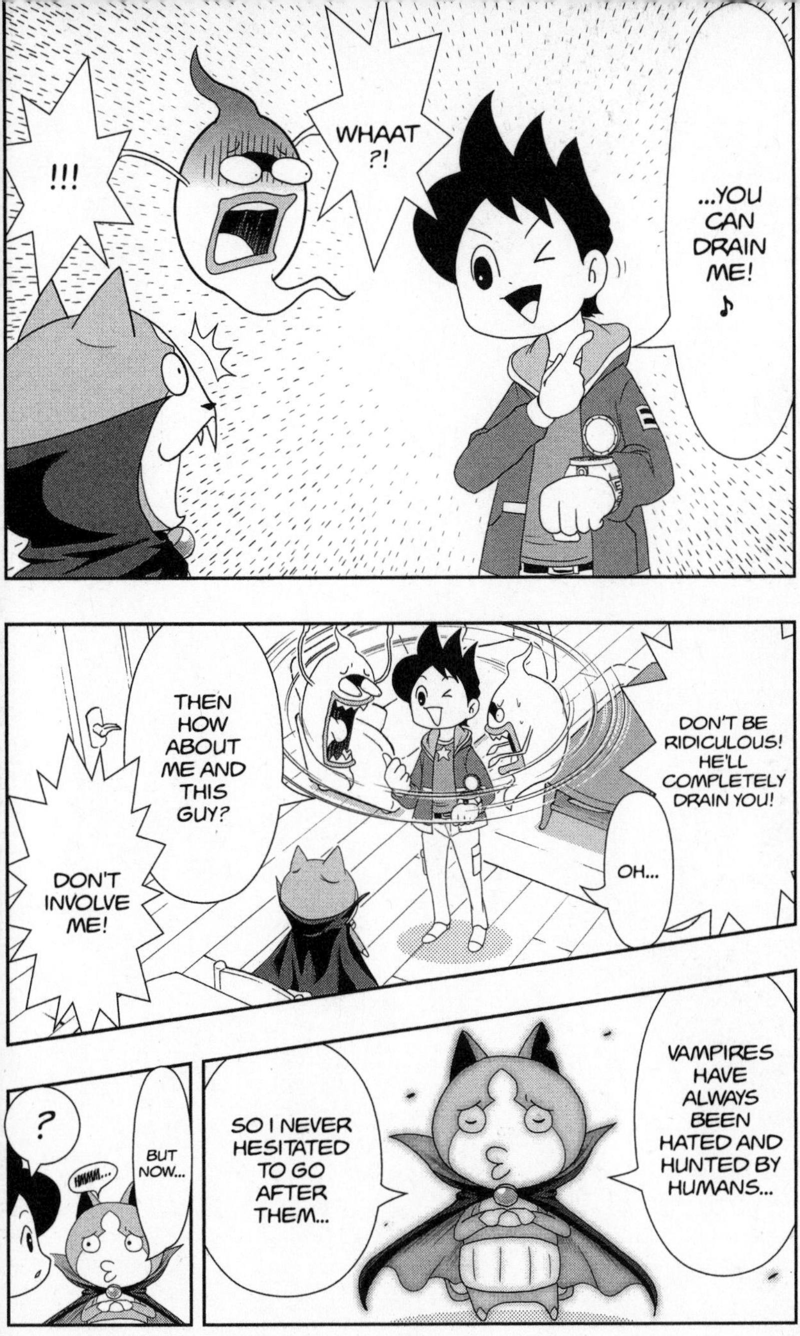
...YOU CAN DRAIN ME! ♪
WHAAT ?!
!!!
DON'T BE RIDICULOUS! HE'LL COMPLETELY DRAIN YOU!
OH...
THEN HOW ABOUT ME AND THIS GUY?
DON'T INVOLVE ME!
VAMPIRES HAVE ALWAYS BEEN HATED AND HUNTED BY HUMANS...
SO I NEVER HESITATED TO GO AFTER THEM...
BUT NOW...
?

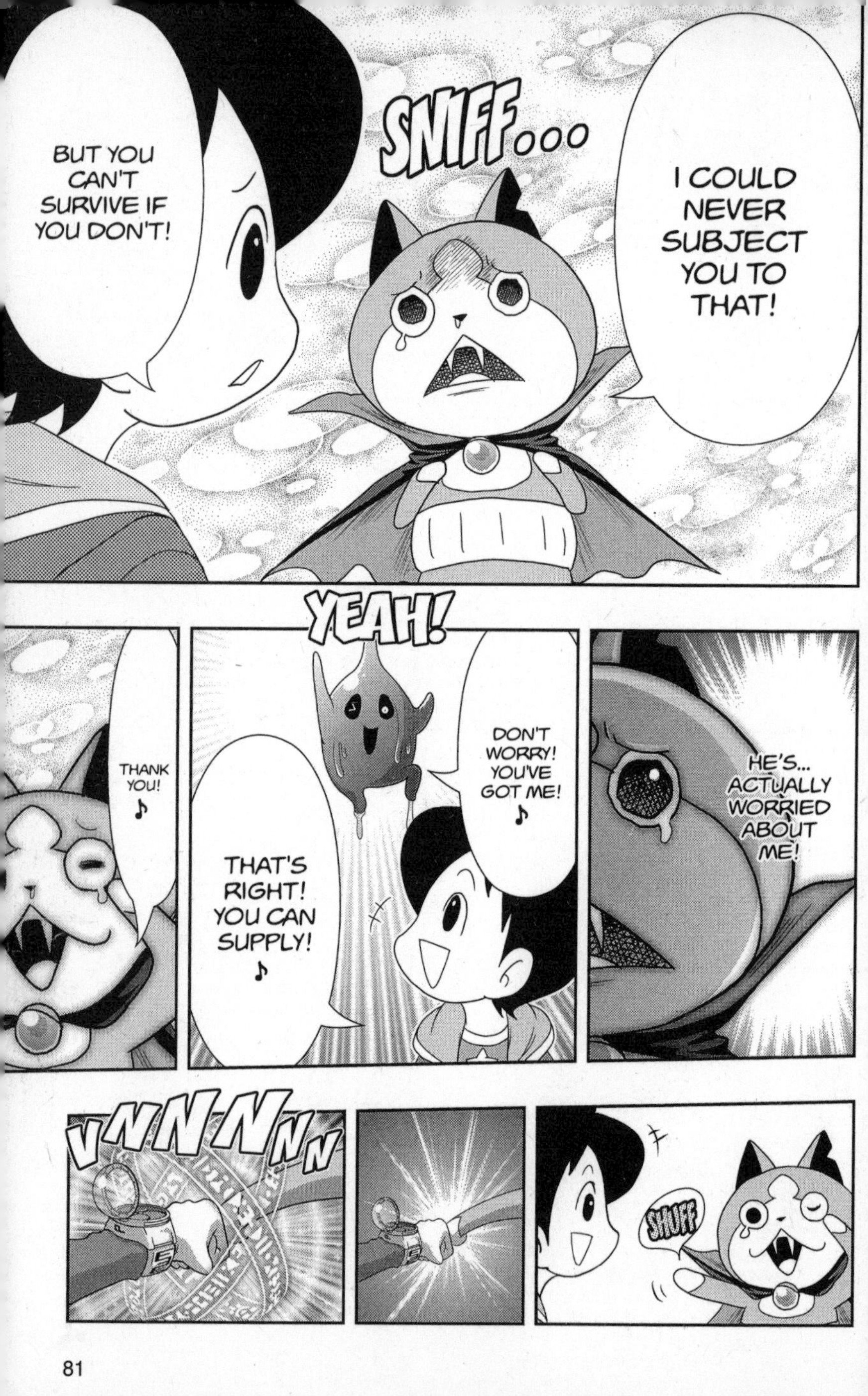
I COULD NEVER SUBJECT YOU TO THAT!
SNIFFooo
BUT YOU CAN'T SURVIVE IF YOU DON'T!
HE'S... ACTUALLY WORRIED ABOUT ME!
YEAH!
DON'T WORRY! YOU'VE GOT ME! ♪
THAT'S RIGHT! YOU CAN SUPPLY! ♪
THANK YOU! ♪
SHUFF
VNNNNN

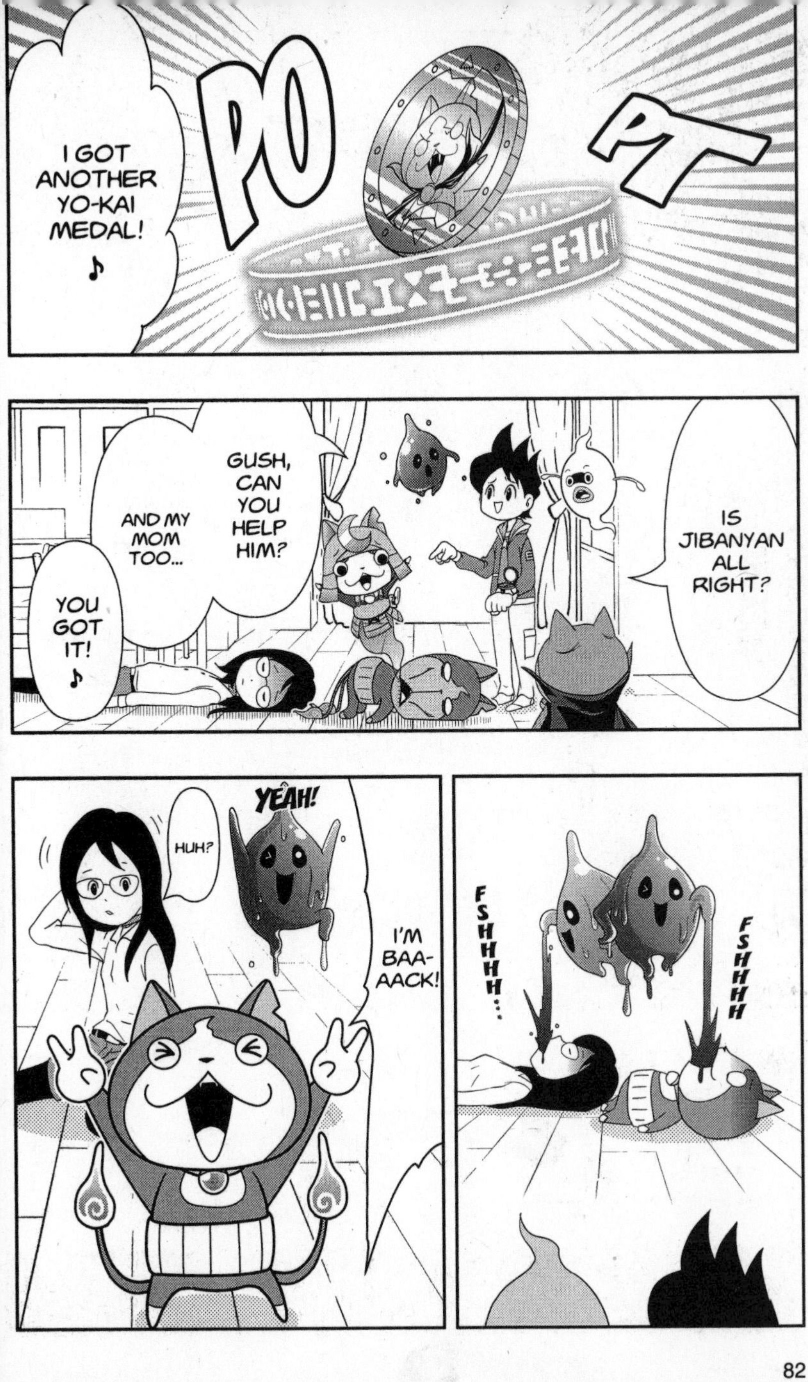

PO
PT
I GOT ANOTHER YO-KAI MEDAL! ♪
IS JIBANYAN ALL RIGHT?
GUSH, CAN YOU HELP HIM?
AND MY MOM TOO...
YOU GOT IT! ♪
FSHHHH
FSHHHH...
YEAH!
I'M BAA-AACK!
HUH?

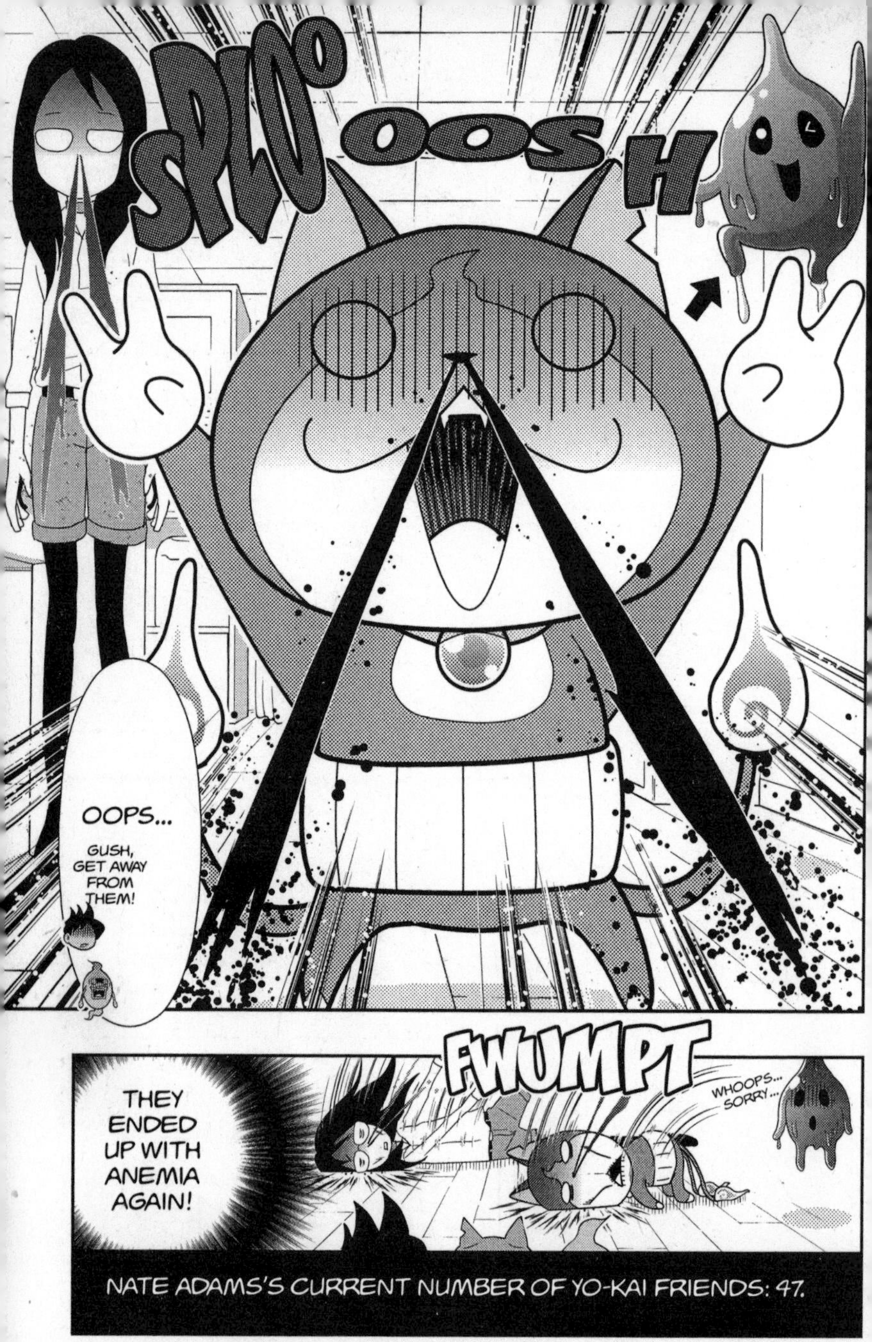
SPLOOOOSH
OOPS...
GUSH, GET AWAY FROM THEM!
FWUMPT
WHOOPS... SORRY...
THEY ENDED UP WITH ANEMIA AGAIN!
NATE ADAMS'S CURRENT NUMBER OF YO-KAI FRIENDS: 47.

## DRACUNYAN

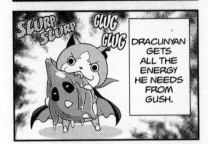

DRACUNYAN GETS ALL THE ENERGY HE NEEDS FROM GUSH.
GLUG GLUG
SLURP SLURP
SLURP SLURP
YOU SURE DO NEED A LOT...
NO MATTER HOW MUCH I GET...
...I'M NEVER FULL... WHY IS THAT?
GLUG GLUG
SO... STRANGE...
YOUR NOSE IS STILL BLEEDING!
YOUR NOSE BLEEDS WHENEVER GUSH IS AROUND.

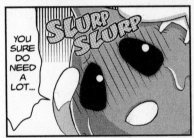

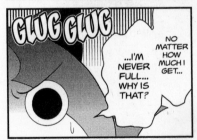

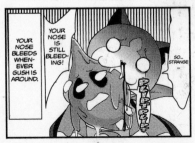

# CHAPTER 63
# I'LL STICK MY NECK OUT FOR YOU
## FEATURING LONG NECK YO-KAI LADY LONGNEK

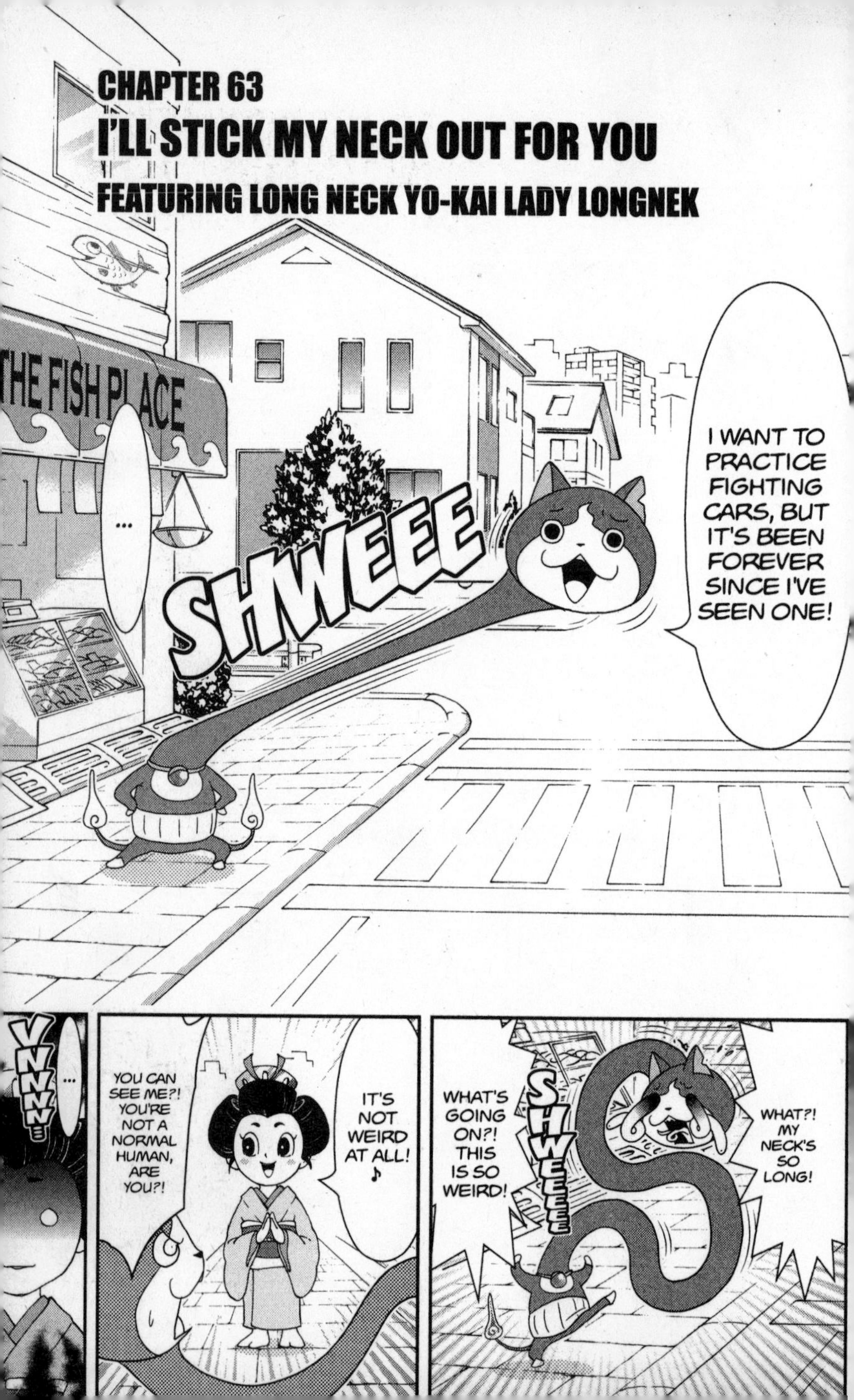
THE FISH PLACE
I WANT TO PRACTICE FIGHTING CARS, BUT IT'S BEEN FOREVER SINCE I'VE SEEN ONE!
SHWEEE
...
WHAT?! MY NECK'S SO LONG!
SHWEEEE
WHAT'S GOING ON?! THIS IS SO WEIRD!
IT'S NOT WEIRD AT ALL! ♪
YOU CAN SEE ME?! YOU'RE NOT A NORMAL HUMAN, ARE YOU?!
...
VNNNN

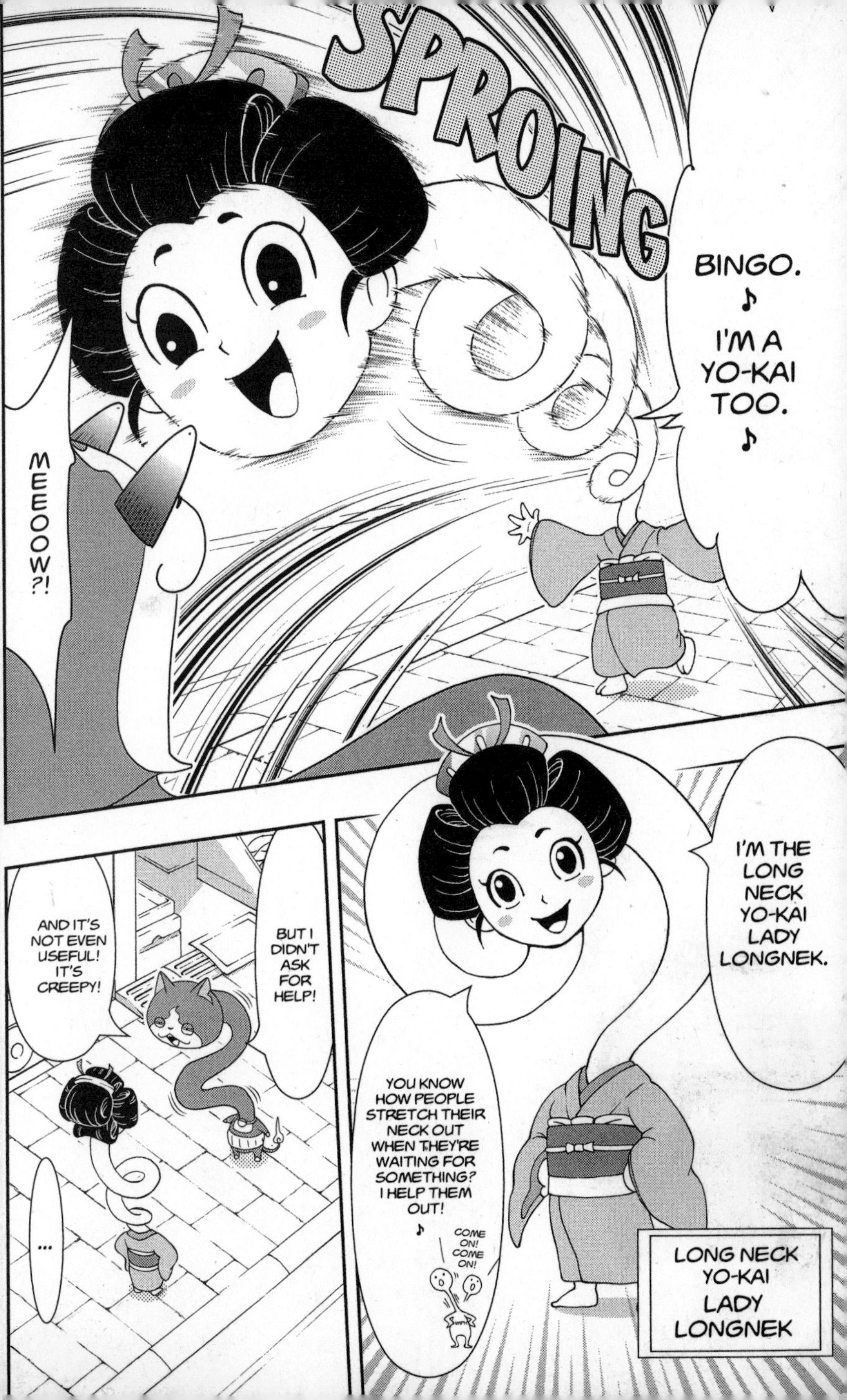
SPROING
BINGO. ♪
I'M A YO-KAI TOO. ♪
MEEOOOW?!
I'M THE LONG NECK YO-KAI LADY LONGNEK.
YOU KNOW HOW PEOPLE STRETCH THEIR NECK OUT WHEN THEY'RE WAITING FOR SOMETHING? I HELP THEM OUT! ♪
COME ON! COME ON!
LONG NECK YO-KAI LADY LONGNEK
BUT I DIDN'T ASK FOR HELP!
AND IT'S NOT EVEN USEFUL! IT'S CREEPY!
...

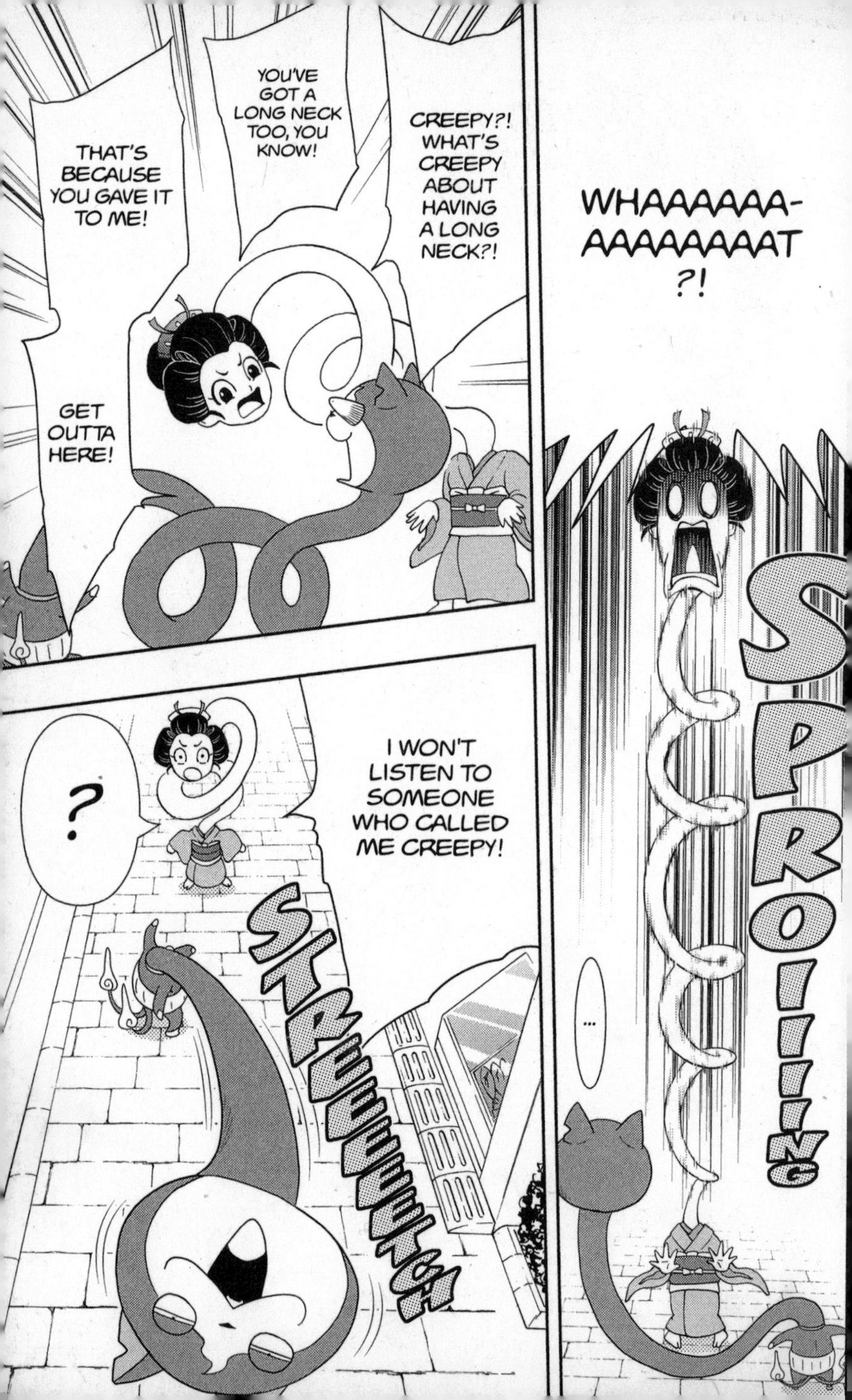
WHAAAAAA-
AAAAAAAAT
?!
SPROIIIING
...
CREEPY?! WHAT'S CREEPY ABOUT HAVING A LONG NECK?!
YOU'VE GOT A LONG NECK TOO, YOU KNOW!
THAT'S BECAUSE YOU GAVE IT TO ME!
GET OUTTA HERE!
I WON'T LISTEN TO SOMEONE WHO CALLED ME CREEPY!
?
STREEEEETCH

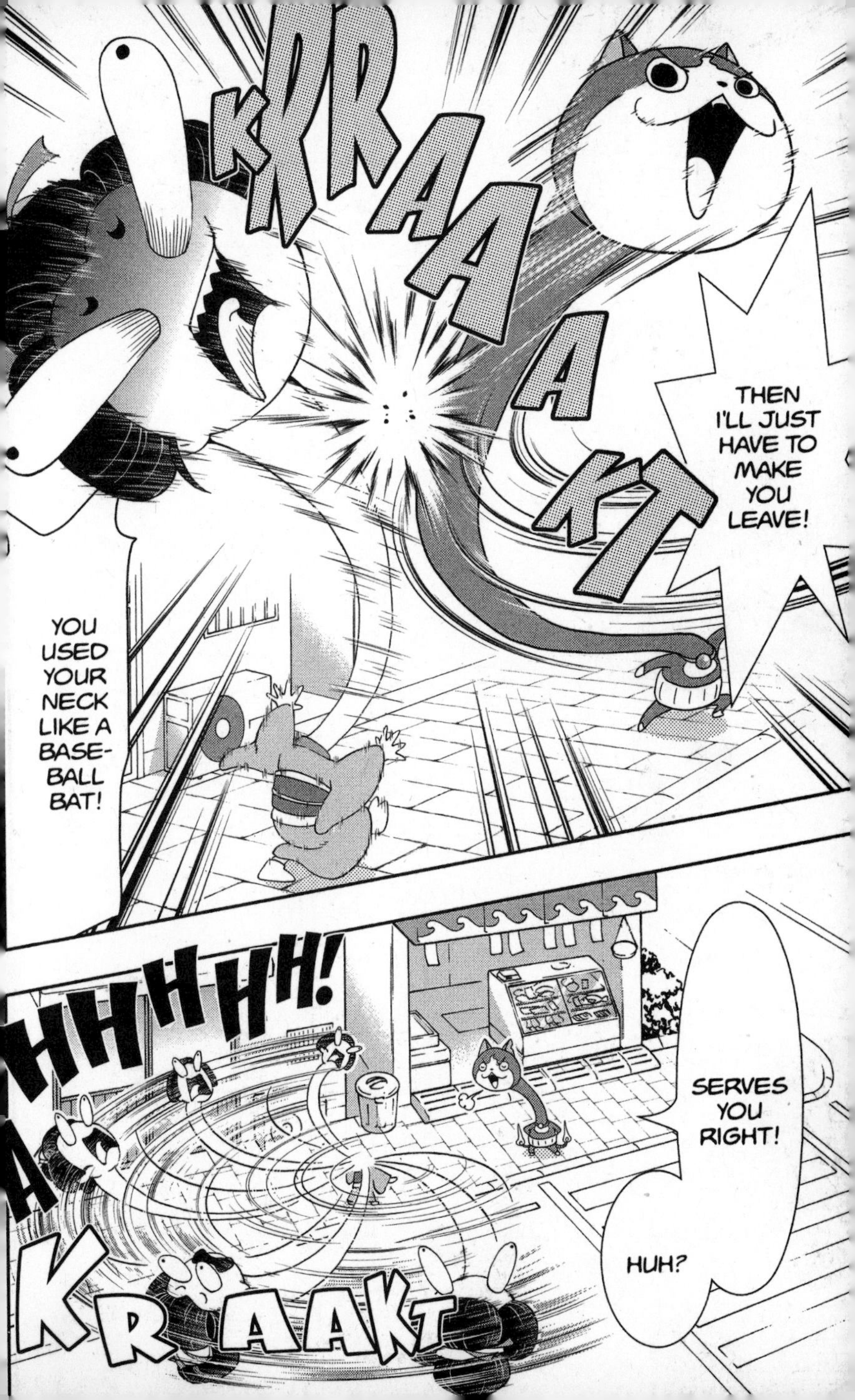
THEN I'LL JUST HAVE TO MAKE YOU LEAVE!
KRRAAAAKT
YOU USED YOUR NECK LIKE A BASE-BALL BAT!
SERVES YOU RIGHT!
HUH?
AHHHHH!
KRAAKT

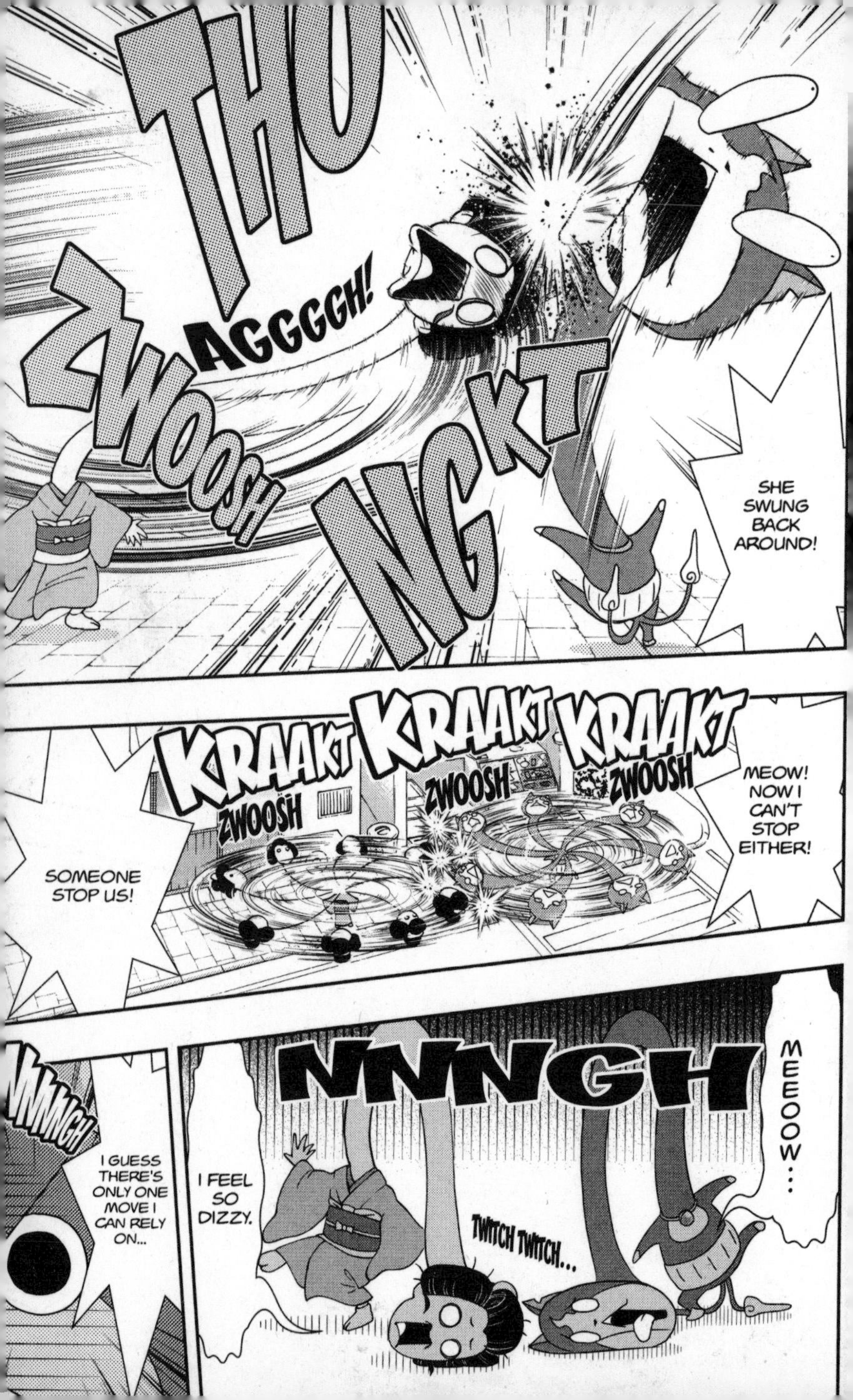

THU
AGGGGH!
NGKT
ZWOOSH
SHE SWUNG BACK AROUND!
MEOW! NOW I CAN'T STOP EITHER!
KRAAKT KRAAKT KRAAKT
ZWOOSH
ZWOOSH
ZWOOSH
SOMEONE STOP US!
MEEEOOW...
NNNGH
TWITCH TWITCH...
I FEEL SO DIZZY.
NNNNGH
I GUESS THERE'S ONLY ONE MOVE I CAN RELY ON...

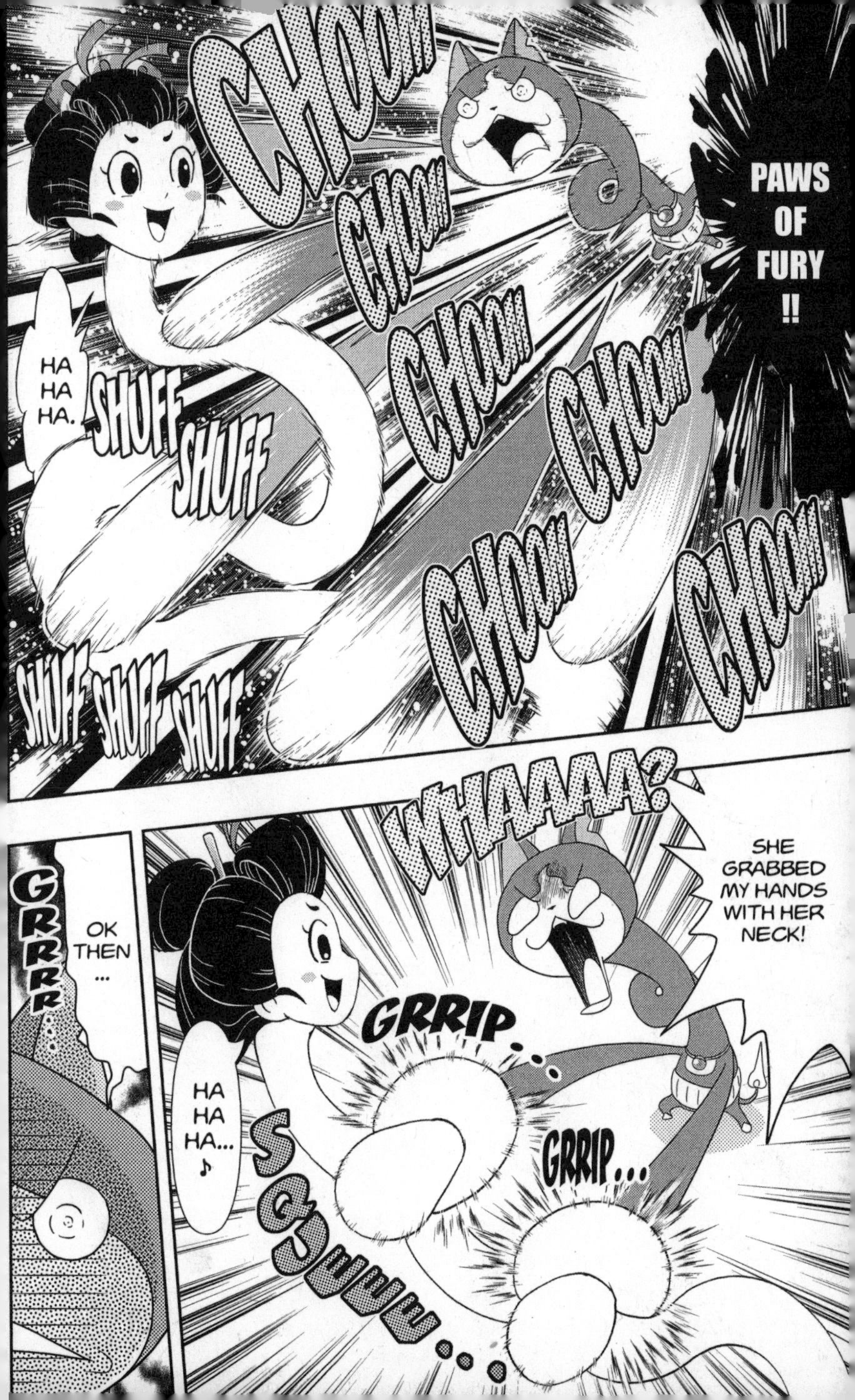
PAWS OF FURY !!
CHOOM
CHOOM
CHOOM
CHOOM
CHOOM
CHOOM
CHOOM
HA HA HA.
SHUFF
SHUFF
SHUFF SHUFF SHUFF
WHAAAA?!
SHE GRABBED MY HANDS WITH HER NECK!
GRRIP...
GRRIP...
HA HA HA... ♪
SQUEEEE...
OK THEN ...
GRRRR...

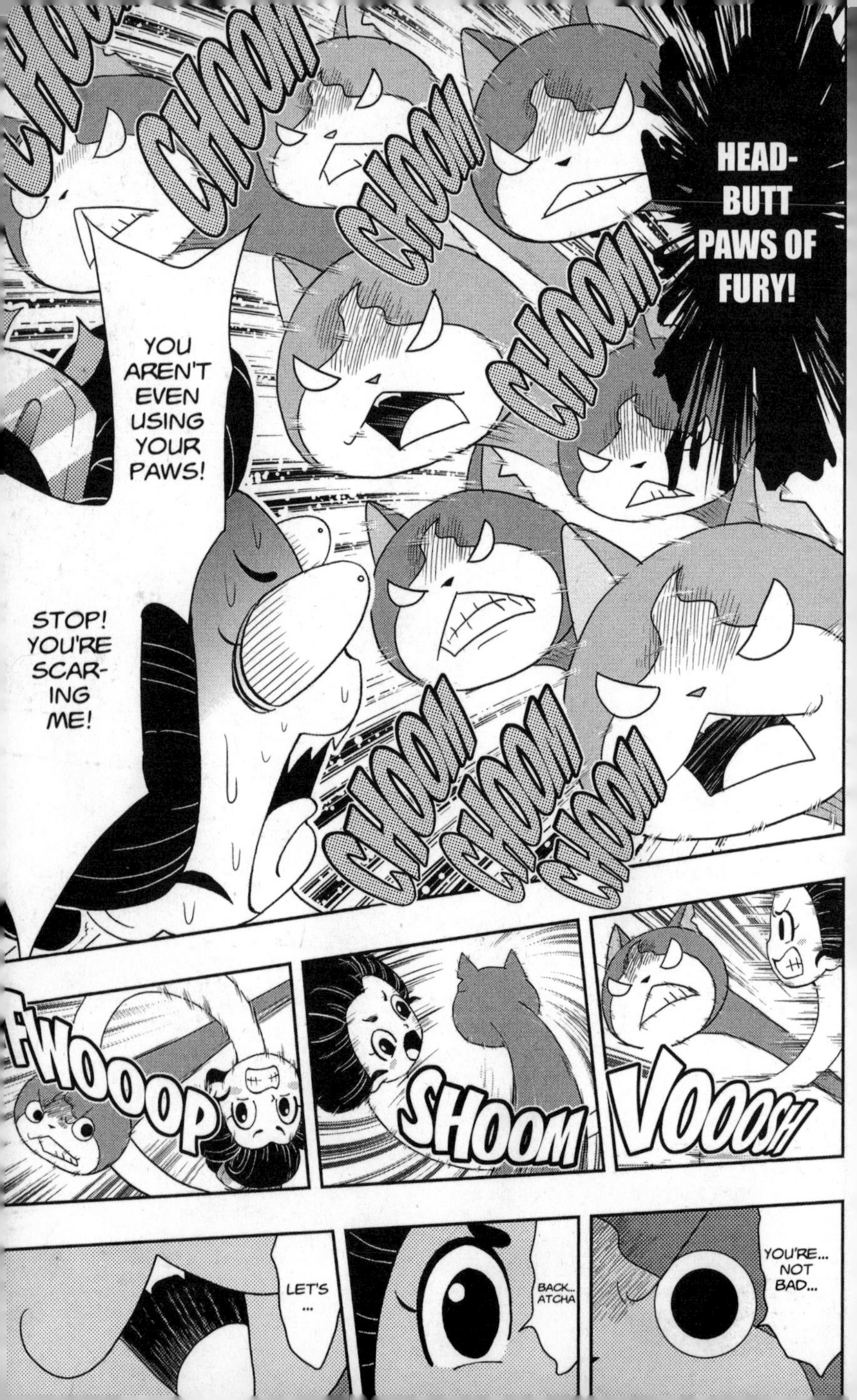

HEAD-BUTT PAWS OF FURY!
CHOOM!!
CHOOM!!
CHOOM!!
YOU AREN'T EVEN USING YOUR PAWS!
STOP! YOU'RE SCAR-ING ME!
CHOOM!!
CHOOM!!
CHOOM!!
VOOOSH
SHOOM
FWOOOP
YOU'RE... NOT BAD...
BACK... ATCHA
LET'S ...

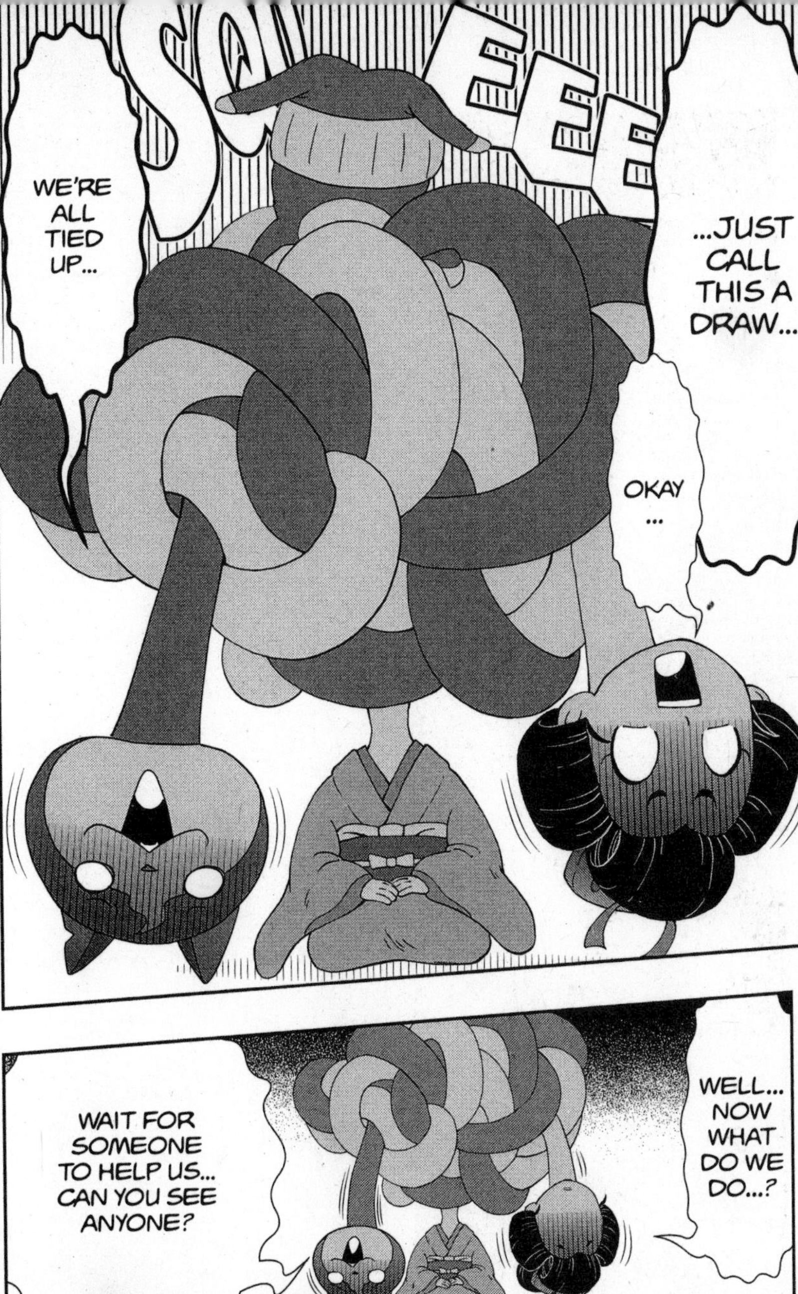
...JUST CALL THIS A DRAW...
WE'RE ALL TIED UP...
OKAY ...
WELL... NOW WHAT DO WE DO...?
WAIT FOR SOMEONE TO HELP US... CAN YOU SEE ANYONE?

LADY LONGNEK

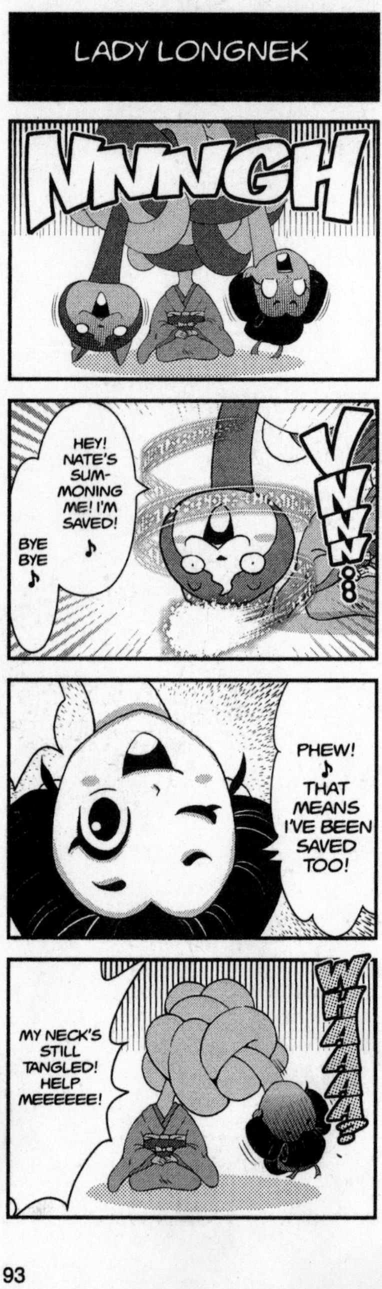
NNNGH
VNNN
HEY! NATE'S SUMMONING ME! I'M SAVED! ♪
BYE BYE ♪
PHEW! ♪ THAT MEANS I'VE BEEN SAVED TOO!
WHAAAA
MY NECK'S STILL TANGLED! HELP MEEEEEE!

# CHAPTER 64

# A HAIRY SITUATION!

## FEATURING HAIRY YO-KAI FURDINAND

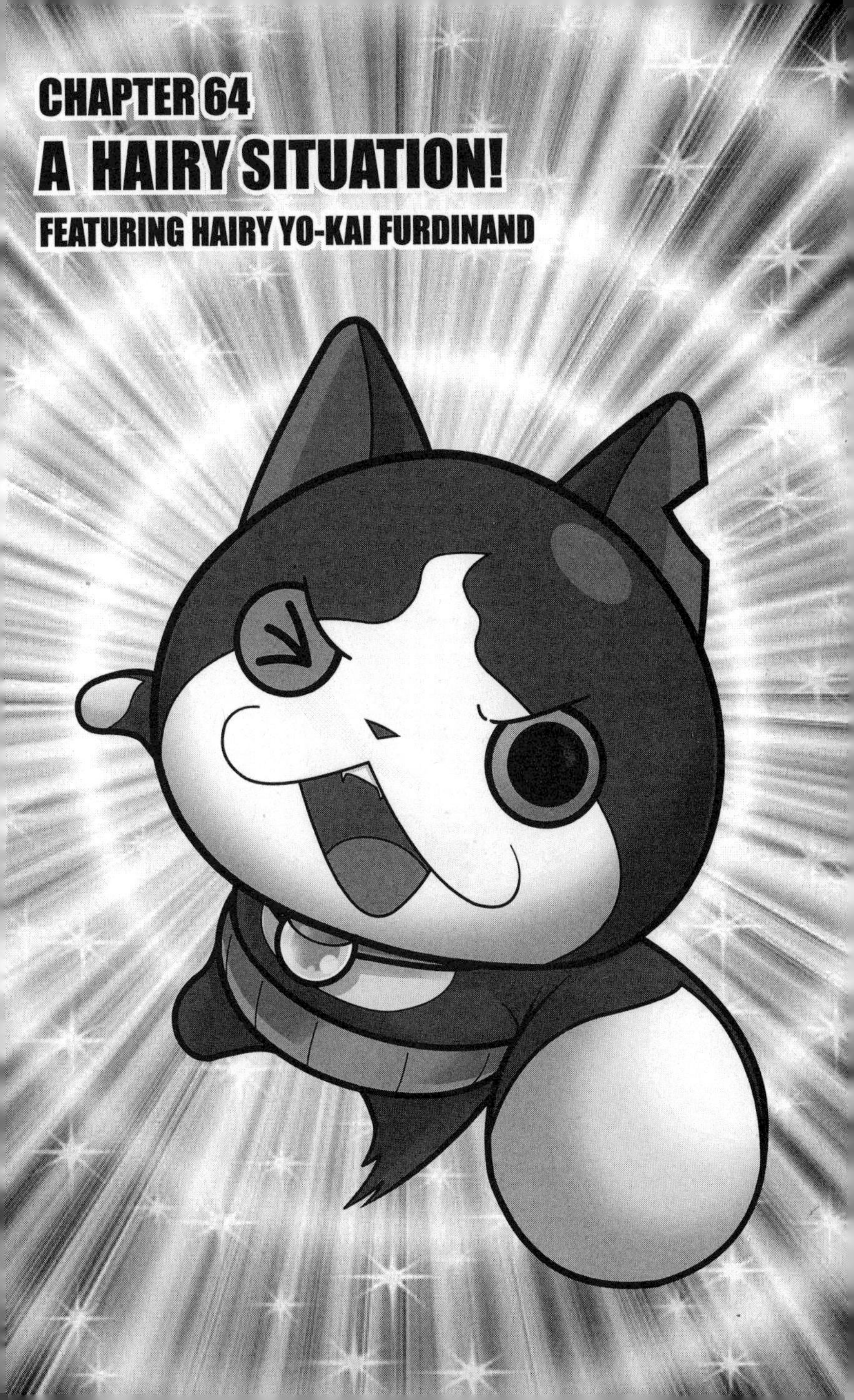

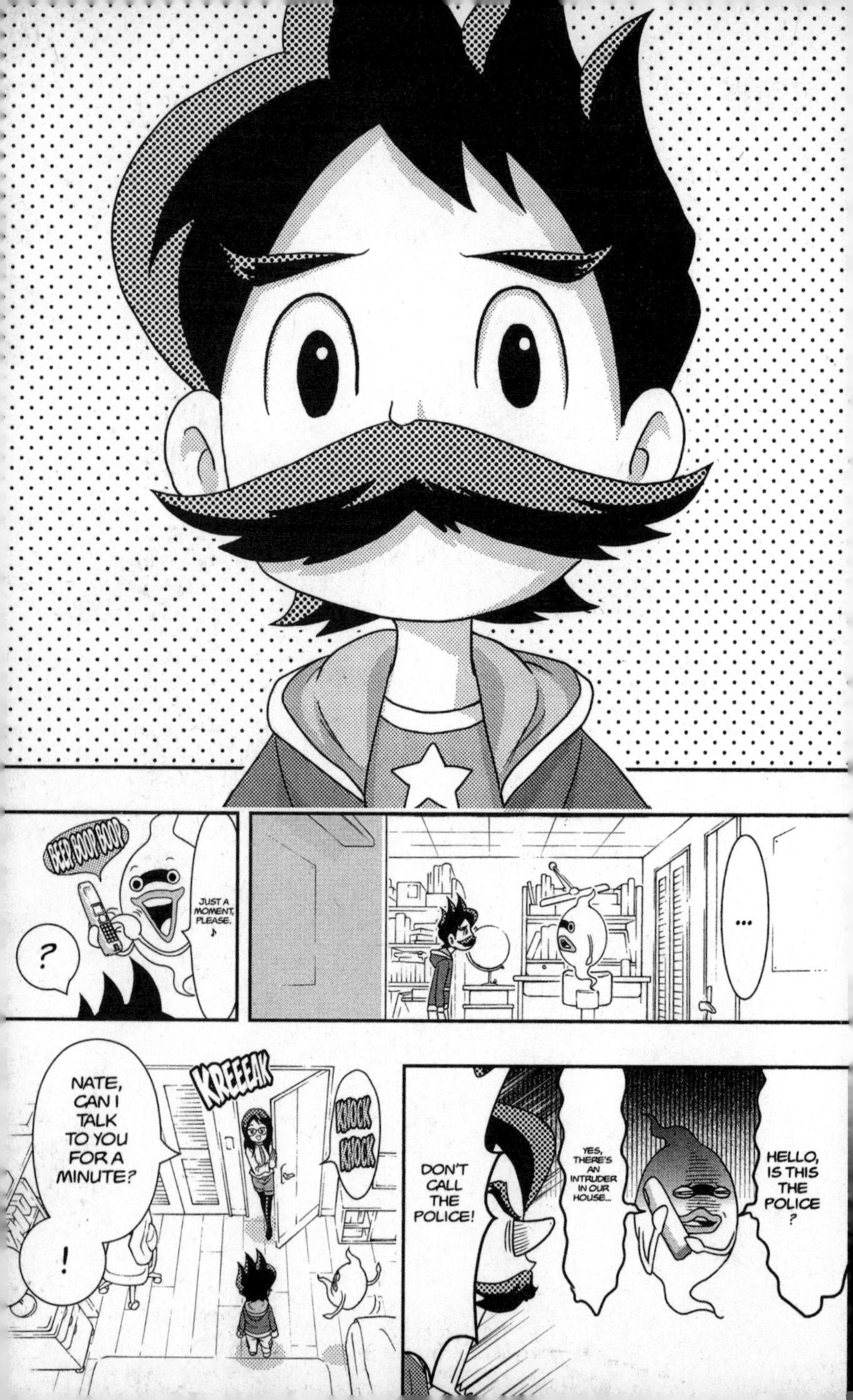
...
JUST A MOMENT, PLEASE. ♪
BEEP BOOP BOOP
?
HELLO, IS THIS THE POLICE?
YES, THERE'S AN INTRUDER IN OUR HOUSE...
DON'T CALL THE POLICE!
KNOCK KNOCK
KREEEAK
NATE, CAN I TALK TO YOU FOR A MINUTE?
!

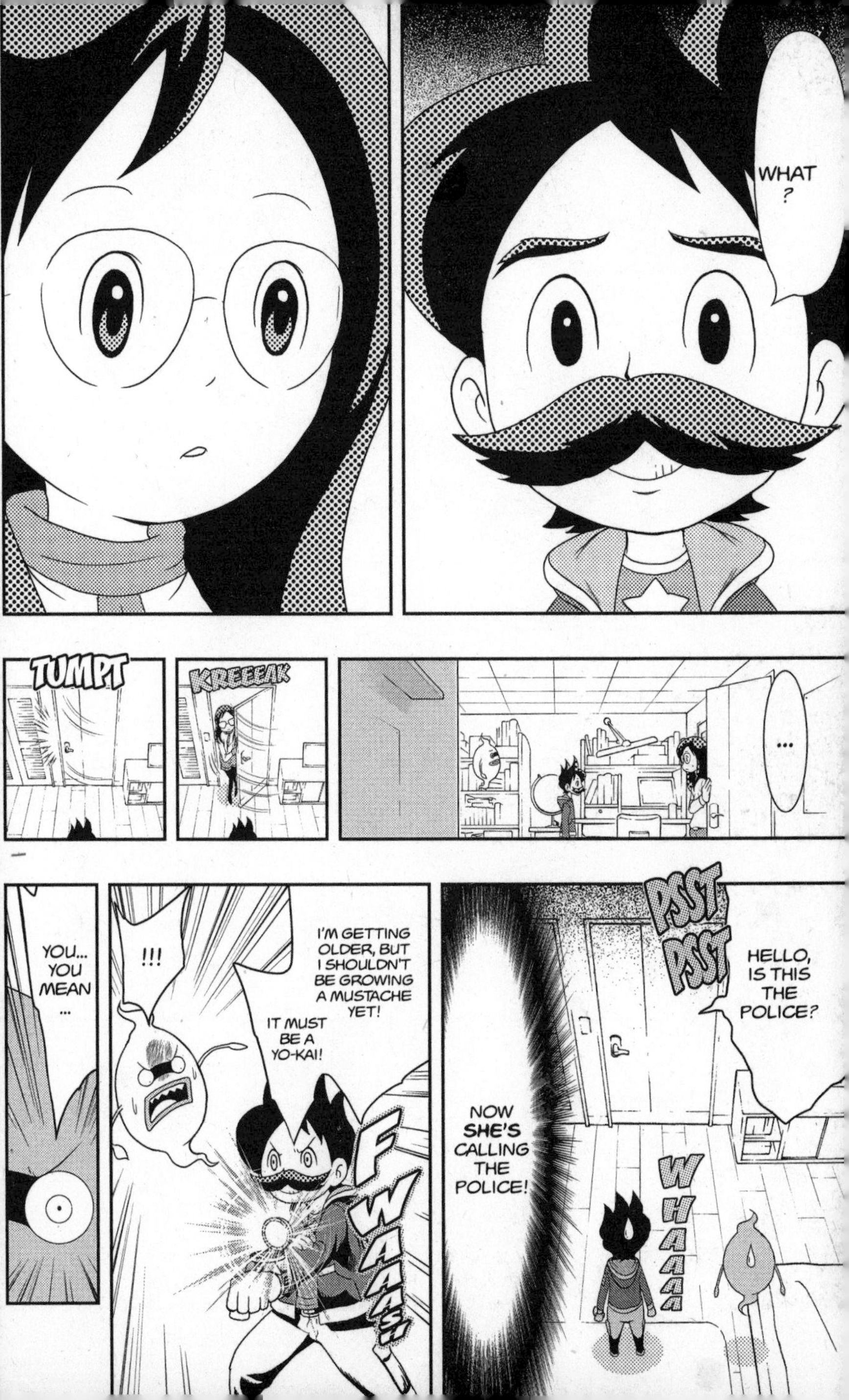
WHAT ?
...
KREEEAK
TUMPT
PSST PSST
HELLO, IS THIS THE POLICE?
NOW SHE'S CALLING THE POLICE!
WHAAAAA
I'M GETTING OLDER, BUT I SHOULDN'T BE GROWING A MUSTACHE YET!
!!!
IT MUST BE A YO-KAI!
FWAAAS!
YOU... YOU MEAN ...

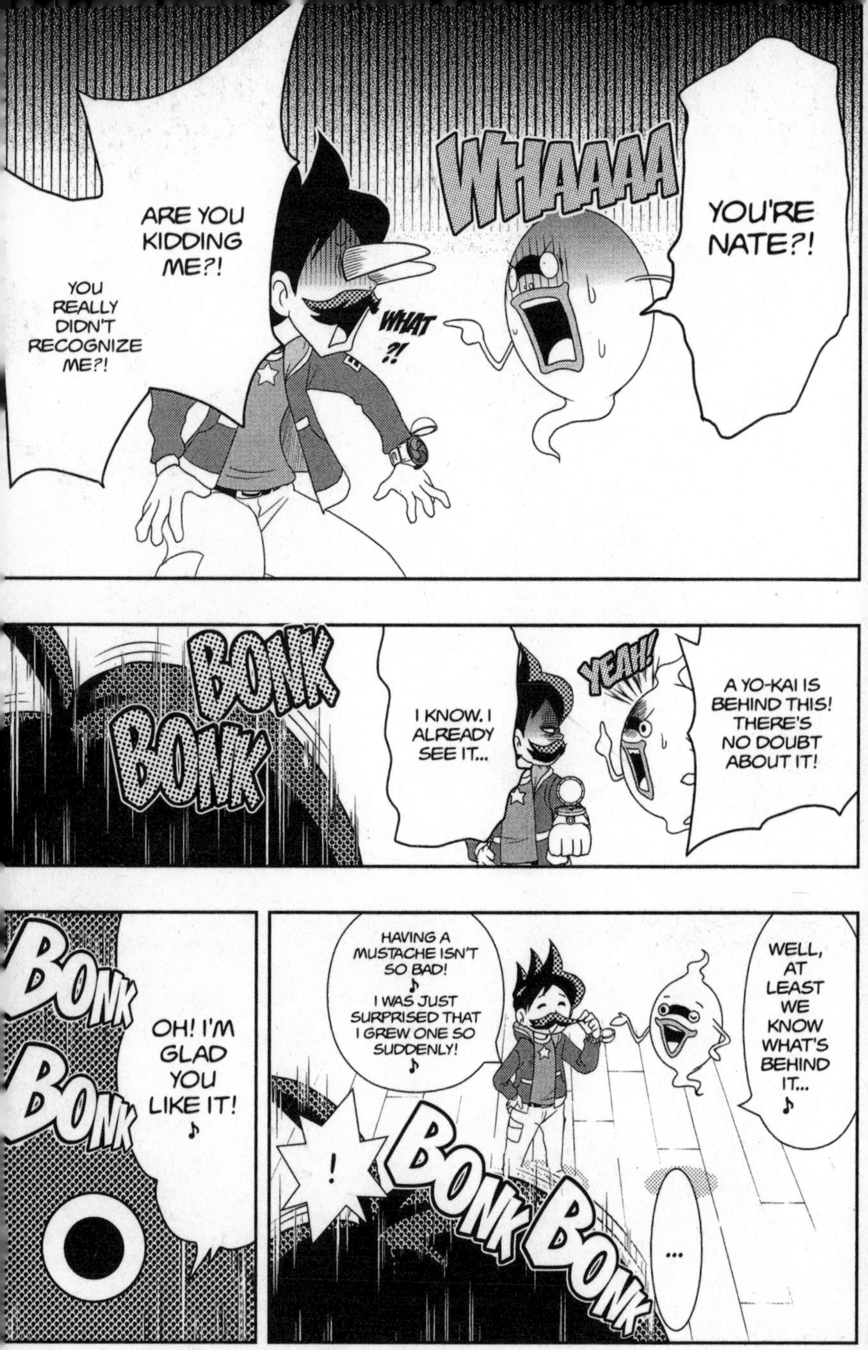
YOU'RE NATE?!
WHAAAA
WHAT ?!
ARE YOU KIDDING ME?!
YOU REALLY DIDN'T RECOGNIZE ME?!
A YO-KAI IS BEHIND THIS! THERE'S NO DOUBT ABOUT IT!
YEAH!
I KNOW. I ALREADY SEE IT...
BONK BONK
WELL, AT LEAST WE KNOW WHAT'S BEHIND IT... ♪
HAVING A MUSTACHE ISN'T SO BAD! ♪ I WAS JUST SURPRISED THAT I GREW ONE SO SUDDENLY! ♪
!
BONK BONK
...
OH! I'M GLAD YOU LIKE IT! ♪
BONK BONK

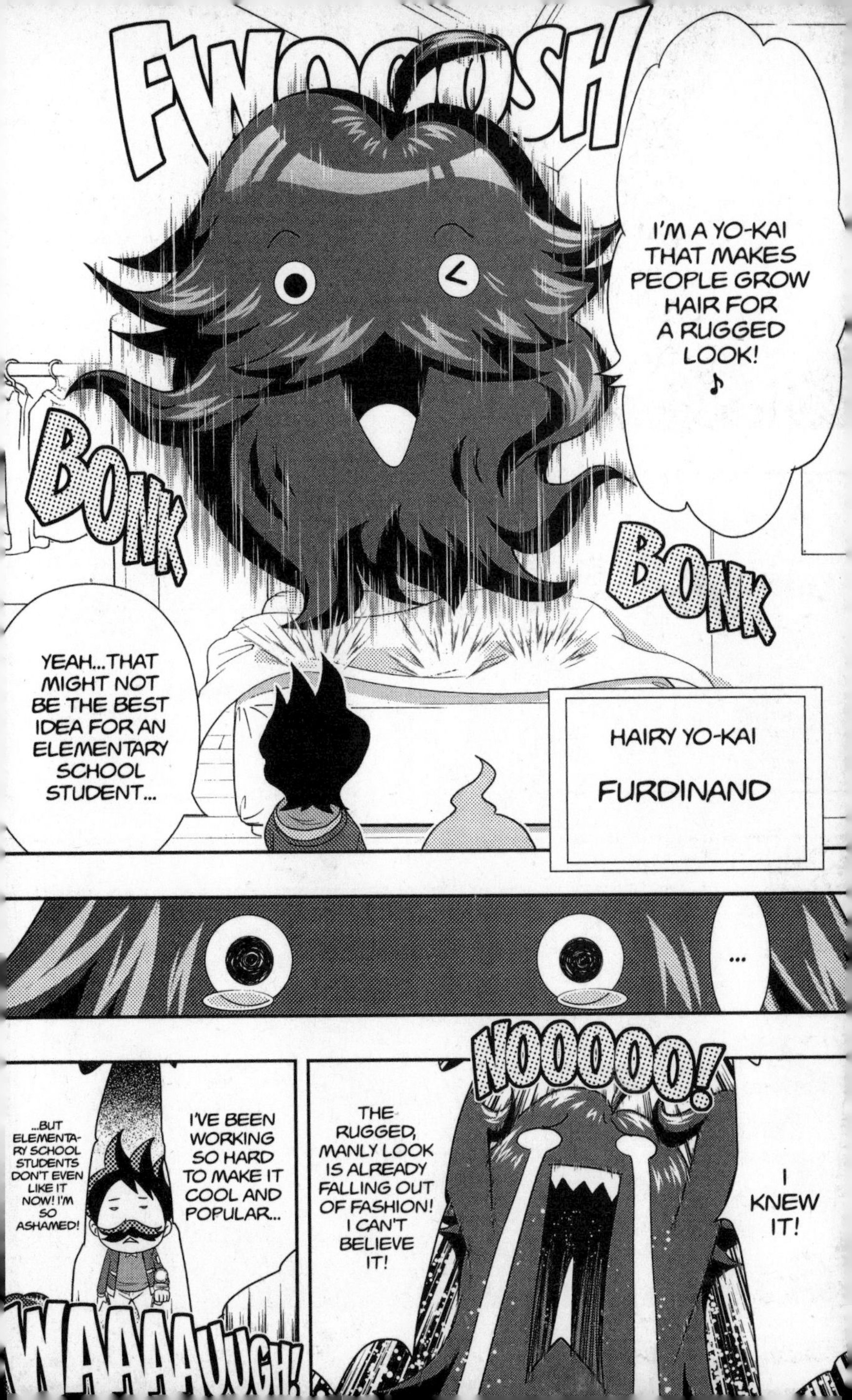
FWOOOSH
I'M A YO-KAI THAT MAKES PEOPLE GROW HAIR FOR A RUGGED LOOK! ♪
BONK
BONK
HAIRY YO-KAI
FURDINAND
YEAH...THAT MIGHT NOT BE THE BEST IDEA FOR AN ELEMENTARY SCHOOL STUDENT...
...
NOOOOO!
I KNEW IT!
THE RUGGED, MANLY LOOK IS ALREADY FALLING OUT OF FASHION! I CAN'T BELIEVE IT!
I'VE BEEN WORKING SO HARD TO MAKE IT COOL AND POPULAR...
...BUT ELEMENTARY SCHOOL STUDENTS DON'T EVEN LIKE IT NOW! I'M SO ASHAMED!
WAAAAUGH!

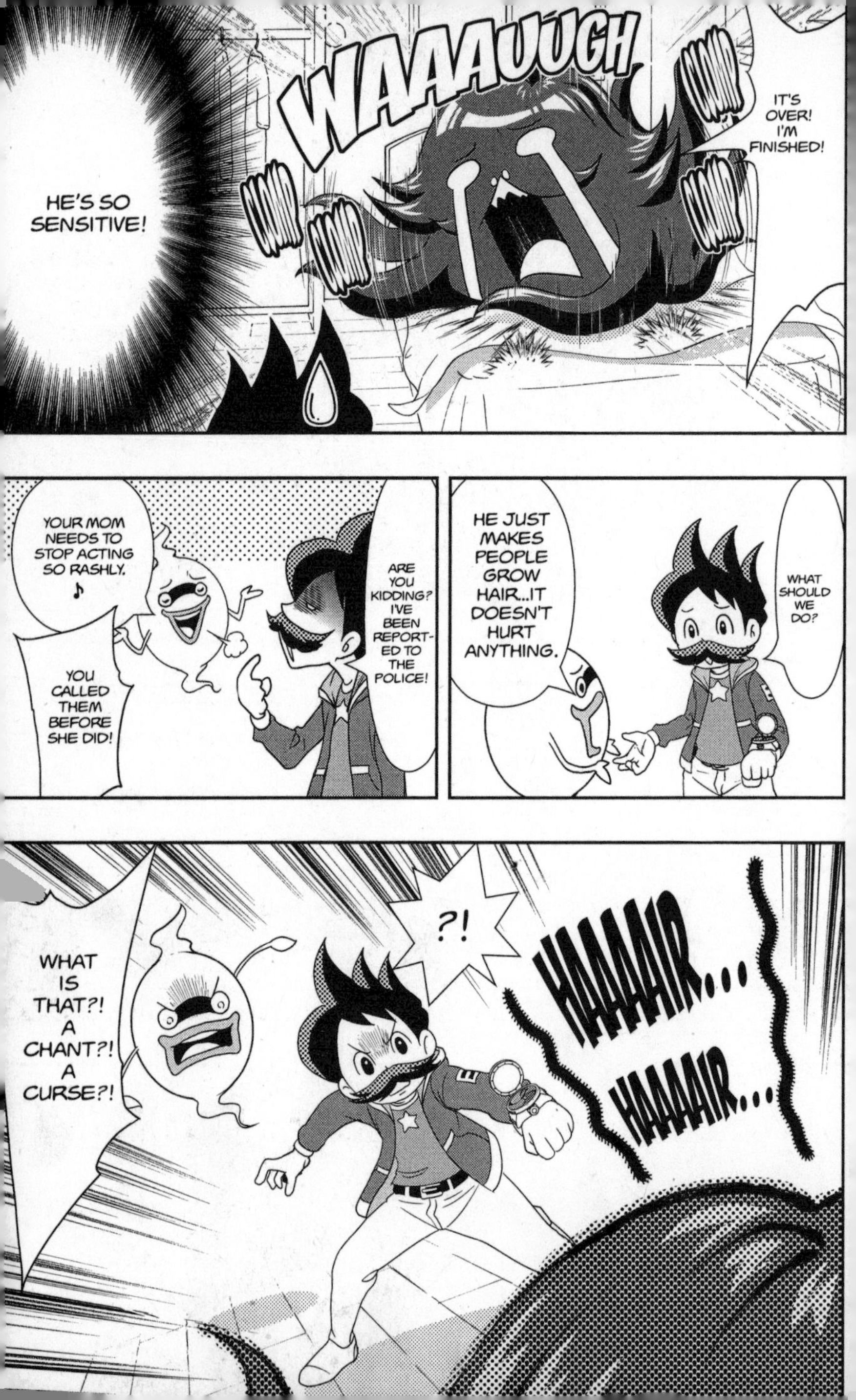
IT'S OVER! I'M FINISHED!
WAAAUUGH
HE'S SO SENSITIVE!
WHAT SHOULD WE DO?
HE JUST MAKES PEOPLE GROW HAIR...IT DOESN'T HURT ANYTHING.
ARE YOU KIDDING? I'VE BEEN REPORTED TO THE POLICE!
YOUR MOM NEEDS TO STOP ACTING SO RASHLY. ♪
YOU CALLED THEM BEFORE SHE DID!
HAAAAIR...
HAAAAIR...
?!
WHAT IS THAT?! A CHANT?! A CURSE?!

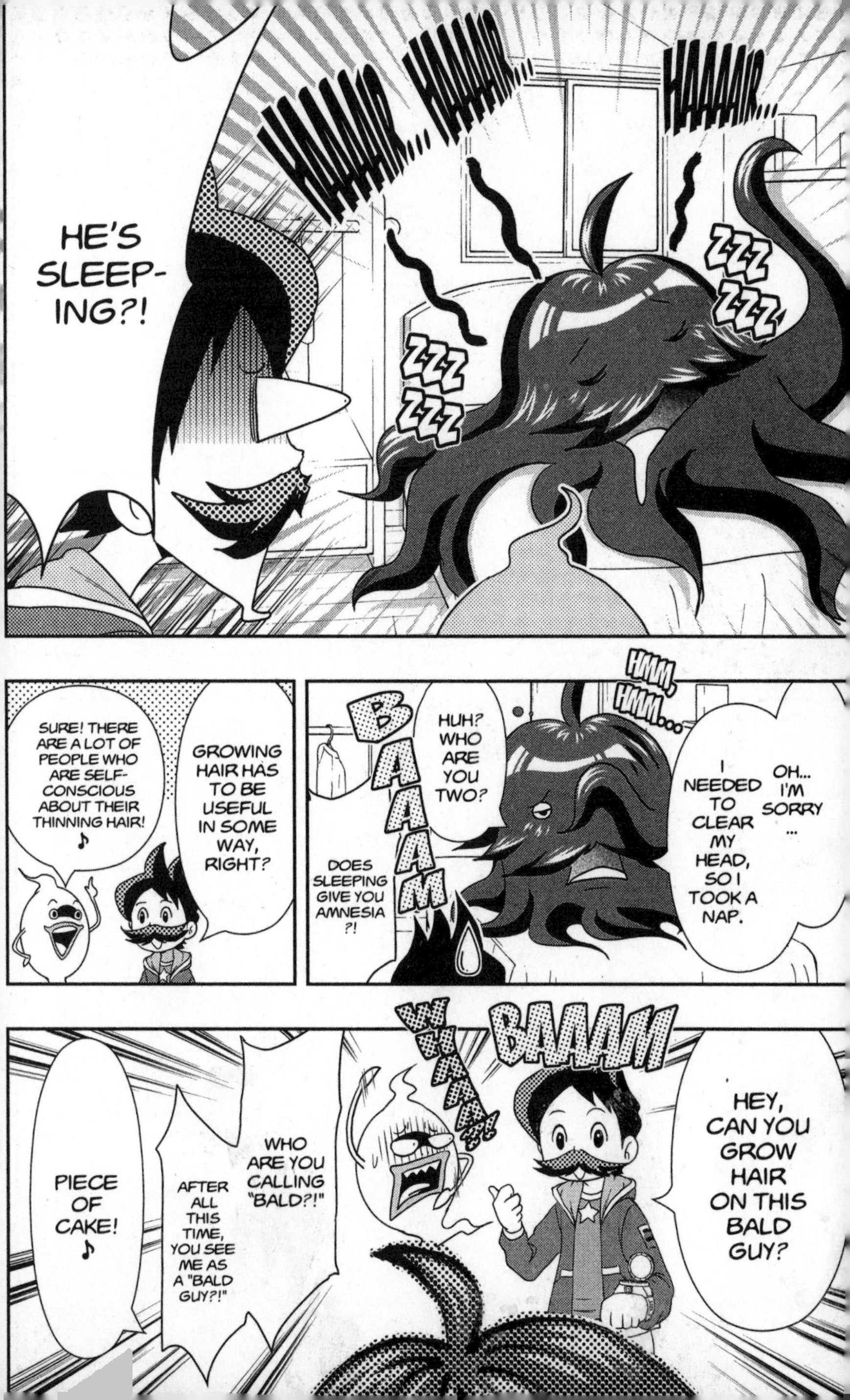
HAAAAIR...
HAAAIR... HAAAIR...
ZZZ ZZZ
ZZZ ZZZ
HE'S SLEEPING?!
HMM, HMM...
OH... I'M SORRY...
I NEEDED TO CLEAR MY HEAD, SO I TOOK A NAP.
HUH? WHO ARE YOU TWO?
BAAAM
DOES SLEEPING GIVE YOU AMNESIA?!
GROWING HAIR HAS TO BE USEFUL IN SOME WAY, RIGHT?
SURE! THERE ARE A LOT OF PEOPLE WHO ARE SELF-CONSCIOUS ABOUT THEIR THINNING HAIR! ♪
HEY, CAN YOU GROW HAIR ON THIS BALD GUY?
BAAAM
WHO ARE YOU CALLING "BALD?!"
AFTER ALL THIS TIME, YOU SEE ME AS A "BALD GUY?!"
PIECE OF CAKE! ♪

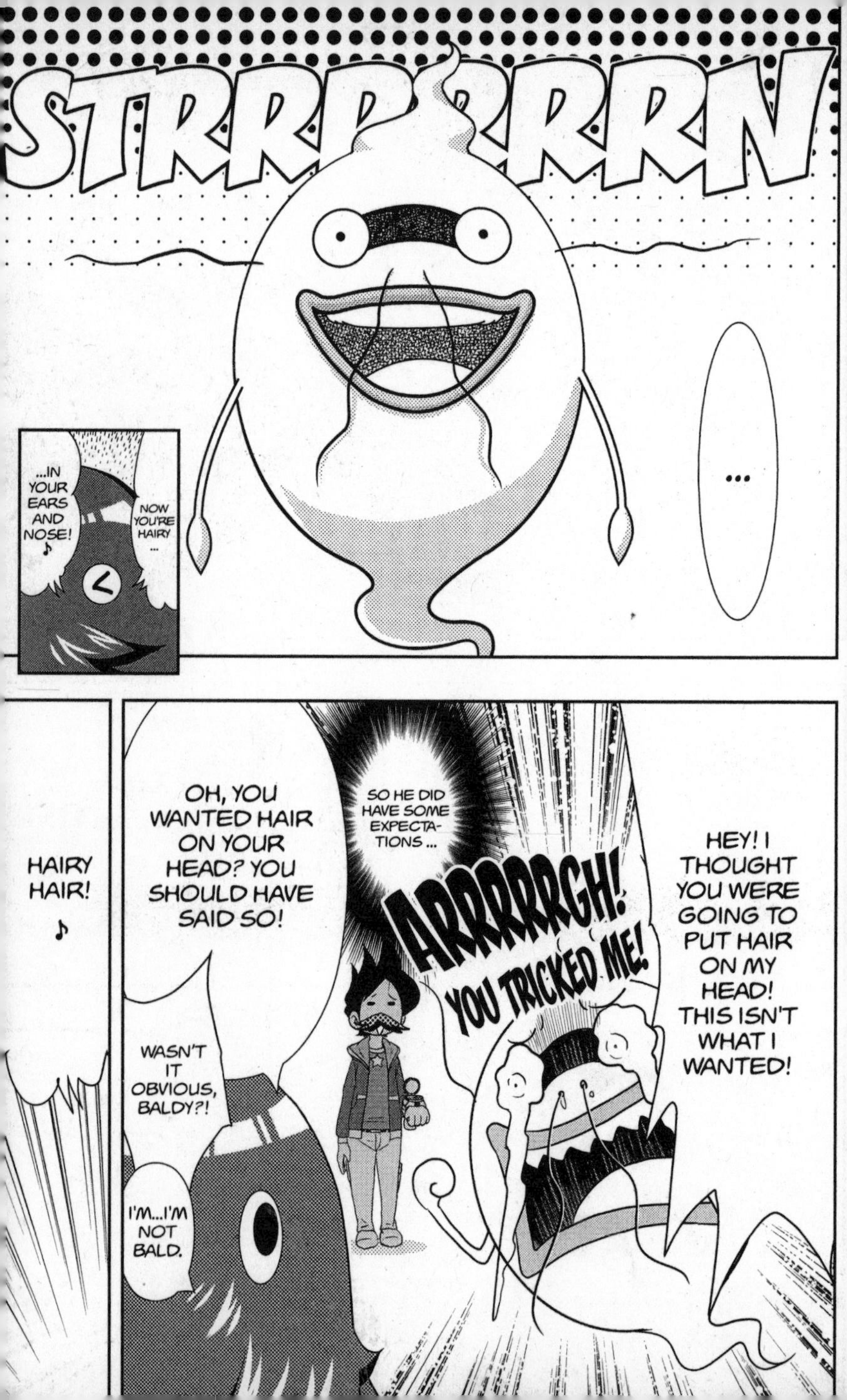
STRRRRRRN
...
NOW YOU'RE HAIRY ...
...IN YOUR EARS AND NOSE! ♪
HEY! I THOUGHT YOU WERE GOING TO PUT HAIR ON MY HEAD! THIS ISN'T WHAT I WANTED!
ARRRRRGH! YOU TRICKED ME!
SO HE DID HAVE SOME EXPECTA-TIONS ...
OH, YOU WANTED HAIR ON YOUR HEAD? YOU SHOULD HAVE SAID SO!
WASN'T IT OBVIOUS, BALDY?!
I'M...I'M NOT BALD.
HAIRY HAIR! ♪

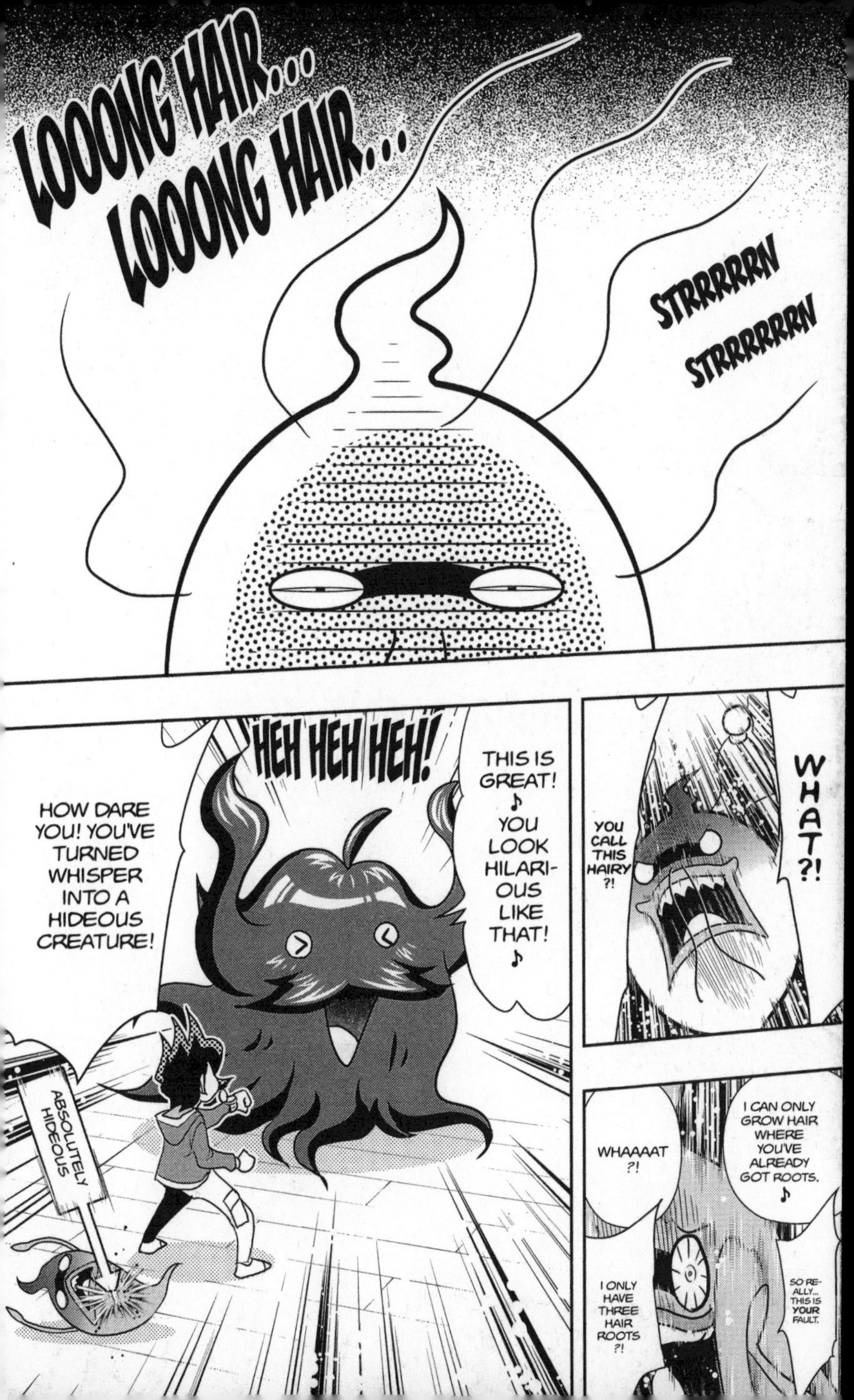
LOOONG HAIR... LOOONG HAIR...
STRRRRRN STRRRRRN
WHAT?!
YOU CALL THIS HAIRY?!
I CAN ONLY GROW HAIR WHERE YOU'VE ALREADY GOT ROOTS. ♪
WHAAAAT?!
SO REALLY... THIS IS YOUR FAULT.
I ONLY HAVE THREE HAIR ROOTS?!
HEH HEH HEH!
THIS IS GREAT! ♪ YOU LOOK HILARIOUS LIKE THAT! ♪
HOW DARE YOU! YOU'VE TURNED WHISPER INTO A HIDEOUS CREATURE!
ABSOLUTELY HIDEOUS

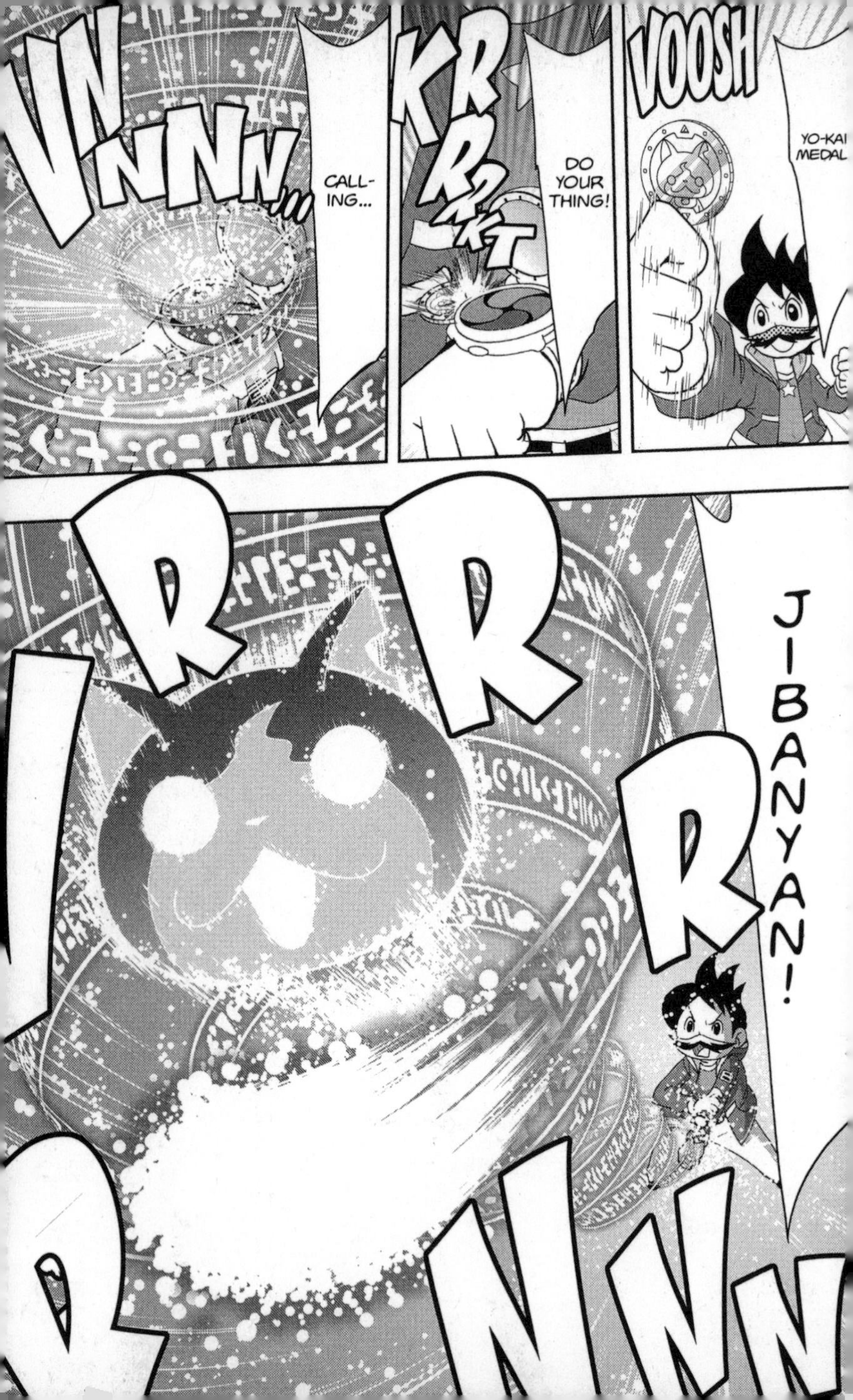
VOOSH
YO-KAI MEDAL
DO YOUR THING!
CALL-
ING...
JIBANYAN!

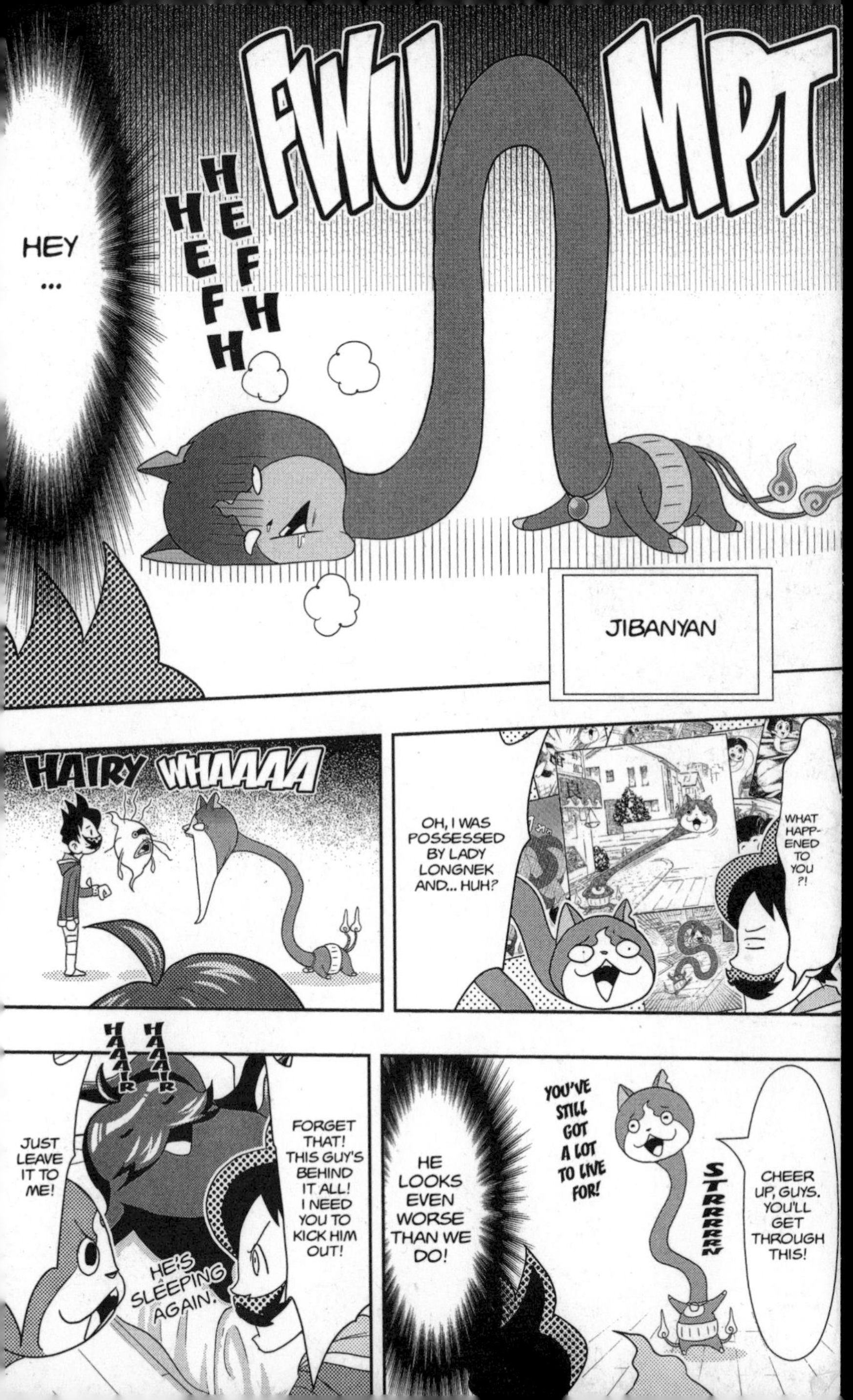
FWUMPT
HEEFH
HEFH
HEY ...
JIBANYAN
WHAT HAPPENED TO YOU?!
OH, I WAS POSSESSED BY LADY LONGNEK AND... HUH?
HAIRY
WHAAAAA
CHEER UP, GUYS. YOU'LL GET THROUGH THIS!
STRRRRN
YOU'VE STILL GOT A LOT TO LIVE FOR!
HE LOOKS EVEN WORSE THAN WE DO!
HAAAIR
HAAAIR
FORGET THAT! THIS GUY'S BEHIND IT ALL! I NEED YOU TO KICK HIM OUT!
JUST LEAVE IT TO ME!
HE'S SLEEPING AGAIN.

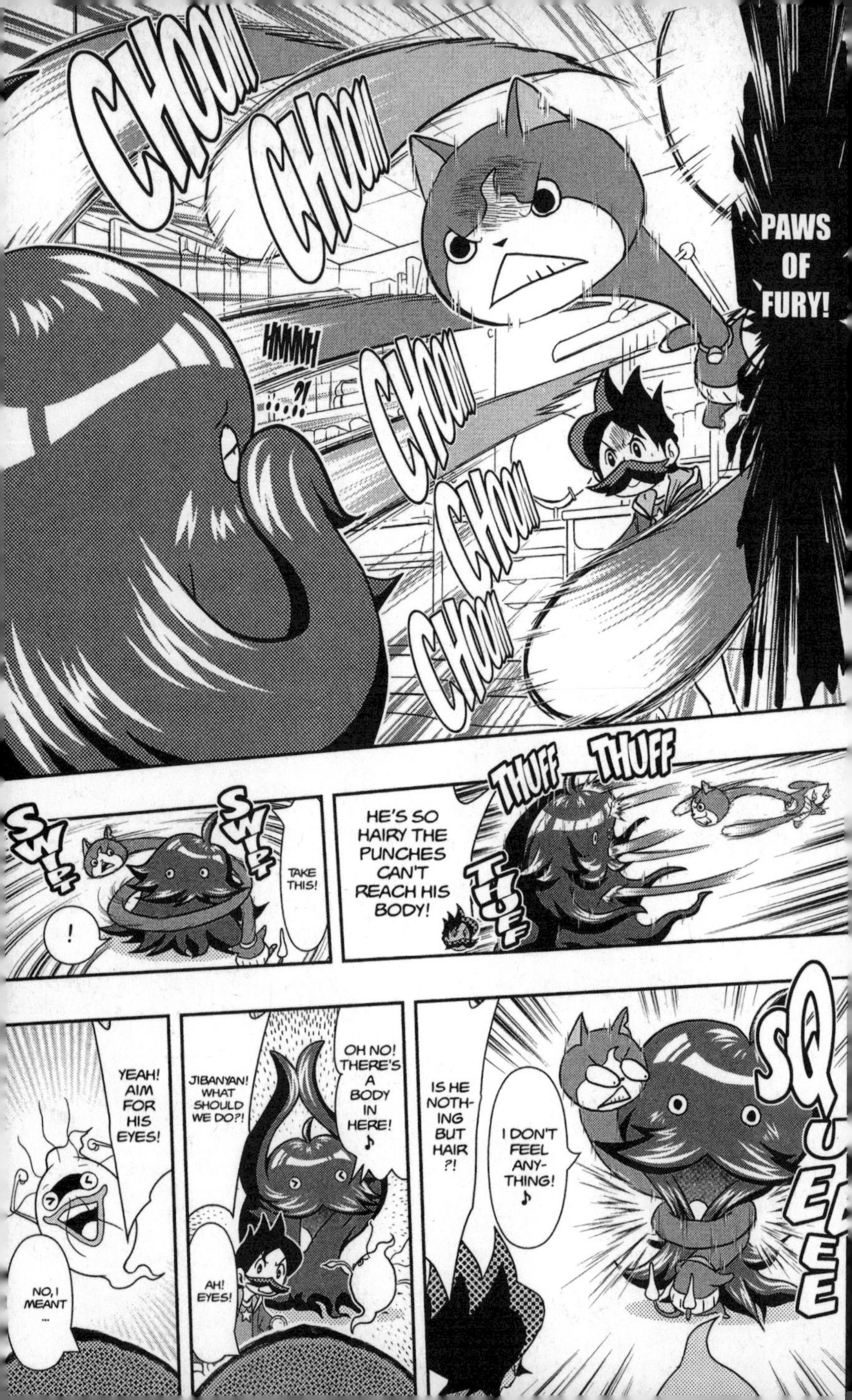
PAWS OF FURY!
CHOOM
CHOOM
HMMNH
...?!
CHOOM
CHOOM
CHOOM
CHOOM
THUFF
THUFF
HE'S SO HAIRY THE PUNCHES CAN'T REACH HIS BODY!
THUFF
TAKE THIS!
SWIP
SWIP
!
SQUEEE
I DON'T FEEL ANYTHING! ♪
IS HE NOTHING BUT HAIR?!
OH NO! THERE'S A BODY IN HERE! ♪
JIBANYAN! WHAT SHOULD WE DO?!
AH! EYES!
YEAH! AIM FOR HIS EYES!
NO, I MEANT ...

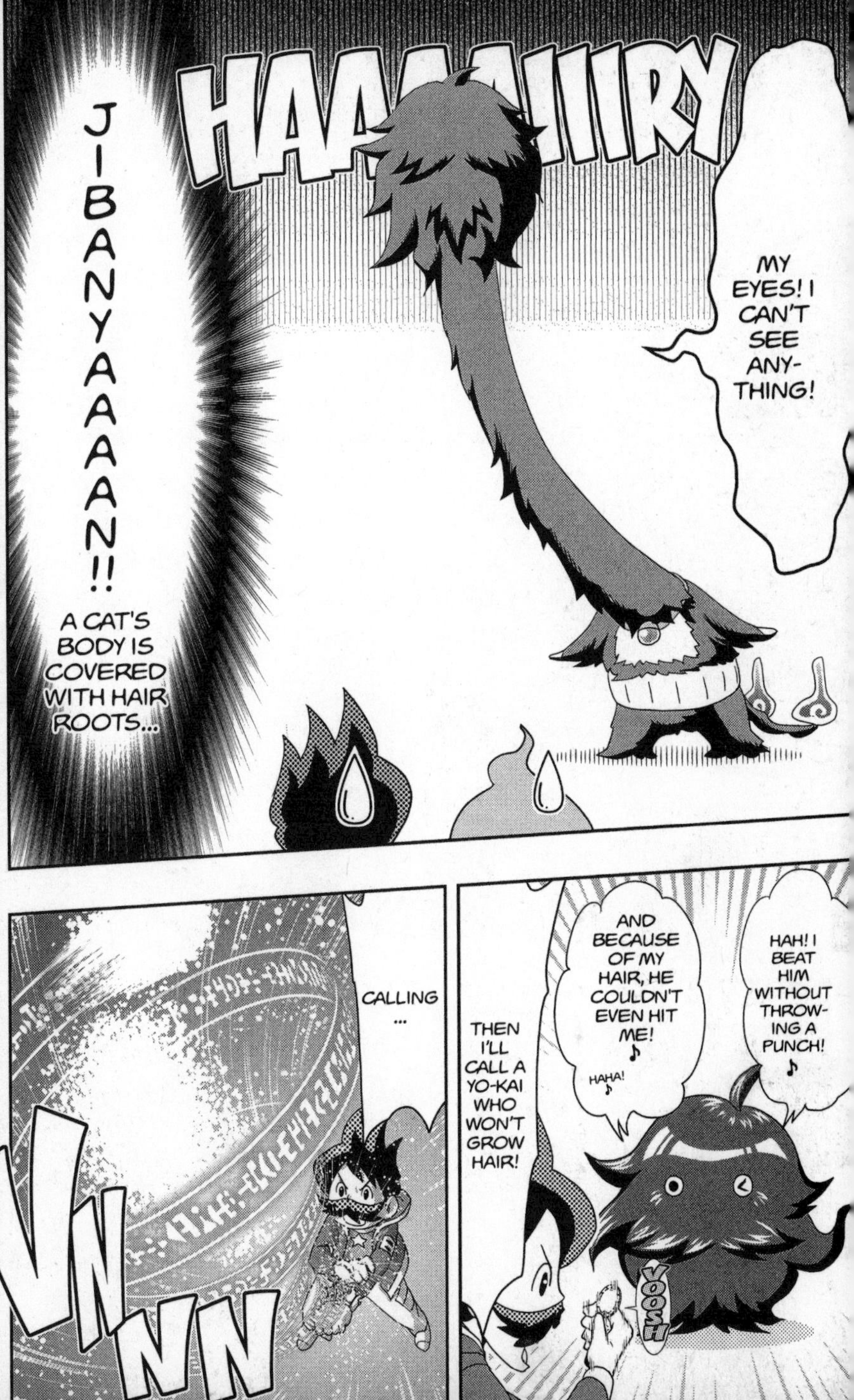

HAAAIIIRY
MY EYES! I CAN'T SEE ANYTHING!
JIBANYAAAAAN!!
A CAT'S BODY IS COVERED WITH HAIR ROOTS...
HAH! I BEAT HIM WITHOUT THROWING A PUNCH! ♪
AND BECAUSE OF MY HAIR, HE COULDN'T EVEN HIT ME! ♪
HAHA! ♪
THEN I'LL CALL A YO-KAI WHO WON'T GROW HAIR!
VOOSH
CALLING ...
VNNN

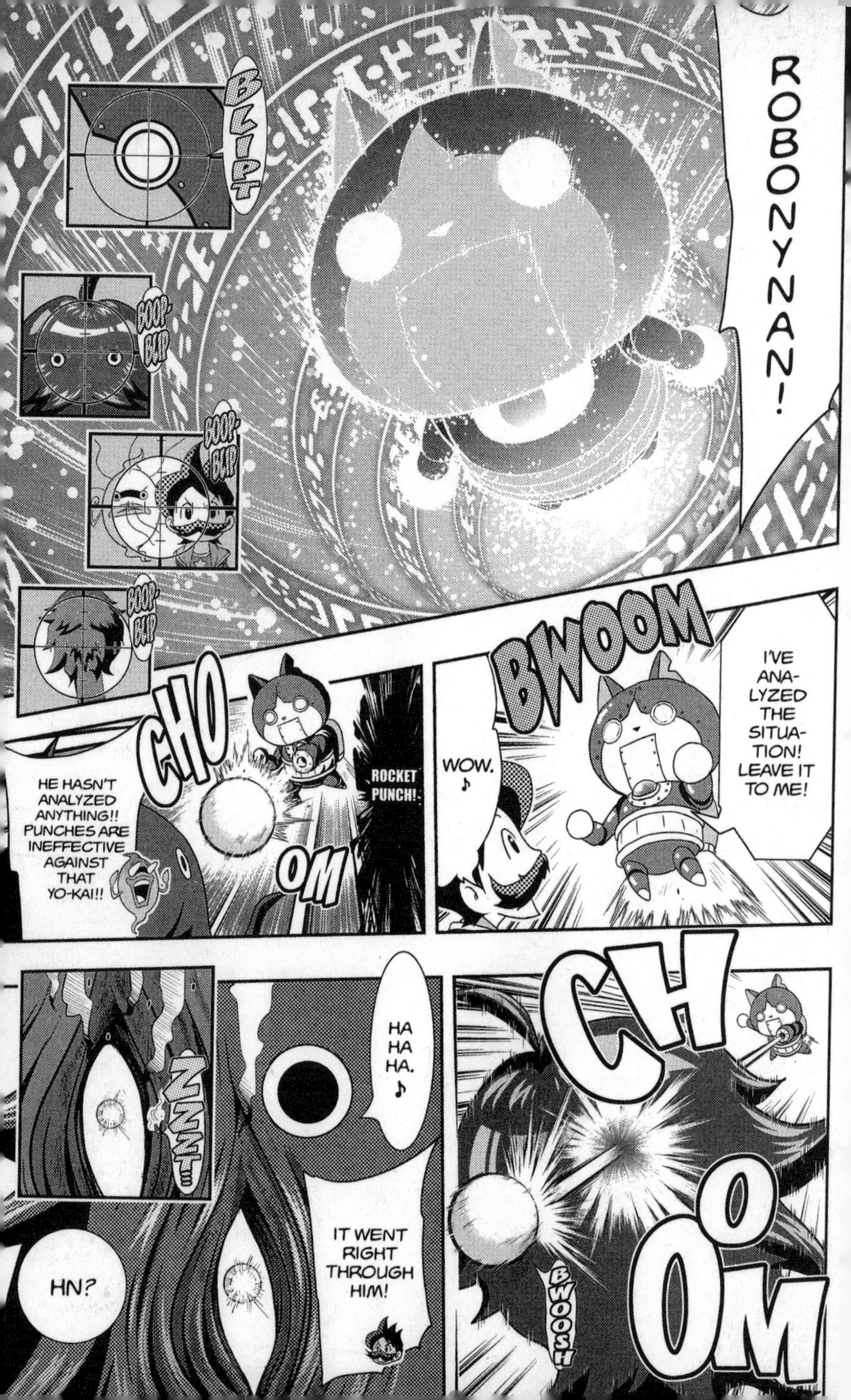
ROBONYNAN!
BLIPT
BOOP-BLIP
BOOP-BLIP
BOOP-BLIP
BWOOM
I'VE ANALYZED THE SITUATION! LEAVE IT TO ME!
WOW. ♪
CHO
OM
ROCKET PUNCH!
HE HASN'T ANALYZED ANYTHING!! PUNCHES ARE INEFFECTIVE AGAINST THAT YO-KAI!!
CH
O
O
OM
BWOOSH
HA HA HA. ♪
IT WENT RIGHT THROUGH HIM!
ZNNT...
HN?

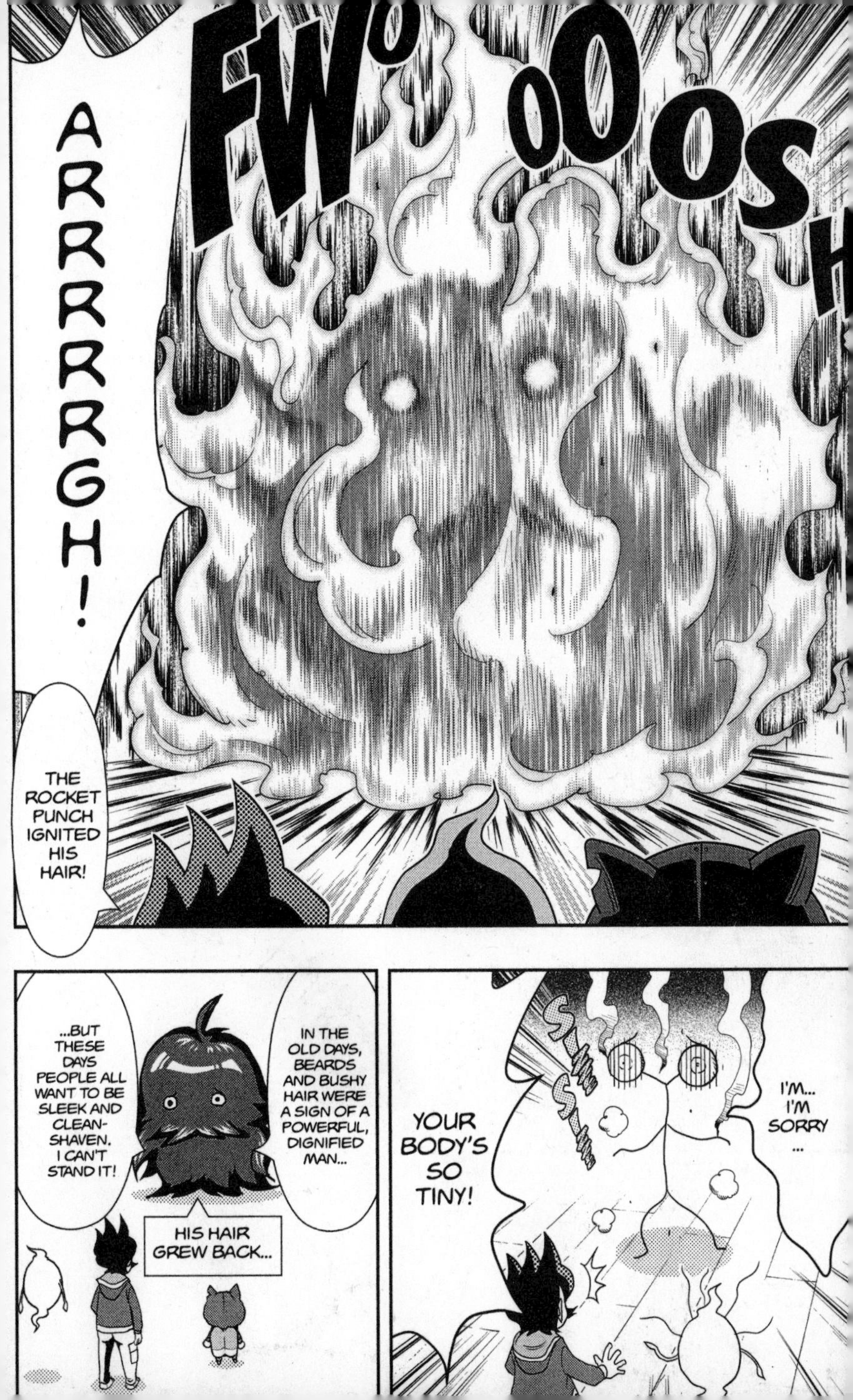
FWOOOOSH
ARRRRRGH!
THE ROCKET PUNCH IGNITED HIS HAIR!
I'M... I'M SORRY...
YOUR BODY'S SO TINY!
IN THE OLD DAYS, BEARDS AND BUSHY HAIR WERE A SIGN OF A POWERFUL, DIGNIFIED MAN...
...BUT THESE DAYS PEOPLE ALL WANT TO BE SLEEK AND CLEAN-SHAVEN. I CAN'T STAND IT!
HIS HAIR GREW BACK...

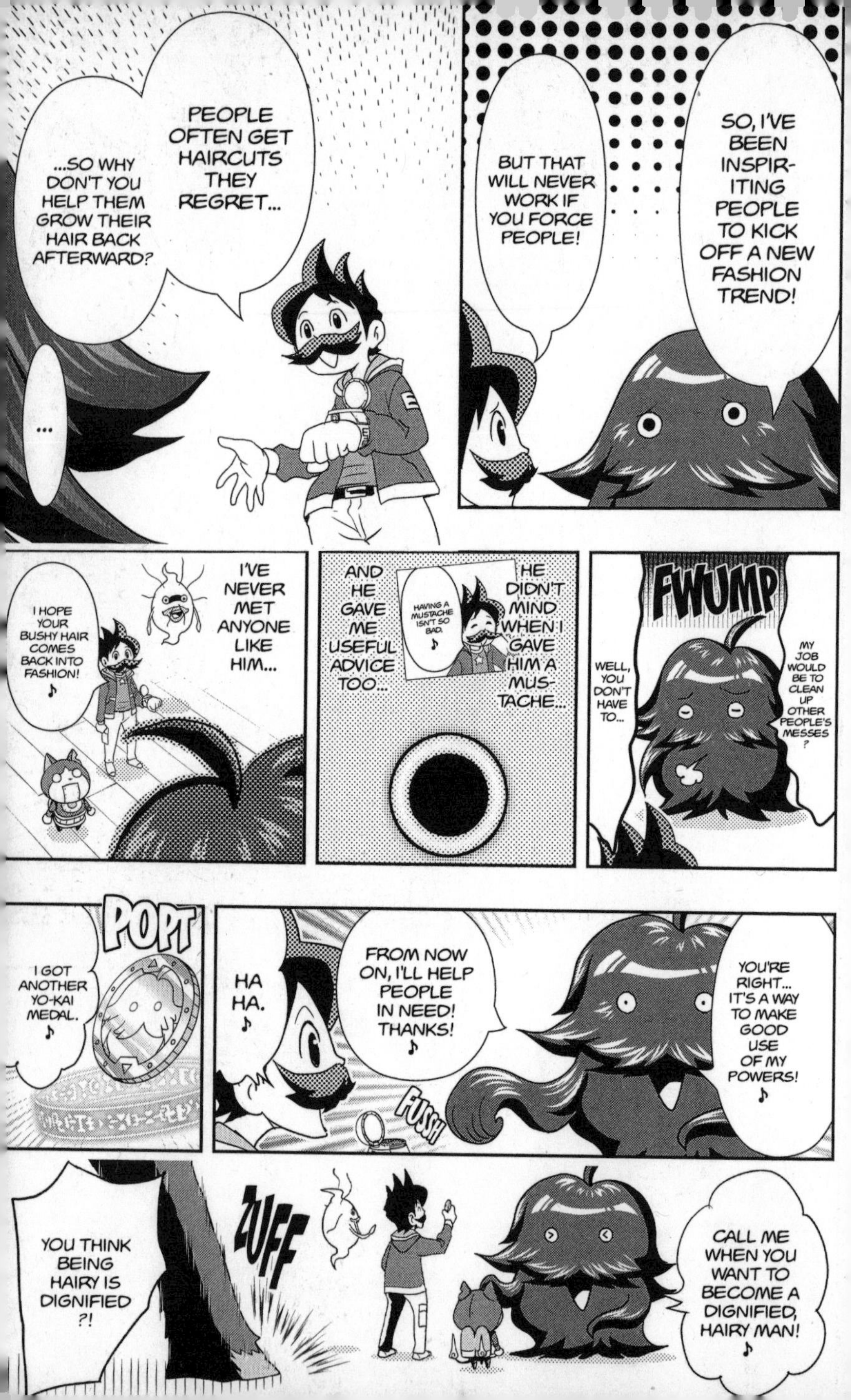
SO, I'VE BEEN INSPIR-ITING PEOPLE TO KICK OFF A NEW FASHION TREND!
BUT THAT WILL NEVER WORK IF YOU FORCE PEOPLE!
PEOPLE OFTEN GET HAIRCUTS THEY REGRET...
...SO WHY DON'T YOU HELP THEM GROW THEIR HAIR BACK AFTERWARD?
...
FWUMP
MY JOB WOULD BE TO CLEAN UP OTHER PEOPLE'S MESSES?
WELL, YOU DON'T HAVE TO...
HE DIDN'T MIND WHEN I GAVE HIM A MUS-TACHE...
HAVING A MUSTACHE ISN'T SO BAD. ♪
AND HE GAVE ME USEFUL ADVICE TOO...
I'VE NEVER MET ANYONE LIKE HIM...
I HOPE YOUR BUSHY HAIR COMES BACK INTO FASHION! ♪
YOU'RE RIGHT... IT'S A WAY TO MAKE GOOD USE OF MY POWERS! ♪
FROM NOW ON, I'LL HELP PEOPLE IN NEED! THANKS! ♪
HA HA. ♪
FUSSH
POPT
I GOT ANOTHER YO-KAI MEDAL. ♪
CALL ME WHEN YOU WANT TO BECOME A DIGNIFIED, HAIRY MAN! ♪
ZUFF
YOU THINK BEING HAIRY IS DIGNIFIED?!

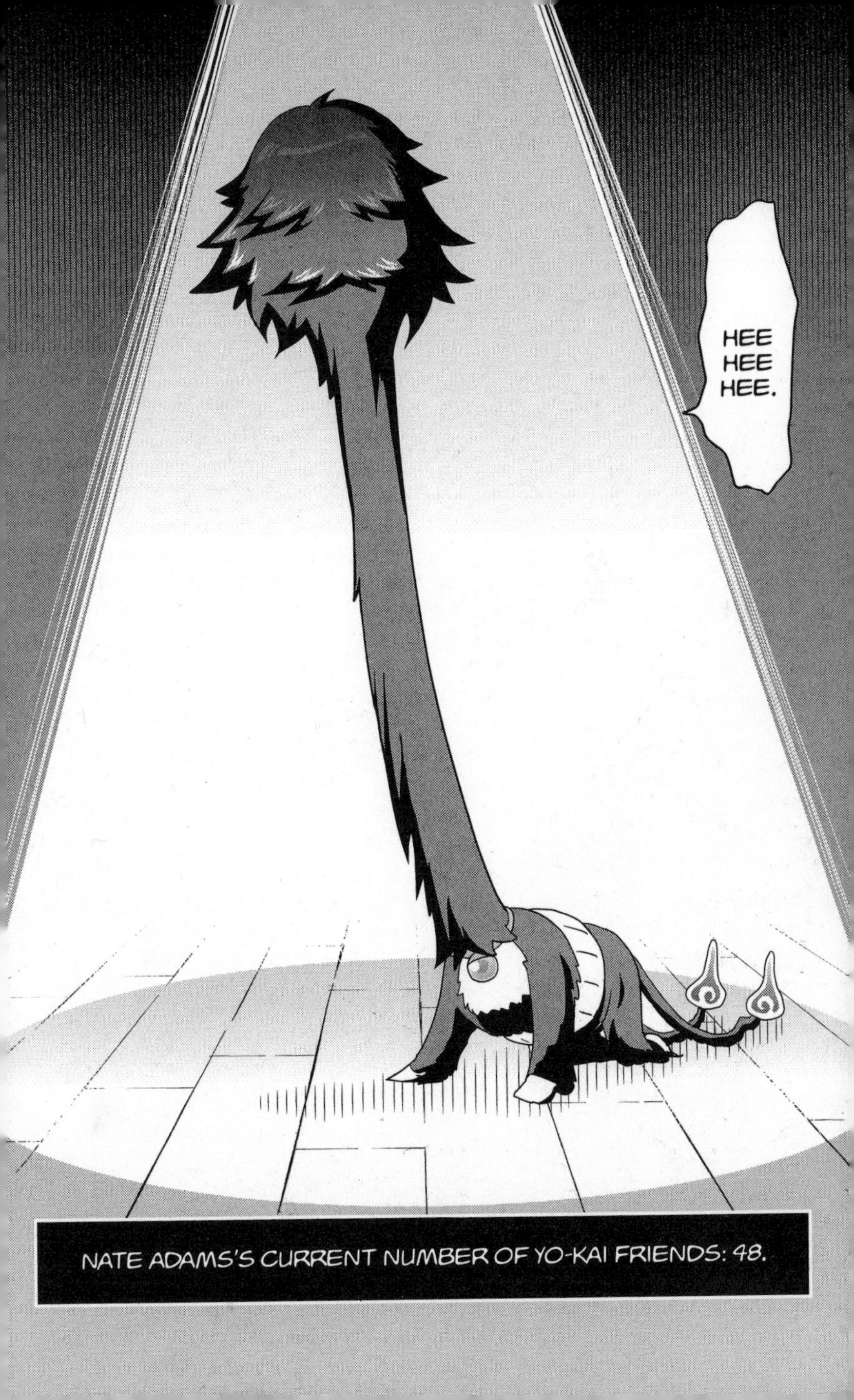
HEE HEE HEE.
NATE ADAMS'S CURRENT NUMBER OF YO-KAI FRIENDS: 48.

# CHAPTER 65
# A MIRROR IMAGE... BUT WHICH ONE'S REAL?!

FEATURING MIMIC YO-KAI MIMIKIN

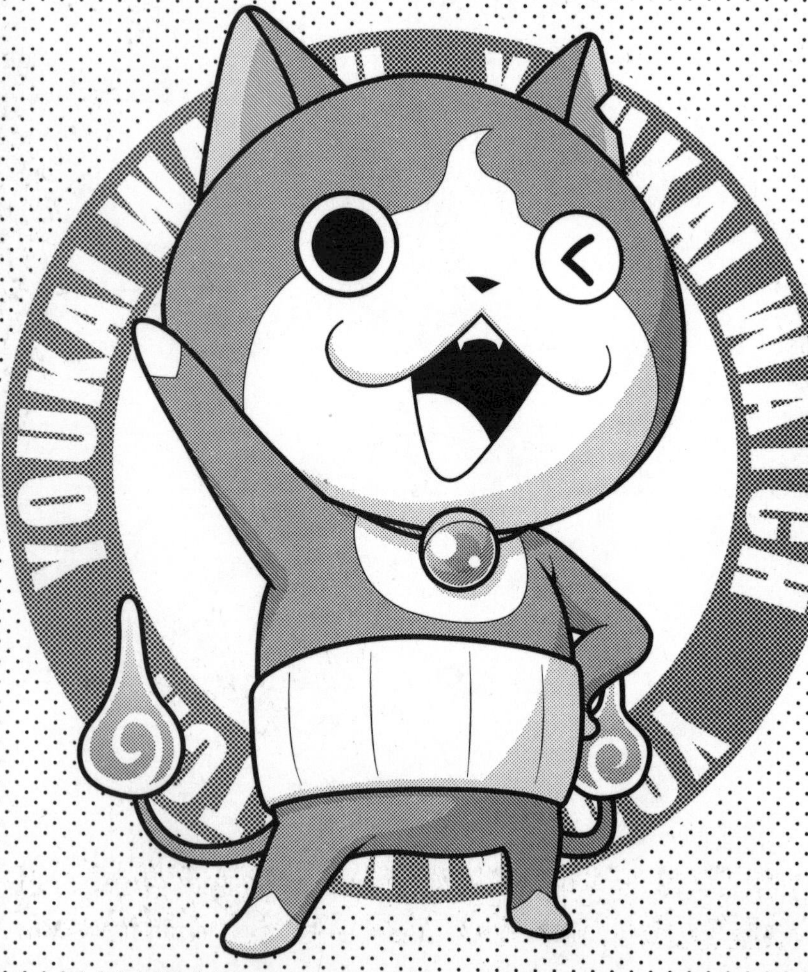
KAI WATCH

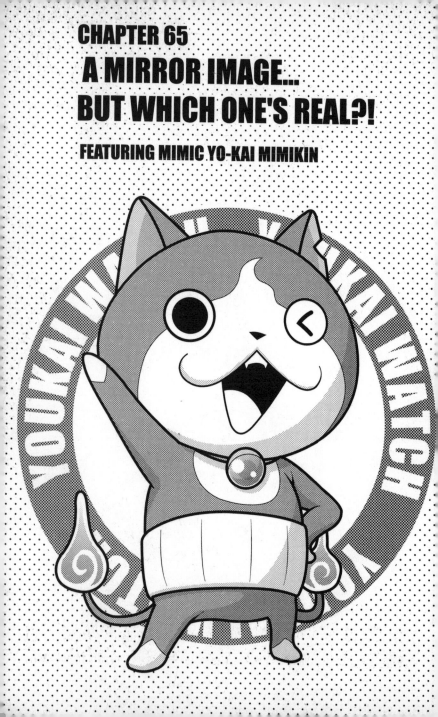

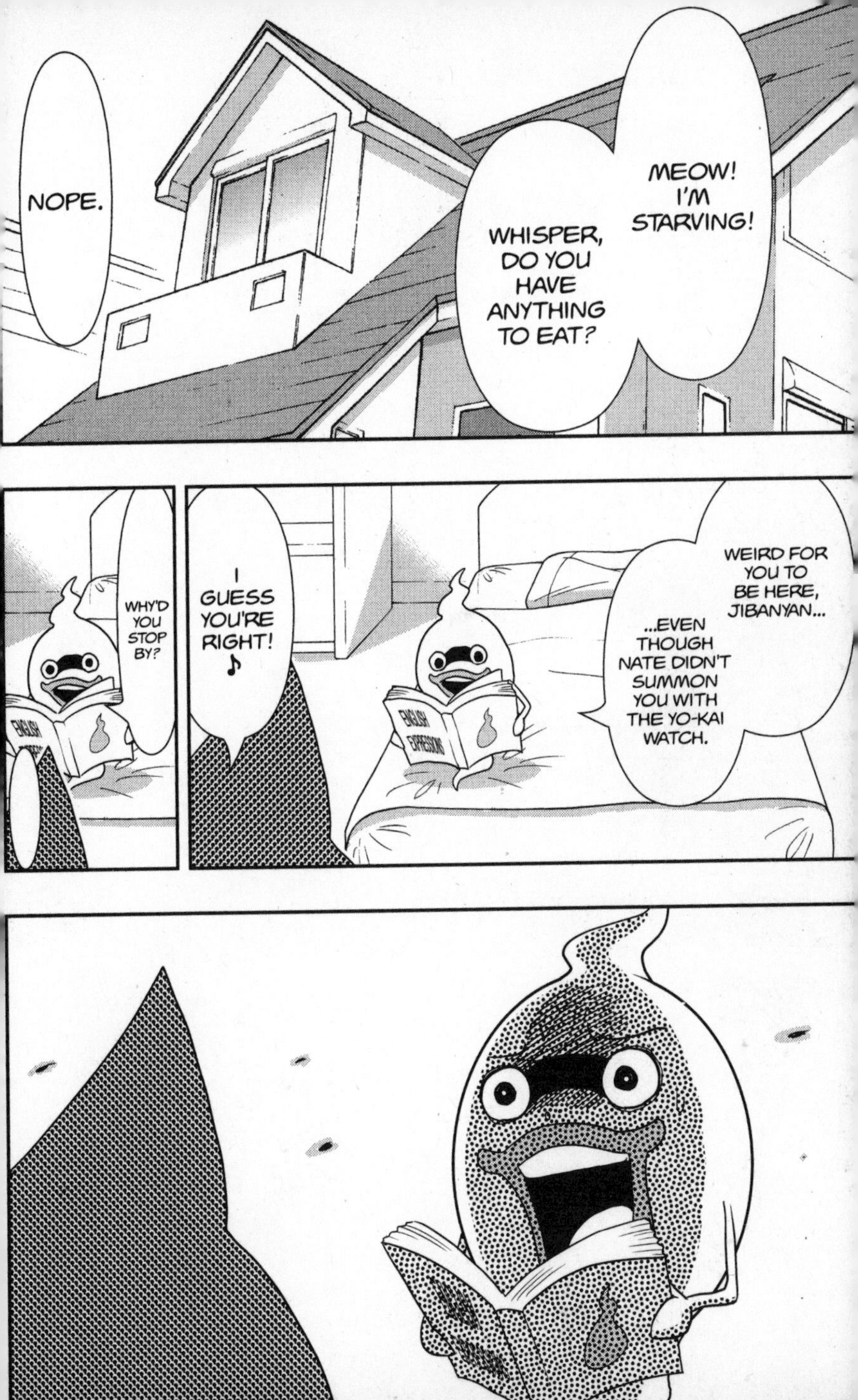
MEOW! I'M STARVING!
WHISPER, DO YOU HAVE ANYTHING TO EAT?
NOPE.
WEIRD FOR YOU TO BE HERE, JIBANYAN...
...EVEN THOUGH NATE DIDN'T SUMMON YOU WITH THE YO-KAI WATCH.
ENGLISH EXPRESSIONS
I GUESS YOU'RE RIGHT! ♪
WHY'D YOU STOP BY?

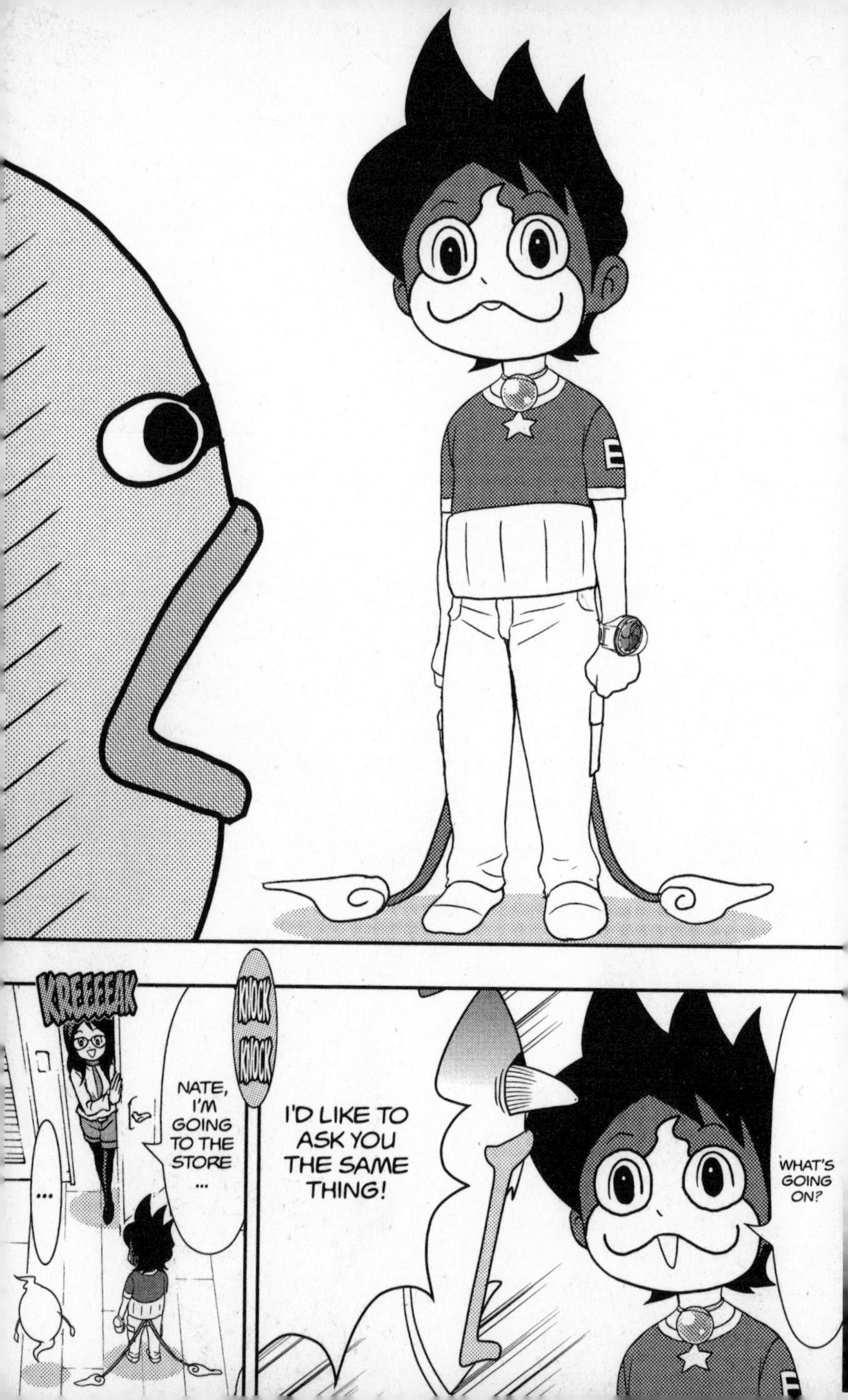
WHAT'S GOING ON?
I'D LIKE TO ASK YOU THE SAME THING!
KNOCK KNOCK
KREEEEAK
NATE, I'M GOING TO THE STORE ...
...

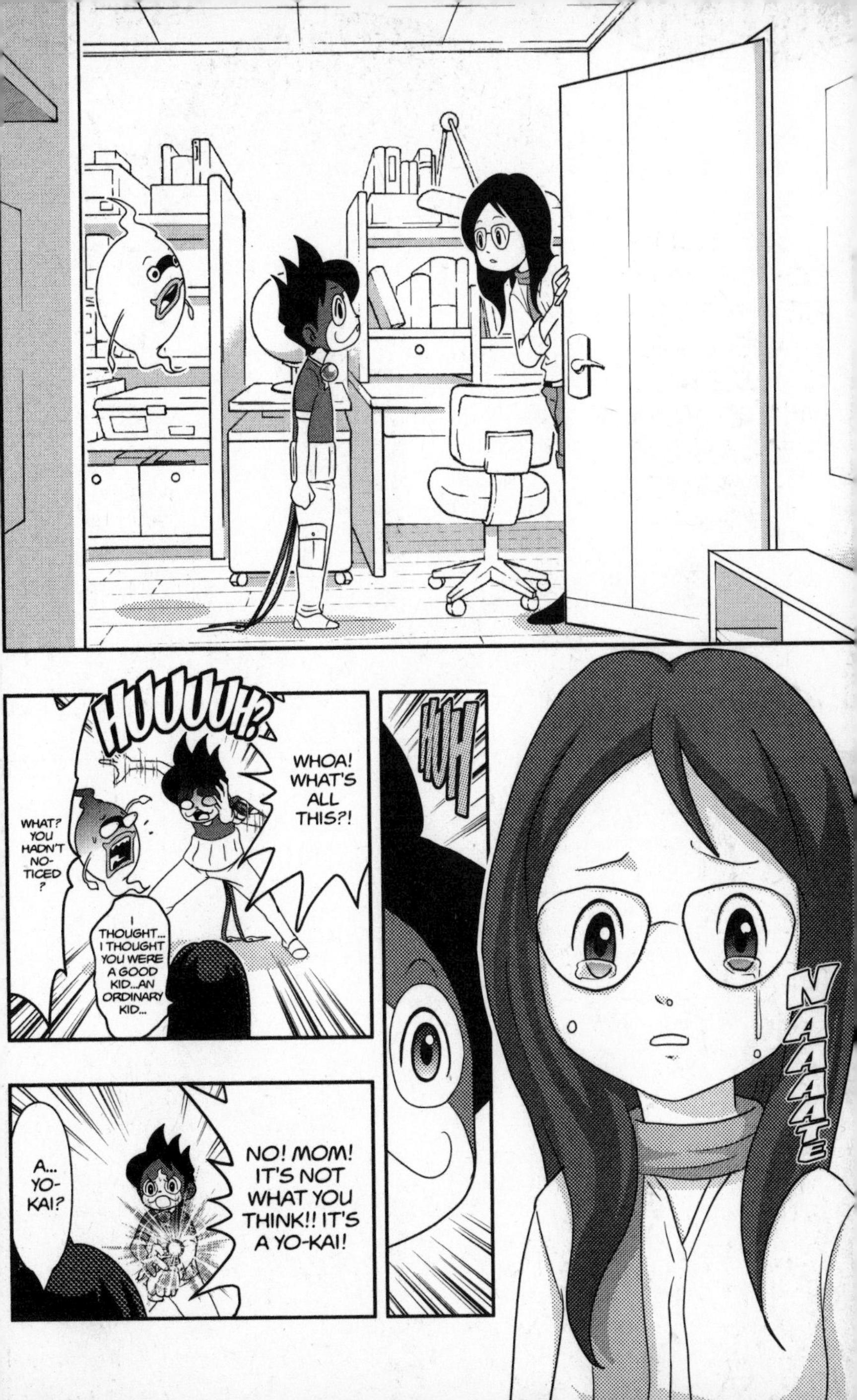
NAAAATE
HUH
HUUUUH?!
WHOA! WHAT'S ALL THIS?!
WHAT? YOU HADN'T NO-TICED?
I THOUGHT... I THOUGHT YOU WERE A GOOD KID...AN ORDINARY KID...
NO! MOM! IT'S NOT WHAT YOU THINK!! IT'S A YO-KAI!
A... YO-KAI?

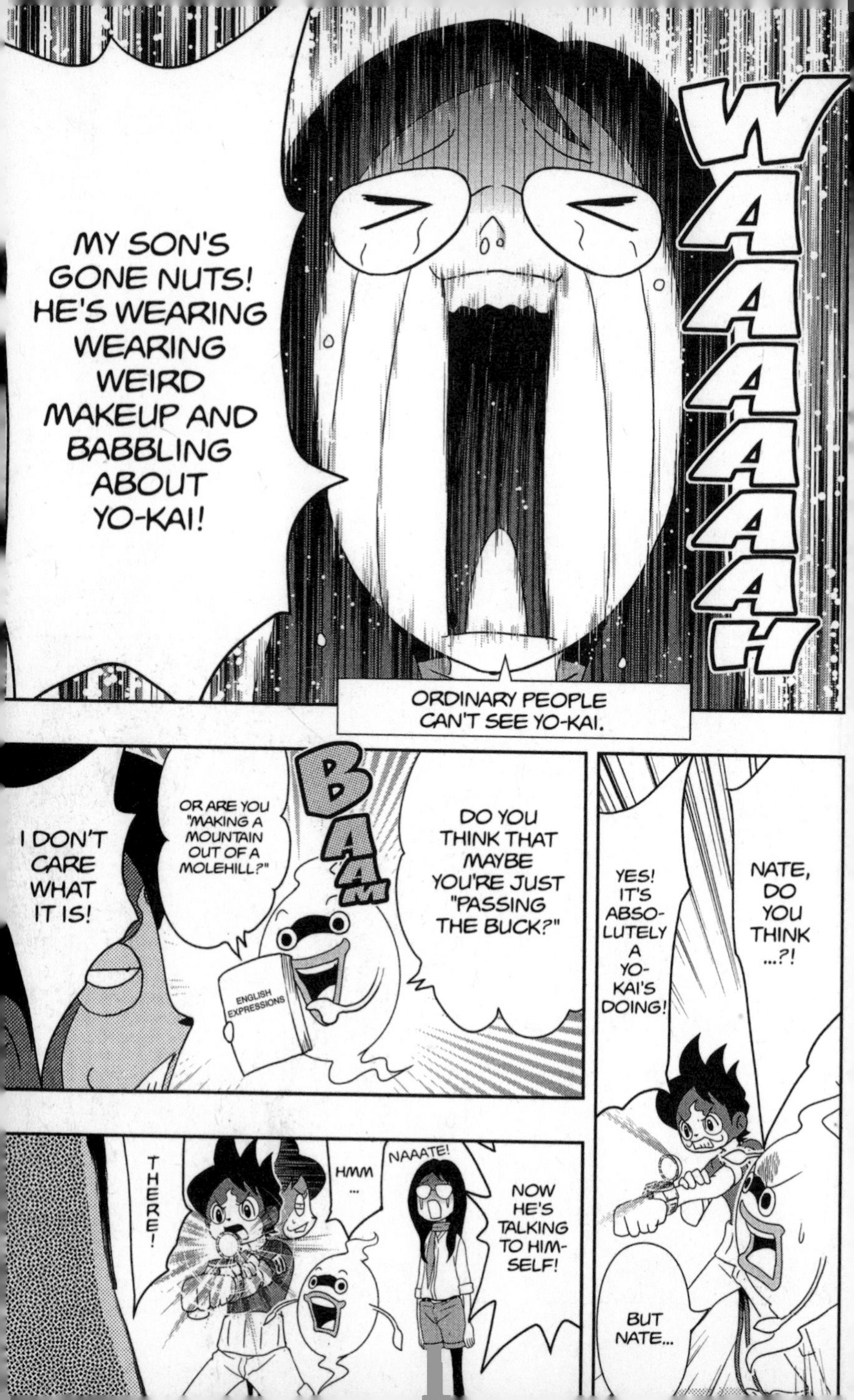
MY SON'S GONE NUTS! HE'S WEARING WEARING WEIRD MAKEUP AND BABBLING ABOUT YO-KAI!
WAAAAAAAH
ORDINARY PEOPLE CAN'T SEE YO-KAI.
NATE, DO YOU THINK ...?!
YES! IT'S ABSO-LUTELY A YO-KAI'S DOING!
BUT NATE...
DO YOU THINK THAT MAYBE YOU'RE JUST "PASSING THE BUCK?"
BAAM
OR ARE YOU "MAKING A MOUNTAIN OUT OF A MOLEHILL?"
ENGLISH EXPRESSIONS
I DON'T CARE WHAT IT IS!
NOW HE'S TALKING TO HIM-SELF!
NAAATE!
HMM ...
THERE!

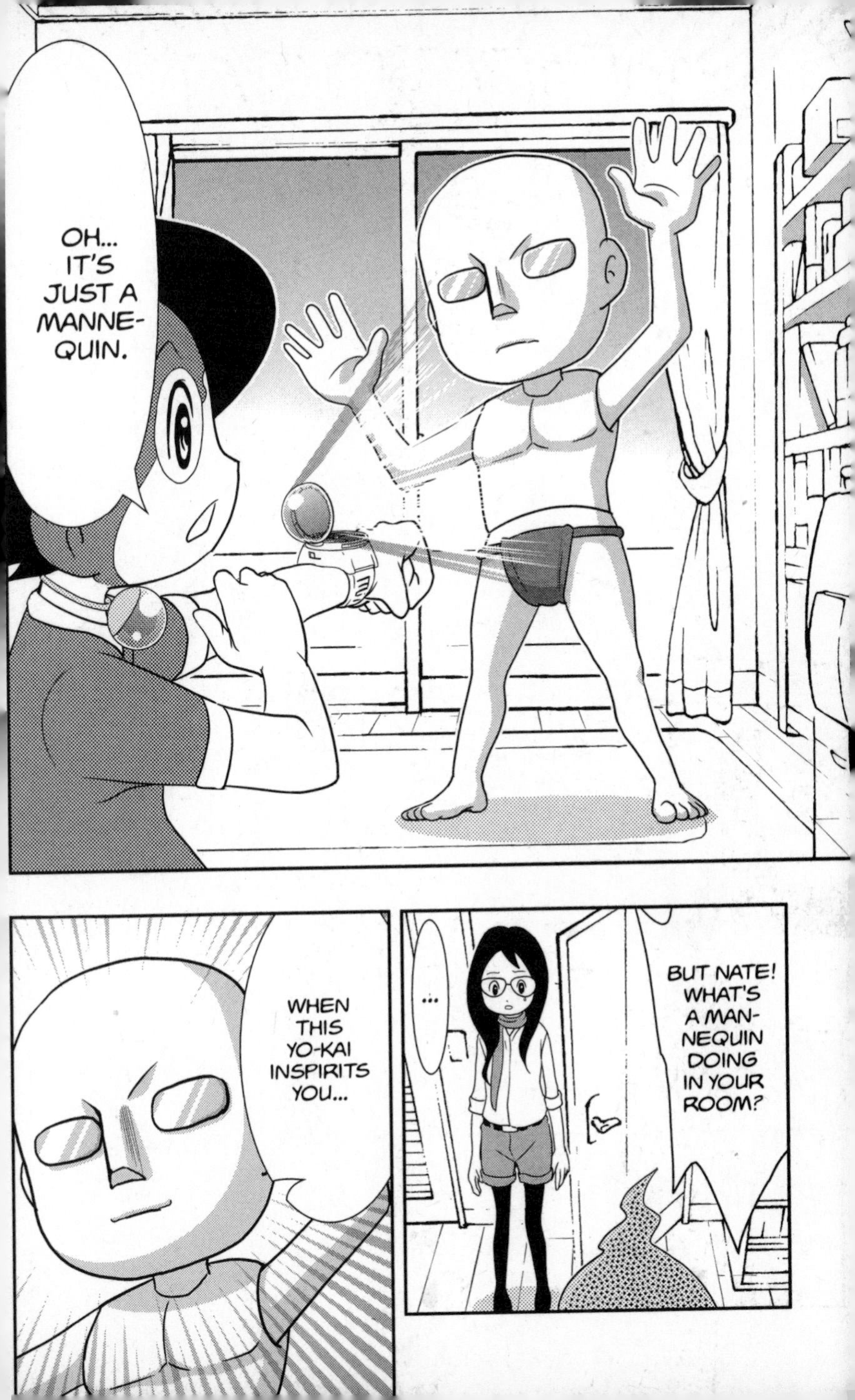
OH... IT'S JUST A MANNE-QUIN.
BUT NATE! WHAT'S A MAN-NEQUIN DOING IN YOUR ROOM?
...
WHEN THIS YO-KAI INSPIRITS YOU...

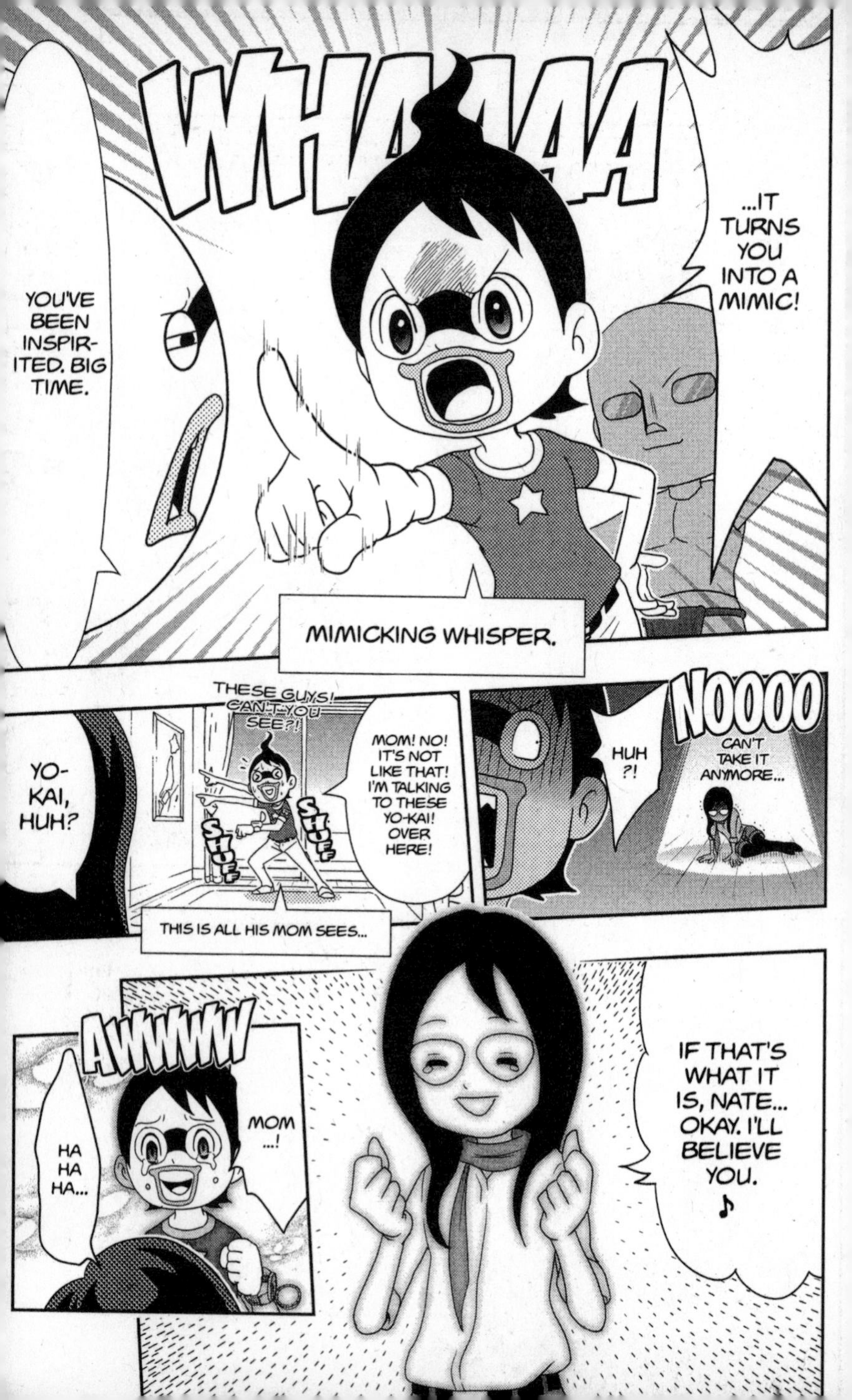
...IT TURNS YOU INTO A MIMIC!
WHAAAA
YOU'VE BEEN INSPIRITED. BIG TIME.
MIMICKING WHISPER.
NOOOO
CAN'T TAKE IT ANYMORE...
HUH ?!
MOM! NO! IT'S NOT LIKE THAT! I'M TALKING TO THESE YO-KAI! OVER HERE!
THESE GUYS! CAN'T YOU SEE?!
SHUFF
SHUFF
THIS IS ALL HIS MOM SEES...
YO-KAI, HUH?
IF THAT'S WHAT IT IS, NATE... OKAY. I'LL BELIEVE YOU. ♪
AWWWW
MOM ...!
HA HA HA...

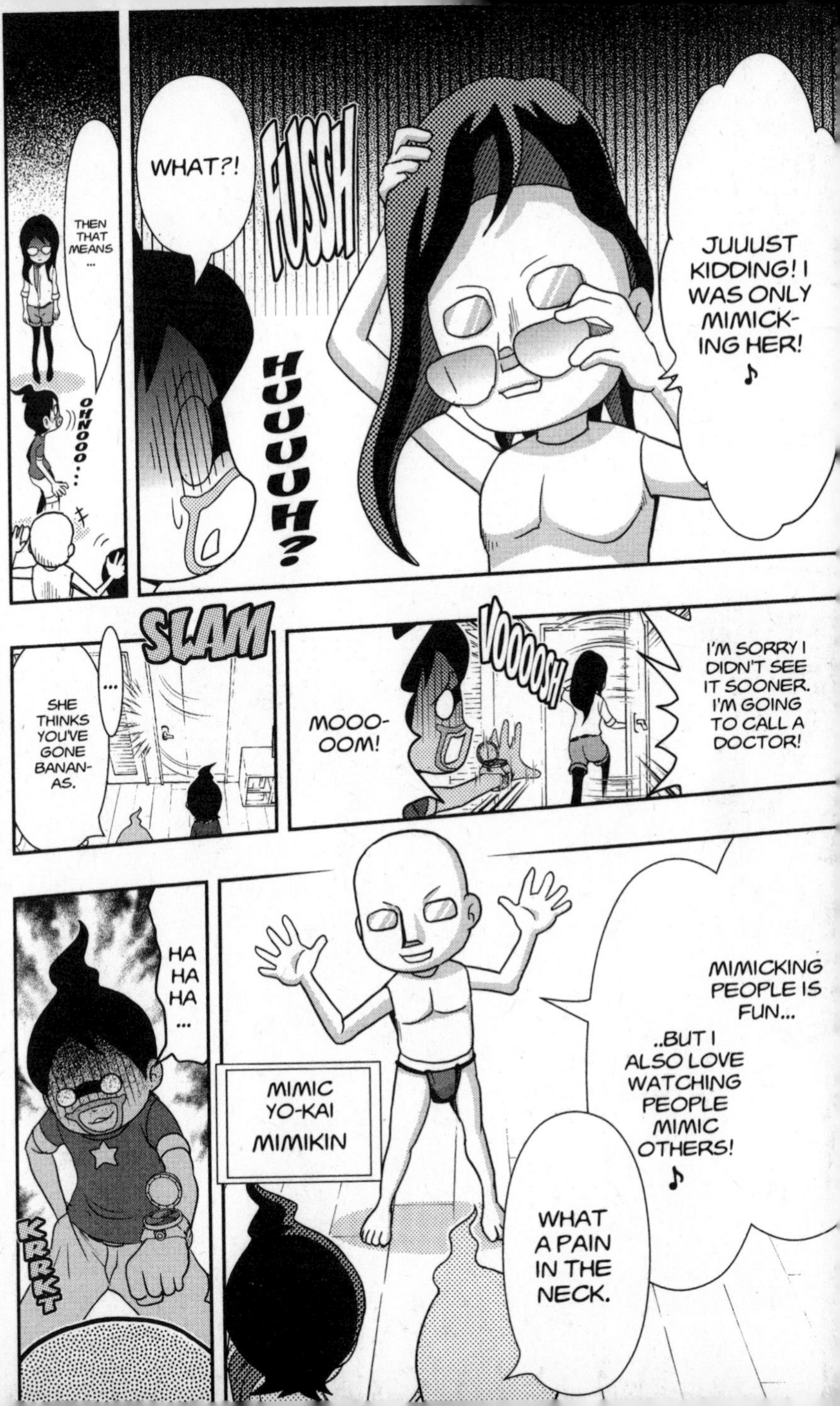

FUSSH
JUUUST KIDDING! I WAS ONLY MIMICK-ING HER! ♪
WHAT?!
HUUUUUH?
THEN THAT MEANS ...
OHNOOOO...
VOOOOSH
I'M SORRY I DIDN'T SEE IT SOONER. I'M GOING TO CALL A DOCTOR!
MOOO-OOM!
SLAM
...
SHE THINKS YOU'VE GONE BANAN-AS.
MIMICKING PEOPLE IS FUN...
..BUT I ALSO LOVE WATCHING PEOPLE MIMIC OTHERS! ♪
MIMIC YO-KAI MIMIKIN
WHAT A PAIN IN THE NECK.
HA HA HA ...
KRRKT

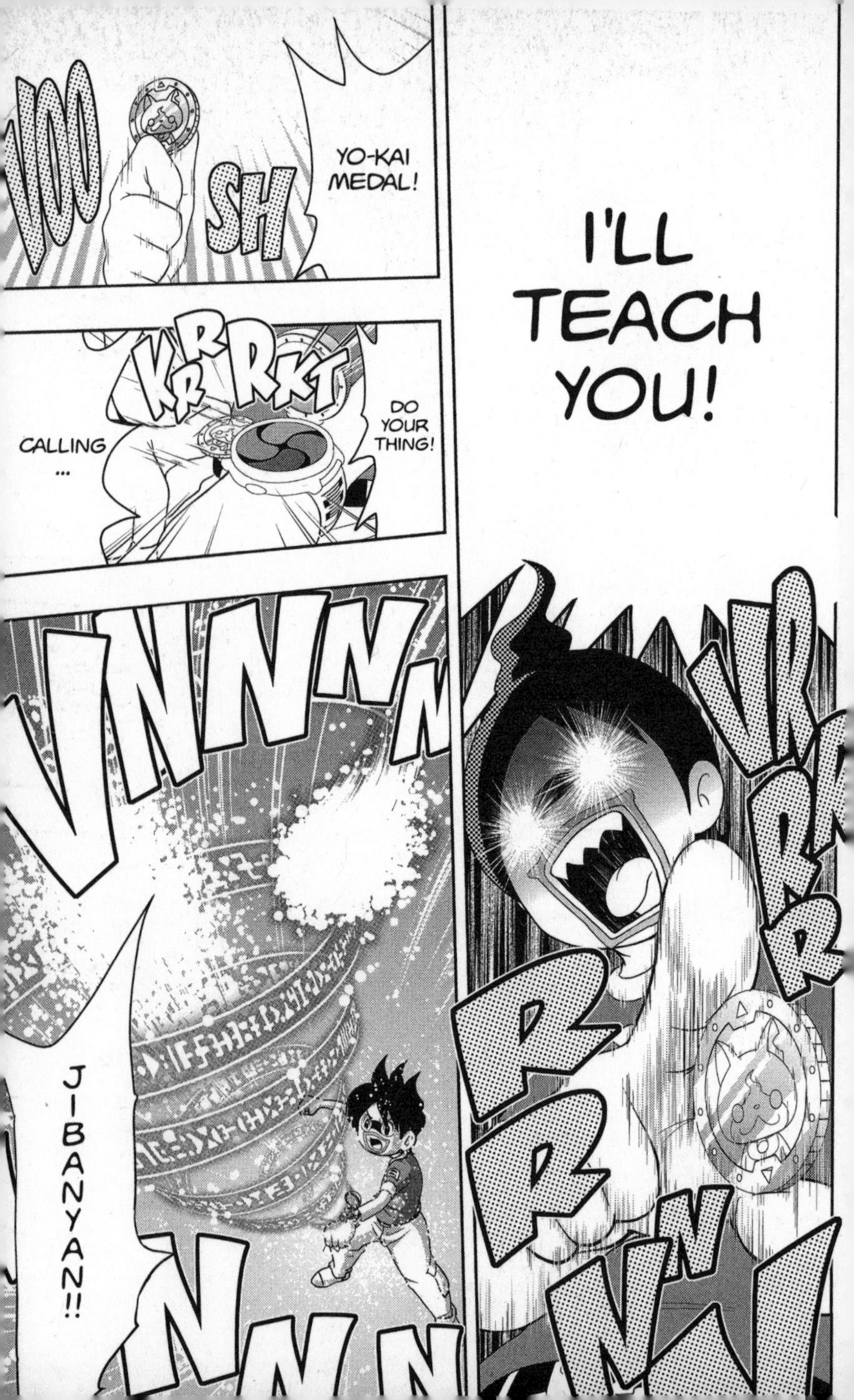
I'LL TEACH YOU!
YO-KAI MEDAL!
WOOSH
KRRRKT
DO YOUR THING!
CALLING ...
VRRRRRNNN
VNNNNNN
JIBANYAN!!
NNNN

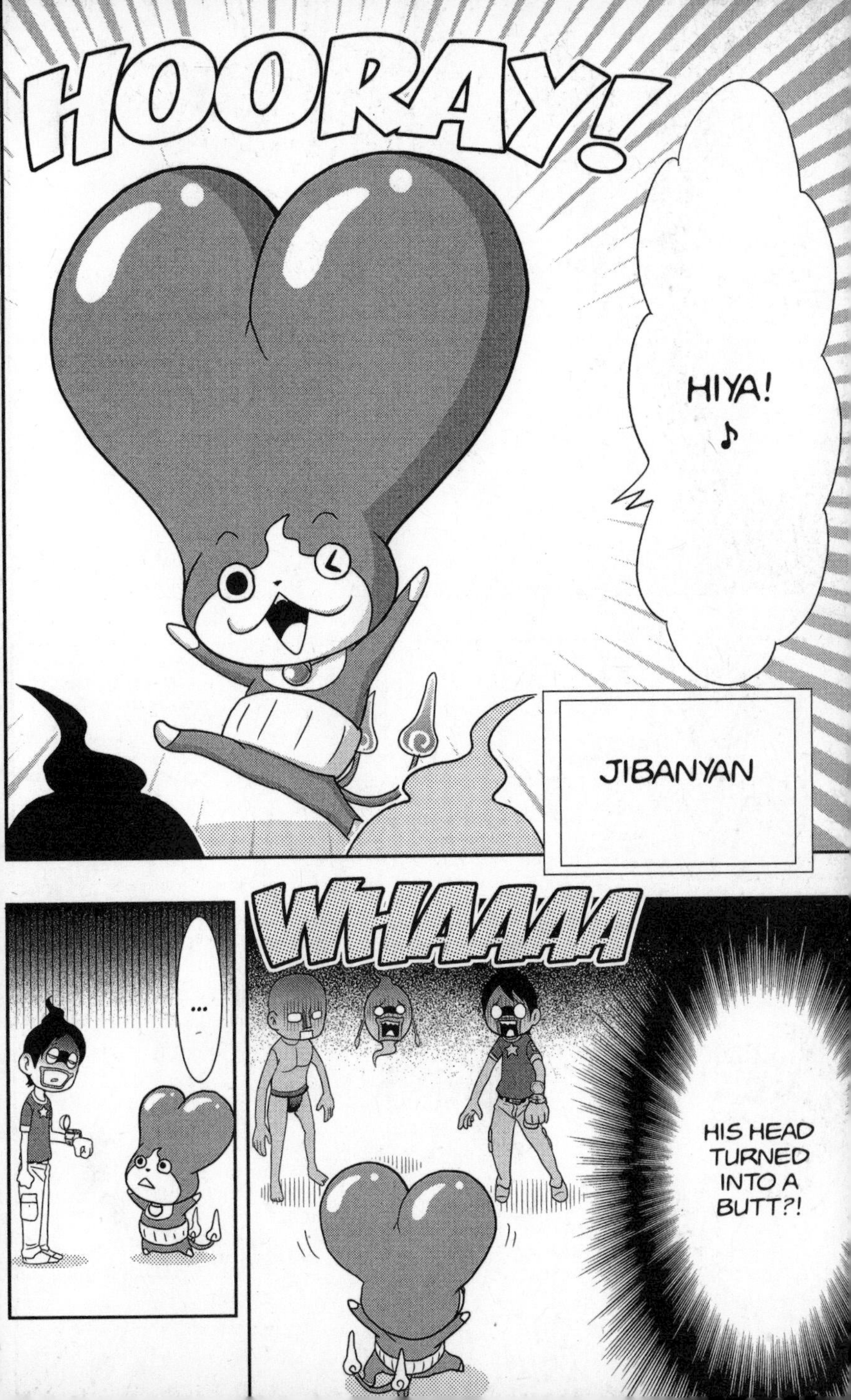
HOORAY!
HIYA! ♪
JIBANYAN
WHAAAAA
HIS HEAD TURNED INTO A BUTT?!
...

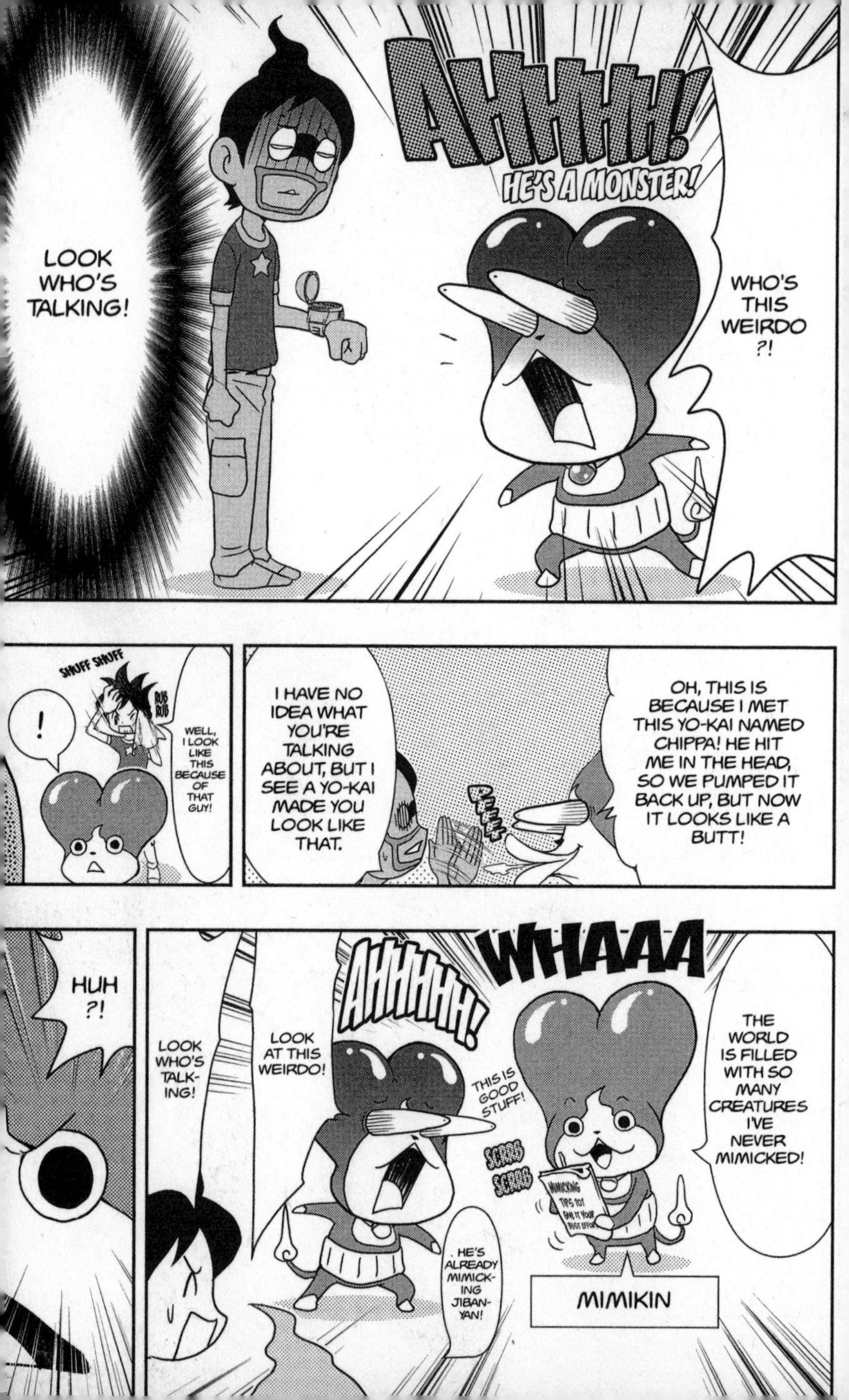
AHHHH! HE'S A MONSTER!
WHO'S THIS WEIRDO ?!
LOOK WHO'S TALKING!
OH, THIS IS BECAUSE I MET THIS YO-KAI NAMED CHIPPA! HE HIT ME IN THE HEAD, SO WE PUMPED IT BACK UP, BUT NOW IT LOOKS LIKE A BUTT!
I HAVE NO IDEA WHAT YOU'RE TALKING ABOUT, BUT I SEE A YO-KAI MADE YOU LOOK LIKE THAT.
SHUFF SHUFF
RUB RUB
WELL, I LOOK LIKE THIS BECAUSE OF THAT GUY!
!
WHAAAA
THE WORLD IS FILLED WITH SO MANY CREATURES I'VE NEVER MIMICKED!
AHHHHH!
LOOK AT THIS WEIRDO!
THIS IS GOOD STUFF!
MIMICKING TIPS 101
LOOK WHO'S TALK-ING!
HE'S ALREADY MIMICK-ING JIBAN-YAN!
MIMIKIN
HUH ?!

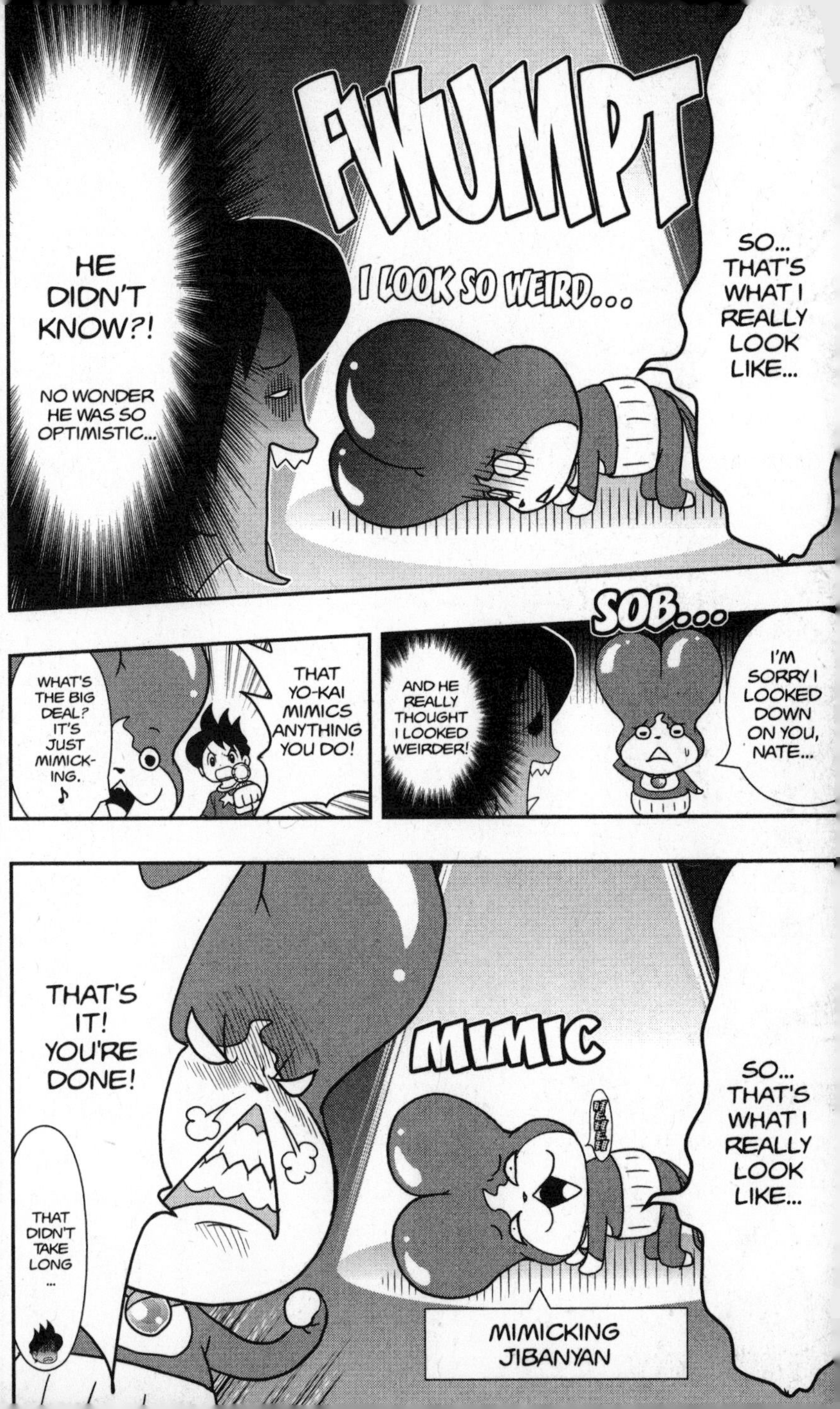
FWUMPT
SO... THAT'S WHAT I REALLY LOOK LIKE...
I LOOK SO WEIRD...
HE DIDN'T KNOW?!
NO WONDER HE WAS SO OPTIMISTIC...
SOB...
I'M SORRY I LOOKED DOWN ON YOU, NATE...
AND HE REALLY THOUGHT I LOOKED WEIRDER!
THAT YO-KAI MIMICS ANYTHING YOU DO!
WHAT'S THE BIG DEAL? IT'S JUST MIMICK-ING. ♪
MIMIC
SO... THAT'S WHAT I REALLY LOOK LIKE...
THAT'S IT! YOU'RE DONE!
MIMICKING JIBANYAN
THAT DIDN'T TAKE LONG...

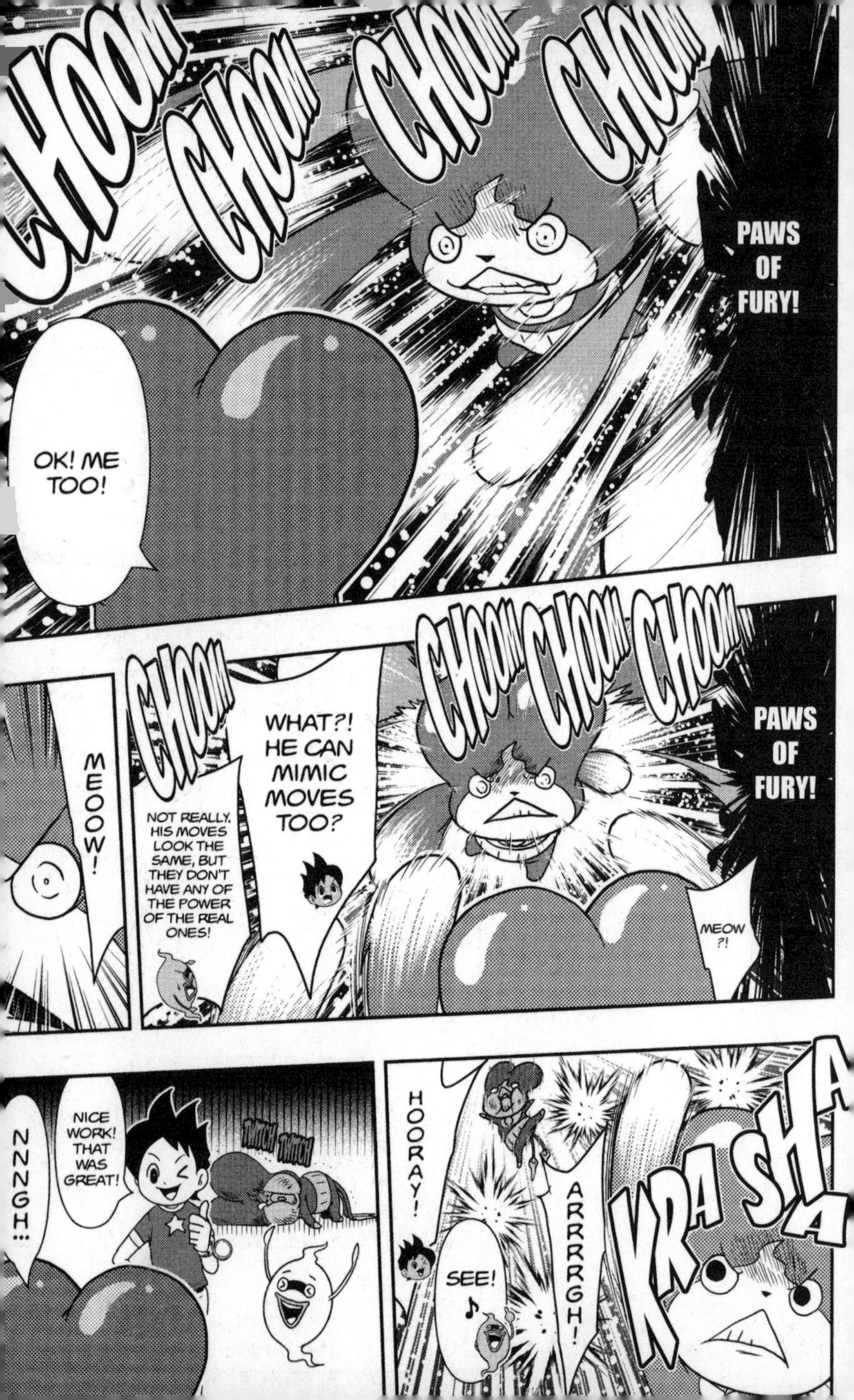
PAWS OF FURY!
CHOOM CHOOM CHOOM CHOOM
OK! ME TOO!
PAWS OF FURY!
CHOOM CHOOM CHOOM
MEOW ?!
WHAT?! HE CAN MIMIC MOVES TOO?
NOT REALLY. HIS MOVES LOOK THE SAME, BUT THEY DON'T HAVE ANY OF THE POWER OF THE REAL ONES!
CHOOM
MEOOOW!
KRASHA
ARRRRGH!
HOORAY!
SEE! ♪
NICE WORK! THAT WAS GREAT!
TWITCH TWITCH
NNNGH!!

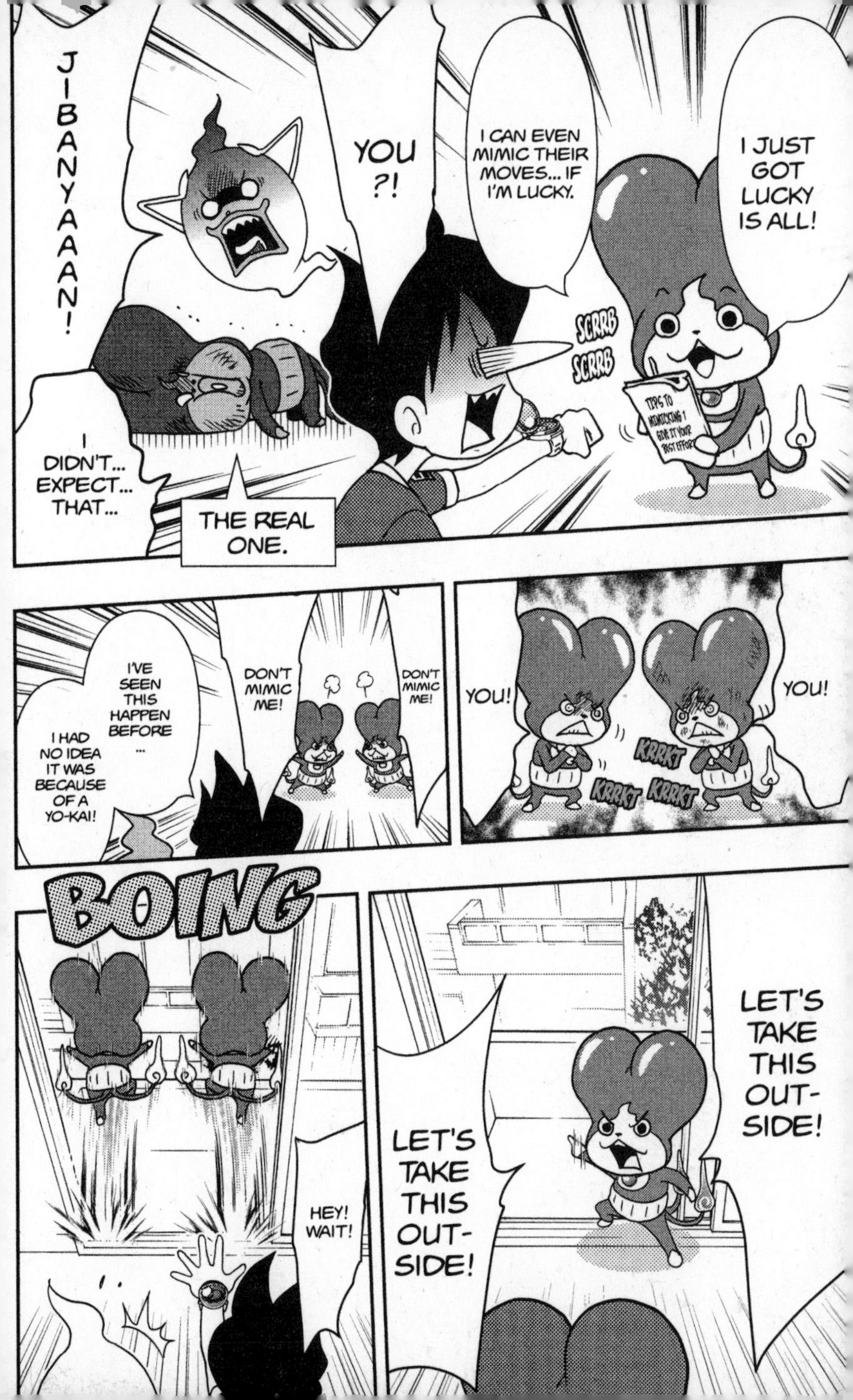
I JUST GOT LUCKY IS ALL!
I CAN EVEN MIMIC THEIR MOVES... IF I'M LUCKY.
SCRRB SCRRB
YOU ?!
JIBANYAAAAN!
THE REAL ONE.
I DIDN'T... EXPECT... THAT...
YOU!
YOU!
KRRKT KRRKT KRRKT
DON'T MIMIC ME!
DON'T MIMIC ME!
I'VE SEEN THIS HAPPEN BEFORE...
I HAD NO IDEA IT WAS BECAUSE OF A YO-KAI!
LET'S TAKE THIS OUT-SIDE!
LET'S TAKE THIS OUT-SIDE!
BOING
HEY! WAIT!

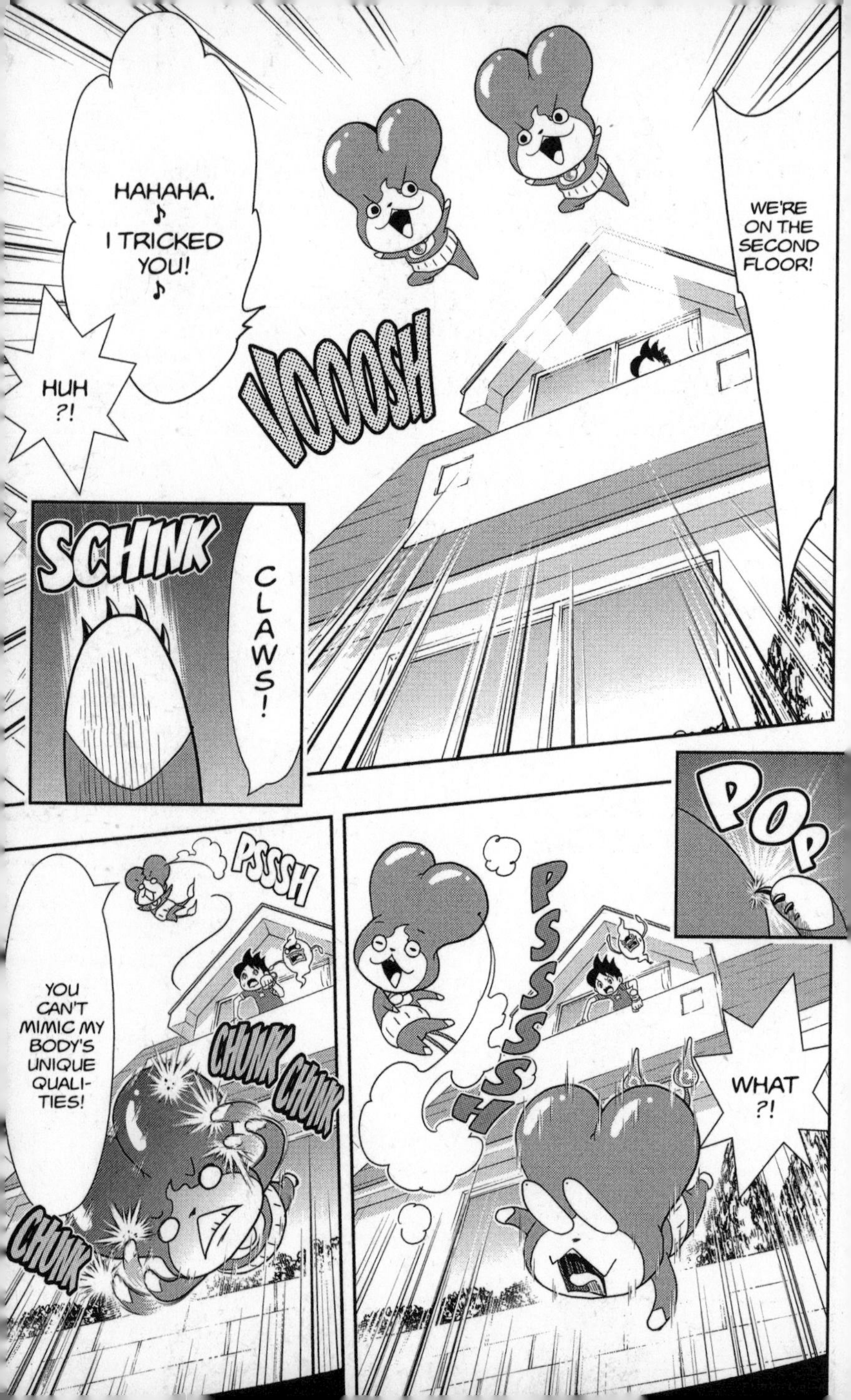
WE'RE ON THE SECOND FLOOR!
VOOOSH
HAHAHA. ♪ I TRICKED YOU! ♪
HUH ?!
CLAWS!
SCHINK
POP
PSSSSH
WHAT ?!
PSSSH
YOU CAN'T MIMIC MY BODY'S UNIQUE QUALI-TIES!
CHUNK CHUNK
CHUNK

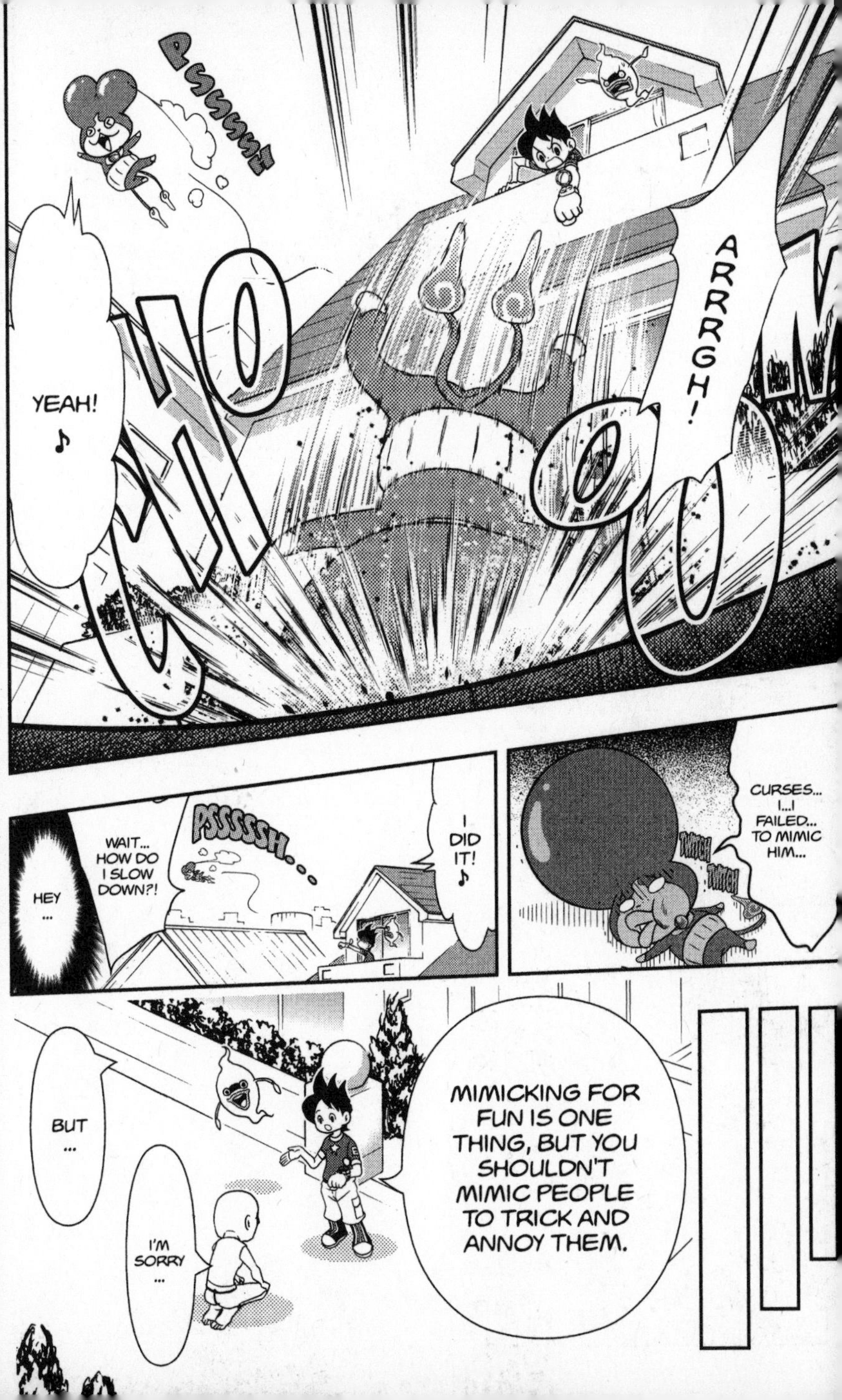
PSSSSSH!
ARRRGH!
YEAH! ♪
CURSES... I...I FAILED... TO MIMIC HIM...
TWITCH
TWITCH
I DID IT! ♪
PSSSSSH...
WAIT... HOW DO I SLOW DOWN?!
HEY ...
MIMICKING FOR FUN IS ONE THING, BUT YOU SHOULDN'T MIMIC PEOPLE TO TRICK AND ANNOY THEM.
BUT ...
I'M SORRY ...

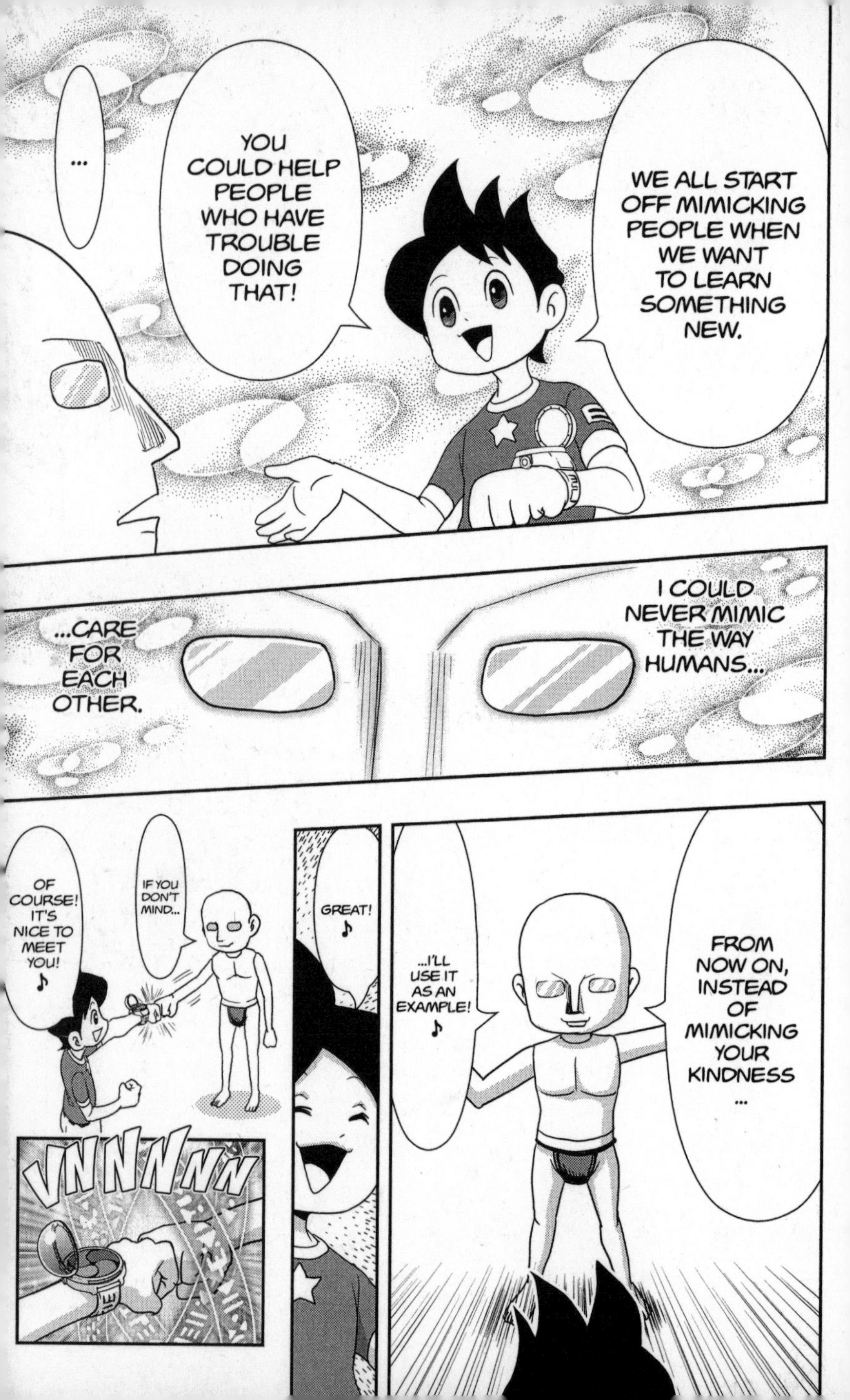
WE ALL START OFF MIMICKING PEOPLE WHEN WE WANT TO LEARN SOMETHING NEW.
YOU COULD HELP PEOPLE WHO HAVE TROUBLE DOING THAT!
...
I COULD NEVER MIMIC THE WAY HUMANS...
...CARE FOR EACH OTHER.
FROM NOW ON, INSTEAD OF MIMICKING YOUR KINDNESS ...
...I'LL USE IT AS AN EXAMPLE! ♪
GREAT! ♪
IF YOU DON'T MIND...
OF COURSE! IT'S NICE TO MEET YOU! ♪
VNNNNNN

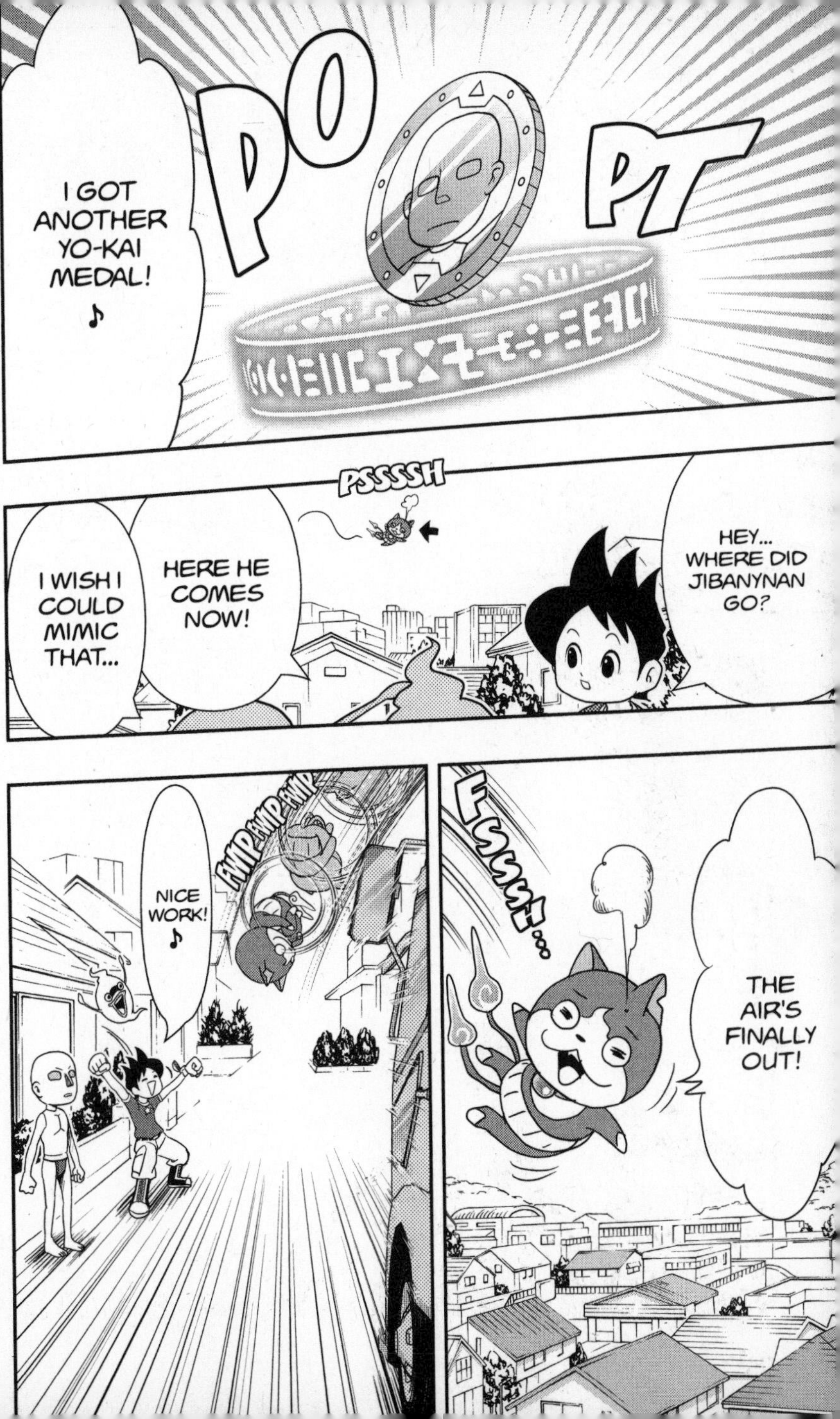
POOPT
I GOT ANOTHER YO-KAI MEDAL! ♪
HEY... WHERE DID JIBANYNAN GO?
PSSSSH
HERE HE COMES NOW!
I WISH I COULD MIMIC THAT...
FSSSSH...
THE AIR'S FINALLY OUT!
FWIP FWIP FWIP
NICE WORK! ♪

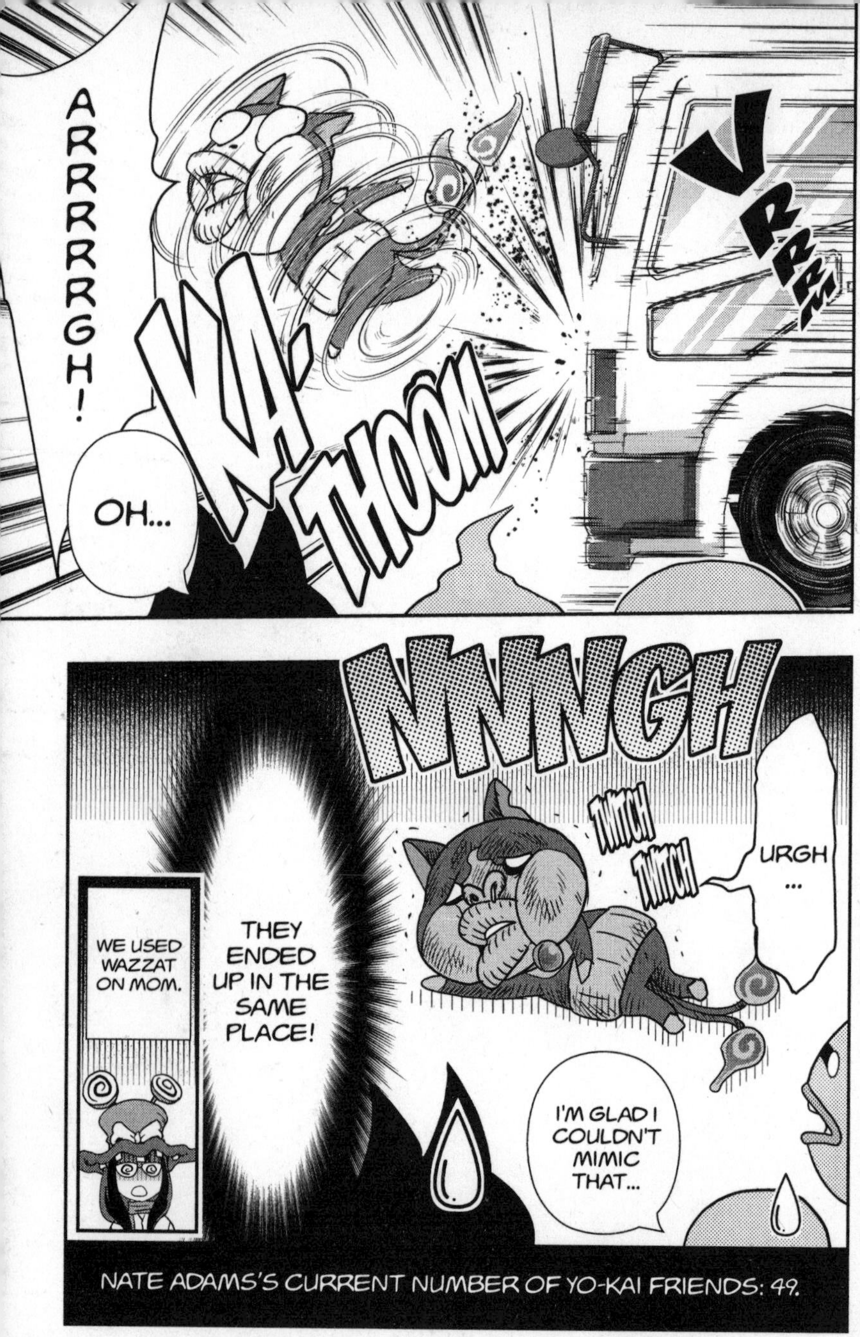
VRRRM
KA-THOOM
ARRRRRGH!
OH...
NNNNGH
TWITCH
TWITCH
URGH ...
THEY ENDED UP IN THE SAME PLACE!
I'M GLAD I COULDN'T MIMIC THAT...
WE USED WAZZAT ON MOM.
NATE ADAMS'S CURRENT NUMBER OF YO-KAI FRIENDS: 49.

# CHAPTER 66

# YO-KAI BUTLER WHISPER'S STARTLING SECRET!

## FEATURING KNOW-IT-ALL YO-KAI NONUTTIN

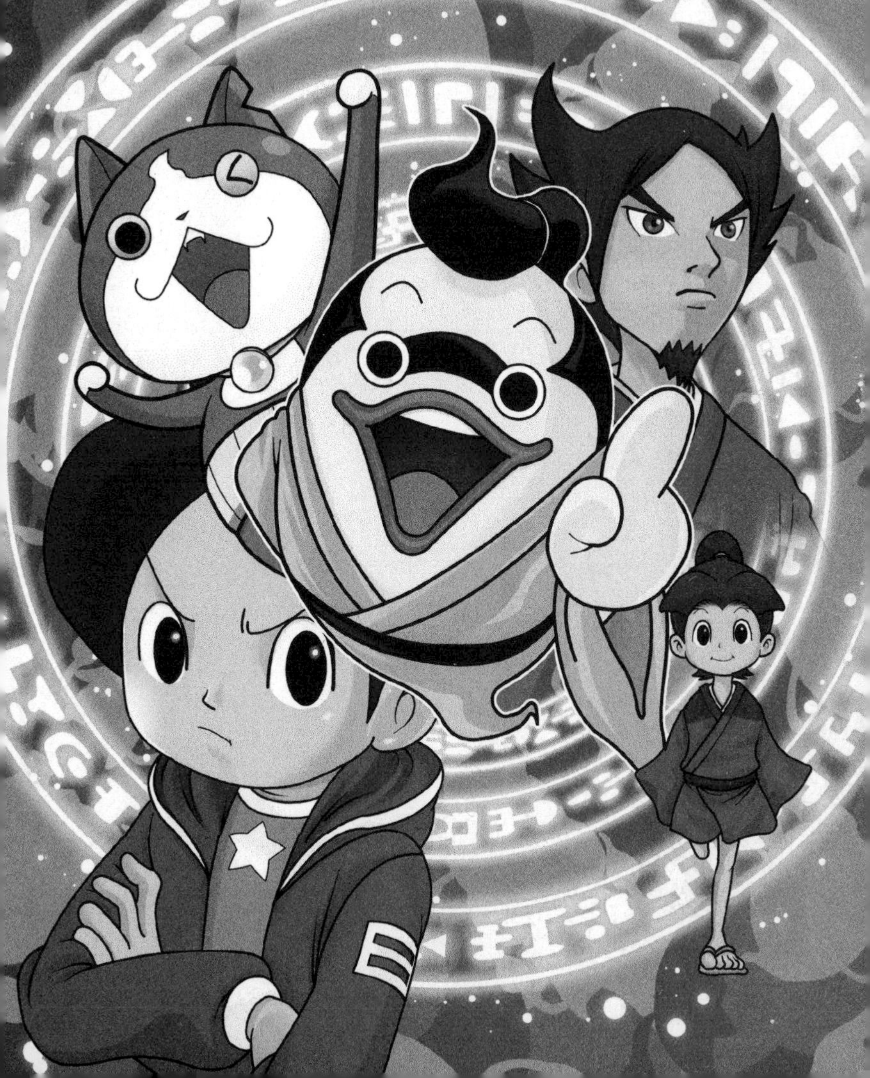

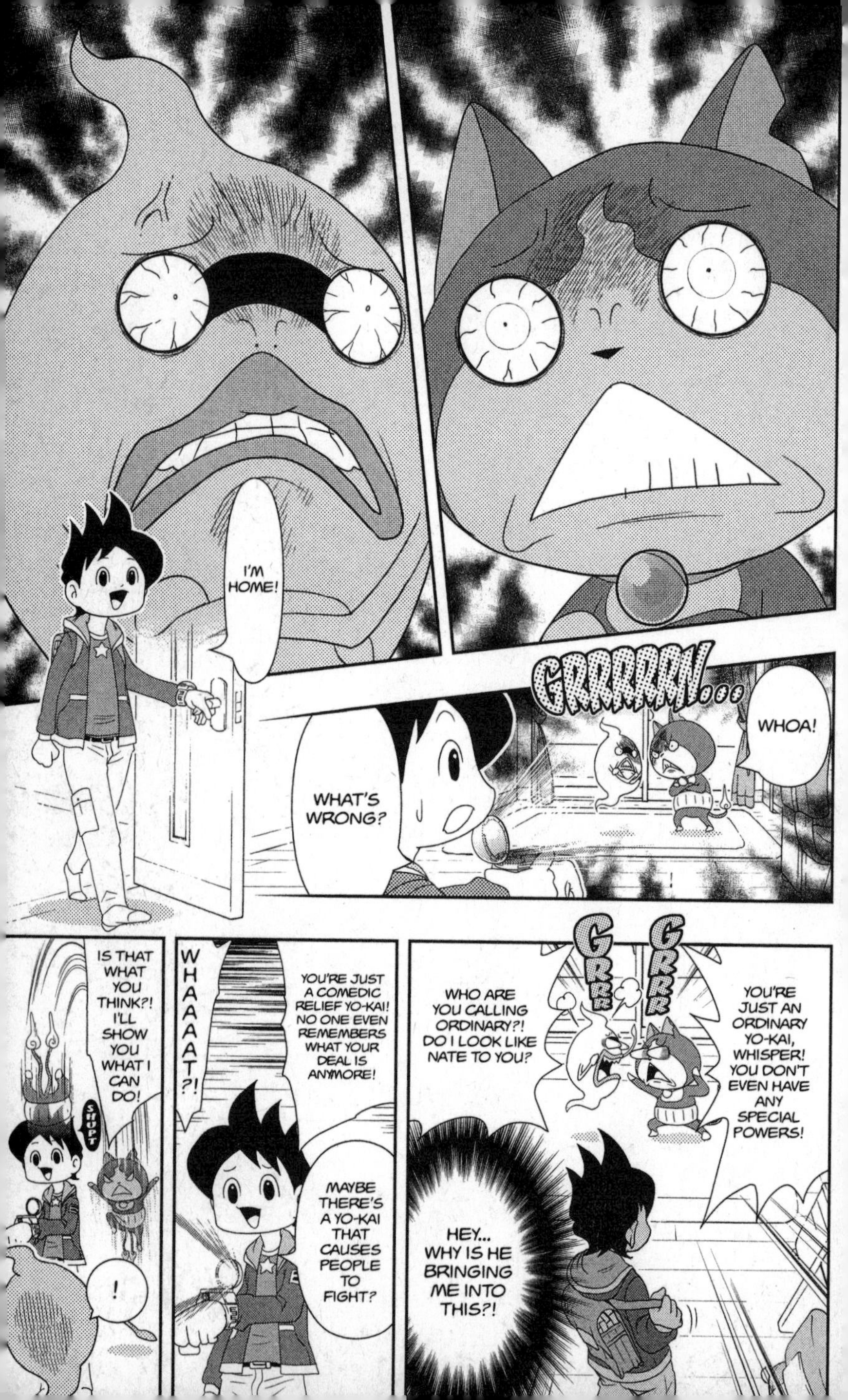
I'M HOME!
GRRRRRN...
WHOA!
WHAT'S WRONG?
YOU'RE JUST AN ORDINARY YO-KAI, WHISPER! YOU DON'T EVEN HAVE ANY SPECIAL POWERS!
GRRR
GRRR
WHO ARE YOU CALLING ORDINARY?! DO I LOOK LIKE NATE TO YOU?
HEY... WHY IS HE BRINGING ME INTO THIS?!
YOU'RE JUST A COMEDIC RELIEF YO-KAI! NO ONE EVEN REMEMBERS WHAT YOUR DEAL IS ANYMORE!
WHAAAAAT?!
MAYBE THERE'S A YO-KAI THAT CAUSES PEOPLE TO FIGHT?
IS THAT WHAT YOU THINK?! I'LL SHOW YOU WHAT I CAN DO!
SHUPT
!

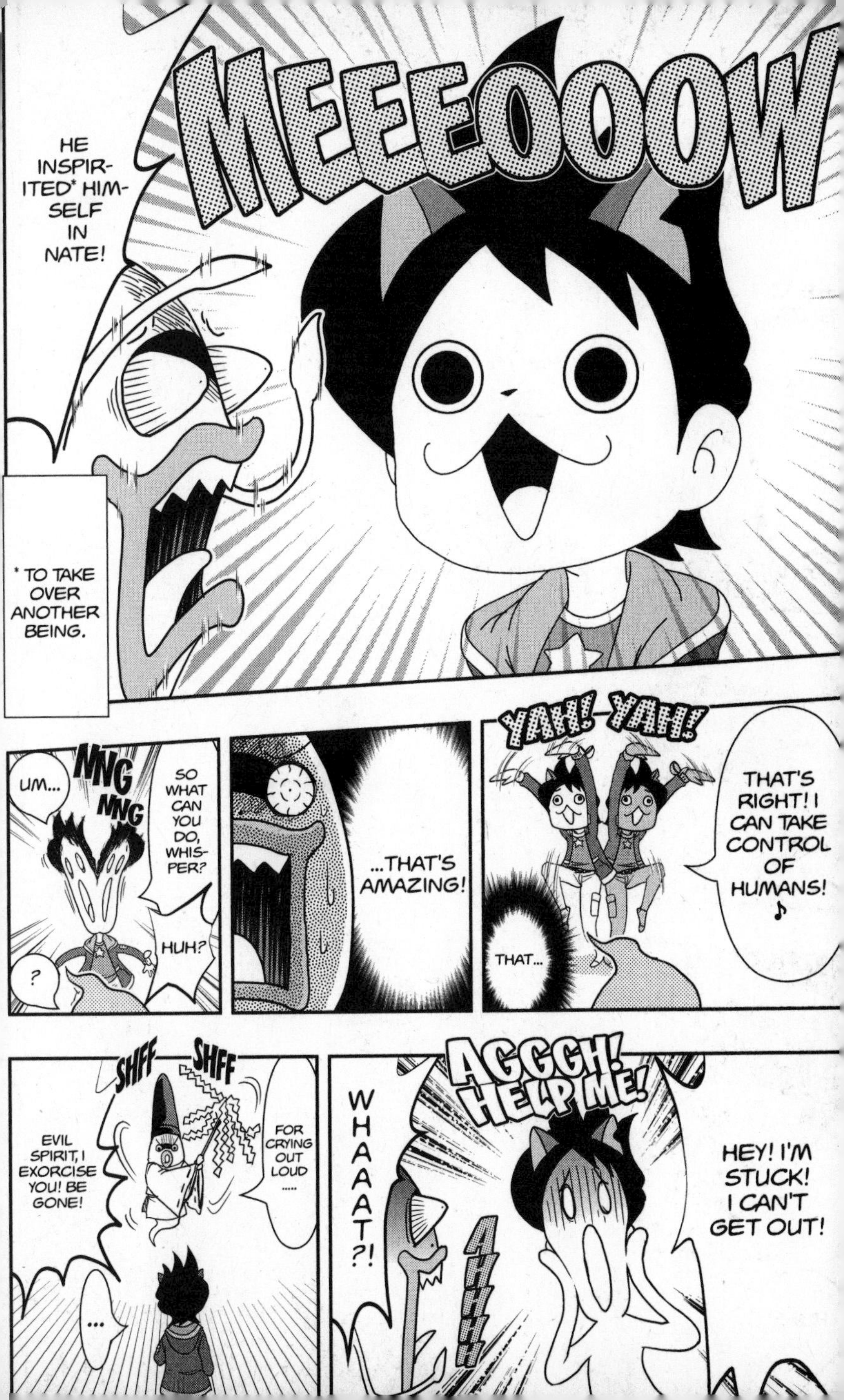
MEEEOOOW
HE INSPIRITED* HIMSELF IN NATE!
* TO TAKE OVER ANOTHER BEING.
YAH! YAH!
THAT'S RIGHT! I CAN TAKE CONTROL OF HUMANS! ♪
THAT...
...THAT'S AMAZING!
SO WHAT CAN YOU DO, WHISPER?
NNG NNG
UM...
HUH?
?
AGGGH! HELP ME!
HEY! I'M STUCK! I CAN'T GET OUT!
WHAAAT?!
FOR CRYING OUT LOUD.....
SHFF SHFF
EVIL SPIRIT, I EXORCISE YOU! BE GONE!
...

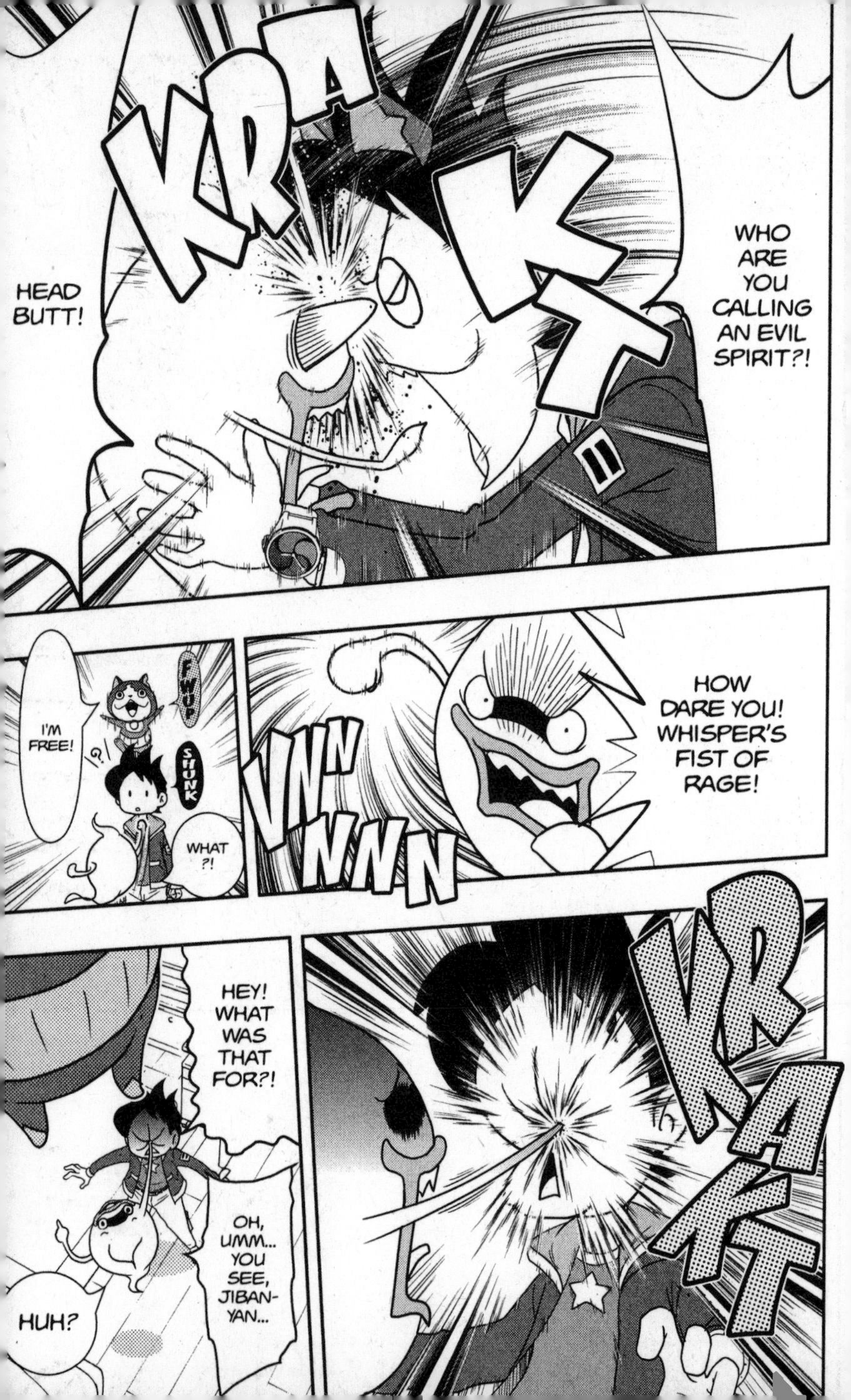
WHO ARE YOU CALLING AN EVIL SPIRIT?!
KRAKT
HEAD BUTT!
HOW DARE YOU! WHISPER'S FIST OF RAGE!
VNNN NNNN
FWUP
SHUNK
I'M FREE!
?
WHAT ?!
KRAKT
HEY! WHAT WAS THAT FOR?!
OH, UMM... YOU SEE, JIBAN-YAN...
HUH?

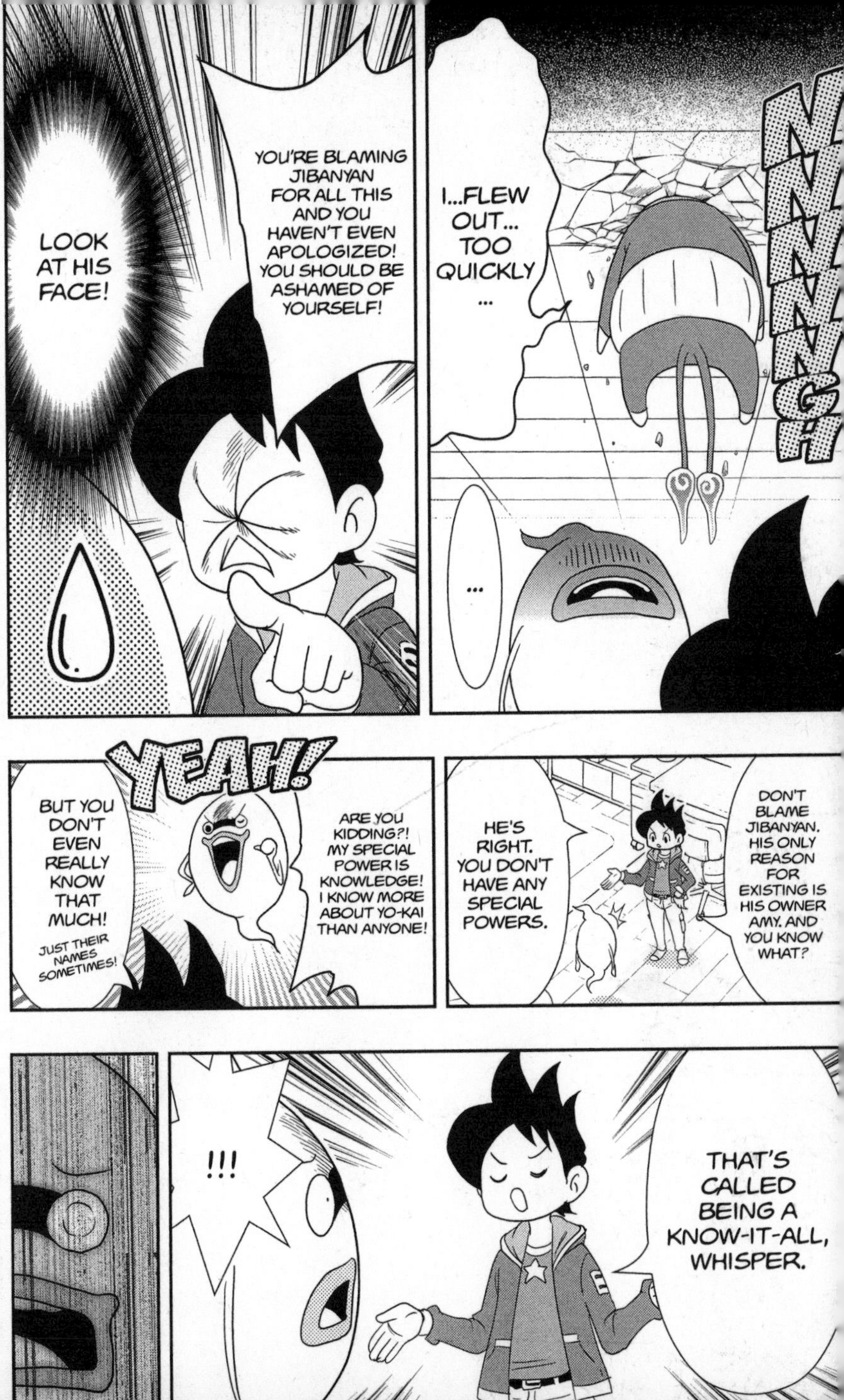
NNNNNGH
I...FLEW OUT... TOO QUICKLY ...
...
YOU'RE BLAMING JIBANYAN FOR ALL THIS AND YOU HAVEN'T EVEN APOLOGIZED! YOU SHOULD BE ASHAMED OF YOURSELF!
LOOK AT HIS FACE!
DON'T BLAME JIBANYAN. HIS ONLY REASON FOR EXISTING IS HIS OWNER AMY. AND YOU KNOW WHAT?
HE'S RIGHT. YOU DON'T HAVE ANY SPECIAL POWERS.
ARE YOU KIDDING?! MY SPECIAL POWER IS KNOWLEDGE! I KNOW MORE ABOUT YO-KAI THAN ANYONE!
YEAH!
BUT YOU DON'T EVEN REALLY KNOW THAT MUCH!
JUST THEIR NAMES SOMETIMES!
THAT'S CALLED BEING A KNOW-IT-ALL, WHISPER.
!!!

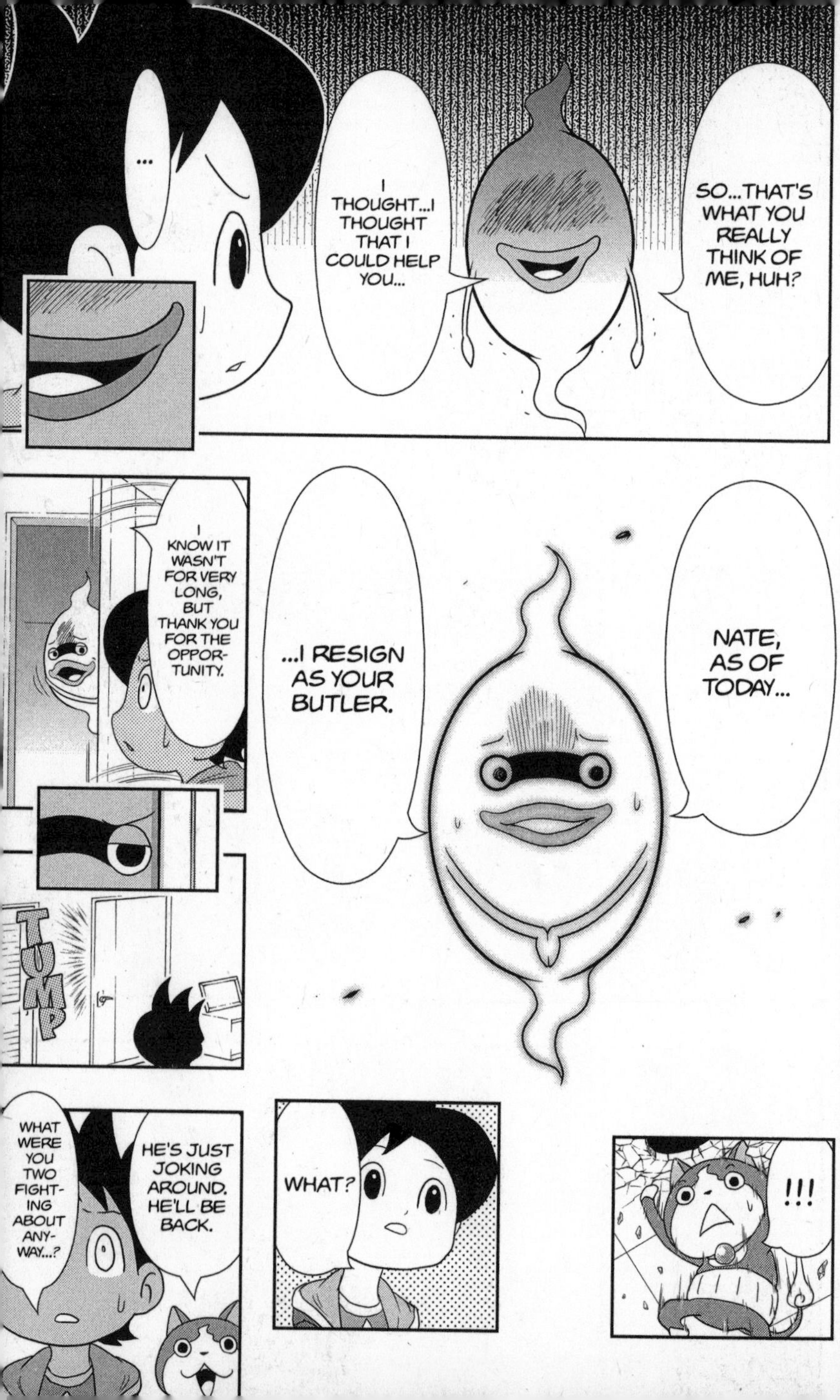
SO...THAT'S WHAT YOU REALLY THINK OF ME, HUH?
I THOUGHT...I THOUGHT THAT I COULD HELP YOU...
...
NATE, AS OF TODAY...
...I RESIGN AS YOUR BUTLER.
I KNOW IT WASN'T FOR VERY LONG, BUT THANK YOU FOR THE OPPOR-TUNITY.
TUMP
!!!
WHAT?
HE'S JUST JOKING AROUND. HE'LL BE BACK.
WHAT WERE YOU TWO FIGHT-ING ABOUT ANY-WAY...?

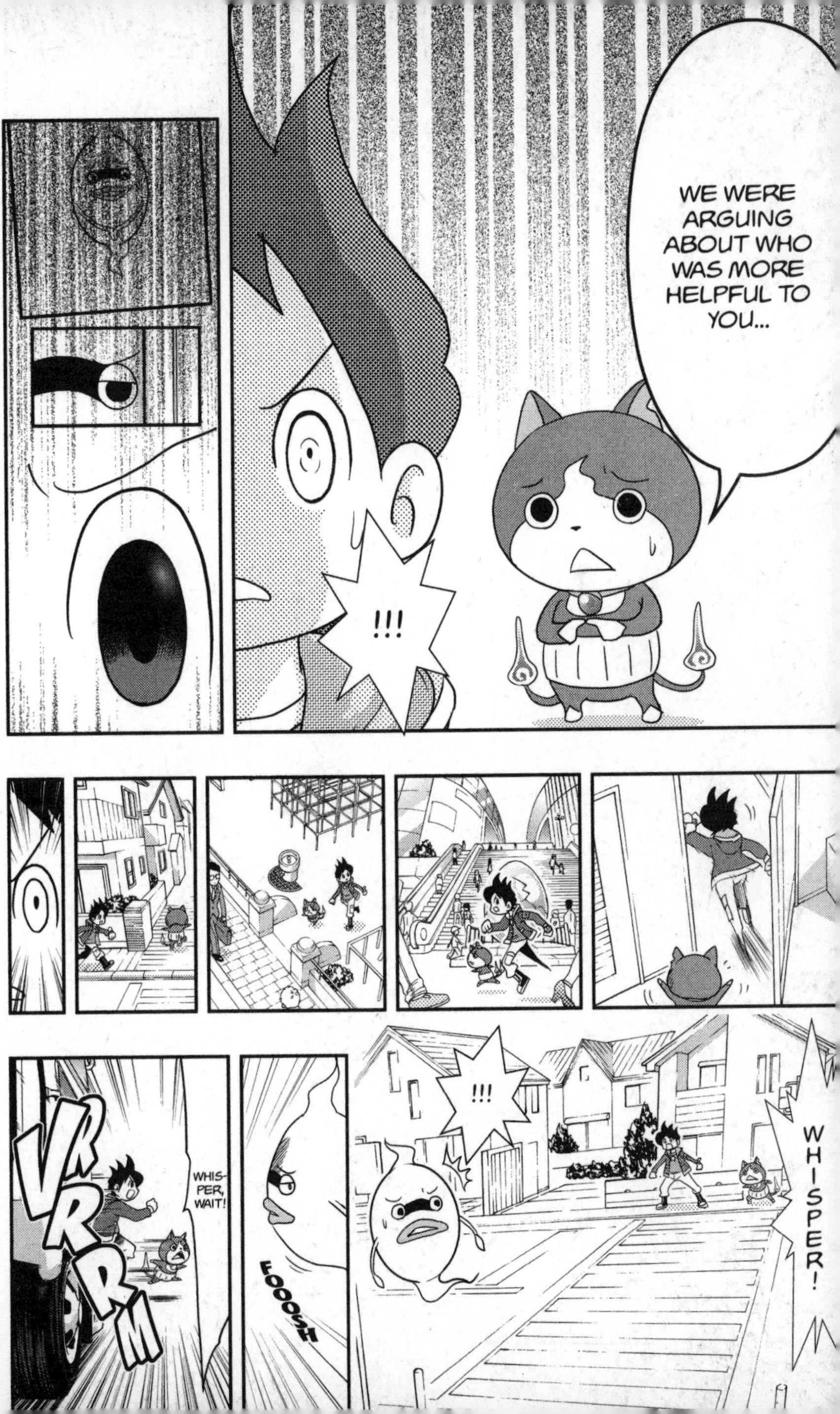
WE WERE ARGUING ABOUT WHO WAS MORE HELPFUL TO YOU...
!!!
WHISPER!
!!!
FOOOSH
WHIS-PER, WAIT!
VRRRM

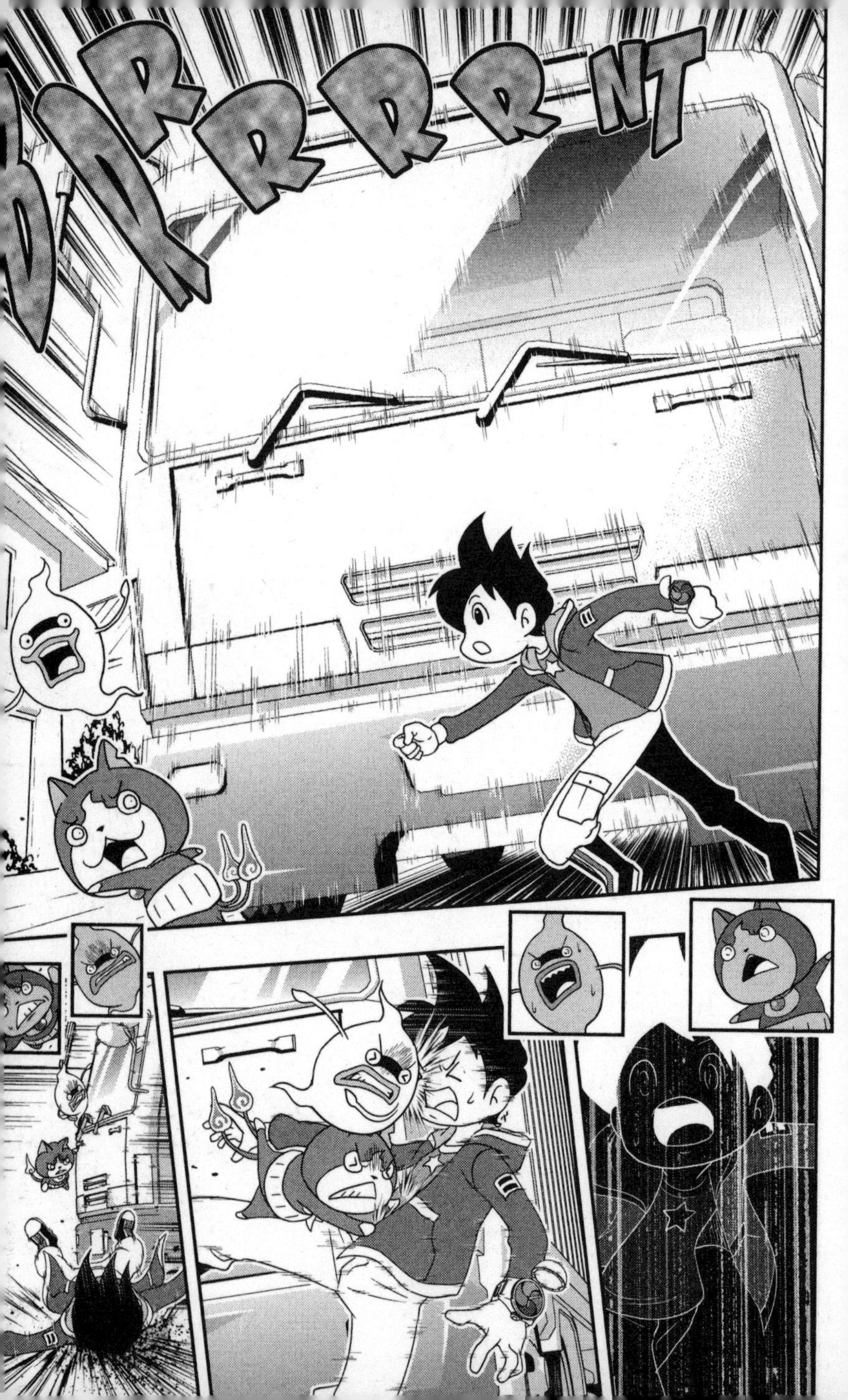
BRRRRNT

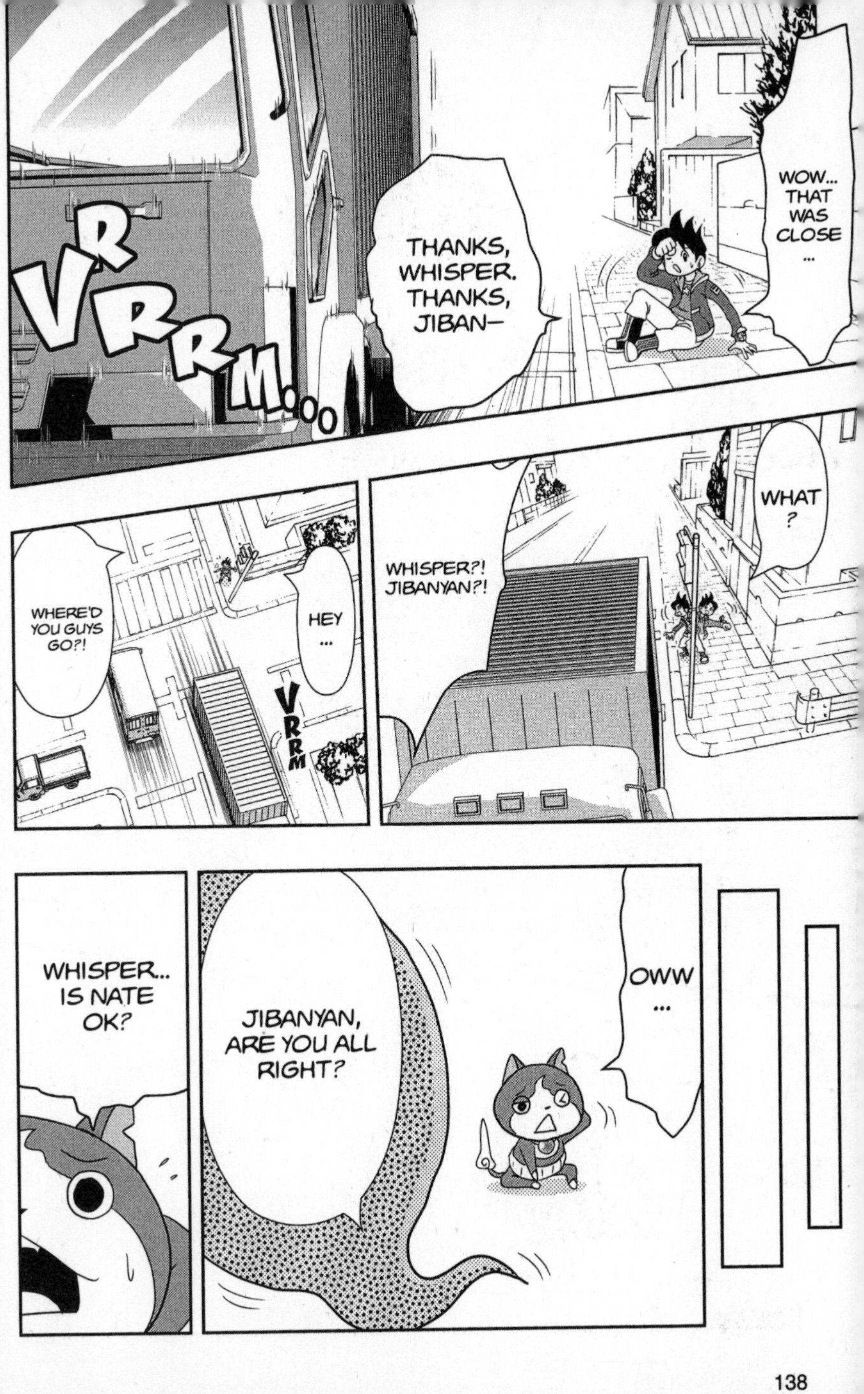
WOW... THAT WAS CLOSE ...
THANKS, WHISPER. THANKS, JIBAN—
VRRRM...
WHAT ?
WHISPER?! JIBANYAN?!
HEY ...
VRRM
WHERE'D YOU GUYS GO?!
OWW ...
JIBANYAN, ARE YOU ALL RIGHT?
WHISPER... IS NATE OK?

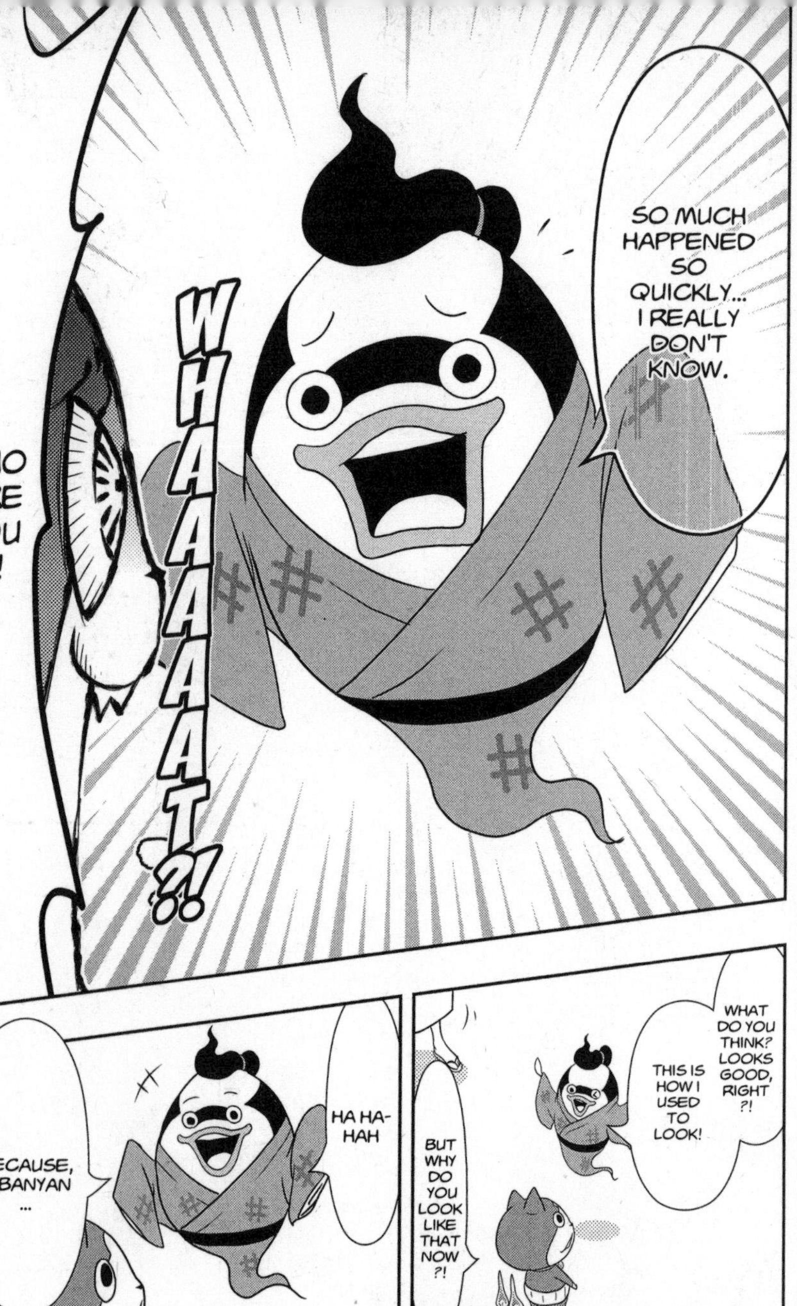
SO MUCH HAPPENED SO QUICKLY... I REALLY DON'T KNOW.
WHAAAAAT?!
WHO ARE YOU ?!
WHAT DO YOU THINK? LOOKS GOOD, RIGHT ?!
THIS IS HOW I USED TO LOOK!
BUT WHY DO YOU LOOK LIKE THAT NOW ?!
HA HA-HAH
BECAUSE, JIBANYAN ...

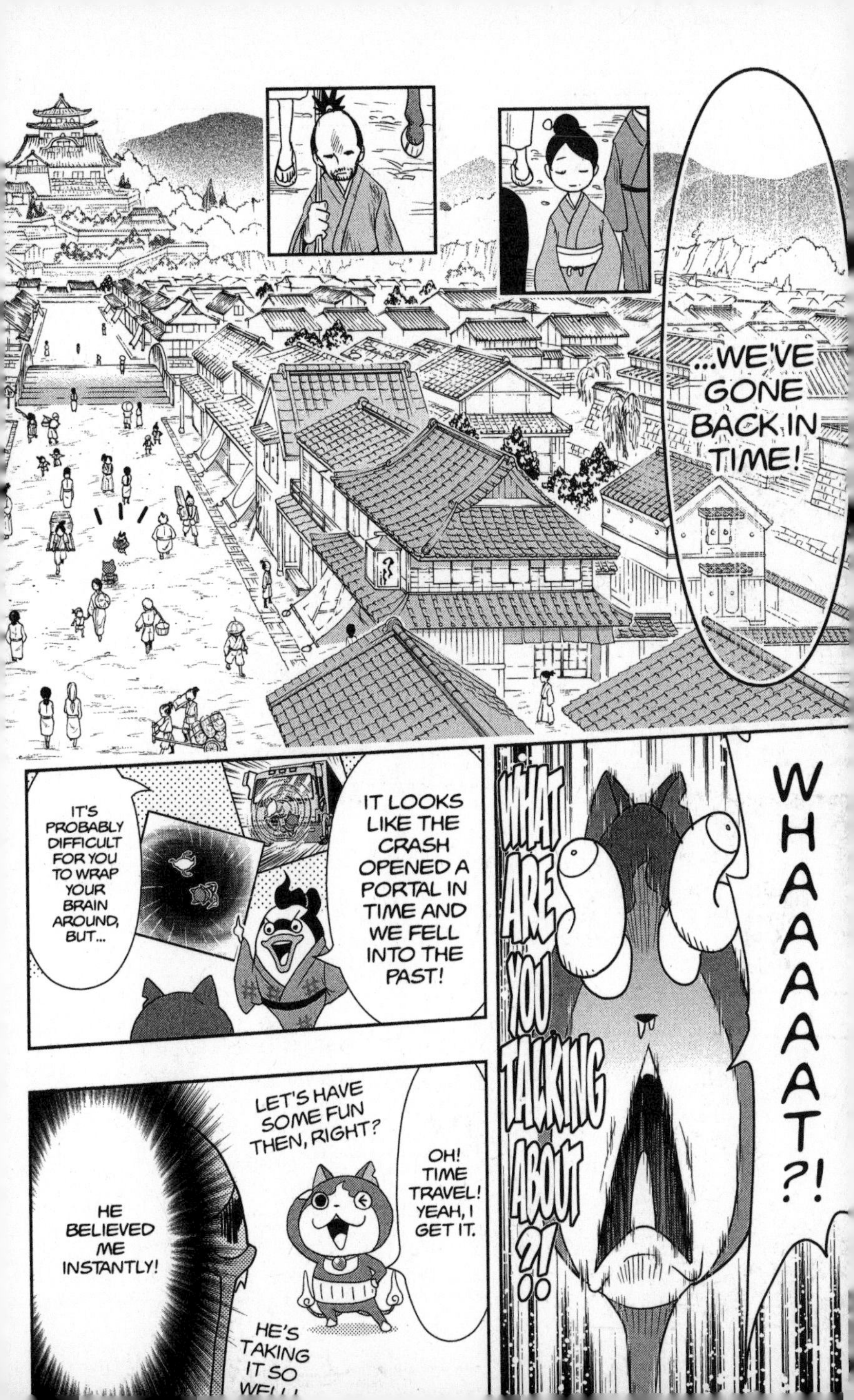
...WE'VE GONE BACK IN TIME!
WHAAAAAT?!
WHAT ARE YOU TALKING ABOUT?!
IT LOOKS LIKE THE CRASH OPENED A PORTAL IN TIME AND WE FELL INTO THE PAST!
IT'S PROBABLY DIFFICULT FOR YOU TO WRAP YOUR BRAIN AROUND, BUT...
LET'S HAVE SOME FUN THEN, RIGHT?
OH! TIME TRAVEL! YEAH, I GET IT.
HE BELIEVED ME INSTANTLY!
HE'S TAKING IT SO WELL

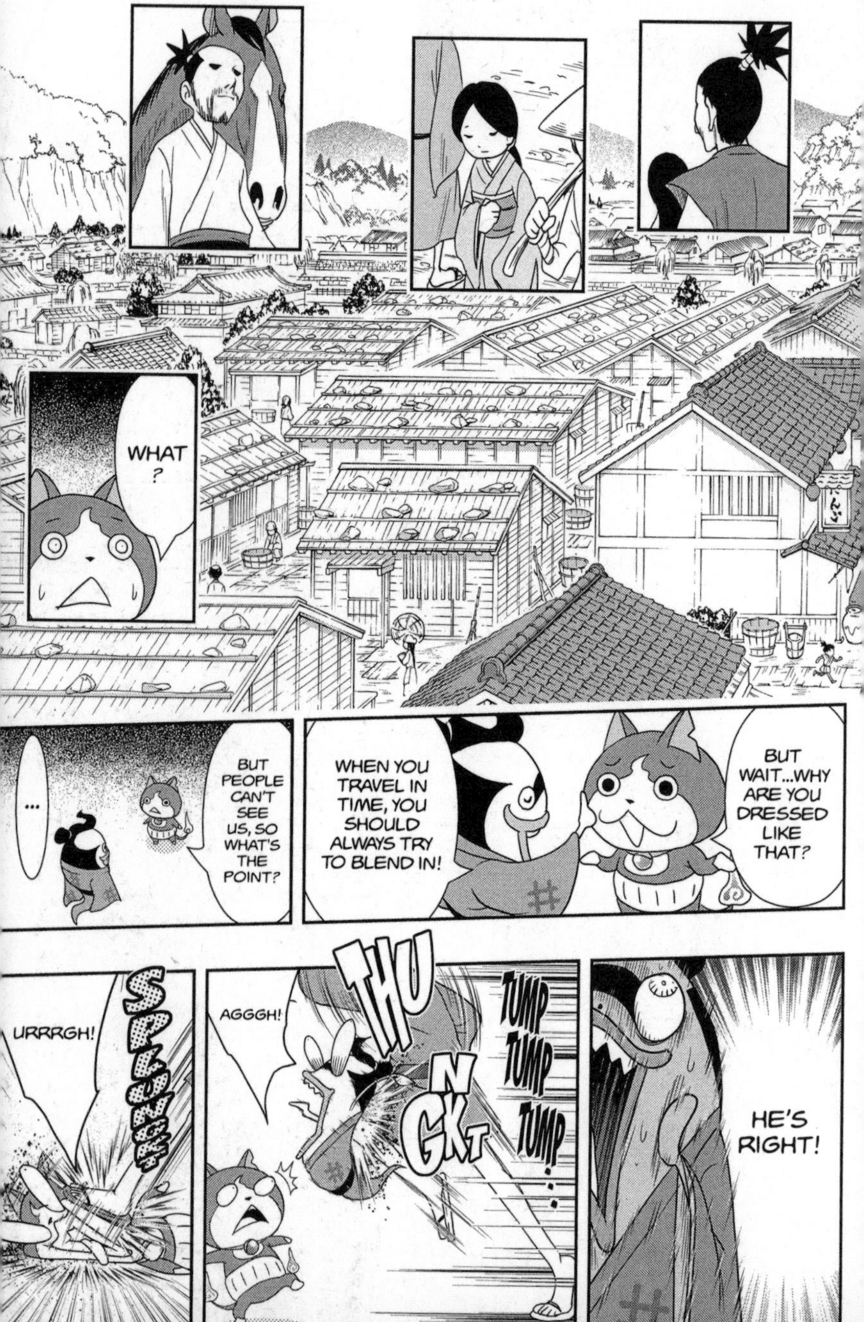
WHAT?
BUT WAIT...WHY ARE YOU DRESSED LIKE THAT?
WHEN YOU TRAVEL IN TIME, YOU SHOULD ALWAYS TRY TO BLEND IN!
BUT PEOPLE CAN'T SEE US, SO WHAT'S THE POINT?
...
HE'S RIGHT!
TUMP TUMP TUMP
THUNGK
AGGGH!
URRRGH!

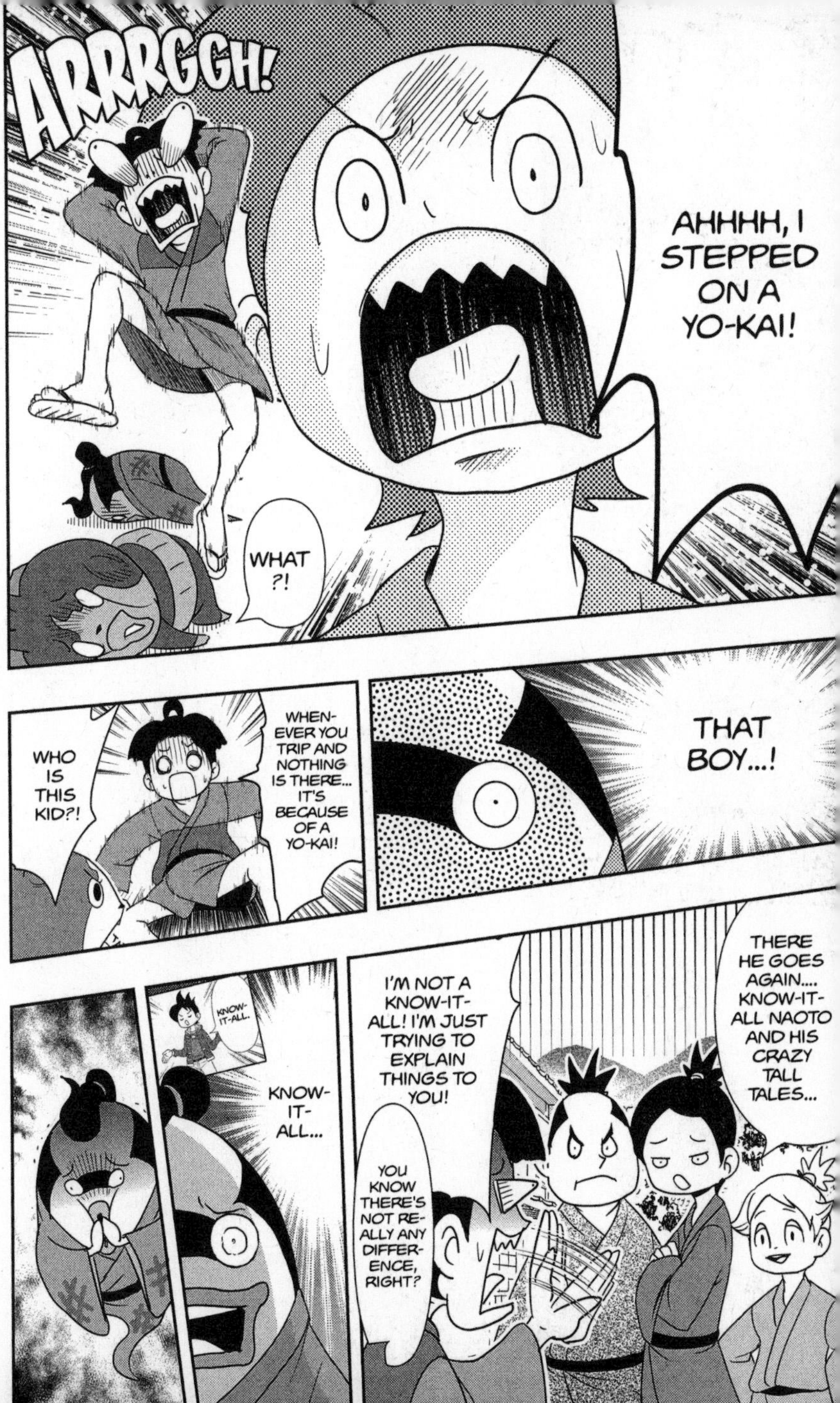
AHHHH, I STEPPED ON A YO-KAI!
ARRRGGH!
WHAT ?!
THAT BOY...!
WHENEVER YOU TRIP AND NOTHING IS THERE... IT'S BECAUSE OF A YO-KAI!
WHO IS THIS KID?!
THERE HE GOES AGAIN.... KNOW-IT-ALL NAOTO AND HIS CRAZY TALL TALES...
I'M NOT A KNOW-IT-ALL! I'M JUST TRYING TO EXPLAIN THINGS TO YOU!
YOU KNOW THERE'S NOT REALLY ANY DIFFERENCE, RIGHT?
KNOW-IT-ALL.
KNOW-IT-ALL...

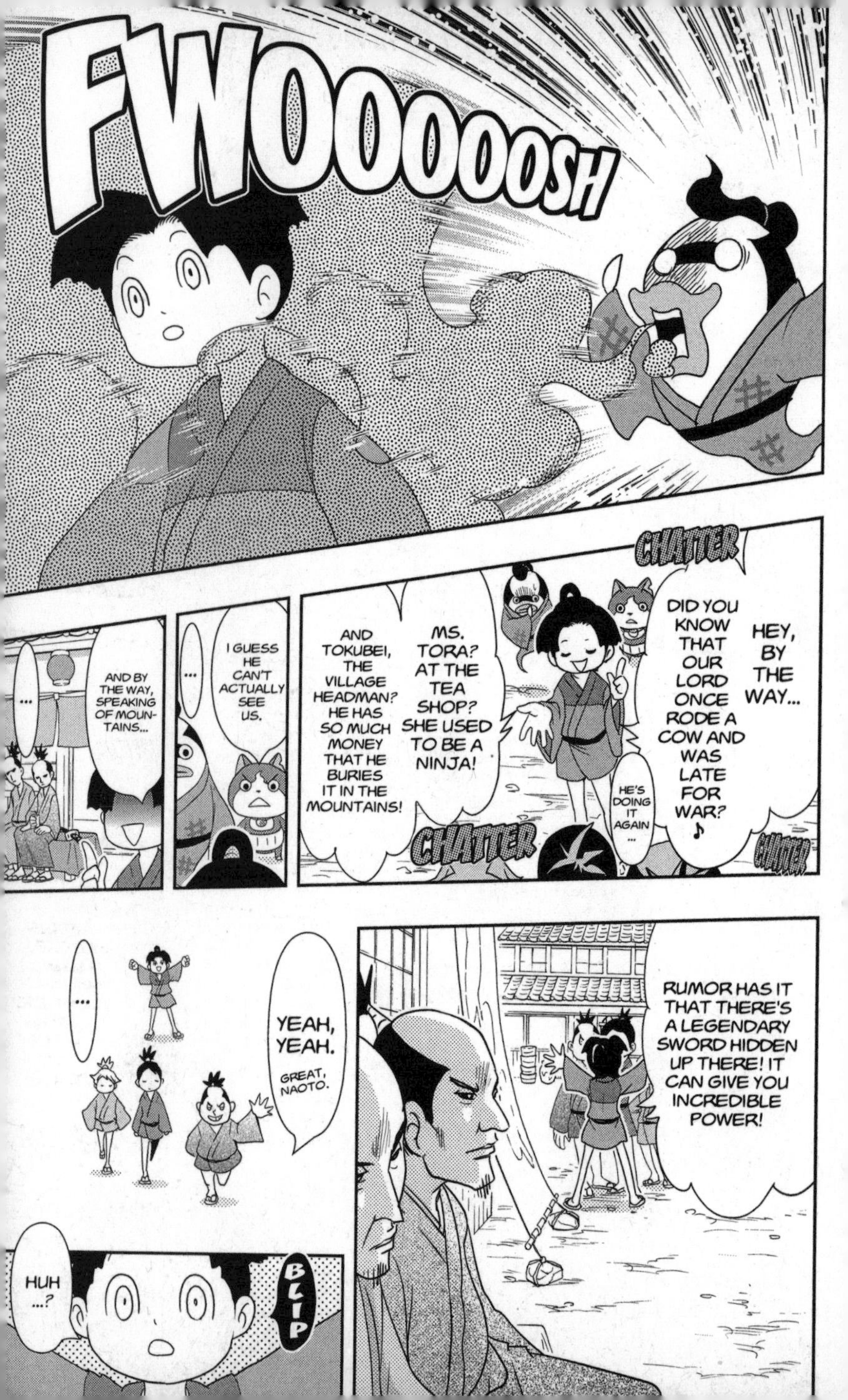
FWOOOOOSH
CHATTER
HEY, BY THE WAY...
DID YOU KNOW THAT OUR LORD ONCE RODE A COW AND WAS LATE FOR WAR? ♪
CHATTER
HE'S DOING IT AGAIN...
MS. TORA? AT THE TEA SHOP? SHE USED TO BE A NINJA!
AND TOKUBEI, THE VILLAGE HEADMAN? HE HAS SO MUCH MONEY THAT HE BURIES IT IN THE MOUNTAINS!
CHATTER
I GUESS HE CAN'T ACTUALLY SEE US.
...
AND BY THE WAY, SPEAKING OF MOUN-TAINS...
...
RUMOR HAS IT THAT THERE'S A LEGENDARY SWORD HIDDEN UP THERE! IT CAN GIVE YOU INCREDIBLE POWER!
YEAH, YEAH.
GREAT, NAOTO.
...
BLIP
HUH ...?

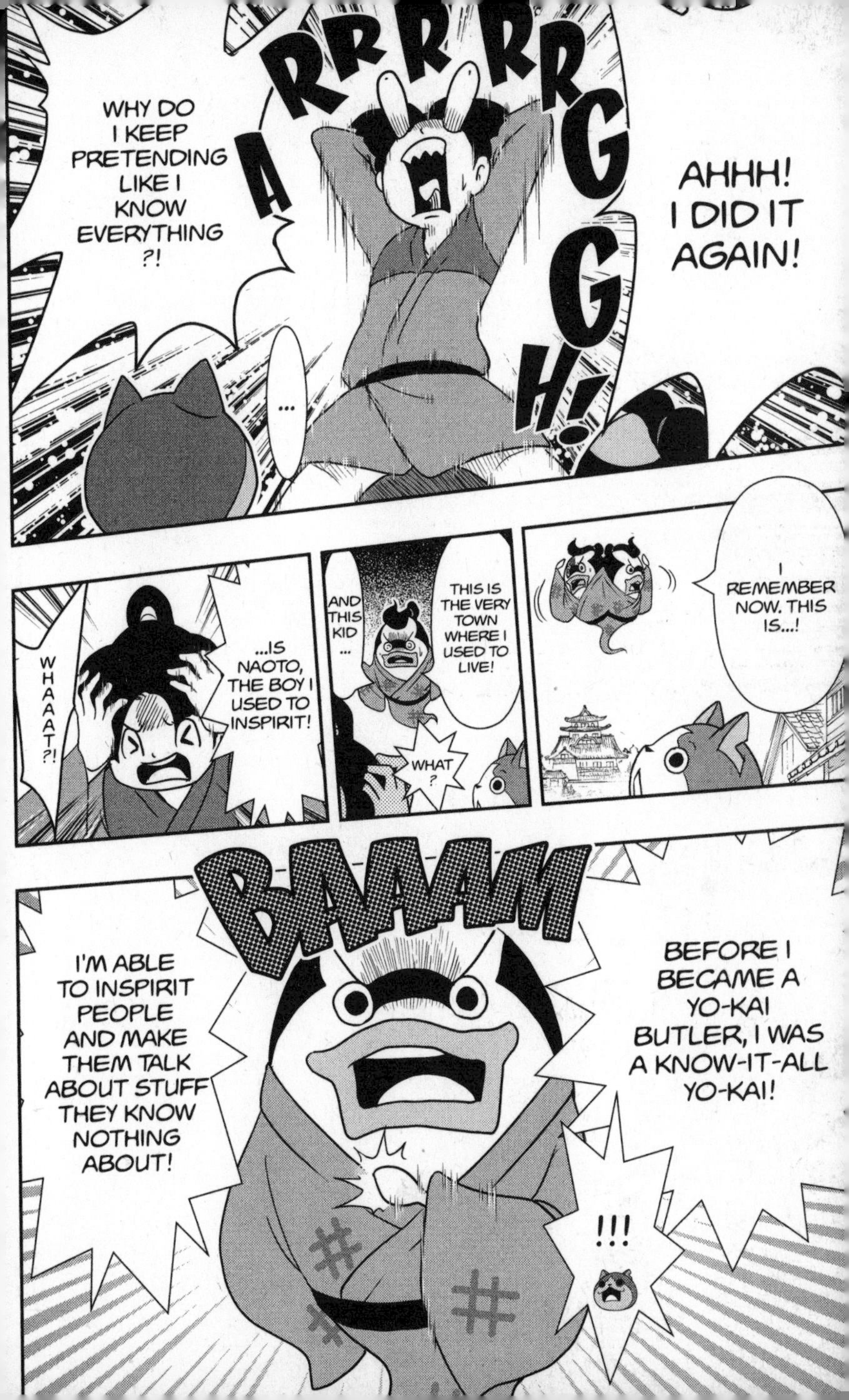
AHHH! I DID IT AGAIN!
ARRRRRGGH!
WHY DO I KEEP PRETENDING LIKE I KNOW EVERYTHING?!
...
I REMEMBER NOW. THIS IS...!
THIS IS THE VERY TOWN WHERE I USED TO LIVE!
AND THIS KID ...
WHAT?
...IS NAOTO, THE BOY I USED TO INSPIRIT!
WHAAAAT?!
BAAAM
BEFORE I BECAME A YO-KAI BUTLER, I WAS A KNOW-IT-ALL YO-KAI!
I'M ABLE TO INSPIRIT PEOPLE AND MAKE THEM TALK ABOUT STUFF THEY KNOW NOTHING ABOUT!
!!!

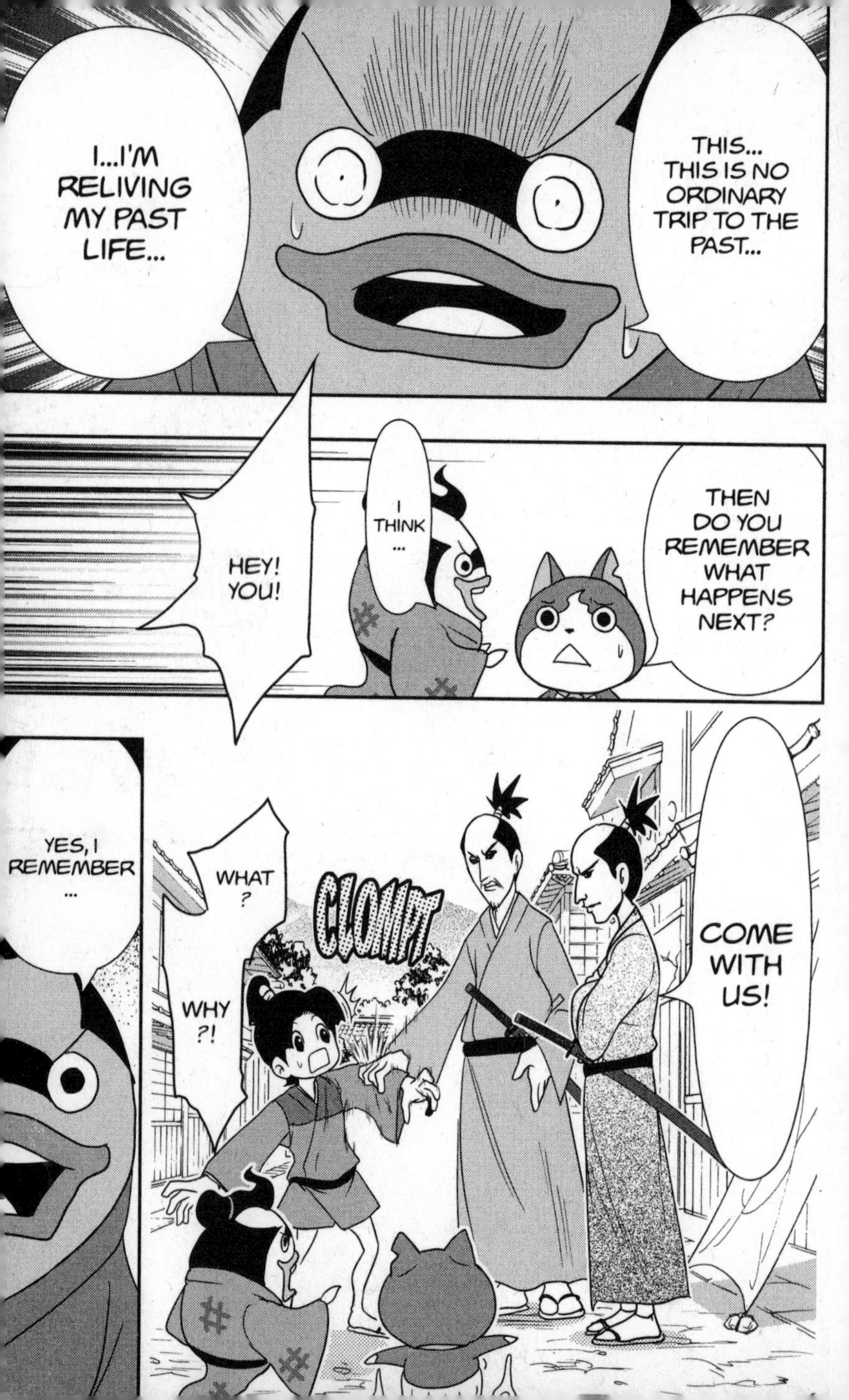
THIS... THIS IS NO ORDINARY TRIP TO THE PAST...
I...I'M RELIVING MY PAST LIFE...
THEN DO YOU REMEMBER WHAT HAPPENS NEXT?
I THINK ...
HEY! YOU!
COME WITH US!
CLOMP!
WHAT ?
WHY ?!
YES, I REMEMBER ...

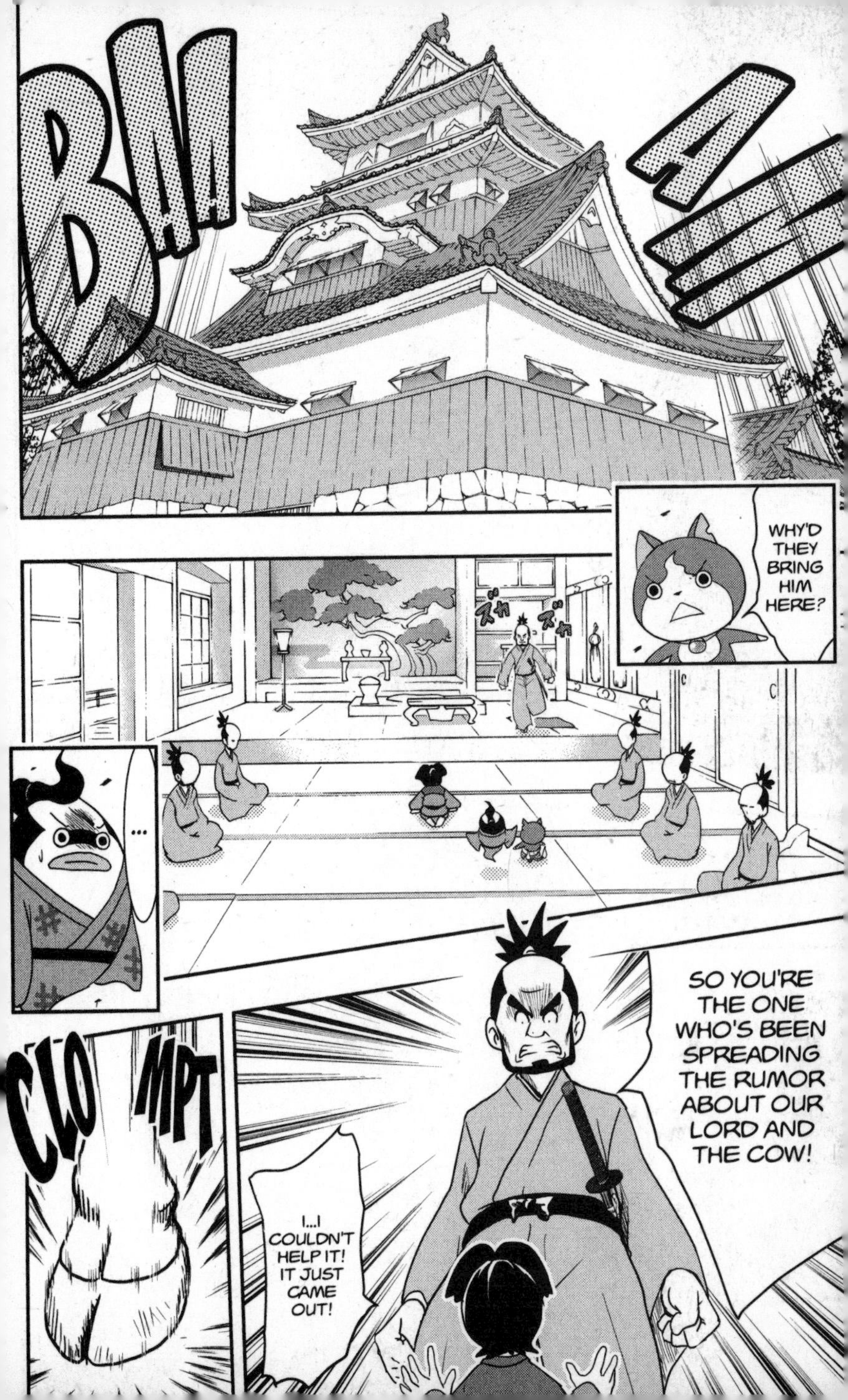
BAA
A
WHY'D THEY BRING HIM HERE?
...
SO YOU'RE THE ONE WHO'S BEEN SPREADING THE RUMOR ABOUT OUR LORD AND THE COW!
I...I COULDN'T HELP IT! IT JUST CAME OUT!
CLOMPT

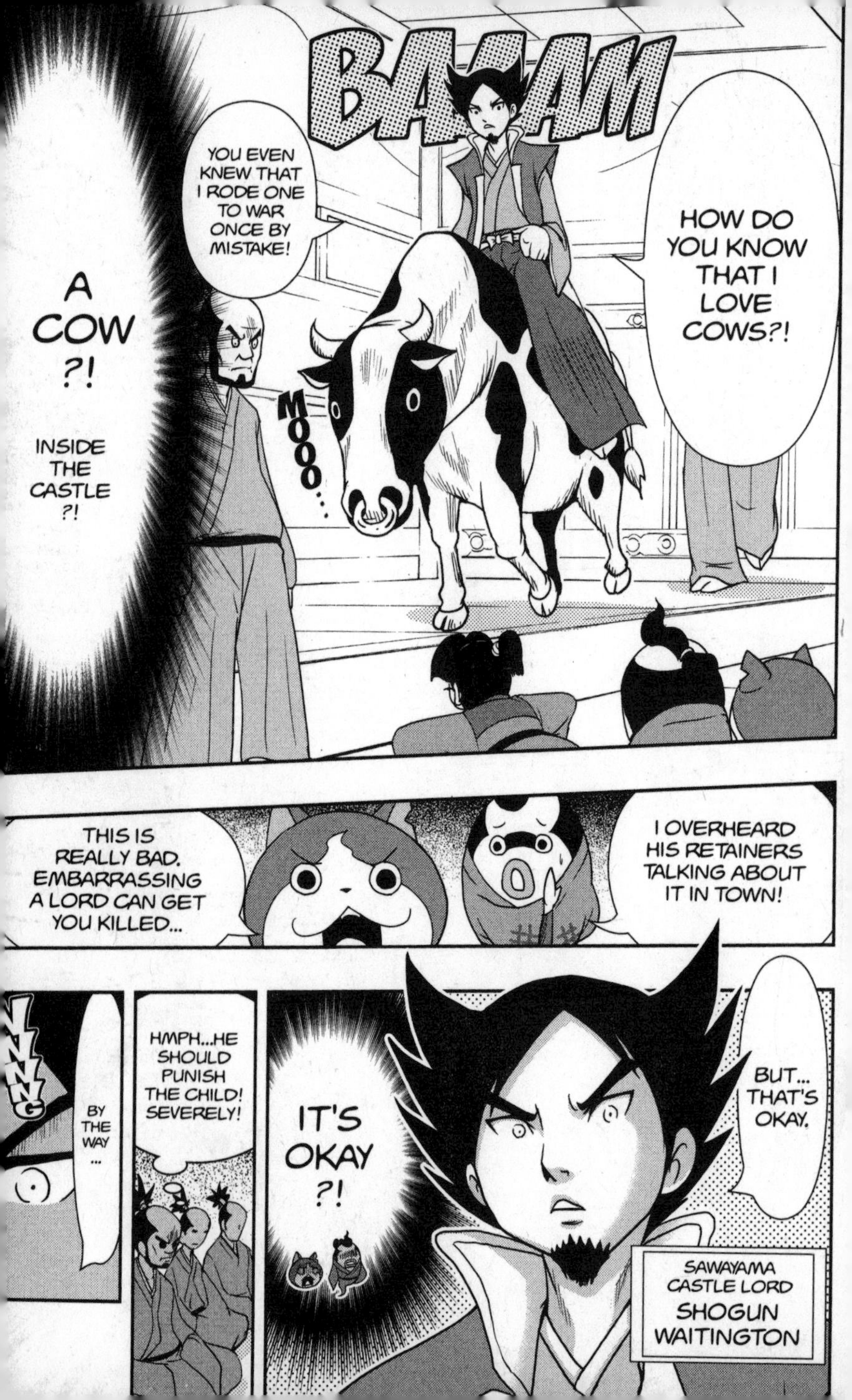
BAAM
HOW DO YOU KNOW THAT I LOVE COWS?!
YOU EVEN KNEW THAT I RODE ONE TO WAR ONCE BY MISTAKE!
MOOO...
A COW ?!
INSIDE THE CASTLE ?!
I OVERHEARD HIS RETAINERS TALKING ABOUT IT IN TOWN!
THIS IS REALLY BAD. EMBARRASSING A LORD CAN GET YOU KILLED...
BUT... THAT'S OKAY.
IT'S OKAY ?!
SAWAYAMA CASTLE LORD SHOGUN WAITINGTON
HMPH...HE SHOULD PUNISH THE CHILD! SEVERELY!
VNNNG
BY THE WAY ...

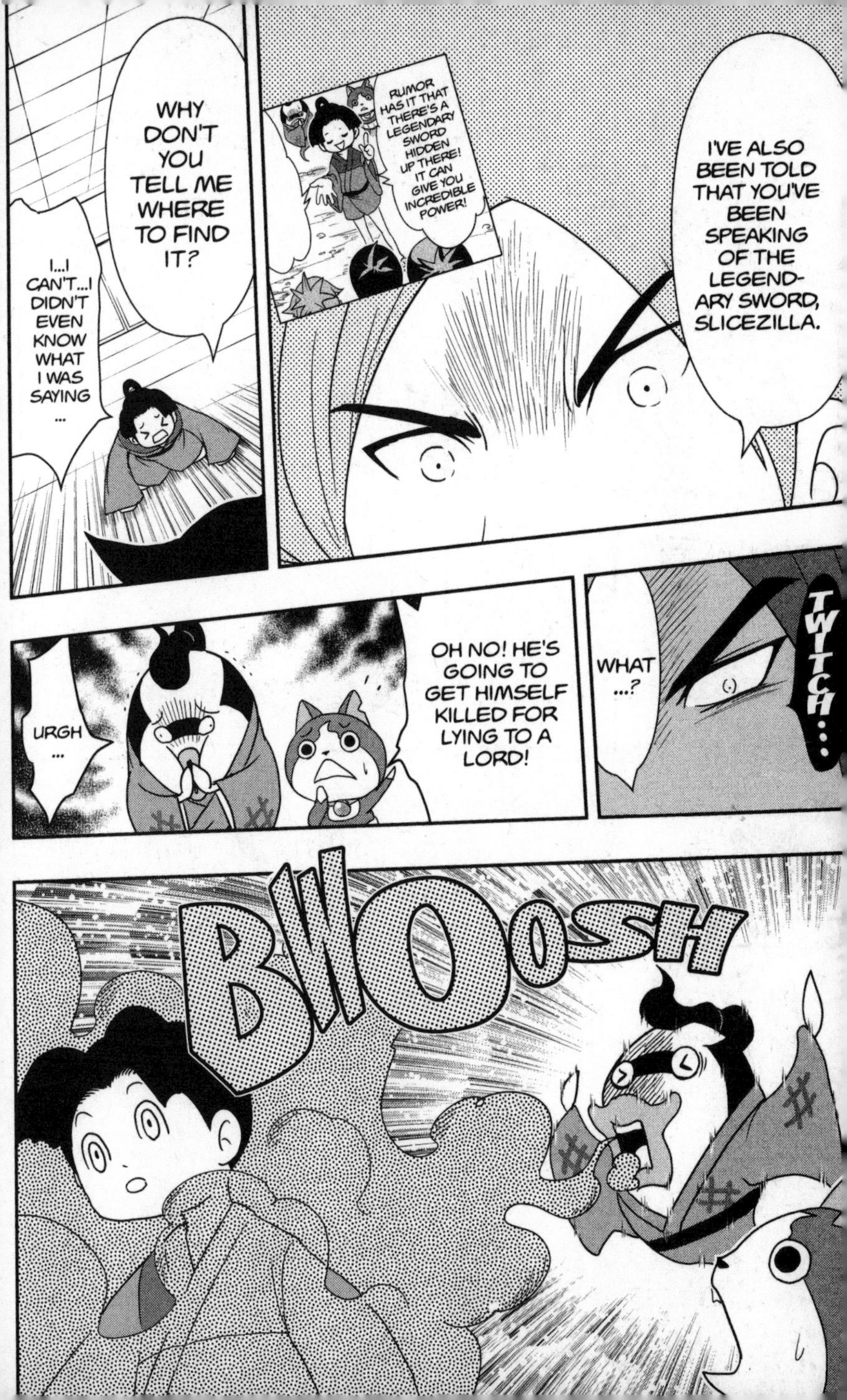
I'VE ALSO BEEN TOLD THAT YOU'VE BEEN SPEAKING OF THE LEGENDARY SWORD, SLICEZILLA.
RUMOR HAS IT THAT THERE'S A LEGENDARY SWORD HIDDEN UP THERE! IT CAN GIVE YOU INCREDIBLE POWER!
WHY DON'T YOU TELL ME WHERE TO FIND IT?
I...I CAN'T...I DIDN'T EVEN KNOW WHAT I WAS SAYING...
TWITCH...
WHAT...?
OH NO! HE'S GOING TO GET HIMSELF KILLED FOR LYING TO A LORD!
URGH...
BWOOSH

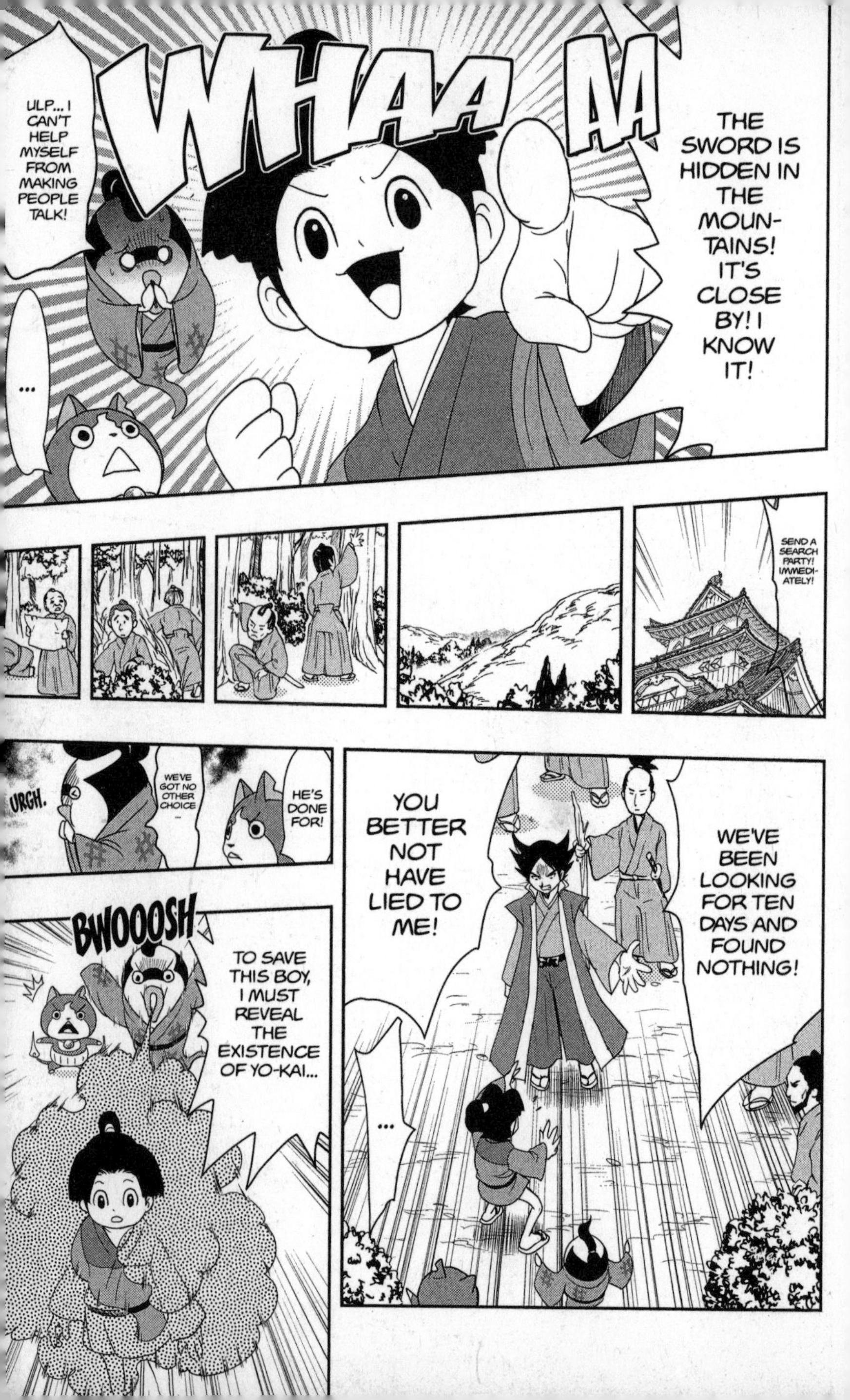
THE SWORD IS HIDDEN IN THE MOUNTAINS! IT'S CLOSE BY!! I KNOW IT!
WHAA M
ULP... I CAN'T HELP MYSELF FROM MAKING PEOPLE TALK!
...
SEND A SEARCH PARTY! IMMEDI-ATELY!
WE'VE BEEN LOOKING FOR TEN DAYS AND FOUND NOTHING!
YOU BETTER NOT HAVE LIED TO ME!
...
HE'S DONE FOR!
WE'VE GOT NO OTHER CHOICE...
URGH.
TO SAVE THIS BOY, I MUST REVEAL THE EXISTENCE OF YO-KAI...
BWOOOSH

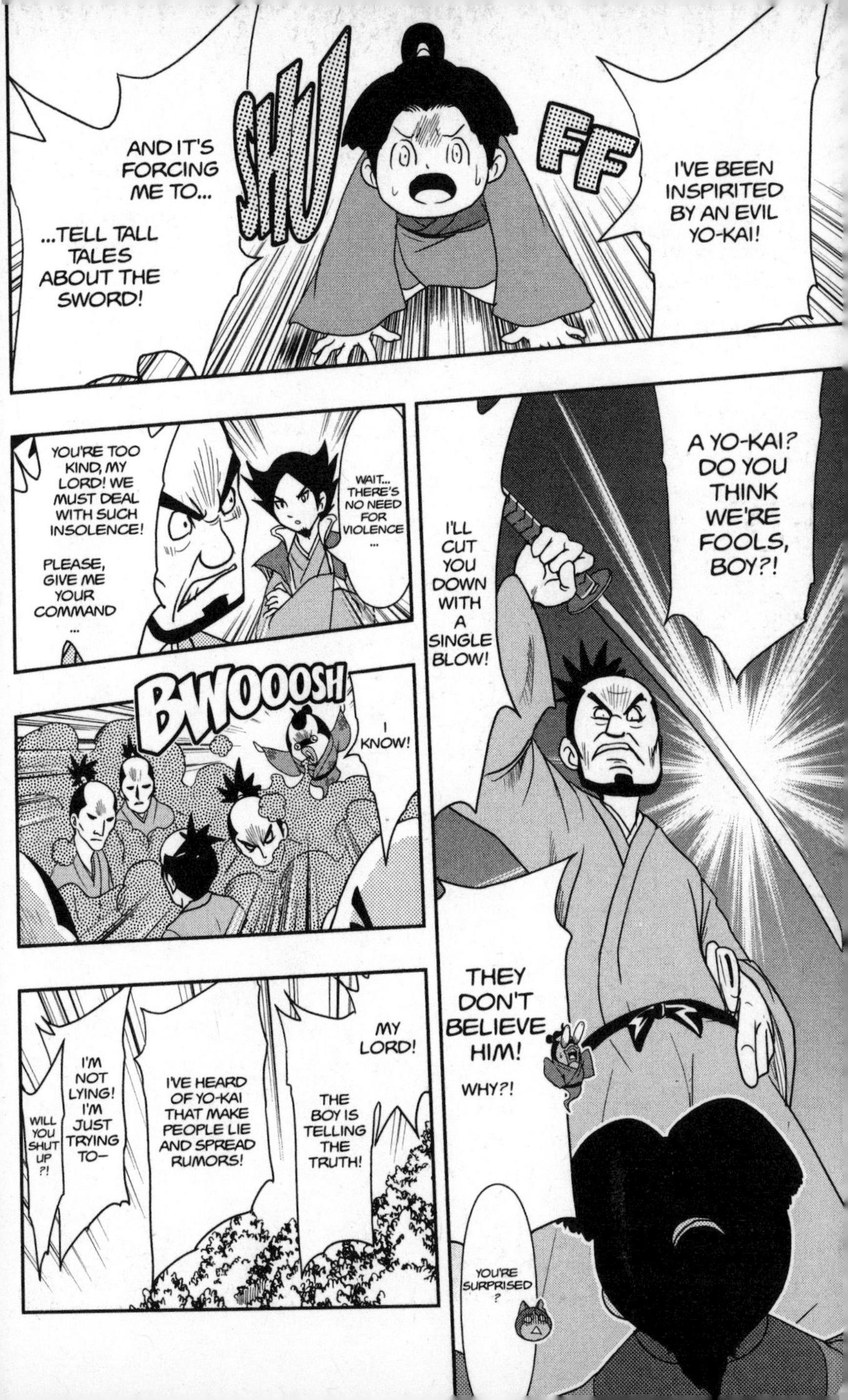
I'VE BEEN INSPIRITED BY AN EVIL YO-KAI!
SHUFF
AND IT'S FORCING ME TO...
...TELL TALL TALES ABOUT THE SWORD!
A YO-KAI? DO YOU THINK WE'RE FOOLS, BOY?!
I'LL CUT YOU DOWN WITH A SINGLE BLOW!
THEY DON'T BELIEVE HIM!
WHY?!
YOU'RE SURPRISED?
WAIT... THERE'S NO NEED FOR VIOLENCE...
YOU'RE TOO KIND, MY LORD! WE MUST DEAL WITH SUCH INSOLENCE!
PLEASE, GIVE ME YOUR COMMAND...
I KNOW!
BWOOOSH
MY LORD!
THE BOY IS TELLING THE TRUTH!
I'VE HEARD OF YO-KAI THAT MAKE PEOPLE LIE AND SPREAD RUMORS!
I'M NOT LYING! I'M JUST TRYING TO—
WILL YOU SHUT UP?!

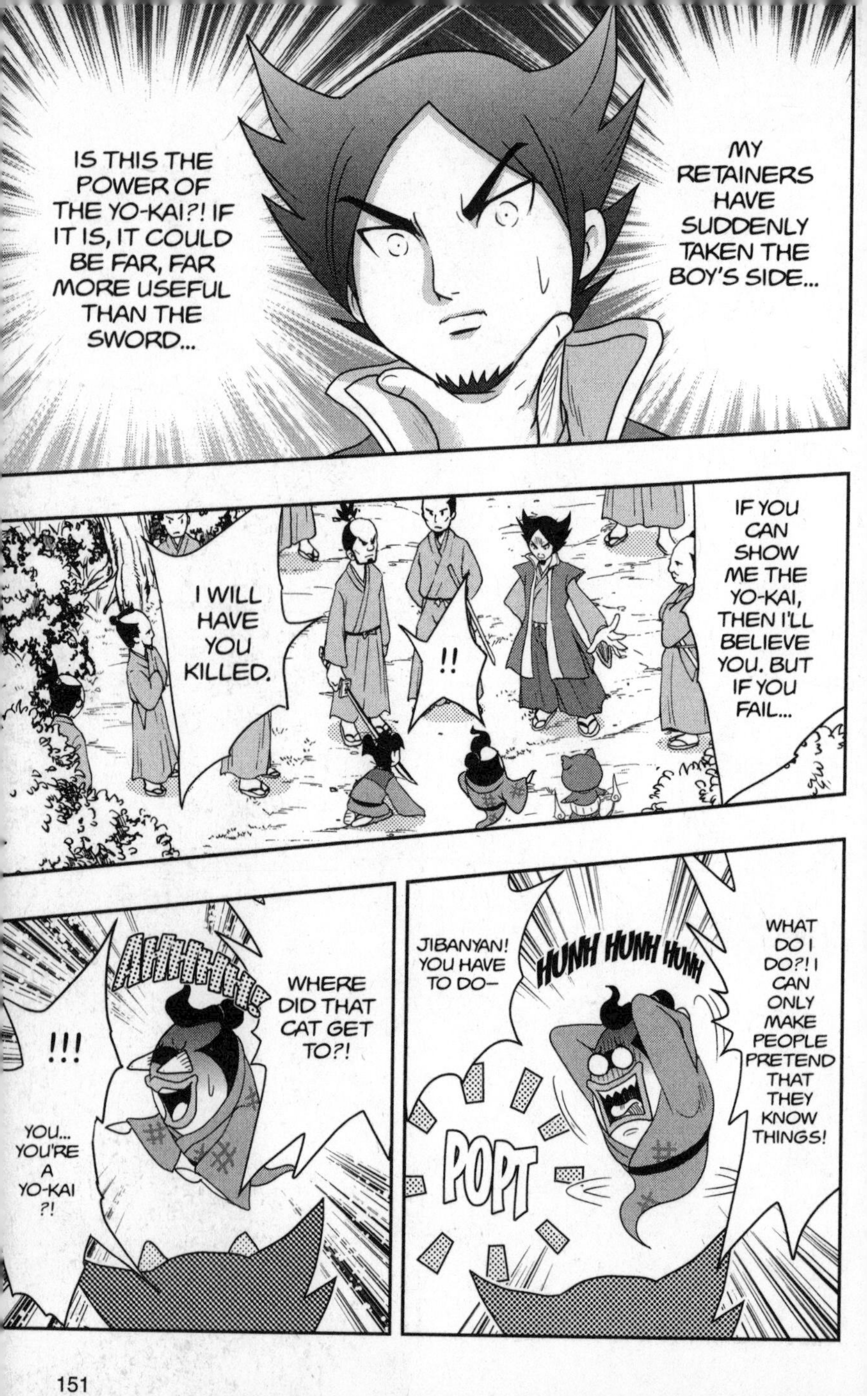
MY RETAINERS HAVE SUDDENLY TAKEN THE BOY'S SIDE...
IS THIS THE POWER OF THE YO-KAI?! IF IT IS, IT COULD BE FAR, FAR MORE USEFUL THAN THE SWORD...
IF YOU CAN SHOW ME THE YO-KAI, THEN I'LL BELIEVE YOU. BUT IF YOU FAIL...
!!
I WILL HAVE YOU KILLED.
WHAT DO I DO?! I CAN ONLY MAKE PEOPLE PRETEND THAT THEY KNOW THINGS!
HUNH HUNH HUNH
JIBANYAN! YOU HAVE TO DO—
POPT
AHHHHHH!
WHERE DID THAT CAT GET TO?!
!!!
YOU... YOU'RE A YO-KAI ?!

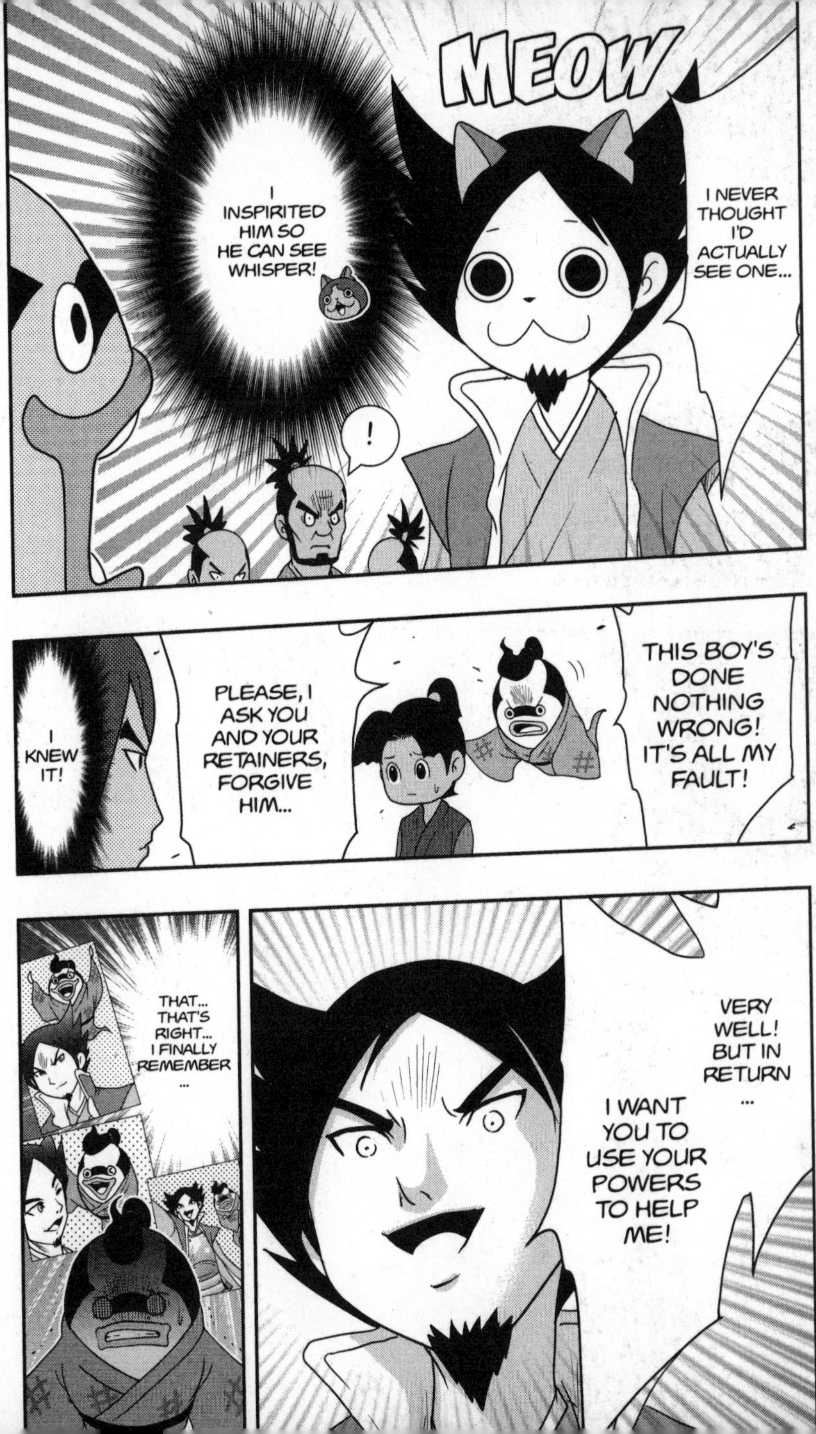
MEOW
I NEVER THOUGHT I'D ACTUALLY SEE ONE...
I INSPIRITED HIM SO HE CAN SEE WHISPER!
!
THIS BOY'S DONE NOTHING WRONG! IT'S ALL MY FAULT!
PLEASE, I ASK YOU AND YOUR RETAINERS, FORGIVE HIM...
I KNEW IT!
VERY WELL! BUT IN RETURN...
I WANT YOU TO USE YOUR POWERS TO HELP ME!
THAT... THAT'S RIGHT... I FINALLY REMEMBER...

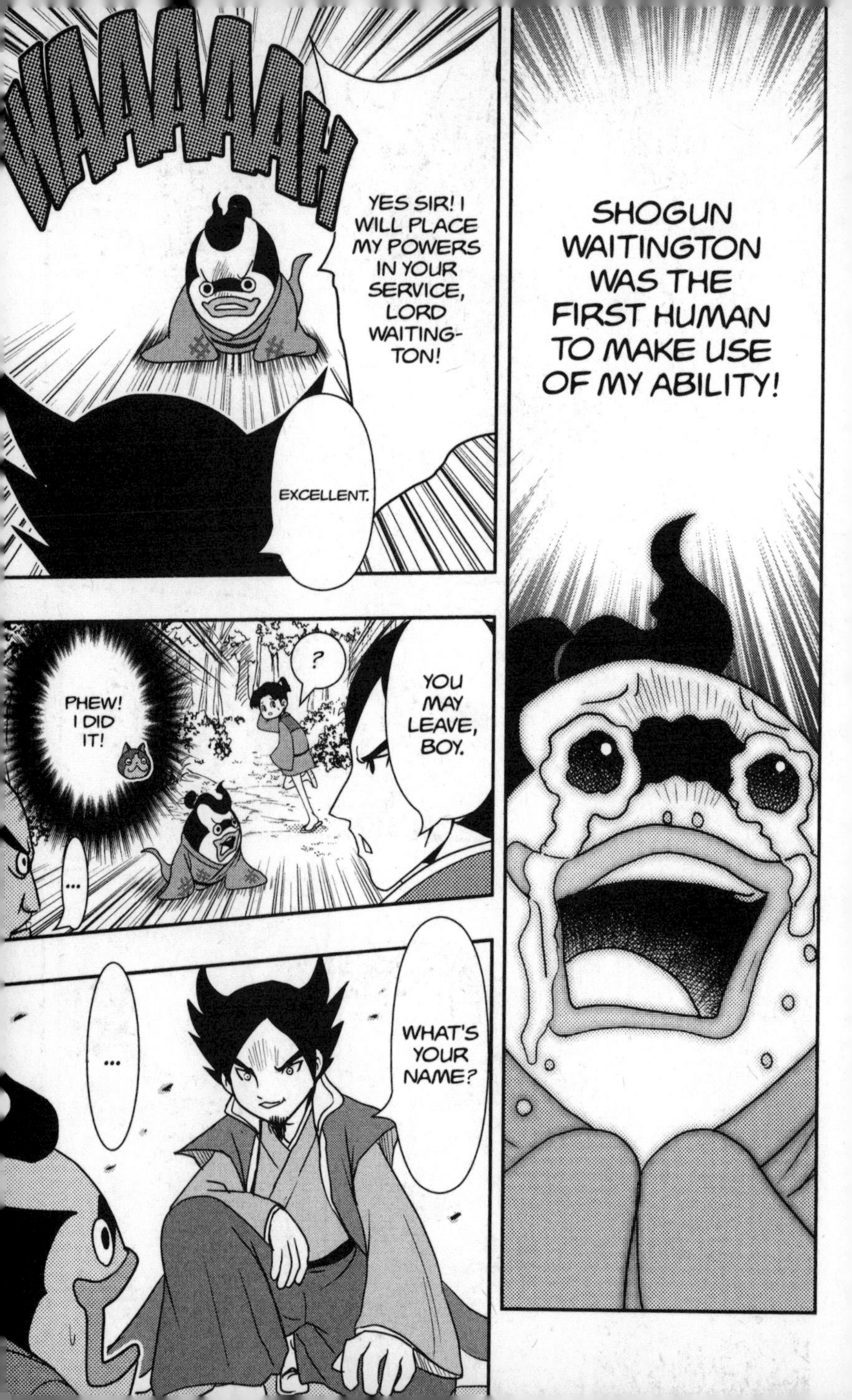
SHOGUN WAITINGTON WAS THE FIRST HUMAN TO MAKE USE OF MY ABILITY!
WAAAAAH
YES SIR! I WILL PLACE MY POWERS IN YOUR SERVICE, LORD WAITING-TON!
EXCELLENT.
YOU MAY LEAVE, BOY.
?
PHEW! I DID IT!
...
WHAT'S YOUR NAME?
...

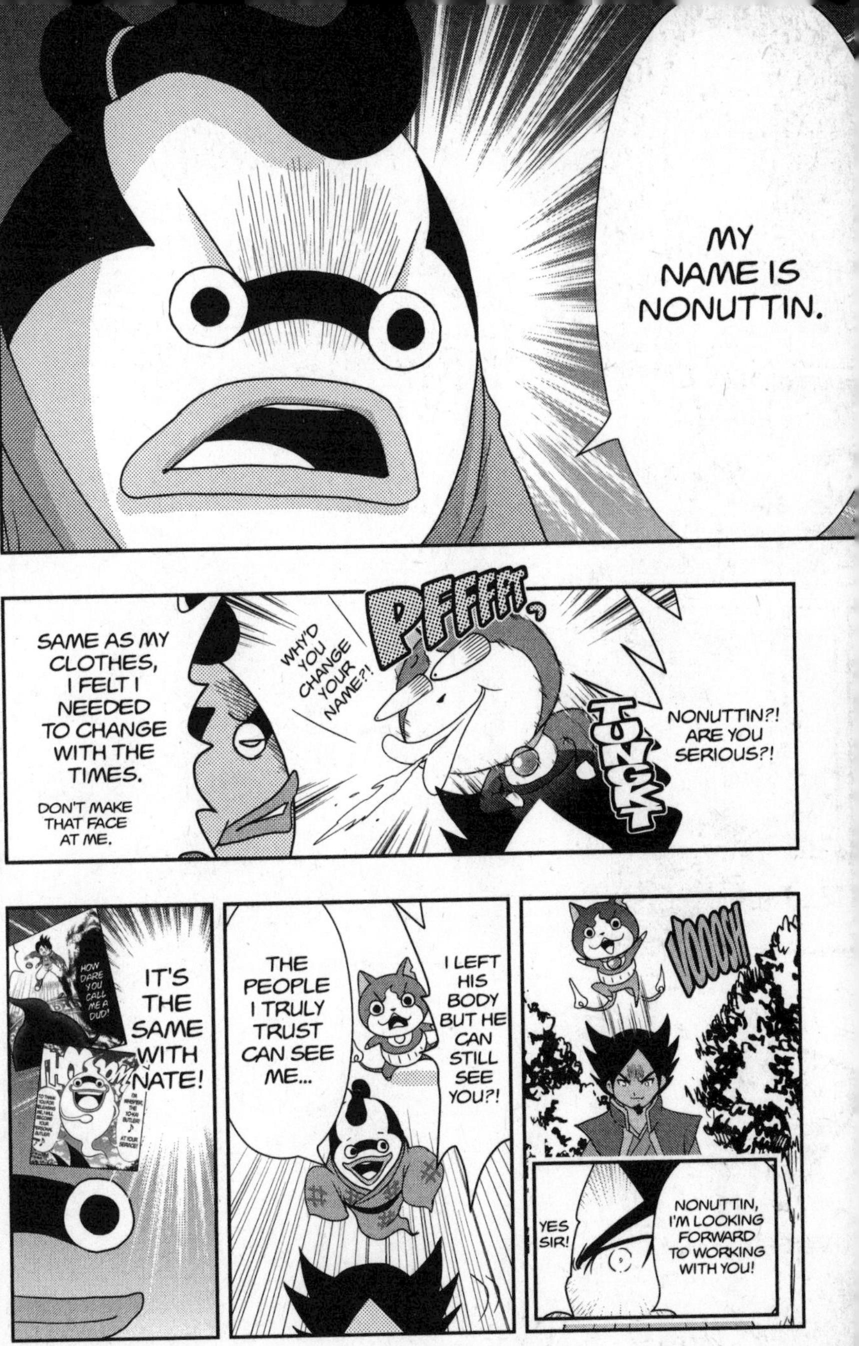
MY NAME IS NONUTTIN.
NONUTTIN?! ARE YOU SERIOUS?!
TUNGK
PFFFFT
WHY'D YOU CHANGE YOUR NAME?!
SAME AS MY CLOTHES, I FELT I NEEDED TO CHANGE WITH THE TIMES.
DON'T MAKE THAT FACE AT ME.
VOOOSH
NONUTTIN, I'M LOOKING FORWARD TO WORKING WITH YOU!
YES SIR!
I LEFT HIS BODY BUT HE CAN STILL SEE YOU?!
THE PEOPLE I TRULY TRUST CAN SEE ME...
IT'S THE SAME WITH NATE!
HOW DARE YOU CALL ME A DUD!

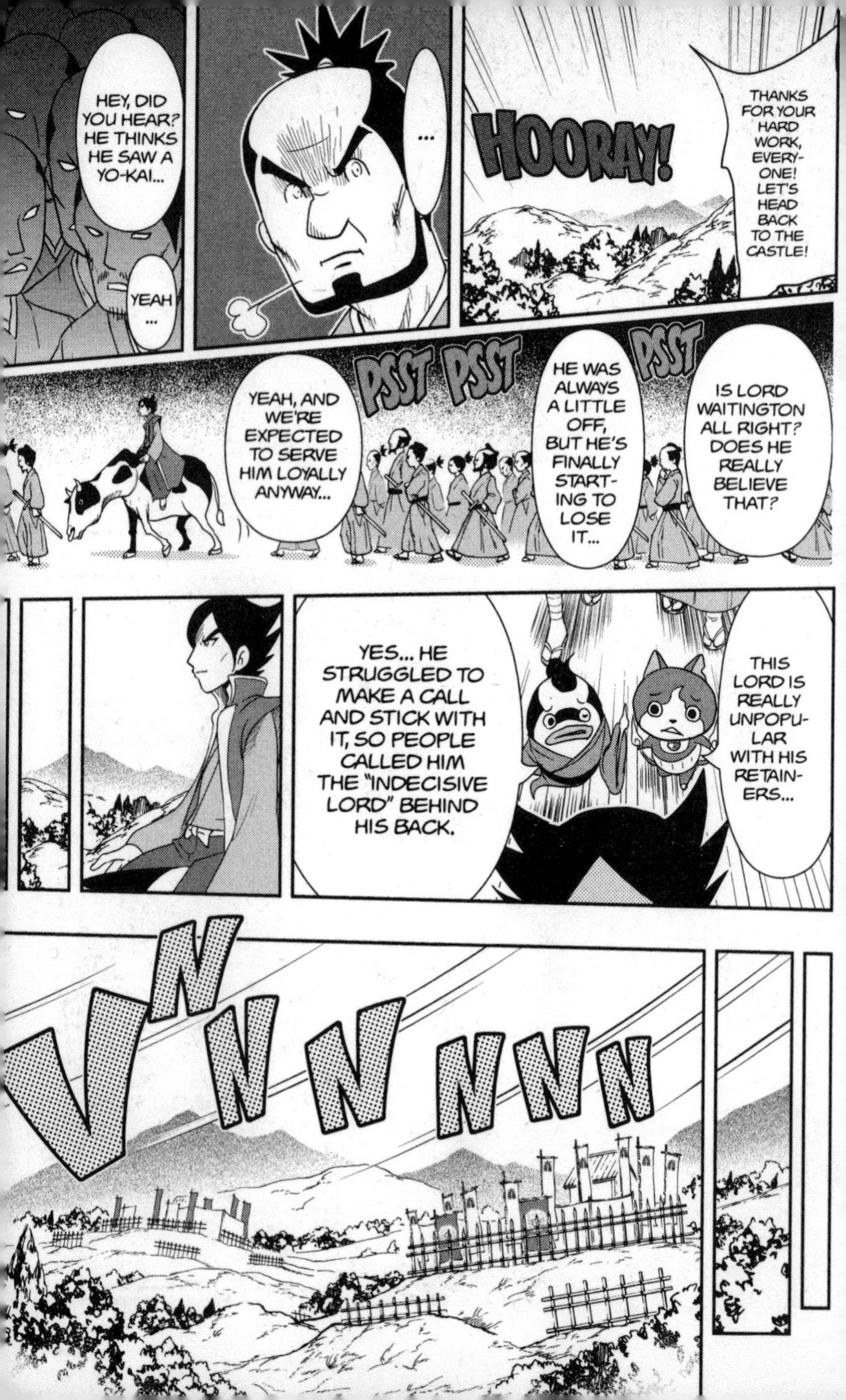
THANKS FOR YOUR HARD WORK, EVERYONE! LET'S HEAD BACK TO THE CASTLE!
HOORAY!
...
HEY, DID YOU HEAR? HE THINKS HE SAW A YO-KAI...
YEAH...
IS LORD WAITINGTON ALL RIGHT? DOES HE REALLY BELIEVE THAT?
PSST
HE WAS ALWAYS A LITTLE OFF, BUT HE'S FINALLY STARTING TO LOSE IT...
PSST PSST
YEAH, AND WE'RE EXPECTED TO SERVE HIM LOYALLY ANYWAY...
THIS LORD IS REALLY UNPOPULAR WITH HIS RETAINERS...
YES... HE STRUGGLED TO MAKE A CALL AND STICK WITH IT, SO PEOPLE CALLED HIM THE "INDECISIVE LORD" BEHIND HIS BACK.
VNNNNNN

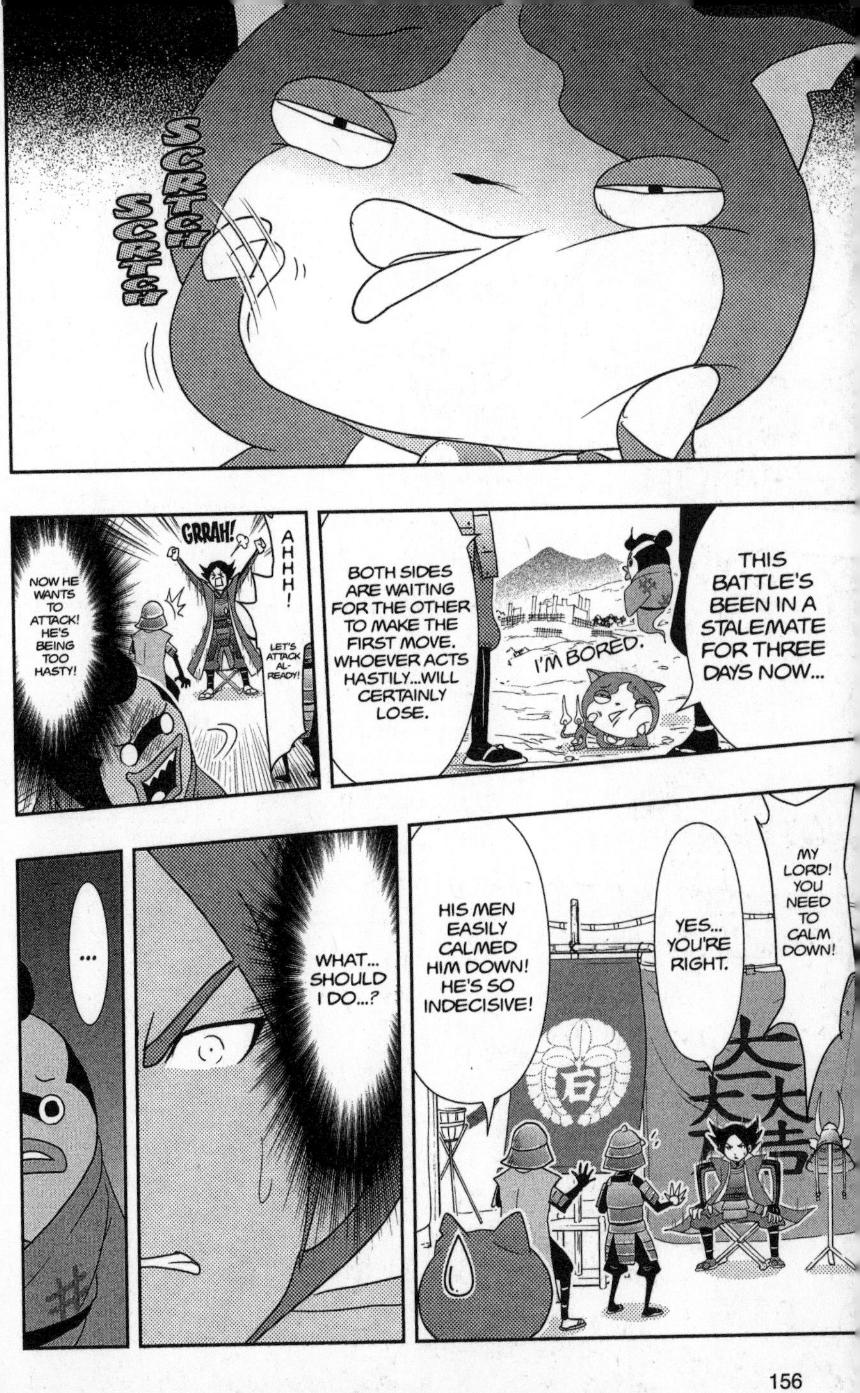
SCRTCH
SCRTCH
THIS BATTLE'S BEEN IN A STALEMATE FOR THREE DAYS NOW...
I'M BORED.
BOTH SIDES ARE WAITING FOR THE OTHER TO MAKE THE FIRST MOVE. WHOEVER ACTS HASTILY...WILL CERTAINLY LOSE.
AHHHH!
GRRAH!
LET'S ATTACK AL-READY!
NOW HE WANTS TO ATTACK! HE'S BEING TOO HASTY!
MY LORD! YOU NEED TO CALM DOWN!
YES... YOU'RE RIGHT.
HIS MEN EASILY CALMED HIM DOWN! HE'S SO INDECISIVE!
WHAT... SHOULD I DO...?
...

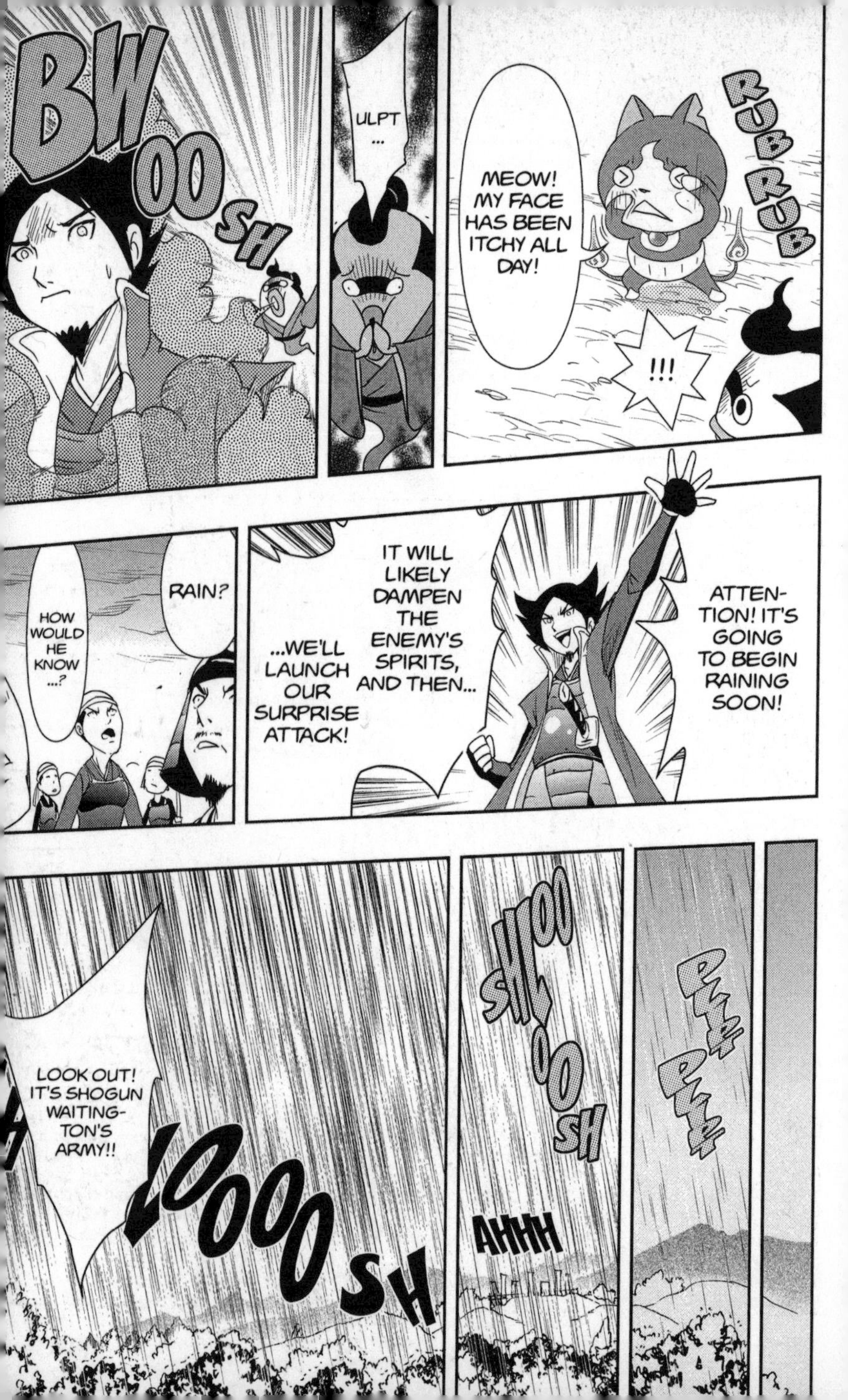
RUB RUB
MEOW! MY FACE HAS BEEN ITCHY ALL DAY!
!!!
ULPT ...
BWOOSH
ATTEN-TION! IT'S GOING TO BEGIN RAINING SOON!
IT WILL LIKELY DAMPEN THE ENEMY'S SPIRITS, AND THEN...
...WE'LL LAUNCH OUR SURPRISE ATTACK!
RAIN?
HOW WOULD HE KNOW ...?
SHOOOOSH
AHHH
LOOK OUT! IT'S SHOGUN WAITING-TON'S ARMY!!
OOOOSH

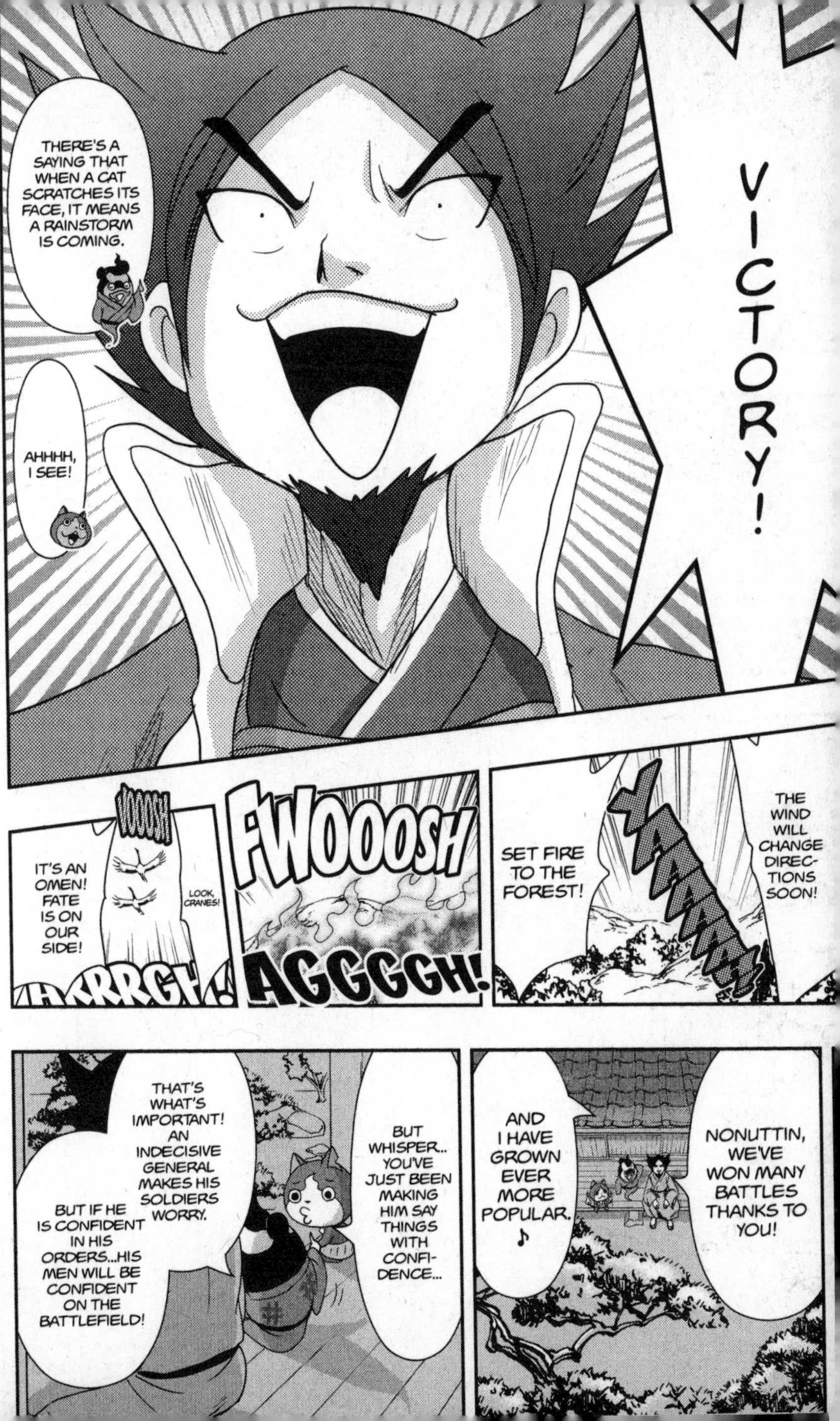
VICTORY!
THERE'S A SAYING THAT WHEN A CAT SCRATCHES ITS FACE, IT MEANS A RAINSTORM IS COMING.
AHHHH, I SEE!
THE WIND WILL CHANGE DIRECTIONS SOON!
SET FIRE TO THE FOREST!
FWOOOSH
AGGGGH!
IT'S AN OMEN! FATE IS ON OUR SIDE!
LOOK, CRANES!
NONUTTIN, WE'VE WON MANY BATTLES THANKS TO YOU!
AND I HAVE GROWN EVER MORE POPULAR. ♪
BUT WHISPER.. YOU'VE JUST BEEN MAKING HIM SAY THINGS WITH CONFIDENCE...
THAT'S WHAT'S IMPORTANT! AN INDECISIVE GENERAL MAKES HIS SOLDIERS WORRY.
BUT IF HE IS CONFIDENT IN HIS ORDERS...HIS MEN WILL BE CONFIDENT ON THE BATTLEFIELD!

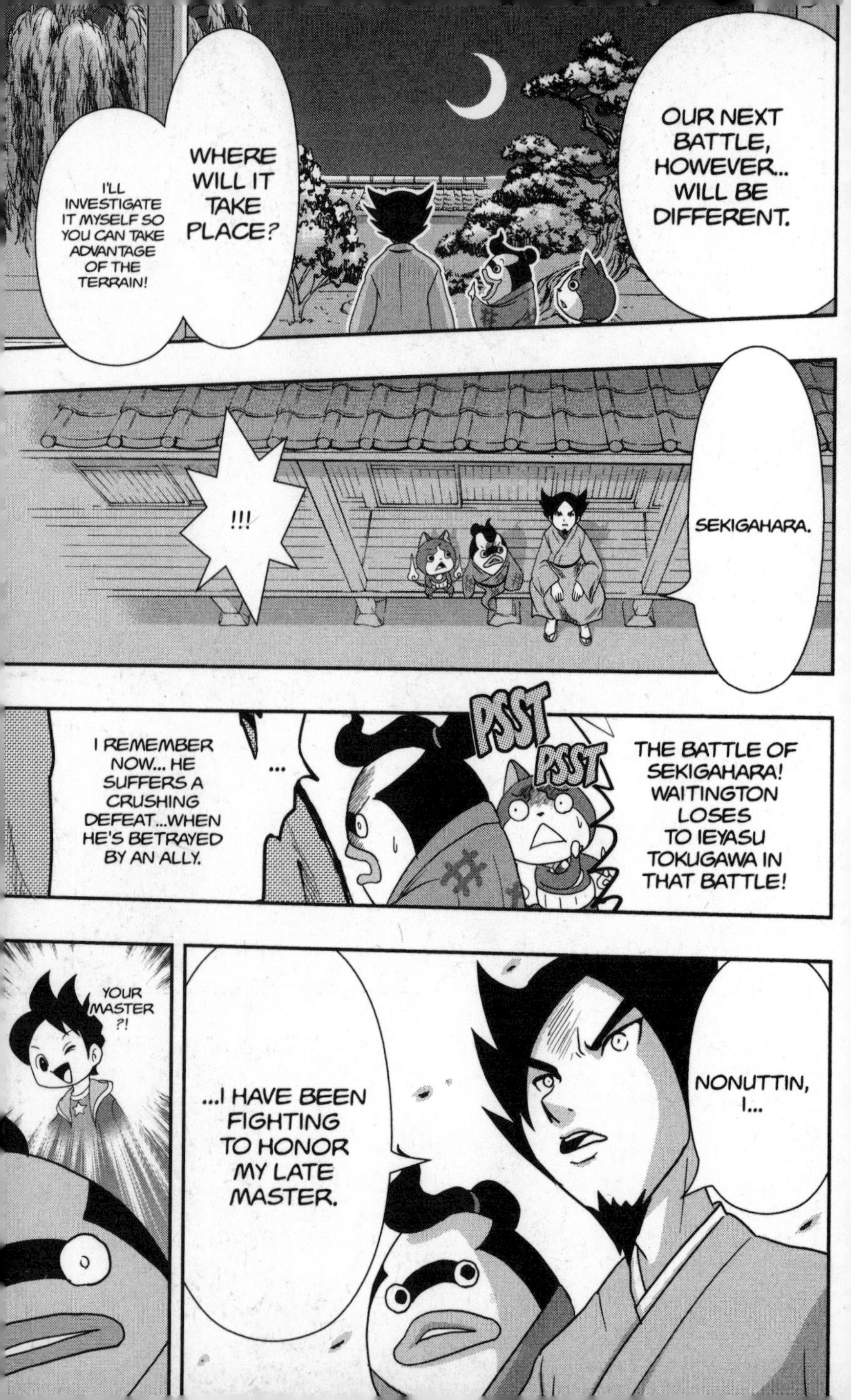
OUR NEXT BATTLE, HOWEVER... WILL BE DIFFERENT.
WHERE WILL IT TAKE PLACE?
I'LL INVESTIGATE IT MYSELF SO YOU CAN TAKE ADVANTAGE OF THE TERRAIN!
SEKIGAHARA.
!!!
PSST PSST
THE BATTLE OF SEKIGAHARA! WAITINGTON LOSES TO IEYASU TOKUGAWA IN THAT BATTLE!
...
I REMEMBER NOW... HE SUFFERS A CRUSHING DEFEAT...WHEN HE'S BETRAYED BY AN ALLY.
NONUTTIN, I...
...I HAVE BEEN FIGHTING TO HONOR MY LATE MASTER.
YOUR MASTER ?!

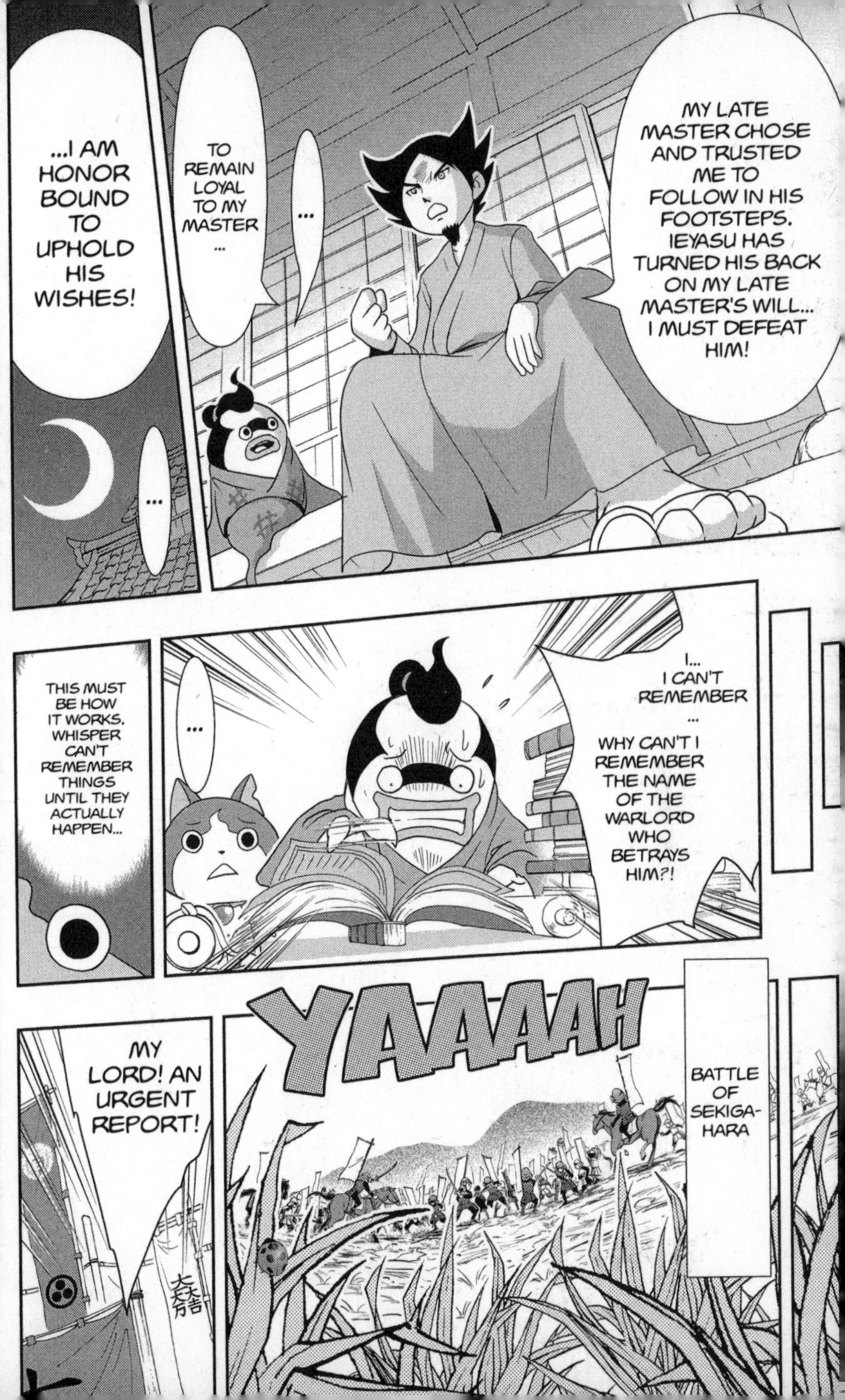
MY LATE MASTER CHOSE AND TRUSTED ME TO FOLLOW IN HIS FOOTSTEPS. IEYASU HAS TURNED HIS BACK ON MY LATE MASTER'S WILL... I MUST DEFEAT HIM!
...
TO REMAIN LOYAL TO MY MASTER...
...I AM HONOR BOUND TO UPHOLD HIS WISHES!
...
I... I CAN'T REMEMBER...
WHY CAN'T I REMEMBER THE NAME OF THE WARLORD WHO BETRAYS HIM?!
...
THIS MUST BE HOW IT WORKS. WHISPER CAN'T REMEMBER THINGS UNTIL THEY ACTUALLY HAPPEN...
BATTLE OF SEKIGA-HARA
YAAAAH
MY LORD! AN URGENT REPORT!

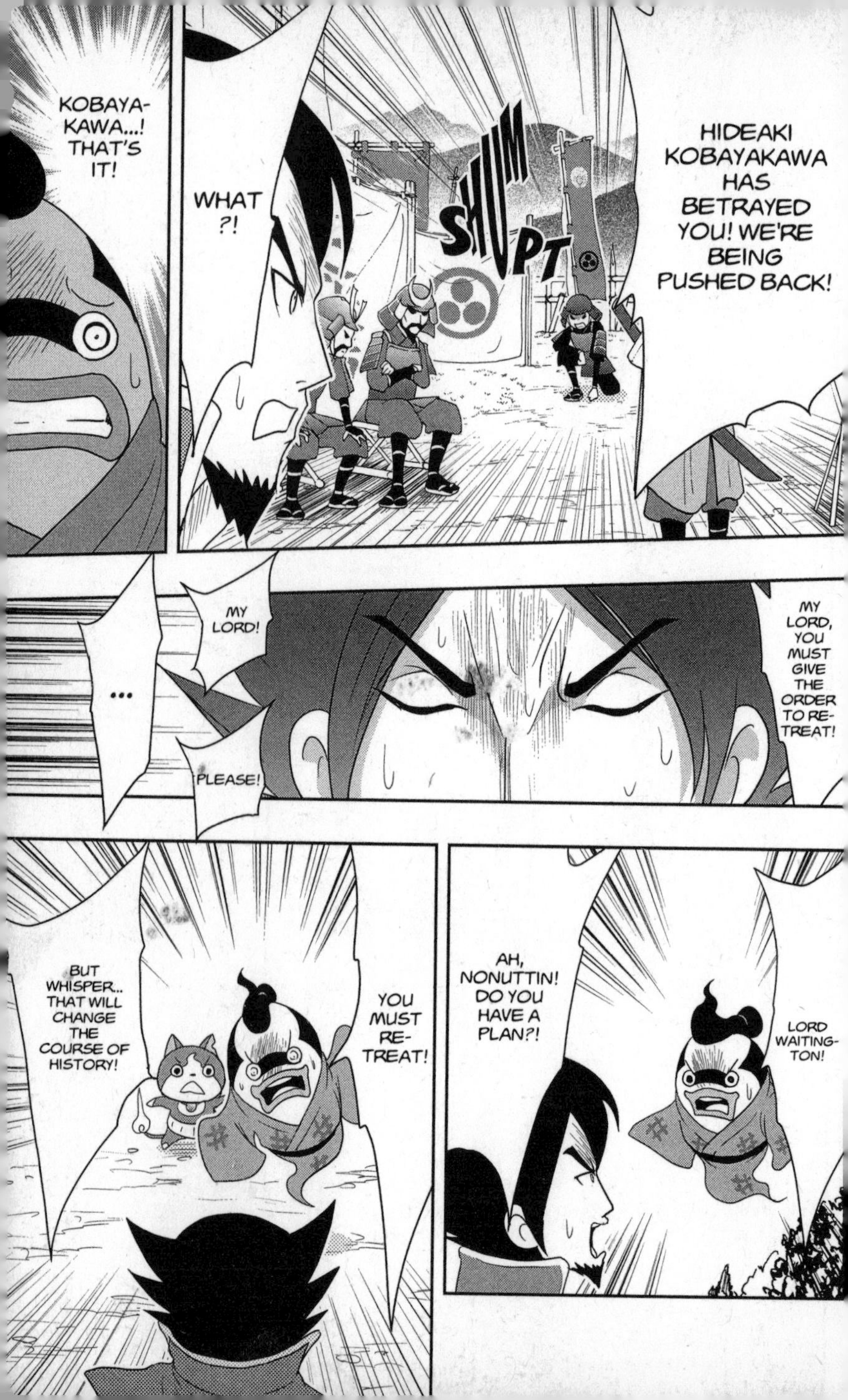
HIDEAKI KOBAYAKAWA HAS BETRAYED YOU! WE'RE BEING PUSHED BACK!
SHUMPT
WHAT?!
KOBAYAKAWA...! THAT'S IT!
MY LORD, YOU MUST GIVE THE ORDER TO RETREAT!
MY LORD!
PLEASE!
...
LORD WAITINGTON!
AH, NONUTTIN! DO YOU HAVE A PLAN?!
YOU MUST RETREAT!
BUT WHISPER.. THAT WILL CHANGE THE COURSE OF HISTORY!

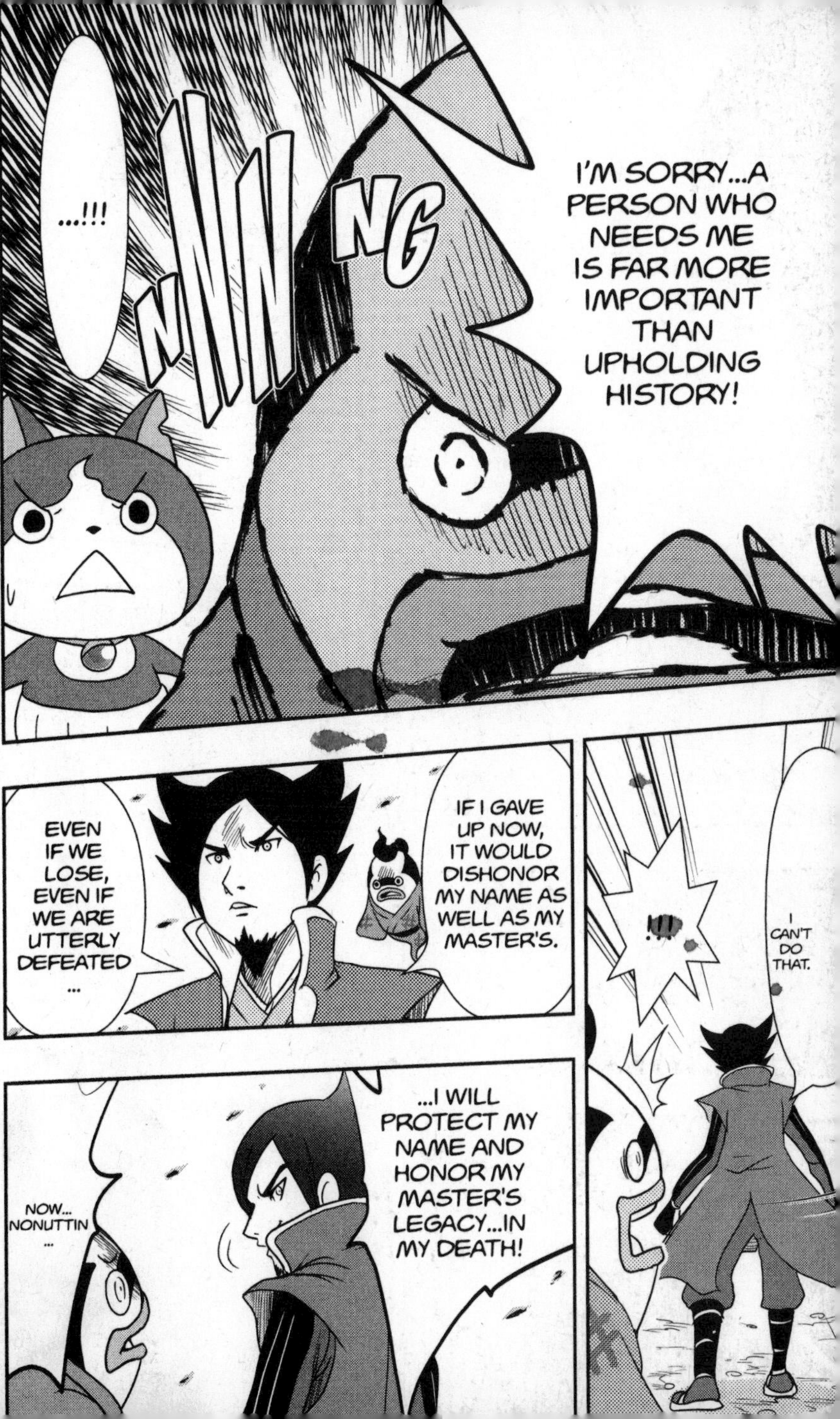
I'M SORRY...A PERSON WHO NEEDS ME IS FAR MORE IMPORTANT THAN UPHOLDING HISTORY!
NNNNG
...!!!
I CAN'T DO THAT.
!!!
IF I GAVE UP NOW, IT WOULD DISHONOR MY NAME AS WELL AS MY MASTER'S.
EVEN IF WE LOSE, EVEN IF WE ARE UTTERLY DEFEATED...
...I WILL PROTECT MY NAME AND HONOR MY MASTER'S LEGACY...IN MY DEATH!
NOW... NONUTTIN...

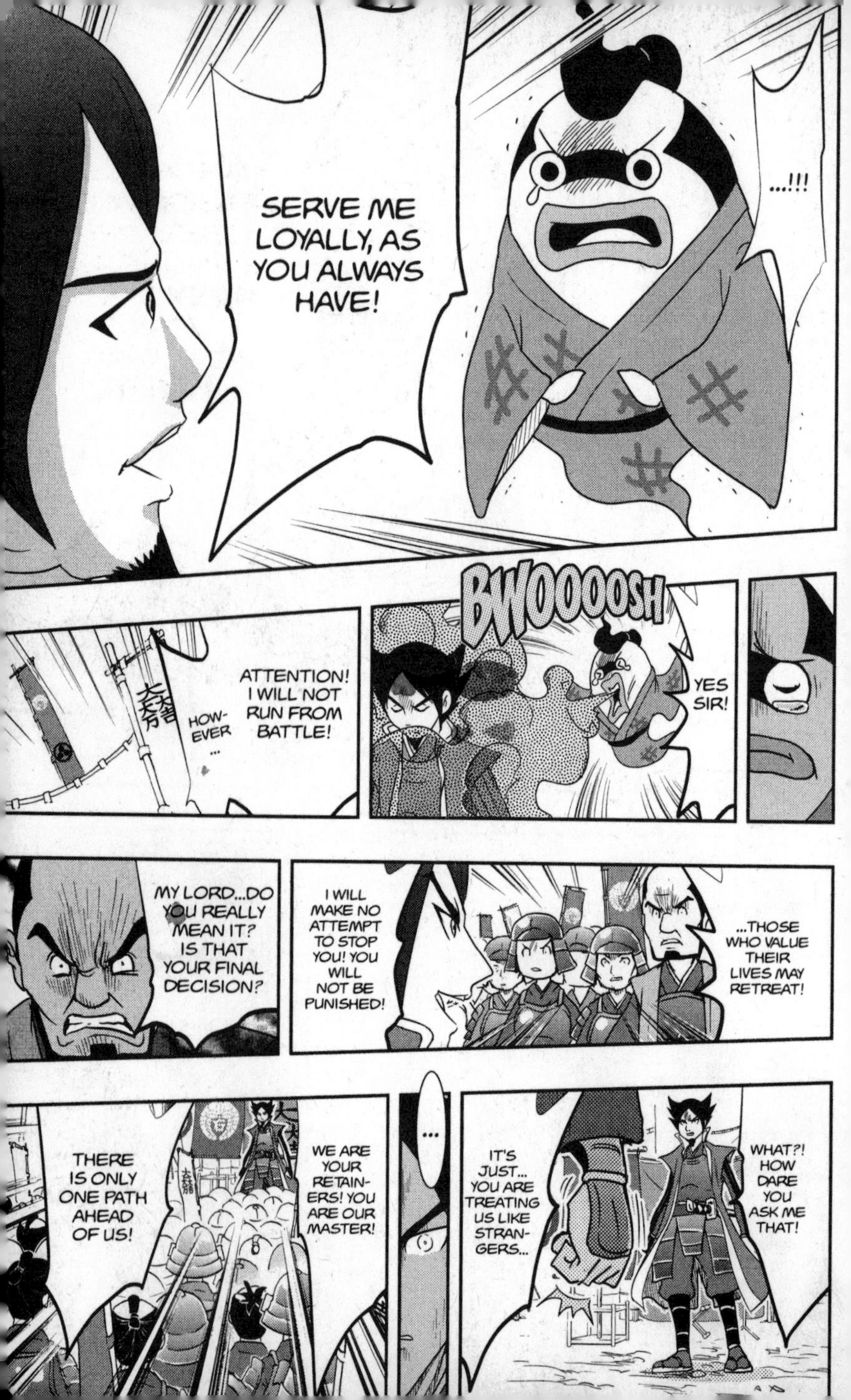
...!!!
SERVE ME LOYALLY, AS YOU ALWAYS HAVE!
BWOOOOSH
YES SIR!
ATTENTION! I WILL NOT RUN FROM BATTLE!
HOW-EVER ...
...THOSE WHO VALUE THEIR LIVES MAY RETREAT!
I WILL MAKE NO ATTEMPT TO STOP YOU! YOU WILL NOT BE PUNISHED!
MY LORD...DO YOU REALLY MEAN IT? IS THAT YOUR FINAL DECISION?
WHAT?! HOW DARE YOU ASK ME THAT!
IT'S JUST... YOU ARE TREATING US LIKE STRAN-GERS...
...
WE ARE YOUR RETAIN-ERS! YOU ARE OUR MASTER!
THERE IS ONLY ONE PATH AHEAD OF US!

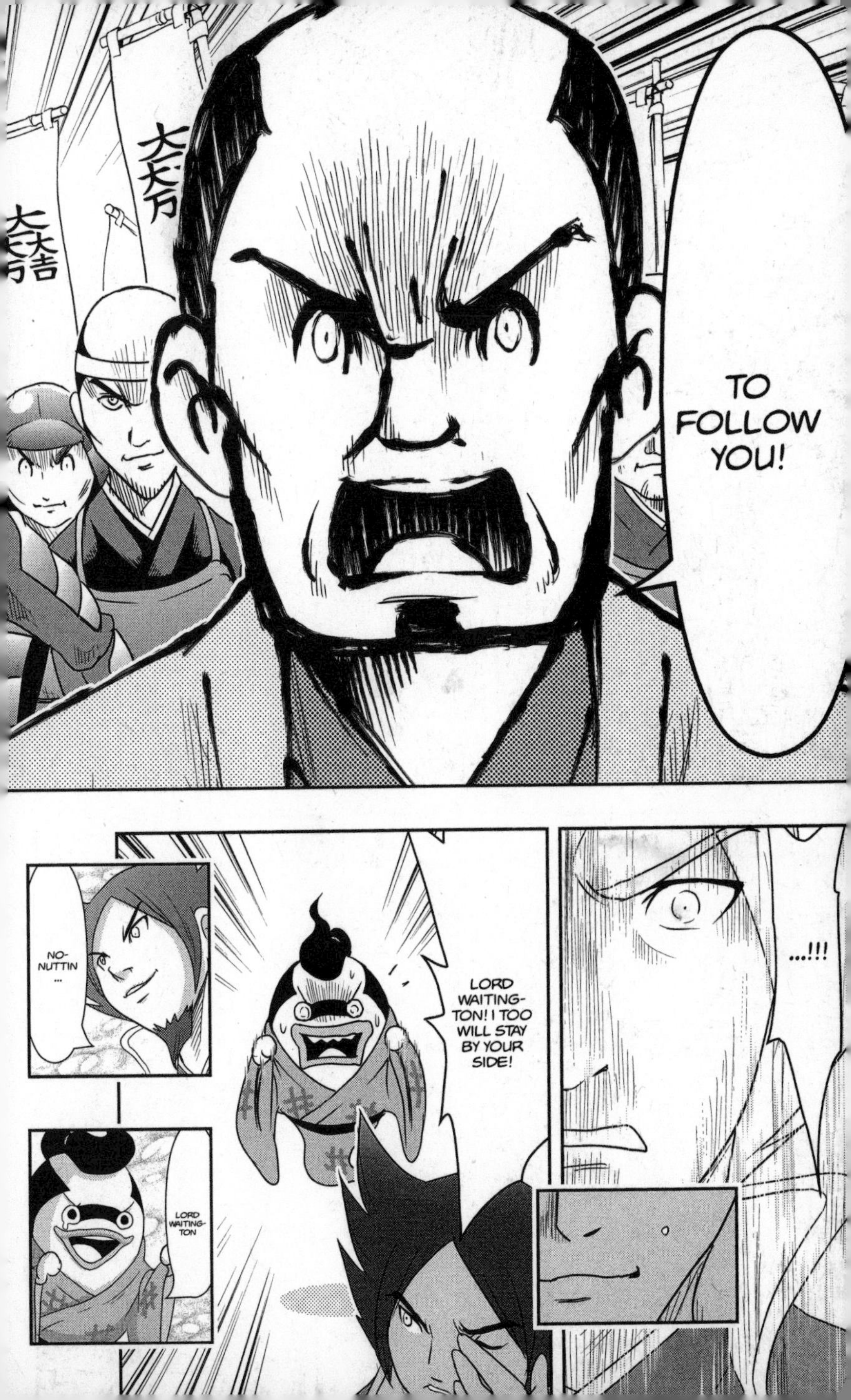
TO FOLLOW YOU!
...!!!
LORD WAITING-TON! I TOO WILL STAY BY YOUR SIDE!
NO-NUTTIN ...
LORD WAITING-TON

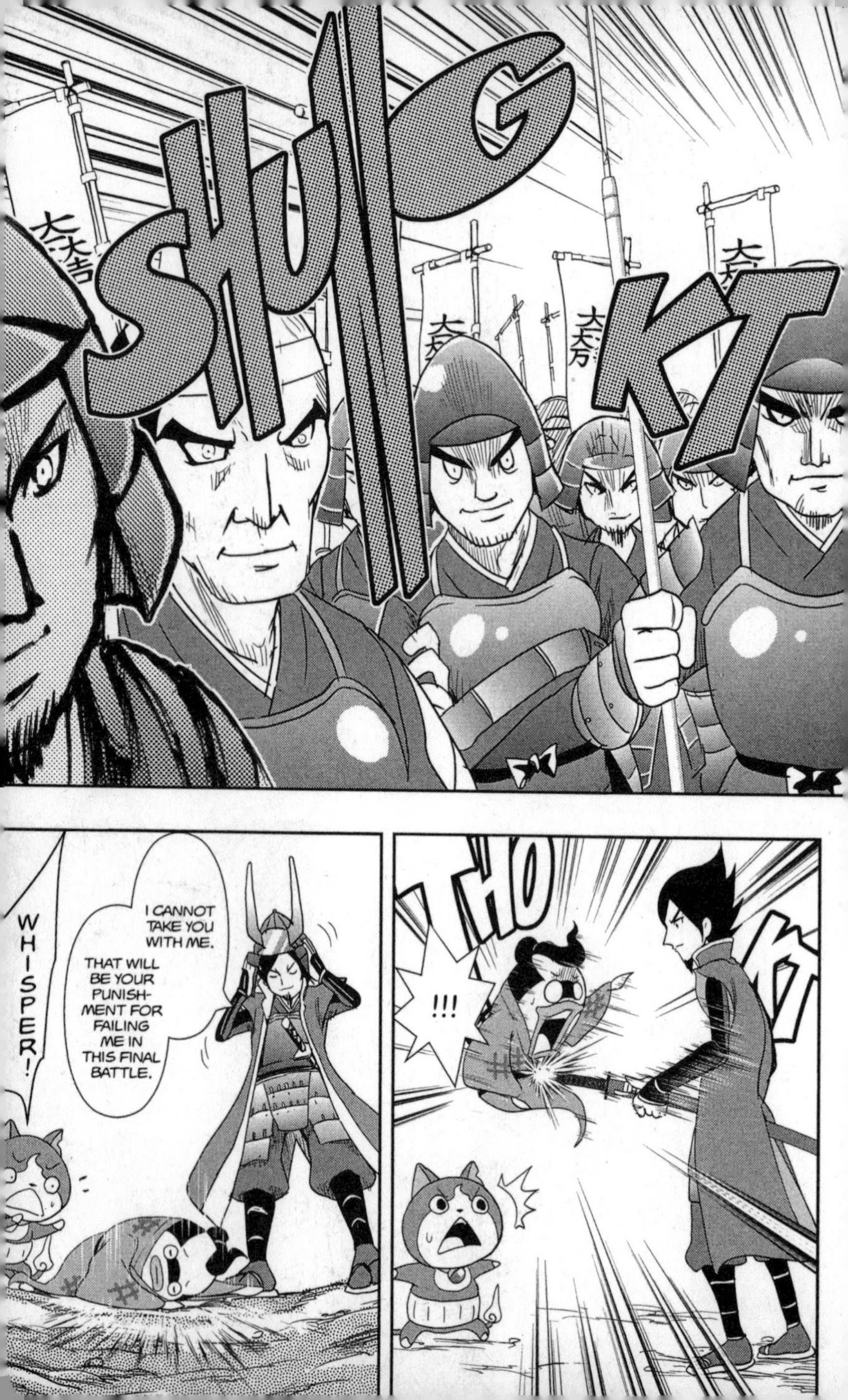
KT
!!!
I CANNOT TAKE YOU WITH ME. THAT WILL BE YOUR PUNISHMENT FOR FAILING ME IN THIS FINAL BATTLE.
WHISPER!

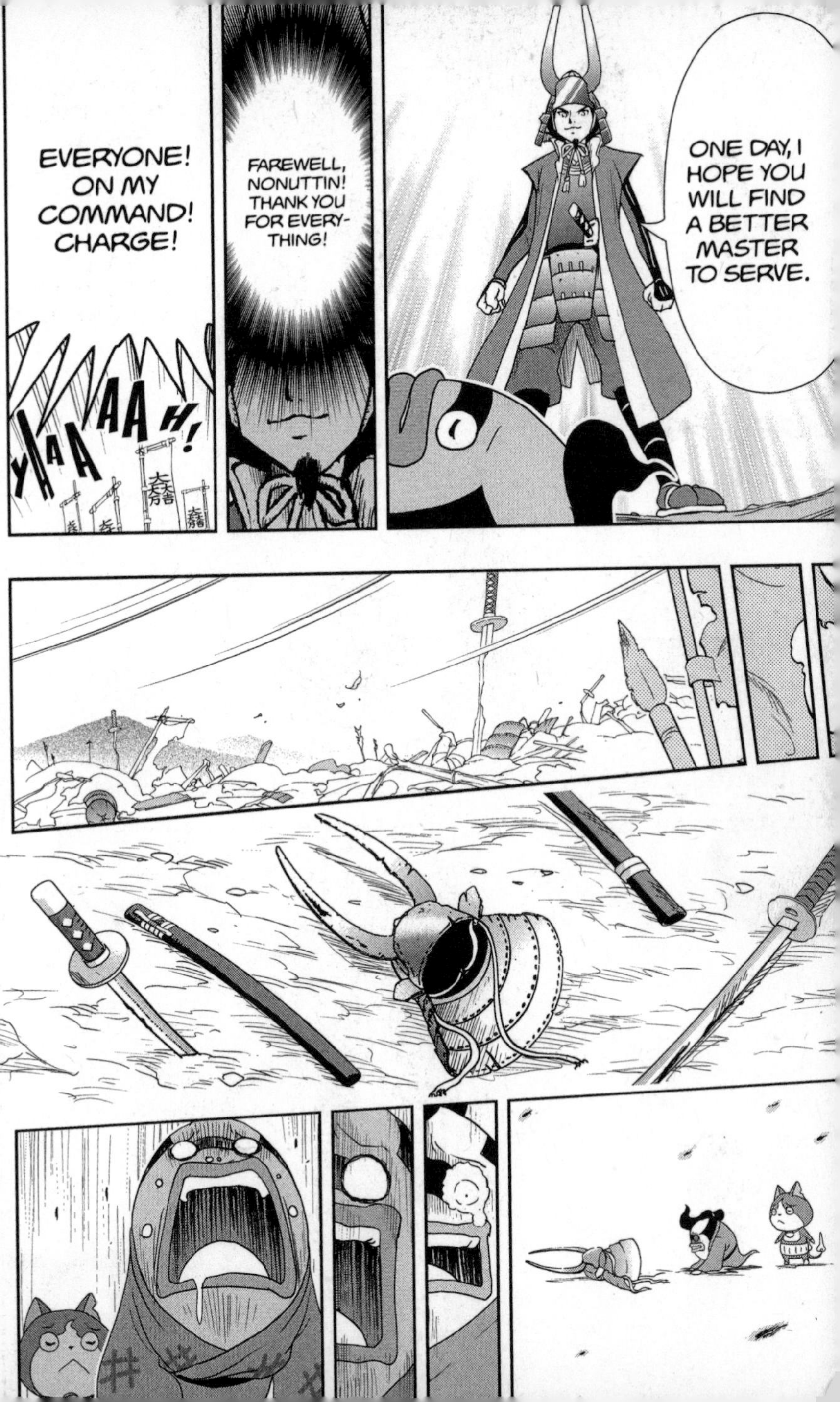
ONE DAY, I HOPE YOU WILL FIND A BETTER MASTER TO SERVE.
FAREWELL, NONUTTIN! THANK YOU FOR EVERY-THING!
EVERYONE! ON MY COMMAND! CHARGE!
YAAAAAH!

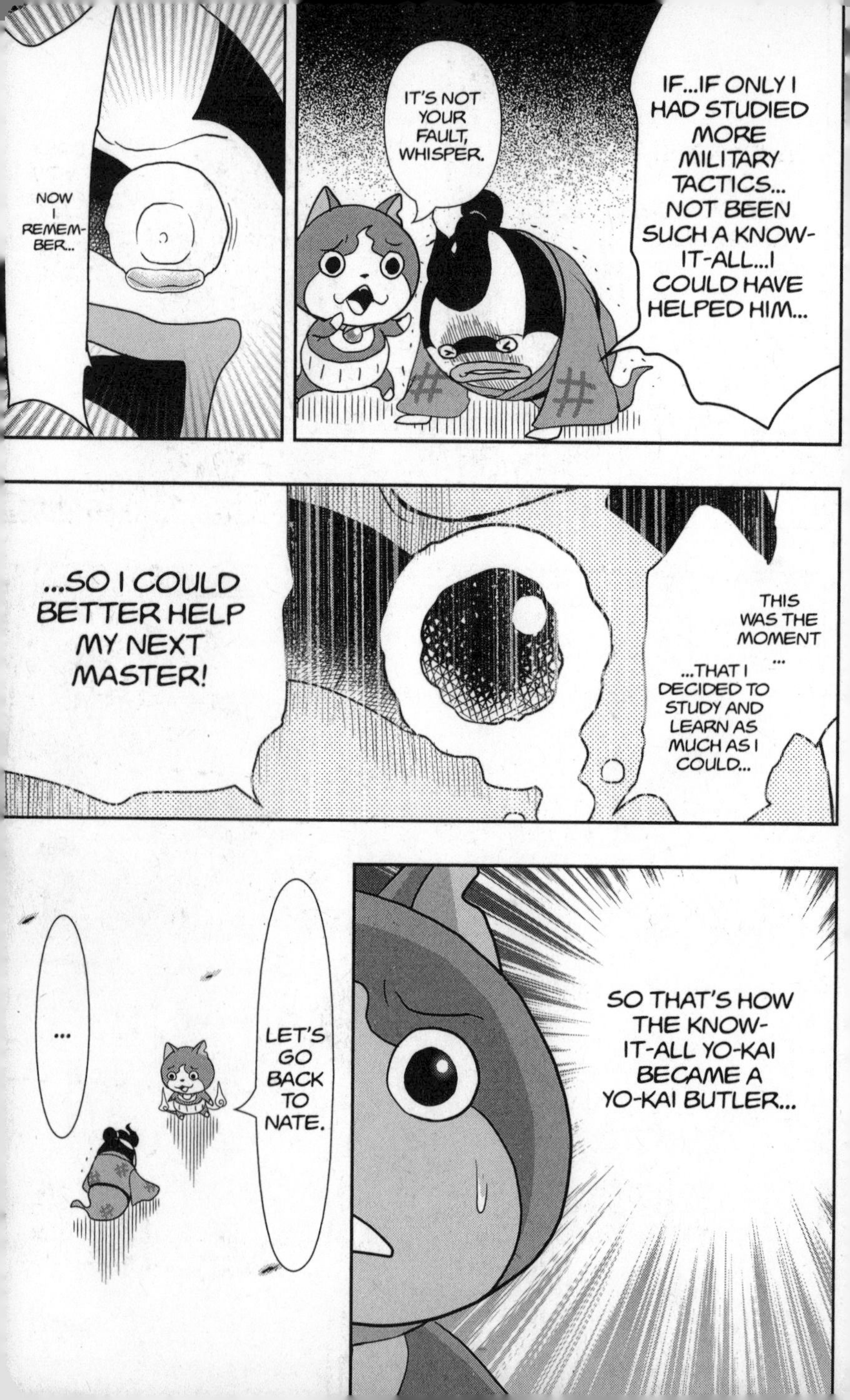
IF...IF ONLY I HAD STUDIED MORE MILITARY TACTICS... NOT BEEN SUCH A KNOW-IT-ALL...I COULD HAVE HELPED HIM...
IT'S NOT YOUR FAULT, WHISPER.
NOW I REMEMBER...
THIS WAS THE MOMENT...
...THAT I DECIDED TO STUDY AND LEARN AS MUCH AS I COULD...
...SO I COULD BETTER HELP MY NEXT MASTER!
SO THAT'S HOW THE KNOW-IT-ALL YO-KAI BECAME A YO-KAI BUTLER...
LET'S GO BACK TO NATE.
...

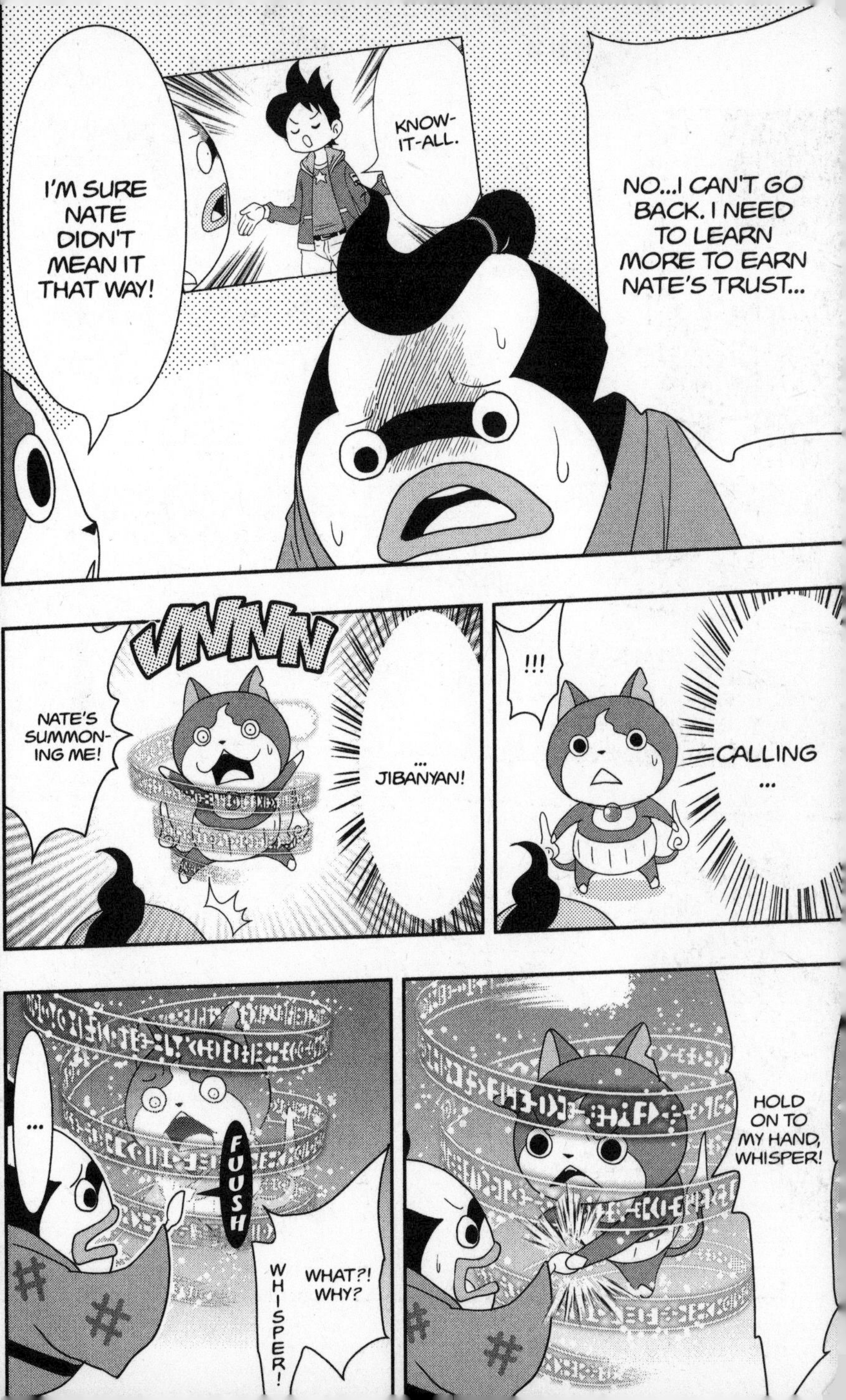
NO...I CAN'T GO BACK. I NEED TO LEARN MORE TO EARN NATE'S TRUST...
KNOW-IT-ALL.
I'M SURE NATE DIDN'T MEAN IT THAT WAY!
CALLING ...
!!!
... JIBANYAN!
VNNNN
NATE'S SUMMON-ING ME!
HOLD ON TO MY HAND, WHISPER!
WHISPER!
WHAT?! WHY?
FUUSH
...

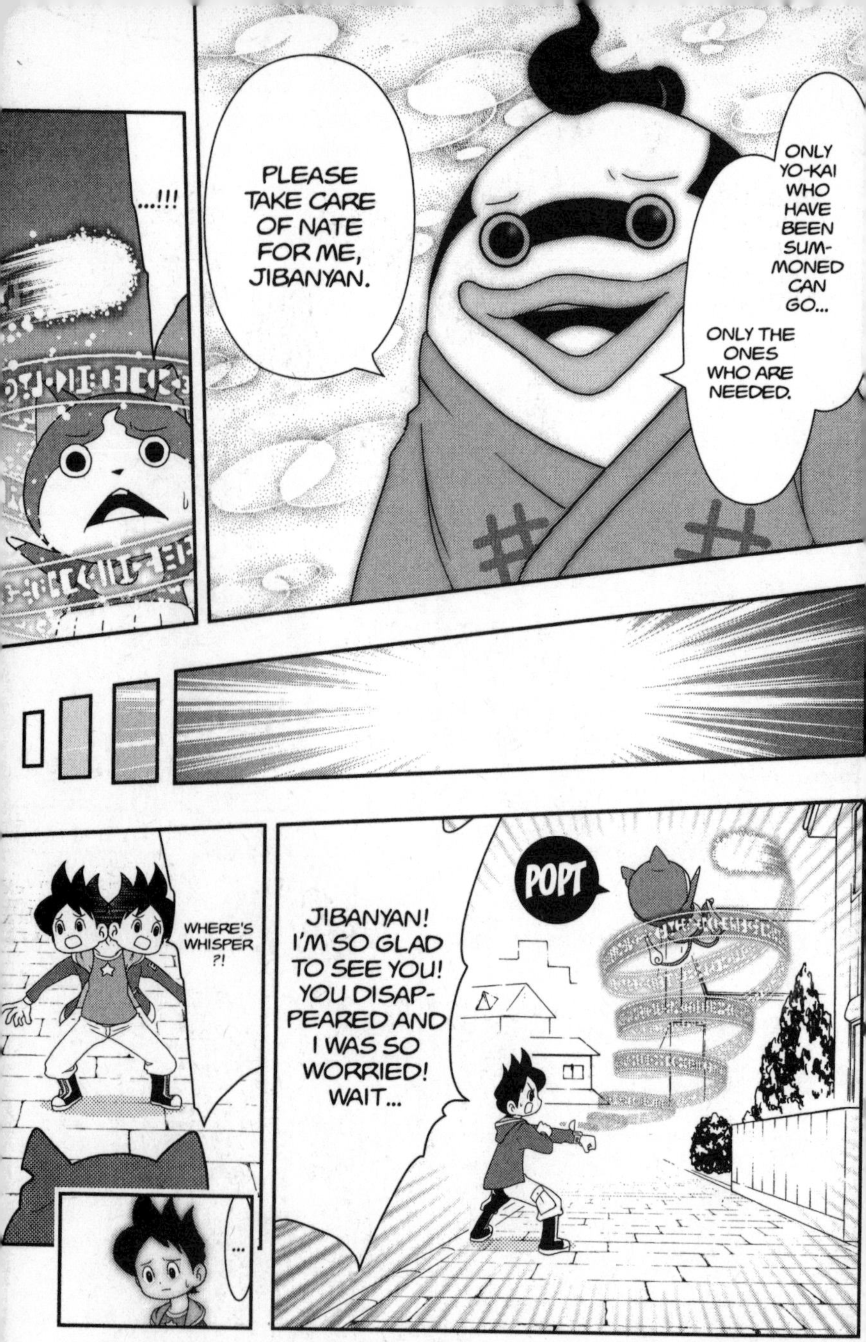
ONLY YO-KAI WHO HAVE BEEN SUM-MONED CAN GO... ONLY THE ONES WHO ARE NEEDED.
PLEASE TAKE CARE OF NATE FOR ME, JIBANYAN.
...!!!
POPT
JIBANYAN! I'M SO GLAD TO SEE YOU! YOU DISAP-PEARED AND I WAS SO WORRIED! WAIT...
WHERE'S WHISPER ?!
...

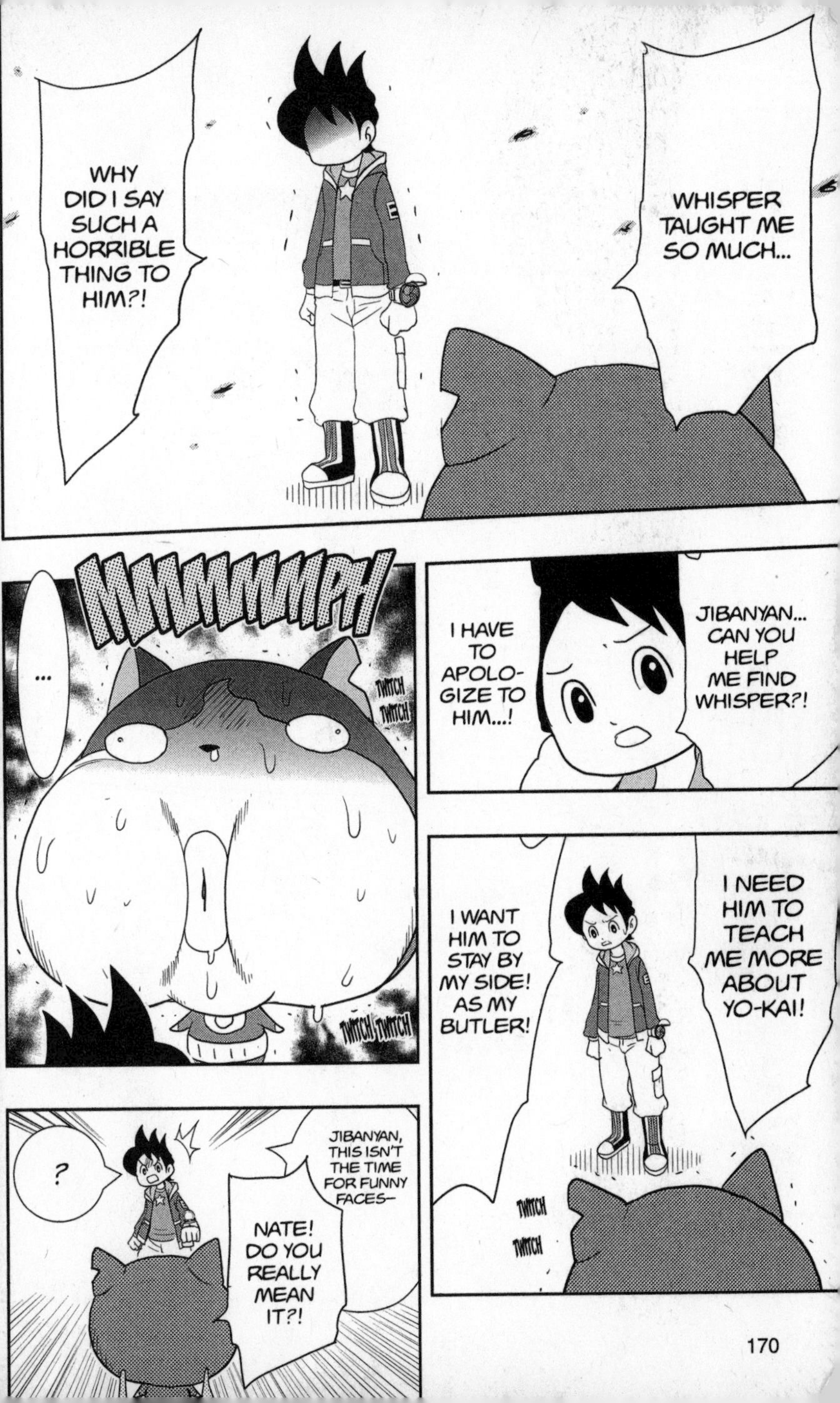
WHISPER TAUGHT ME SO MUCH...
WHY DID I SAY SUCH A HORRIBLE THING TO HIM?!
JIBANYAN... CAN YOU HELP ME FIND WHISPER?!
I HAVE TO APOLOGIZE TO HIM...!
I NEED HIM TO TEACH ME MORE ABOUT YO-KAI!
I WANT HIM TO STAY BY MY SIDE! AS MY BUTLER!
TWITCH
TWITCH
MMMMMMMPH
...
TWITCH TWITCH
TWITCH, TWITCH
JIBANYAN, THIS ISN'T THE TIME FOR FUNNY FACES–
?
NATE! DO YOU REALLY MEAN IT?!

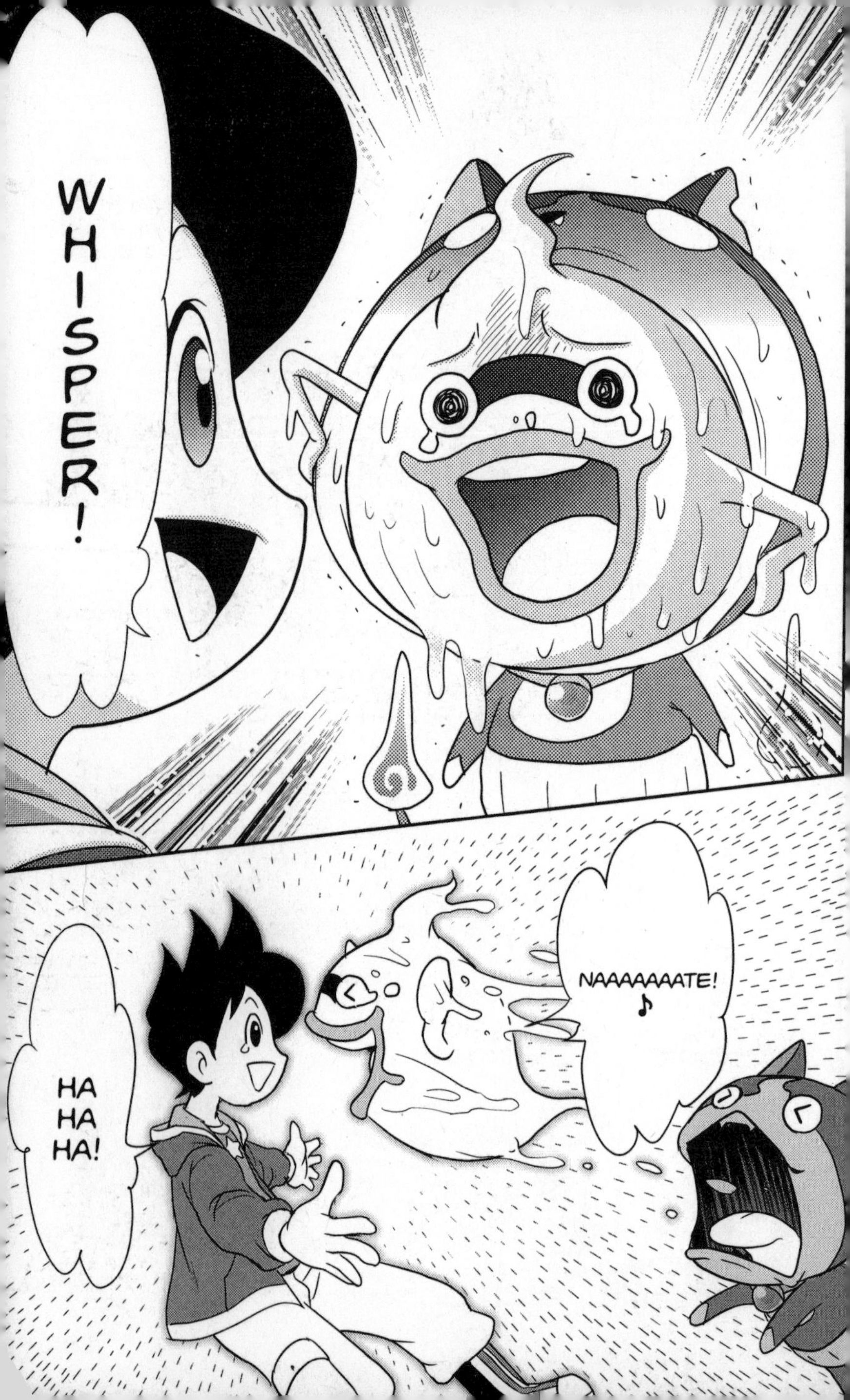
WHISPER!
NAAAAAAATE! ♪
HA HA HA!

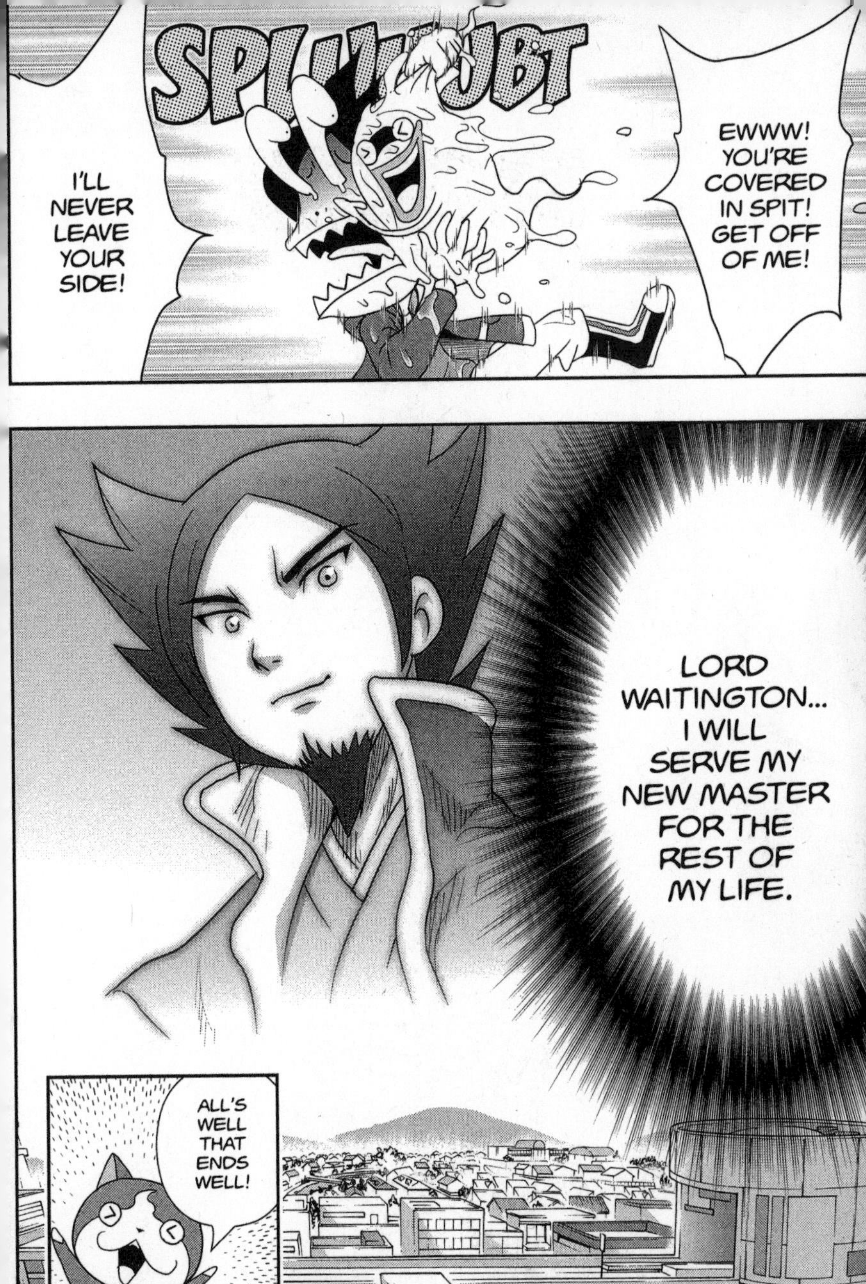
EWWW! YOU'RE COVERED IN SPIT! GET OFF OF ME!
I'LL NEVER LEAVE YOUR SIDE!
LORD WAITINGTON... I WILL SERVE MY NEW MASTER FOR THE REST OF MY LIFE.
ALL'S WELL THAT ENDS WELL!

# HOMEBOUND

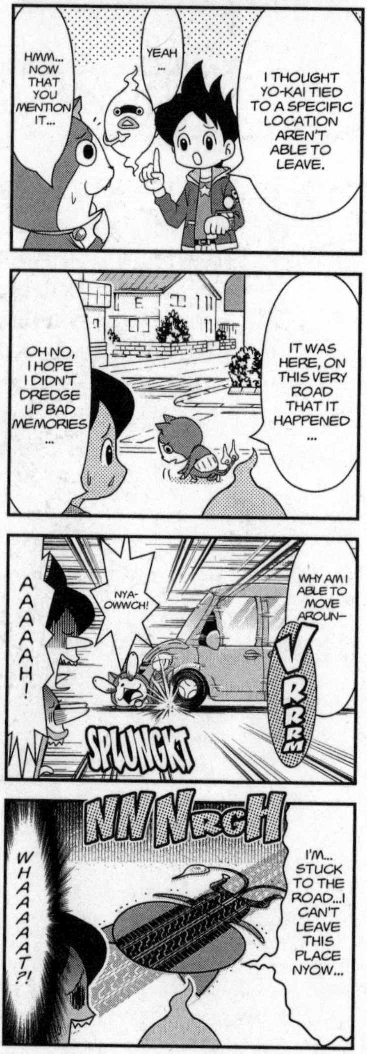
I THOUGHT YO-KAI TIED TO A SPECIFIC LOCATION AREN'T ABLE TO LEAVE.
YEAH...
HMM... NOW THAT YOU MENTION IT...
IT WAS HERE, ON THIS VERY ROAD THAT IT HAPPENED...
OH NO, I HOPE I DIDN'T DREDGE UP BAD MEMORIES...
WHY AM I ABLE TO MOVE AROUN-
VRRRM
NYA-OWWCH!
SPLUNGKT
AAAAAAH!
NNNRGH
I'M... STUCK TO THE ROAD...I CAN'T LEAVE THIS PLACE NYOW...
WHAAAAAAAT?!

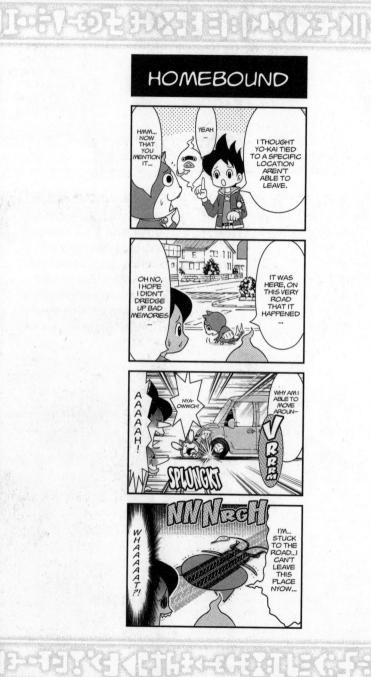

# Little Battlers eXperience

## LBX

### LITTLE BATTLERS EXPERIENCE™

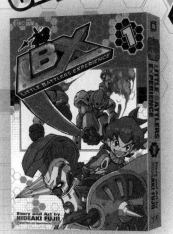

## Story and Art by
## HIDEAKI FUJII

Welcome to the world of Little Battlers eXperience! In the near future, a boy named Van Yamano owns Achilles, a miniaturized robot that battles on command! But Achilles is no ordinary LBX. Hidden inside him is secret data that Van must keep out of the hands of evil at all costs!

## All six volumes available now!

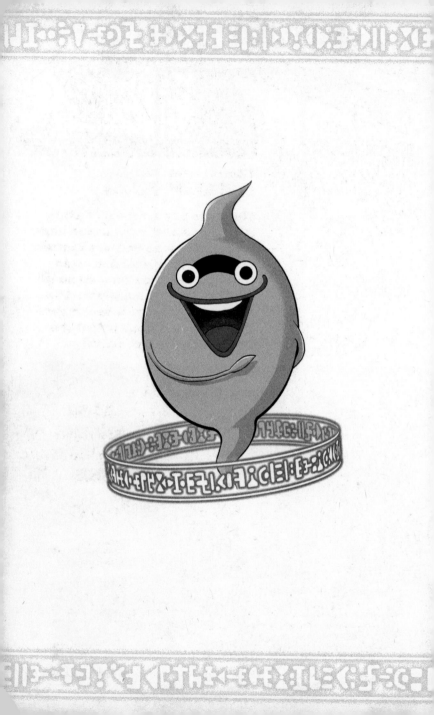

# THIS IS THE END OF THIS GRAPHIC NOVEL.

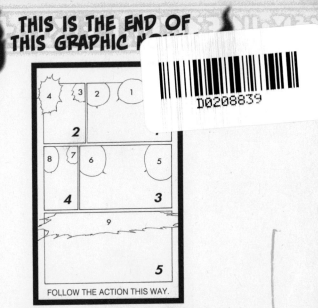

FOLLOW THE ACTION THIS WAY.

**To properly enjoy this Perfect Square graphic novel, please turn it around and begin reading from right to left.**

# AUTHOR BIO

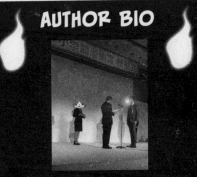

I was super nervous....

—Noriyuki Konishi

Noriyuki Konishi hails from Shimabara City in Nagasaki Prefecture, Japan. He debuted with the one-shot *E-CUFF* in *Monthly Shonen Jump Original* in 1997. He is known for writing manga adaptations of *AM Driver* and *Mushiking: King of the Beetles*, along with *Saiyuki Hiro Go-Kū Den!*, *Chōhenshin Gag Gaiden!! Card Warrior Kamen Riders*, *Go-Go-Go Saiyuki: Shin Gokūden* and more. Konishi was the recipient of the 38th Kodansha manga award in 2014 and the 60th Shogakukan manga award in 2015.